# THE LOST GOSPEL

## An Archaeological Thriller

## JOE EDD MORRIS

Black Rose Writing | Texas

ISBN: 978-1-68433-848-1 (Paperback); 978-1-68433-849-8 (Hardcover)
PUBLISHED BY BLACK ROSE WRITING
www.blackrosewriting.com

Printed in the United States of America
Suggested Retail Price (SRP) $20.95 (Paperback); $25.95 (Hardcover)

*The Lost Gospel* is printed in Chaparral Pro

*As a planet-friendly publisher, Black Rose Writing does its best to eliminate unnecessary waste to reduce paper usage and energy costs, while never compromising the reading experience. As a result, the final word count vs. page count may not meet common expectations.

Map Artwork by Jan Cobb
Author Photo by Thomas Wells

To The Rev. Dr. Embra Jackson, my pastor and a living gospel

In Memory of Reverends Garland "Bo" and Floy Holloman


and


In honor of The Holloman Covenant Class

First United Methodist Church, Tupelo, Mississippi

Praise for

# THE LOST GOSPEL

"*The Lost Gospel* combines a clear understanding of current tensions in Israel with a historian's knowledge of the first century Jewish revolt against the Roman Empire and the dangers inherent in both situations. The author's expert knowledge of archaeology and ancient manuscripts, and the uncertainties of the budding love relationship of the two main characters make for a fast-paced, suspenseful thriller that I couldn't put down."
**–Joseph T. Reiff, Emeritus Professor of Religion at Emory & Henry College and author of *Born of Conviction: White Methodists and Mississippi's Closed Society***

"*The Lost Gospel* is a splendid novel written with the lyrical prose and the meticulous research I've come to expect from Joe Edd Morris. As the author once again sends his beloved archeologist, Dr. Chris Jordan, in search of ancient Biblical scrolls, along with his feisty and endearing companion, Dr. Kate Ferguson, he is also carving out a sub-genre to a famous movie thriller franchise – 'the thinking man's Indiana Jones.'"
**–Peggy Webb, USA Today Bestselling Author of *The Language of Silence***

"Joe Edd Morris once again mines his interest in spiritual issues and history with this archaeological mystery which seamlessly cross-cuts between the earliest years of Christianity (50 A.D.) and the present turmoil surrounding the Holy Land. A highly-original take which suggests that the true message of those earliest years has been lost and has morphed into something counterproductive."
**–R. J. Lee, author of the *Bridge to Death Mysteries***

# THE LOST GOSPEL

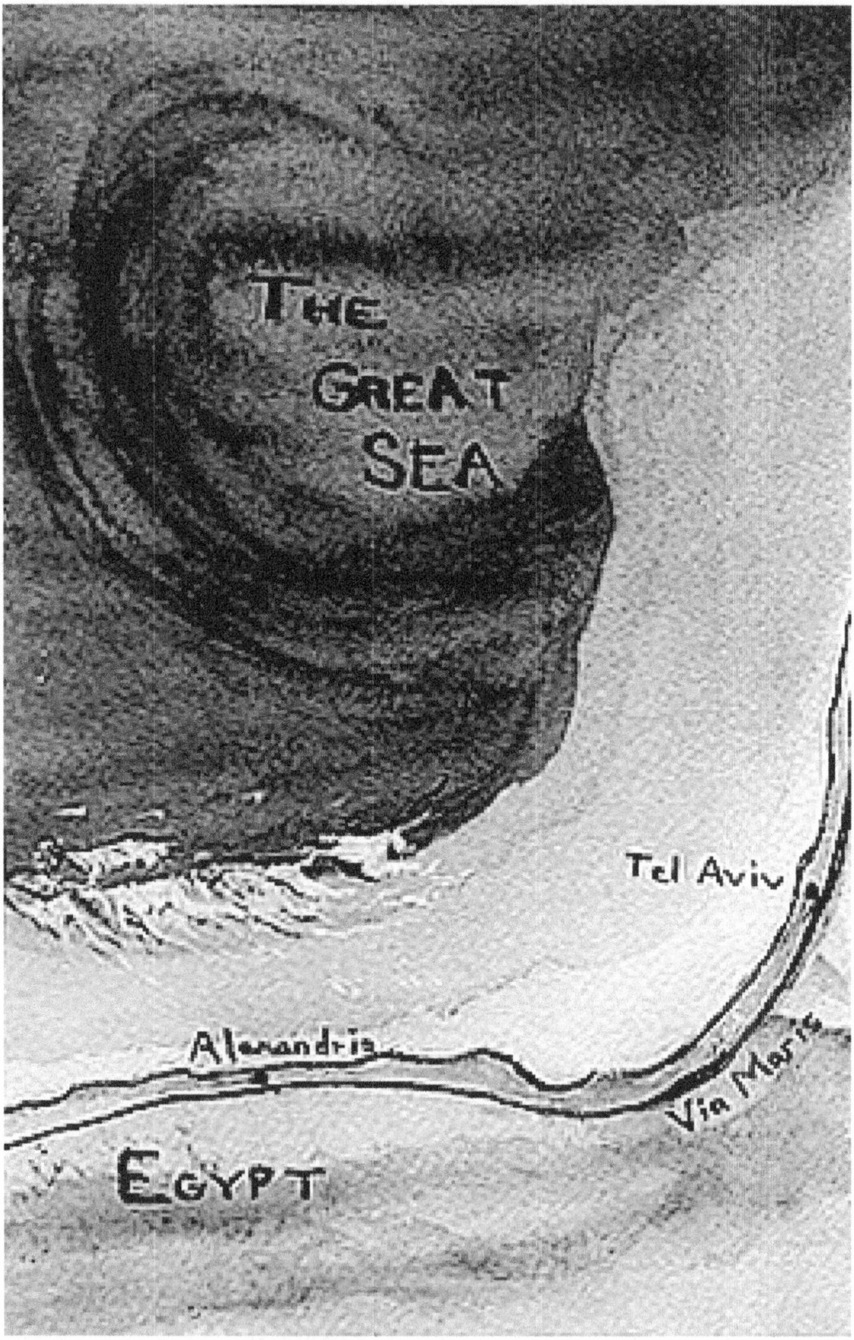
THE GREAT SEA
Tel Aviv
Alexandria
Via Maris
EGYPT

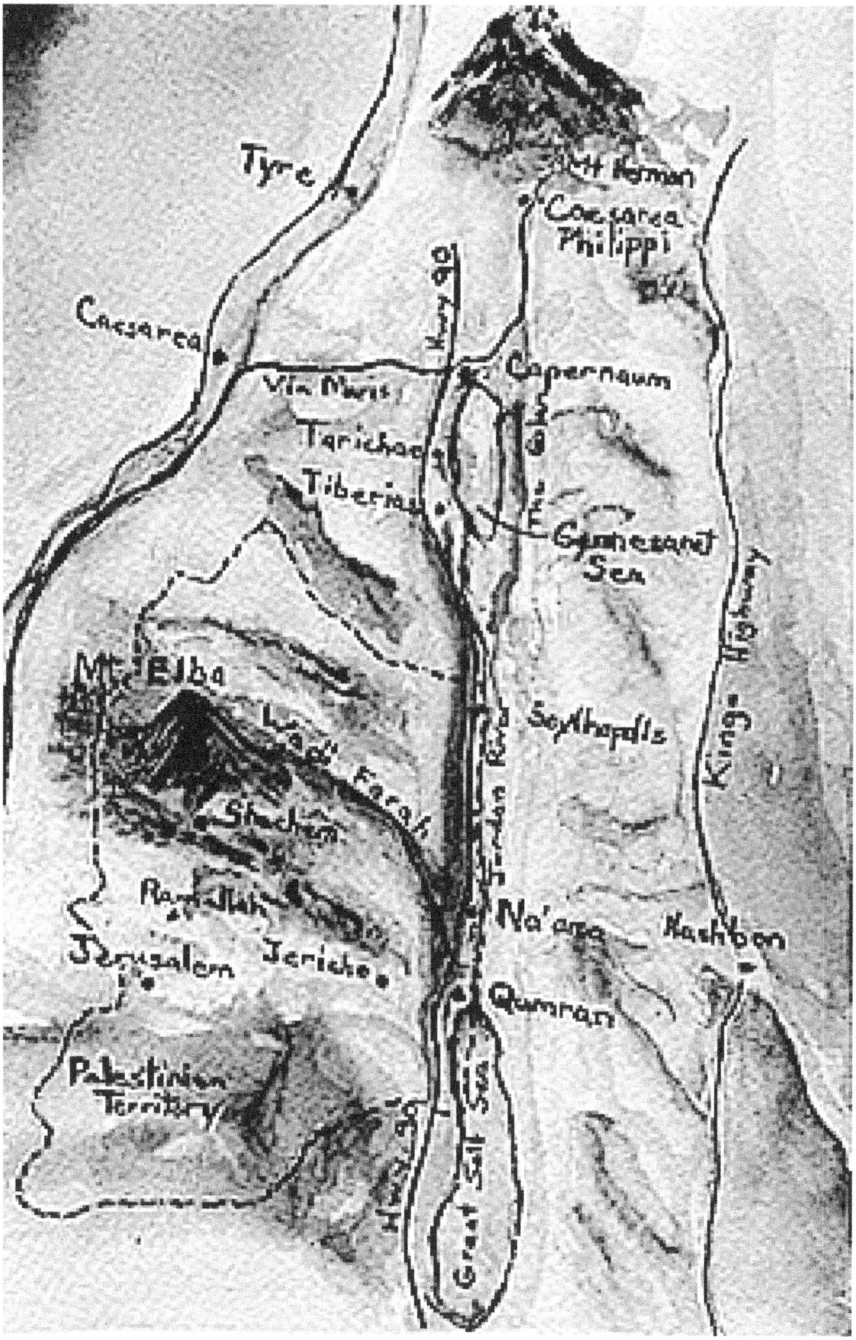

Tyre
Caesarea
Caesarea Philippi
Capernaum
Via Maris
Tiberias
Sea
Mt. Ebal
Wadi Faragh
Shechem
Jordan River
King's Highway
Jerusalem
Jericho
Qumran
Palestinian Territory
Great Salt Sea

# CHAPTER ONE

*Flagstaff, Arizona, May 24, 2012*

Christopher Jordan shot up in bed. The sound was coming from his cellphone on his nightstand. Calls don't come in the middle of the night unless … Anxiously, he managed a starchy "Hello!"

"Chris?"

"What?" he replied, straightening up. "Kate?"

"Yes."

He glanced at the time on the phone. "Do you realize it's two a.m."

"Oh, my!" She gasped. "I am sorry. It's ten a.m. here in London. I was excited and didn't think about the time difference."

"That excitement was six months ago," he said, referring to their discovery of Mark's gospel in Syria in the midst of Arab spring.

"But this is new."

"I'm listening," he said, struggling to calm down and wake up.

"Just moments ago I got a call from Dr. Townsend, head of the ancient manuscripts department. She received a phone call from Israel. Two jars have been discovered in a cave."

Chris rolled his eyes. "That's not news. Jars are discovered there all the time."

"I've seen the photos," she said excitedly. "These urns have Qumran written all over them; same cylindrical shape, same lids. Except they were found near Jericho, not Qumran."

"Jericho?" Chris questioned. "The caves between Jericho and Qumran have been scavenged and picked clean."

"These jars were not found *between* Jericho and Qumran but *north* of Jericho, east of Nablus, along the Wadi Faria in the lower Jordan River basin, the valley rift."

"I'm familiar with that area. No jars containing manuscripts have ever been found north of Jericho."

"I don't know," she allowed. "But other scrolls *have* been found in that area. In the third century, Eusebius found a manuscript of Psalms in a jar in Jericho and—"

He held the phone away from his ear as she rattled off papyrus discoveries in the area, ran his hand through his hair and pressed the phone back to his ear.

"In the eighth century books were found in a small cave in Jericho. This could be huge."

He sensed she was upset with him for not being excited with her. "Who called Dr. Townsend?" he asked, switching gears, attempting to tone both of them down.

"An American student working on a dig east of Shechem. He told her he was there on a college study-work program."

"Why did he call the British Museum and not the Israeli or Palestinian antiquities department?"

"Actually, he called the Museum asking for me. You and I have become famous."

"Unfortunately!" he mumbled.

"Due to the crank calls the museum gets, Dr. Townsend intercepted it. She said that caller had heard about my involvement with the discovery in Syria, that he was aware the jars resembled those found at Qumran and thought they might contain rare scrolls."

"Again, why you and not the authorities there."

"Dr. Townsend asked him the same question. He said he was concerned that, given the conflicts between the Israelis and Palestinians over archaeological discoveries, they might fall into the wrong hands. He said he was in a delicate situation. Dr. Townsend interpreted his reaching out as a cry for help, not knowing what to do or where to turn."

"Besides the Israel, Palestine conflict, what's his *delicate* situation?" Chris probed.

"Dr. Townsend said he didn't go into detail. The young man—she said he sounded young—was not an archaeologist but was working as a student from an American university on invitation from the Israeli Antiquities Authority. In other words, this is their dig."

"Most of them are," he said. "The Israelis use archaeology to control the West Bank and confiscate land from Palestinians for settler organizations."

"I know," she agreed. "The 1993 Oslo Accords gave the Palestinian Authority administrative control over most of the archaeological and heritage sites within the main cities of the West Bank."

"And the Accords included Gaza and East Jerusalem plus joint control over almost all inhabited villages. Israel got control of all the rest, or seventy-five percent," he added, "and the Israelis throw the scraps to the Palestinians. If these are not scraps, and he found them in the East Bank, that could start a war."

"Throw in the Christians," she reminded. "Our young discoverer also told Dr. Townsend that if they were Christian artifacts or manuscripts, they should be in Christian hands."

"Sounds a bit holy-rolly, right-wing fanatic to me," Chris said dubiously. "He's told only the British Museum, none of his team, which suggests subterfuge. Might be a hoax and someone wants the British Museum to give the find legitimacy."

"Chris, I don't think this is subterfuge or a hoax," she responded firmly. "Nor does Dr. Townsend. The story is too unusual, and consistent. He had to pee, walked away a distance from the site up an embankment, stepped behind part of a huge rock. His urine stream didn't run down the cliff and puddle at the bottom, but went straight through the wall and streamed out from the bottom. He went back later on his own with his pick and uncovered what turned out to be the entrance to a cave and found the two jars. One is tall, suggesting a scroll, and the other shorter and wider which, mysteriously, suggests something else."

"Did he retrieve them?" he pressed.

"No. He left them where he found them and recovered the cave entrance. I assume he knows Israeli laws about archaeological finds. The photos show the jars standing, presumably in the cave where he said he left them and recovered the entrance. In a follow-up email to Dr. Townsend, he said both were encased in leather satchels. He pushed the leather down around the jars so he could snap a picture."

"Are the lids intact?"

"From the photos, they appear to be."

"That could be a problem," he said. "The lids become melded over time, cemented to the lip of the jar, like the one we found in Syria."

"Opening them would require *expert* attention."

He sensed the direction the discussion was headed. "At least, he had the presence of mind not to try. You say you've seen the pictures?"

"Yes. Dr. Townsend forwarded them to me from an email attachment he had sent to her. They appear real and not doctored. And, they are in color,"

"Are the jars the same color as the Qumran jars?" he asked, becoming more intrigued.

"The coloration is different, darker than the Qumran jars," she replied. "I'm a manuscript expert: you're the archeologist. You open ancient jars, analyze their age and composition all the time. A carbon thirty-five would determine authenticity."

"Send the pictures to me."

"I just did. They're probably in your in-box now. Chris, you're waking up," she said, a smirk in her voice.

He wasn't going to look at pictures at two in the morning, especially with a bogus air hanging over them. "I'll view them later. I sense there's another angle to all this."

"There is," she said as he heard her take a deep breath. "Townsend is intrigued with the story. She wants me to go and check it out."

He responded quickly. "The museum doesn't have a dog in this fight. The Israelis and Palestinians are at each other's throats over archaeological discoveries. You could be in harm's way."

"That would be nothing new," she said flatly and without emotion. "And museums around the world have a vested interest in archeological discoveries. Dr. Townsend emphasized that the British Museum has a good relationship with both the IAA and its Palestinian counterpart. Both have loaned many of their valuable relics and manuscripts to the museum. My involvement would be solely to offer advice and expertise, if requested. In short, the museum would have some leverage on what could be a huge find."

"Sounds too risky," he said. "I don't think you should get involved."

Kate sighed heavily. "Chris, I have to get involved. Dr. T says the man does not know what to do and is asking for help. This could be a priceless find, part of the Dead Sea Scrolls, the Qumran collection." She paused to catch her breath. "Consider the alternatives. This student loses his nerve, tells no one else and the jars remain lost forever in an unknown cave in the Wadi Faria."

"That's a stretch," he quipped.

"Perhaps, but the other options are real. He could heist them, sell them on the antiquities black market. Or worse, break the jars open, risking damage to the contents."

"What he should do is call the IAA or Palestinian authorities," he admonished,

"And trigger an international conflict? I tell you, Chris, this kid has a bomb on his hands and is reaching out for help."

"The museum could get sucked into a situation where its integrity is compromised," he cautioned. "As an archeologist, I understand your concerns," his tone softening as he took her claims more seriously, weighing his next comment. "But there's more to all of this."

"I want you to go with me," she said.

He took a deep breath. Before he could respond—

"Dr. T said we're a perfect team. She's already given the project a green light."

Silence.

She continued. "We were going to meet in Italy in July anyway. I can't wait that long. I miss you." she said, her voice pleading, almost breaking. "It's been months, seems like years, since you proposed to me. Remember?"

"I do."

"That's what you to say to the minister," she snapped.

He didn't know how to respond. He couldn't tell her that since their sudden fame with the archaeological discovery of the millennia, his ex-wife had muscled her way back into his life, aligning his sons on her side in a massive display of let bygones be bygones and can't we see each other again. He suspected money might be the reason. Allyson had lost her job. There was no one else in her life. He couldn't tell Kate he had softened under the emotional onslaught and had seen his ex. He had felt sorry for her and, after all, she was his sons' mother. He had decided it was the dutiful thing to do.

When he didn't respond right away, she asked nervously, "Are you getting cold feet?"

"No, no," he said, too emphatically. "I'd love to see you. I'm just figuring how to pull this off. What's today? Thursday, May twenty-four. Memorial Day means a long weekend coming up. Classes are over for the summer and

I'm between digs. The next one is an Indian mound in Mississippi. So, yeah, I can manage a week."

"That is decent of you," she said caustically.

"Cut me some slack," he pleaded. "It's two o'clock in the morning. I'm doing good for someone still half asleep."

"I agree, you are. And I apologize again for the poor timing," her tone cold.

He tried to sound more upbeat. "Where will I meet you?" he asked.

Her response was quick. "Jerusalem."

"Where in Jerusalem?"

"The Olive Garden Hotel," she replied. "I've stayed there before. It's quaint and quiet and has beautiful gardens."

He thought of Kate's past, her deceased husband, their roles together in the British Special Forces, his assassination in Syria in 2005. She'd probably stayed in the same hotel with him when they were on assignment or when she joined him on his leaves. "Is that the only one that's quaint and quiet?"

"No. And I was alone at the time."

They might as well be married, he thought, she read him so well. "I'll work on travel plans first thing then e-mail my flight itinerary to you," he said. "I'll try to leave in two days."

"This time you won't have the problem you had in Syria with the Israeli stamp on your passport," she advised.

"That's true. I'll just have bigger problems if I try to re-enter Lebanon and Syria, if we get married amid the ruins of Baalbek like we discussed."

She laughed at the fun she'd had telling the border official in Beirut that they were going to Baalbek to get married. "When we do, perhaps we'll get the same passport official."

Laughing with her, he said, "Good night. I love you. I'll talk to you later, when I'm fully awake."

"In Jerusalem," she affirmed.

Chris hung up, put his head back down and lay thinking.

Kate wouldn't call with some outlandish story just to leverage a chance to see him again. She was too independent and self-assured. This was the woman who had been in the British Army's Special Forces, flew into Syria and reclaimed her husband's body. The woman who spoke multiple languages, was an accomplished violinist and Scottish royalty with a karate black belt. On top of all that, she was a gorgeous redhead. Kate Ferguson was always in control. There were times during their experience in Syria he had seen emotional fissures, times when she almost broke and unloaded on him. But she always recovered quickly, Scottish pride flashing in eyes sucking back the tears.

Allyson Jordan was no Kate Ferguson. There was no comparison between the two women in his life. Why, then, was he feeling a tug back to his ex-wife? The feelings were not related to love or romance or sexual urges. He had had no other relationship, stayed too busy to have one then considered the irony. The only relationship he had now was related to his work, with Kate on the search for Mark's gospel.

Though no knock-out, Allyson was pretty. There was a genuine softness about her he liked, one that made him feel comfortable in her company. She was not pretentious. Everyone liked her. The reasons they divorced were still a mystery. No particular issue stood out. No other men were involved. They didn't fight often. Perhaps a contributing cause was the long periods of separation. Through much of their marriage, she was homesick and he frequently flew her back to Scotland to see her family. When she returned, he was usually off on a dig. At times, he'd wondered if she had someone in Scotland, yet when the divorce was final and the dust had settled, no one was waiting in the wings. She chose to remain in Arizona to be near their two sons.

The years following their divorce, Allyson rarely called him. Though they lived in the same city, their contacts were minimal. Their sons were grown. Occasionally, he'd see her at restaurants. She always had a date, all different men, no one he knew. He sensed she was unhappy. The boys, Ian and Gordon, never talked about her.

Then came the discovery of Mark's Gospel, the original autograph, in Maaloula, Syria. Overnight, he became famous and Allyson's world began spinning backwards, as if to recapture something lost. His sons began telling him positive comments she'd made about him, how proud she was of his discovery, how she wanted to know more of the daring episode.

She called and invited him to lunch. The reason, she said, was to discuss property they owned jointly in Scotland, a lot in St. Andrews they had purchased when they were married and were living in Edinburgh. It was near the golf course and, with the resurgence of the famous club, had increased in value. She was his business partner, the mother of their sons. He could not say no.

For the occasion, she dressed as though she was going to a cocktail party, short sleek dress, patent heels, shoulder-length hair swept to the side. She looked better than he had ever seen her, even when they were dating. She was in her mid-forties but looked early thirties. He knew, through his sons, that she worked out regularly at a fitness center, thanks, in part, to alimony payments. Another reason she may not have remarried.

At lunch, the lot they owned was briefly mentioned, clearing the deck for the real agenda: the famous discovery. She wanted to know all about it; his former professor's involvement, where and how the scroll was found, the details of his escape from Syria with the manuscript. He told her of the high speed chase, the near entrapment at the Syrian-Lebanese border, how the scroll was hidden in the false bottom of his companion's carry-on and, "was almost detected at the airport in Beirut before our flight to Edinburgh which—"

—"Tell me about *her*," she said, interrupting his narration.

He'd said nothing to his sons about Kate. There had been articles and pictures in newspapers, television interviews. Had Allyson been only vaguely interested in the news, she would have known the sex and attractive appearance of his companion. But the way she said it—putting down her drink, leaning across the table, the unblinking flinty gaze—*Tell me about her.* She knew. More than any news clip revealed ... she knew.

Her name, he calmly told her, was Dr. Kathrine Ferguson. She worked for the British Museum and had been contacted by his former New Testament professor at the University in Edinburgh who had found a partial copy of Mark's Gospel in Maaloula, Syria and recruited the two of them to find the original. "I'd never laid eyes on her until then," Chris said apologetically, wishing he could retrieve the line.

Then, he lied. "The mission was all very professional."

His omission of future co-authored books with his "companion," joint lecture series and Kate's accepted marriage proposal was part of the lie. The part that was true—that there had been no sexual intimacy between them—would have sounded like a lie.

He couldn't go back to sleep. Thoughts, questions circulating through his head. The demise of his marriage. The reasons. Kate. Was it *deja vu*? Had this romance flared with adventure, discovery, fame, and then simmered. Had four thousand miles apart—contacts limited to emails, Skype, letters—dimmed this relationship, too. Their communications always ended with "I love you," but the tone seemed different. He sensed it in his own voice, the diminished intensity and thought of the saying, "Absence makes the heart grow fonder," and wondered of its origin ... its fallacy?

Besides distance, there were other issues.

Kate had fallen in love with his place in Arizona, especially the ceiling-to-floor windows, the view of the mountains, two stone fireplaces and wrap-around deck. She was enamored. Her comments about the place were playful, but her voice was completely earnest when she said she could not leave her parent's baronial estate in Dunbar, Scotland, and move to Arizona. She had made it clear. If they married, he'd have to move to Scotland. That involved quitting a tenure position at the University of North Arizona and hopefully getting one—non-tenure—in the University of Edinburgh archaeological program.

She did have a point. He had less bases to cover and could move more easily than she. It would take him away from his two sons, whom he saw infrequently, intentionally failing to mention his ex. Kate had said her job with The British Museum was negotiable, that she could transfer to the Scottish Royal Museum. Another option, not discussed, was his gaining employment with The British Museum. Perhaps that was what the call was ultimately about, getting his foot in the door.

These recourses must be discussed in the right moment and none seemed promising on this trip. Regardless, he wanted, needed, to see her again.

For the present moment, one thing was certain. He wasn't going back to sleep. He got up and brewed a pot of coffee. He needed a clear head for jumping through electronic hoops and making flight reservations.

The computer screen bloomed to life and he went online to Travelocity, scrolled through the options. One flight arrived Tel Aviv at 8:50 a.m. Scrolling down further, he saw a U.S. Airways with connections in Phoenix and Philadelphia, non-stop on United to Tel Aviv, arriving 3:15 p.m. Perfect. He secured the reservation, clicked Business Class. Kate had spoiled him on their trip from Edinburgh to Beirut. Until then, he had only flown coach. He was smitten. The discovery of the millennium had not raised his salary, but he'd made money from speaking engagements and could spring for the higher fare.

Finishing the confirmation, a thought hit him. They should coordinate their arrival time and rent one car, drive to Jerusalem together. He sent her a text with his itinerary and suggested, since they both now had a Priority Pass, they meet at the Dan Lounge in the Ben Gurion Airport.

"Super!" she quickly responded, and said she was changing her flight from Edinburgh, arriving fourish in the afternoon ... "Meet you at the Dan."

Computer in his lap, he sat on the porch enjoying a second cup of coffee and the panoramic scene of Mount Elden and the San Francisco Peaks, shoals of clouds swimming through the sky. He went to his email file and pulled up the attachments Kate had sent. The photos of the two jars did resemble the famous Qumran urns—cylindrical shape, flattening sharply at the top and bottom, wide collared neck, ring base. He could examine them more closely inflight and closed the laptop.

He thought.

If a Christian was in possession of one or more ancient scrolls—if that was, in fact, what the jars contained. And, if this Christian refused to report them to the Israelis or the Palestinians, then he and Kate could get caught in a crossfire, literally. *Would she manage to come up with a gun on this trip, too?*

# CHAPTER TWO

*Capernaum, Galilee, Passover, A.D. 50*

It is the Sabbath. Jairus rises early, careful not to wake his wife sleeping beside him. He swings one leg, then the other over the edge of the bed. He goes to the window and looks east across the sea. Backlit by the dawn's first blush, the Golan looms like a wall of night. Moments later a burst of light, like a star being born, pierces the plateau's crest. A brilliant arc of sun appears, so bright he must raise a hand to shade his eyes. Slowly, in the cloudless diaphanous sky, the sun climbs majestically amid deeper tones of red and gold.

People on the opposite shore rising early and looking west would see the first band of sunlight striking the straw-colored hills above his home. They would watch its slow expanse unveil orchards, tilled fields, scattered mud huts. If they gazed long enough at the falling curtain of light, they would see small fishing villages strung along the western shore. Looking northwest, the village of Capernaum would appear, its blonde stone synagogue gold in the early sunlight, conspicuous from the darker basalt structures surrounding it. Making a diagonal descent down the mountain toward Capernaum, they might see the thin line of a Roman road, the Via Maris, a major highway from Egypt to Damascus, their eyes tracking it around the village, skirting the sea then north toward the folds of hills.

This is Galilee. His world. The world of the Jesus people. He is one of them. Their leader. Later in the morning, they will come again, as they do each Sabbath, to hear him read the master's words.

His wife steps silently behind him, lays a hand on his shoulder and gazes out the window with him. "You are in deep thought, my dear Jairus."

He turns, puts an arm around her and draws her close. Her name is Rebecca. She is nearing her sixtieth year yet her dark olive skin is without wrinkles, a few strands of gray thread her long black hair. He feels strength in her marbled hands whenever, wherever, she touches him.

"Each day I watch the dawn break I wonder, is this the day?" he says.

"The day?"

"The last day. The eschaton. The day of judgment. Jesus said it would happen in our time."

"He also said," she reminds him, "it would be an hour we do not expect."

"All the more reason we must be vigilant and continue following his teachings," he says. "They prepare us for that day."

"But others," she continues, "are less concerned about his teachings. They speak only of his crucifixion and resurrection, that belief in him saves them from this day of which you speak."

Her comment takes his mind back twenty years, almost to the day, when Jesus died. Word had traveled from Jerusalem. Fifty days after his reported resurrection, on Pentecost, a great event had occurred in that city. Disciples of Jesus from Capernaum—Simon Peter, Andrew, James and John—were there. It was said a mighty wind, like one that leaned olive trees, swept through a gathered crowd of the prophet's followers and all were filled with a Holy Spirit, that an ecclesia blossomed overnight and the disciples went in many directions of the world preaching about Jesus' crucifixion and his resurrection. But none returned to Galilee.

"There is no worse death, dear one, than crucifixion," he says, as though to himself. "There is no greater joy over death than resurrection. But crucifixions and resurrections do not teach people how to live. These 'others' of whom you speak know a different Jesus, a martyred hero, a man of myth. They believe *in* him. We *believe him*, his words."

"Verily, verily," she says. "This I know, dear husband. Because of those words of fairness, justice, kindness and love to others, I am guided to the next day and will be ready for the last day."

"The others coming today echo your 'verily,'" he says.

"You know it is the Passover," she says, a cautious timbre in her voice.

"Yes. Some will soon leave their homes to retrieve the Pascal lamb."

"And they will go to the synagogue today," she completes the thought. "They will not join us at the seashore."

"This is true," he agrees. "They are still bound by the old ways. I do not fault my fellow Jews."

"Nor do I. But you are a good teacher, Jairus. If only they would listen to you."

"You listen well, my beloved."

"Because you speak well," and she pats him on the back.

He looks at her and smiles. "The master also said, 'Can the blind lead the blind?'"

She raises a finger. "You are being modest, dear one. You were once the president of the congregation in Capernaum, responsible for the order of the synagogue service. Several times you appointed Jesus to read scriptures and comment on them."

"Yes, and each time with some reluctance," he says, a regretful tone in his voice. "I thought his message too radical. He was baptized by the wild man named John. At the time, I thought the baptizer a maniac."

"Yes, but that 'wild man' drew people from nearby villages and cities, even Jerusalem," she admonishes him. "In the synagogue, you witnessed Jesus cast out a demon and heal a withered hand."

He looks up at her. "Those miracles did not impress me. Miracle workers are everywhere. But when he..." Emotion rises in his throat. His wife puts a comforting arm around him. She knows he always has trouble going back to that time. Their twelve-year-old daughter, Hava, was dying. The doctors did not know the reason. They were rural medics, not as educated as the doctors from the cities. That would mean a journey of several days. Hava could not leave her bed. Jairus was out of options. He grew desperate. He sought out Jesus. He did not send his wife or a servant. He went himself and, unashamedly, on bended knee, pleaded for Jesus to come to his home and heal his daughter. Jesus came and Hava lived. His life was changed. A daughter dying or near death, then rising to become healthy and lead a normal life will turn a man around. He began listening to the man, to his new message. One day Jairus said to himself, someone needs to record what he is saying and he began writing in a codex what he had heard. *His codex!*

"Where is my codex?" he cries out. "I must have it for the service today." His house was larger than most, three rooms on the first level and two on the second, a large patio outside. He could have left it anywhere.

"I saw it by the hearth," Rebecca says, "where you left it after evening meditation."

He leaves the window and walks to the hearth, its smoldering embers glowing orange in the darkened room. There, on the side, next to a few sticks of wood, was the codex. Fearing one would not be sufficient, he had purchased two from a paper vender on a trip to Caesarea Philippi. The notebook was bound with sheepskin. Holes were punched along the sides and its parchment pages bound by leather thongs. Less cumbersome than a scroll, one could write on the backs of pages which could easily be leafed back and forth. The notebook form was more adaptable to a wondering preacher or missionary. He wishes he had had one when Jesus was alive. He could have taken the journal with him and inscribed his teachings as they came fresh from the master's mouth. Now he carried it with him so he could record the sayings when they came to him or when he was speaking with another who recalled them. It was also the source of his own messages when the followers of Jesus met weekly. When he filled this codex, he would continue on the second.

He sits on the hearth and opens it, thumbs the warped leathery pages to a place he had marked with a splinter of wood, then stops.

"Do you know what you will read today?" his wife asks.

"Yes, instructions for the master's followers. Some new seekers, I have been told, are coming," he says. "They are from Bethsaida, a fisherman, his wife and their two sons. The man was a friend of Peter's, often fished with him. They stayed the night with his daughter Miriam. It has been a year, almost to the day her husband drowned."

"That horrible incident, the man trapped in the water under his nets," she cries, hands flying to her cheeks.

"She has been strong. I may ask her to read today," he says.

"Is it a good time?"

"Dear wife, it is never a bad time to read and hear the words of Jesus."

She narrows her eyes and frowns. His remark is condescending. He knows it as the words left his mouth. He walks to her, puts her face in his hands and looks into her eyes. "Rebecca, Rebecca, you are my sensitive side, always vigilant to the frailties of others, ever revealing my own." He kisses her on the forehead. "'How can you look for the splinter in your brother's eye and not notice the stick in your own eye. You hypocrite, first take the stick from your own eye then you can see to remove the splinter from your brother's eye.' I will reconsider. We will see if she volunteers a prayer. That will tell us."

# CHAPTER THREE

*Tel Aviv, Israel: Ben Gurion International Airport, May 26, 2012*

Chris' flight arrived at Ben Gurion International Airport on time. As the jet touched down, he felt a rising excitement about what lay ahead.

He had been through the new Tel Aviv airport several years ago as a visiting professor for some lectures he gave in Jerusalem and Ramallah. He had never been to any of the airport lounges and was dismayed that there was not one but two Dan Lounges, on B and C Concourses. His plane arrived at a B Concourse gate. He checked the monitor for Kate's flight. It was an Air France and on time. The exit gate, to his luck, was on Concourse B.

He decided not to enter the lounge but to wait in a seat at an adjacent gate. He used the downtime to review his messages, take care of matters back home. He'd forgotten to tell his maid to water the plants on the porch and make sure he'd turned off his coffee pot. He opened his note book and reviewed some documents on ancient Palestinian pottery he'd downloaded before leaving, including the photos Kate had sent him along with other relevant archaeological data.

Before pulling up the photos, he looked around to insure privacy. He was sitting on the front row facing the corridor in a vacant seating area at a gate with no planes scheduled. One could never be too careful, not in Israel, especially if you were an archaeologist. He moved to a seat with his back to the wall, so he would be facing the concourse Kate would walk down.

He opened his laptop and pulled up the photos of the two jars. Kate had told him the urns were found in a cave beneath a mound of rubble in leather casings. The pictures revealed that the young discoverer had left the leather casings, which appeared to be in a deteriorated state, collapsed around the respective jars. Judging from their appearance, the casings were probably goat's hide but it was hard to tell from the two photos.

The shape of the jars *was* similar to those found at Qumran. It was accepted knowledge that the Qumran jars were made locally, supplied by a single pottery workshop. The clay, however, came from Jerusalem which means it was imported. The coloration on these jars was different, darker, a yellowish red to reddish brown hue. The only clay in Israel with that particular coloration was in the Galilee region, which would bring a strange twist to the evolution of the jars and take some explaining why they were found out of that region. He would need to collect samples and run chemical tests to be sure. One thing he thought odd. The small jar was shorter and wider than the larger jar with a wider mouth suggesting contents other than a scroll. Perhaps it was not a scroll jar. Perhaps neither were for scrolls and both contained other artifacts.

Perhaps, they contained nothing.

Perhaps, the find was, as he'd thought at first, a hoax.

Perhaps.

He continued scrutinizing the photos and saw something he'd not previously noticed, near the lid on one of the jars: inscriptions. He hit the zoom button for a closer look, magnified the image again. What he saw was faint but discernible—fish images, one after another below the lip of the lid. They were similar to those made by early Christians, one arc intersecting another. He zoomed in on the second jar, saw the same symbols. He was looking at only one side of the jars. He'd be glad when he could see all the sides.

Key questions remained, location being one of them. Transporting large jars by pack animal over the rugged terrain would have been difficult. How did the jars, composed of Galilean clay, get to a cave north of Jericho in the Wadi Faria?

That's what Kate and most people called the valley, though in error. In actuality, there was no Wadi Faria. Having been to Israel in the early days of his archaeological career, he was familiar with the area. Research he'd conducted did show a Wadi Faria on numerous maps and in several Atlases. But the broad valley which made travel into eastern Samaria easy was listed in the earliest surveys as Wadi Farah, which the Palestinian Arabs still called it. He wasn't going to get into an argument with her on a transatlantic call over the error. Despite the name, the elongated depression was near Nablus, the ridge curving away from the city like a scythe aimed at the Jordan Valley. And it was within the West Bank, which always created problems for archaeologists. It was also just south of Galilee, the center of Jesus' ministry which may or may not be a factor.

He also wondered about the location of the place where the young man relieved himself. Was he near the top of the valley, near its ridge? Or close to the bottom of the descending incline? If the cave extended into the side of the valley wall, how deep was it? Did the aperture penetrate the cliff at a slant and, if so, did it slant up or down? The answer to the latter question he probably knew. The cave extended at a downward slant or he would not have heard the flow of his urine.

He chuckled to himself at how great antiquities had been discovered. The Markan scroll was found because a beggar got drunk and fell against a makeshift bogus wall that had stood for two millennia. The Dead Sea Scrolls were discovered when a small boy threw a rock into a cave and heard a strange clink. The Nag Hammadi Texts of Gnostic Gospels, as some have called them, were discovered in 1945 in Egypt when seven Bedouin laborers were digging for *sabakh*, a bird-lime fertilizer to use in their gardens.

He glanced at a clock on the opposite wall. If it was still on time, Kate's plane would be landing. He closed his notebook. Passengers from the plane began scurrying by, trying to get an early spot in line at Passport Control and Customs. He wanted to surprise her. He got up, went to the far side with his back against the wall where she wouldn't see him.

They were faint at first, sounds he knew, the rhythmic click of heels, footfalls set apart from hundreds of others. They grew louder. He turned his head and watched as she drew even, observed the dignity in her walk he remembered, those deliberate wide strides, moving with the confidence of someone who, with each step, was fulfilling her destiny as she passed him.

She was wearing sunglasses, a dark jacket he recognized from their Syrian adventure, a pleated tartan skirt flaring as she strode in black leather pumps. He grabbed the handle of his carry-on and began walking behind her and observed she was pulling the same carry-on with the false bottom where they smuggled the Markan scroll out of Syria and Lebanon.

He accelerated his pace, drew near to her and exaggerated a cough.

She turned and shrieked, "Chris Jordan."

Arms of glee encircled his neck. He pressed her close to him. She wore a light scent he recalled from the last time he had embraced her and held her close. She stood back and pushed her sunglasses up and over her head, spreading her hair away from her face.

"You look better than I remember," he said cheerfully.

"You don't look so bad yourself," she responded with a weary smile, flipping his tie with a playful finger. "I've never seen you in a suit and tie."

"This was special. I wanted to look my best for my best."

Gently, she pushed him back and punched him teasingly on the shoulder. "Oh, there's competition?" she said sarcastically.

"No," he lied, regretting the poor choice of words. "I've read that well-dressed travelers have less trouble negotiating passport authorities and customs." He looked her up and down. "You should sail through."

"I can't sail through customs just yet, darling," she said. "We must go to the baggage claim area. I have a small bag to retrieve."

"But you have your carry-on. That's all you traveled with on our trip to Syria."

"I have to pick up my Glock Seventeen."

He stopped but she kept walking.

"Wait a minute." Quick-stepping, he caught up with her. "I didn't think you could take a gun on a flight."

"I didn't take it with me onto the airplane. I followed protocol. I notified the airlines that I would need to take a firearm to Israel. I provided identification. I am still officially associated and registered with the British Special Forces. I complied with airline directions, placed the gun in a locked hard-sided case, unloaded with ammunition in a separate compartment. It was available for inspection at any time and I had the key."

"You never cease to amaze me."

"Furthermore," she proceeded, "I have been in Israel several times and still have an Israeli permit to own and carry a gun."

"How in the world ... ?"

"Let's just say I'm resourceful and let it go at that."

They came to the escalator to take them down to the baggage claim.

"I recall the problems the last gun you had caused us in Syria," he said as she descended the conveyor ahead of him.

"I'm sure you include in that memory the time it came in handy," she snapped, turned and shot him a gotcha glance.

"The Israelis are more thorough than the Syrians." He decided to drop it. If push came to shove—and in the Middle East, in an eye blink, push could come to shove—he felt safer she had access to a firearm and knew how to use it.

She immediately identified her bag, silver metallic and the size of a briefcase, like those you see in mobster movies only those contain money.

She did sail through passport control and customs. He did not. She had taken the same trip to Syria as he, same dates and itinerary. Yet, he was the one asked to step aside for questions.

She was waiting on the other side of the checkpoint for him. "What was all that about?" she asked as they began walking toward the car rental section.

"The suit and tie didn't work. They wanted to know about the trips to Lebanon and Syria."

"And?"

"I just told them I'd been to both countries as a tourist with a friend, which was the truth."

"That friend, now your fiancé," she said, reminding him. "I saw the officer interrogating you leave and discuss something with the officer in the next booth."

"I don't know what that was about, perhaps checking my time frames."

"Perhaps, it was more," she said. "The officer then went into an office. We are world famous, you know. Perhaps they recognized us."

"I told him the truth. Per Professor Stewart's instructions, we listed ourselves as tourists in Lebanon and Syria."

"But, against Syrian law," she said, "we removed an archaeological artifact from the country."

"Syria is lawless," he countered as they continued walking. "Besides, the Israelis could care less about what we did in Syria."

"Unless they think we're in their country to do the same," she said earnestly. "We need to be careful. After all, our young Christian confidante might be breaking the law and we could be charged with conspiracy and accessory. The Israelis take very seriously any archaeological antiquity leaving the country without legal permission and under the authority of the IAA, which, by the way, has a Robbery Prevention Unit, a kind of antiquities police. Ever heard of it?"

"Have I?" he said. "Somebody has to police over 20,000 antiquities. And Israel is the only country in the Middle East that permits the sale of antiquities."

She made a cautious nod toward a security officer they were approaching.

"But they do more than police sales," she said, lowering her voice. "They prevent looting. They work like an army using the same methods— undercover agents, night-vision binoculars, ambush. Their surveillance of potential looting sites is constant, day and night. They gather information from the field and other sources. They work with the local police, the border patrol, the national guard, Interpol, Scotland Yard, the Italian Carabinieri, F.B.I., with anyone who deals with antiquities, including the media which is probably why you got pulled aside. You can bet they know about our find in Syria."

"I'd be happy to carry your case for you," he offered.

"Thanks but no thanks," she quipped. "I can manage it."

"And you didn't get pulled over," he said still puzzled.

"Not sure why," she said, giving an enigmatic shrug. "Maybe they just wanted to interrogate one of us to see if our stories mesh. I may be next."

"Where were we?" she questioned, slipping a hand through his arm.

"The Robbery Prevention Unit."

"Oh, yes."

"Sounds like a mafia outfit," he said.

"It's close to one," she replied. "Antiquities are big business. A lot of money is at stake. One coin can be worth over four thousand pounds. Recently, in the Old City of Jerusalem, in the neighborhood of Silwan, looters dug down only two meters and discovered the door to a cave from the Second Temple period, the time of Jesus. Some of the items they found, mostly oil lamps, sold for 10,000 pounds each."

"How do they get around this robbery prevention army?" he asked draping his free arm around her shoulders.

"They work in groups, with metal detectors and digging tools," she responded. "Someone, usually an Israeli, takes them to a particular site. They are paid a work rate. If they find something, it is turned over to a middleman who, in turn, gives it to a dealer. There are seventeen licensed antiquity dealers in Israel but many more who are not licensed. Once an item gets to a dealer, and is not detected or determined to have been looted, it can be sold to anyone, an American tourist or wealthy Arab. If the IAA catches them they could pay a huge fine or spend a few years in jail."

She pointed to the car rental sign where they would turn.

"First order of business, then," he says, "is for this young man to report his find ... immediately."

"I agree. But it would be prudent for us to first find out what the find is," she said, stopping at the car rental counter.

Hertz would not have been his choice but she was driving and paying, she had insisted. The clerk rattled off the list of cars available and she picked: a 2010 white Buick LaCrosse sedan.

"Why the Lacrosse?" he asked.

"Because it's sporty, heavy, low slung," she said, popping up fingers with authority, "has a three point zero dynamo engine that gets your heart rate going, and all wheel drive. After all, we *are* in Israel," she raised a brow, "You never know where we might go. Anything else, dear?"

He recalled months earlier, she had picked him up at the Edinburgh airport in a white BMW, 128i coup and drove it like a race car. The woman did know her cars.

They were quickly through the Ben Gurion Exchange and on Highway 1 riding into the hills toward Jerusalem, forty miles away. Predictably, Kate drove intently, fast and skillfully staring straight ahead, both hands on top of the steering wheel. An uneasy silence enclosed them, one he hesitated breaching. He decided to make an attempt and asked her about her estate. Her father was an earl and had acquired property adjacent to the original estate outside of Dunbar, a picturesque fishing village near Edinburgh. When her parents died, the estate was left to her and her brother who wanted little to do with it, so she moved from her flat in Edinburgh and took it over.

"The estate is in good order," she said. "I have excellent help. The place basically runs itself. I've been to your home but you've never been to mine. Perhaps on our way back, you can stop over."

"I've got roundtrip tickets to Phoenix," he advised.

"You can re-route them," she said, throwing him a challenging glance. "Add Edinburgh as a stopover. We've got ample bedrooms. I'm a superb cook. You might decide you want to stay," she said with a cocky smirk.

"We've been there, discussed that," he said. "You know I have tenure at the university which includes archaeological contracts for the next two years, at least. Then, there are my sons." No need to mention his ex-wife. Kate was keenly aware of her.

"You did propose to me, love, and I accepted. Somewhere in our tangled scheme of things our lives will fit."

"They will," he said assuredly. "We may have to move some pieces around."

"Perhaps it's the other way around."

"I'm not sure I understand," he said confused.

She glanced at him smugly. "The pieces remain in place and we move around them. We commute—part of the time in Scotland, part of the time in Arizona."

The suggested arrangement surprised him. She had been adamant. She could not, would not, live in Arizona. Perhaps she was softening. The first half of the equation could work. The second half was questionable. "Part-time" in Scotland was predictable, "part-time" in Arizona predictably unpredictable. He didn't respond and turned his head, as though distracted, observing the passing countryside. An approaching sign said Latrun, a site of many battles. Ironically, it was also the place, he recalled, where Joshua commanded the sun to stand still. He turned his attention back to her.

She was focused on her rearview mirror and had been glancing back and forth at it during their conversation. "Right now, we may need to let something move around us, if it will."

"As in?" he questioned.

"The black Suburban behind us."

He looked left and right. "This is a major highway. There's a lot of traffic."

"It's been behind us since we left the used car parking lot at the airport." She paused. "And it's almost like whoever's in it wants their presence to be obvious."

He leaned forward and observed the vehicle from his side-view mirror.

"We're not in a hurry," she continued. "I'm taking this next exit, see what happens." With no blinker, she swung the car suddenly right and onto the ramp.

The Suburban continued straight.

Kate drove the car up the ramp.

"False alarm," Chris said.

"Maybe so," she sighed and continued across the intersection, down the ramp on the other side and back onto the highway, the Suburban visible in the distance ahead, until an eighteen wheeler slipped in front of them.

"Other than what you've already told me," Chris said changing the subject, "what do you know about this young American?"

"His name is Emmanuel Jones. We spoke a second time and he told me he was from Austin, Texas, played football at Baylor University, majored in religion and is now attending seminary at Liberty Christian Academy." Chris noticed she had slowed down, probably to keep a distance from the Suburban. "He is on a summer archaeological program through his school. He is alone. He said the study program was arranged through the IAA. As I previously shared with you, he told Dr. Townsend he's concerned the jars might contain valuable scrolls or manuscripts that could fall into the wrong hands."

"Based upon what you've told me about him, any but his would be the wrong hands."

"Meaning?" she asked.

"His Christian persuasion is conservative, probably Fundamentalist. Liberty Christian Academy is Liberty University, founded by Jerry Falwell. Ever heard of him?"

"Yes, but enlighten me."

"Jerry Falwell, until his death a few years ago, was a Fundamentalist leader of the Christian Right. He was in tight with the Israeli Government. Members of the Israeli government are not naïve about the beliefs and clout of the Christian Right in the U.S." He peered ahead to see if he could still see the Suburban and could not, but decided to say nothing. "In 1978, Menachem Begin, Zionist and ultranationalist Israeli prime minister, invited the Reverend Falwell to Israel. The following year, Falwell founded the Moral Majority and received a gift from the Israeli government: a Lear Jet." He tapped her on the shoulder. "Are you connecting these dots?"

She nodded. "I know about the Christian Right. I did not know about the Lear Jet. I am somewhat vaguely aware of American Fundamentalism. It's endemic to your country and not much in the British press."

"It is very much in the Israeli press," he continued. "American Fundamentalists are the counterpart to the Jewish Hasidim, radical conservatives, biblical literalists, keepers of the Word. It is their position that any scriptures, found or unfound, belong to them."

"Outrageous!" She exclaimed. "How can they make such a claim?"

"Because they're God's chosen and the only ones qualified to interpret scripture, discovered or undiscovered," he responded.

"If this is true," she said, "and if he took any thing, manuscripts or otherwise, that might be in the jars that had a Christian origin, he would not consider himself a thief."

"Absolutely! The thieves are the Israelis and Palestinians, or anyone else who doesn't agree with them."

"My God! I had no idea what I might have gotten us into," she expressed.

"We don't know yet," Chris said. "I could be wrong. Our man may just be a naïve explorer."

"He's not naïve if he went to the trouble of locating me at the British Museum," she said.

"Let's hope for the best."

"Tensions in the area are running high," she said. "A spark could set off an armed conflict."

"Holy writ has started wars before," he said nonchalantly observing a passing scene. A couple of monuments and old rusted military vehicles, reminders of battles along the Tel Aviv-Jerusalem corridor during Israel's fight for independence in 1948. Arabs had launched violent attacks to prevent the U.N. decision from being implemented. Attacks from both sides continued and have never stopped. "It doesn't take much to trigger conflict in the area. Disagreement over an archaeological find could do it," he said.

They continued on. After a few miles, she began glancing again at her rearview. "It's back," she said.

"What's back?" he asked, his mind still on war and archaeology.

"The Suburban."

"How could he get behind us?"

"When our view was blocked, the driver must have pulled up the next ramp, waited and re-entered," she guessed. "It's several vehicles back."

"They're getting smarter," he said.

"Or dumber," she countered. "They're not being very subtle about it. Black Suburbans stand out."

He thought a moment, then injected, "Maybe their following *is* intentional. They know who we are and want us to know they know we are here." He looked at her to see her reaction but her face was set, eyes steady ahead. "A warning shot across the bow. Hands off our history."

She looked at him. "You're even smarter," and she reached over, patted him on the thigh.

# CHAPTER FOUR

*Capernaum, Galilee, Passover, A.D. 50*

Jairus still feels strange walking past the synagogue without turning and entering. At one time, he had been the president of the assembly which included all of Capernaum, about fifteen hundred people. He was neither a teacher nor a preacher but was responsible for the order of the synagogue service and keeper of the sacred books, which were the property of the community. He was, in a manner of speaking, the head of the city.

Now, he leads a different group, the Jesus people. Some are former members of the synagogue congregation he once led. Jairus thinks often of Jesus' use of the metaphor "shepherd." When others ask him what he does, Jairus says he is shepherding a Jesus flock. While a synagogue leader, he had received a salary from tithes. He is now a farmer. He owns the land behind him to the crest of the hill and has two olive groves. The income is enough for him and his wife to live comfortably.

He likes to arrive early at the place of gathering, a spot on the shore where Simon Peter, Andrew, James and John moored their boats, where Jesus was often in their company. The service is always simple. It involves prayers, readings from *The Scriptures*, usually the Psalms, and recitation of the sayings of Jesus. Members of the fellowship share concerns and prayers for them are offered. Before each gathering, Jairus needs time to pray and meditate, align his thoughts.

He thinks of those who will be coming and all they have endured. He recalls the day the news of Jesus' death reached Capernaum. As leader of the synagogue, he was one of the first to receive the news. He went immediately to Peter's house to console his wife and family, then to the homes of Andrew and James and John. Levi, also called Matthew, had no family but lived alone near the Via Maris where he collected road taxes.

Along the way, Jairus told others, "Did you hear, the Romans killed Jesus." He would never forget the faces, the sheer shock they reflected. Some wailed loudly, as though one of their own had died. Some were struck dumb, so overwhelmed they showed no emotion. Even children wept, the same Jesus had welcomed and gathered in his arms. Some refused to believe. Days later, word arrived that Jesus had risen from the dead. Women followers had found his tomb empty. Many found this incredible, casting doubt on the news of his crucifixion. As far as they were concerned, Jesus was still alive. Within minutes, the entire village knew. Once he was back home from spreading the word of Jesus' death, Jairus broke down and wept. Within three years, Jesus had brought hope and healing to their world. Crucified? Resurrected? It did not matter. He was gone. All that remained were his teachings, words for common people—fishermen, farmers, laborers, homemakers. Words that knitted together the broken places in their lives, that carried them from one day to the next.

People dealt with the loss of Jesus in different ways. Most resorted to their families for comfort. Others, small bands, wandered the countryside. Many were poor people, sparsely dressed, lacking staffs or bags. They traveled from village to village within Galilee. They gathered on the Sabbath at special places and rallied crowds to listen. Some spoke like prophets, some were charismatics. They believed a new age was dawning, a new kingdom was coming. They were the people Jesus had called the "salt of the earth."

Jairus resigned his position at the synagogue. He told his wife he could no longer be a part of a Judaism locked in its law, imprisoned by its past. The man Jesus had shown a new way, a new set of principles for daily living. Jairus became part of the Jesus movement and in short time, because he had been collecting the sayings of Jesus, a leader.

Jairus looks up and sees his wife and daughter, Hava, walking toward him along the road. It is cobbled with chalky stone and their sandaled feet stir white dust puffs. They grow nearer, leave the road and make their way toward him along a worn path beside the shore. Their colorful garments, belted with sashes, shine brightly. They look lovely in the early sunlight. Hava is now in her early thirties and married with three children, two sons and a daughter. The two sons, Asher and Dan, are ten and eight years old. His granddaughter Michal, whose name means "one who is like God," is six.

Rebecca chides Jairus that he breaks the first commandment, worshiping the little one as though she were a goddess.

Hava is devoted to Jesus. She, whose name means "life," owes the Master her life. Her husband Abner and their children will soon follow. Abner was named well by his parents. He is tall and broad shouldered with the first frost of age touching the sides of his long black hair and streaking his beard. He is, in every way, the "father of light" to his wife and children. A stone mason, he never works far from his home, returning each evening to his wife and children in whom he delights. With Hava, he became one of the first followers of Jesus in Capernaum and is a leader in the fellowship.

Others, too, will come. Mary, the woman Jesus healed in Peter's house, will attend. Another woman, whose name will forever remain unnamed, never misses a service. Jairus has a particular fondness for her. She is the woman Jesus healed of a bleeding disease while on his way to heal his daughter Hava. Miriam, the daughter of Peter, also never misses a service. Today she will bring guests along with several of her neighbors who desire to worship and hear again the master's words. Most are illiterate which is the reason he must recite the sayings to them from his codex.

Watching his wife and daughter draw nearer, Jairus sadly reflects on the rest of his family, two sons and their wives and children. Aaron and Benjamin, though they attended some of the Jesus gatherings and listened to the man, could not follow him. They tended to side with the scribes and Pharisees in Galilee, that the man Jesus was attempting to destroy their religion and replace it with radical ideas like those preached by the wild man, John, further south across the Jordan.

Some of the men begin appearing. In the distance, it is difficult to distinguish them. All are bearded with long hair and rectangular cloaks draped across their bodies. When they emerge from the shadow of trees into the light, Jairus can see their faces. Some are new in the community. Most he knows from childhood, others from their experience with Jesus. Occasionally, a Roman centurion comes. Jesus healed the soldier's paralyzed servant. Then there are two men, one healed of leprosy, the other of paralysis. Some who come were in the crowd the day Jesus fed five thousand. They share basic concerns of life, how to provide and care for their families. For most who come, a crucifixion and resurrection are events far removed from day-to-day life.

Everyone approaches the place of worship in silence. Once they leave the road, no one speaks. The silence communicates. They sit on the ground, some on nearby rocks and look at the sea, the play of light on the waters ushering up memories. This was the place where it all began. Here, the first disciples were chosen. Nearby, the first healings took place. Not far from the shore, a storm was calmed.

Before beginning the service, Jairus keeps his head bowed, praying. He waits a long time before speaking. Some have to walk from homes up the mount, others from distances north and south. Even after he begins, worshippers will arrive and collect around the fringes of the crowd. For them he will repeat the sayings.

Mid-morning he begins with a prayer:

"When you pray, say, 'Father, may your name be holy.

May your rule take place.

Give us each day our daily bread.

Pardon our debts, for we ourselves pardon everyone indebted to us.

And do not bring us to trial ...'"

Then he opens his codex and begins reading, "These are the teachings of Jesus:"

When someone said to him, "I will follow you wherever you go," Jesus answered, "Foxes have their dens, and birds of the sky have nests, but the son of man has nowhere to lay his head."

When another said, "Let me first go and bury my father,"

Jesus said, "Leave the dead to bury the dead."

Go, look, I send you out as lambs among wolves.

Do not carry money, or bag, or sandals, or staff; and do not greet anyone on the road.

Whatever house you enter, say, "Peace be to this house!"

And if a child of peace is there, your greeting will be received.

But if not, let your peace return to you ...

One after another, Jairus continues reading those sayings of instruction he has recalled and recorded. Inevitably, at the conclusion of each service, some of those present come forward with their own memories of words Jesus spoke. In the early days of the movement after Jesus' death, Jairus would hurry home to record what others had told him. His mind, like those of his time, had been trained to remember long discourses. But he could not recall everything. Rebecca would help him but she, too, had lapses. Now, he always carries his inkwell and pens with him to add the sayings and events to his codex immediately. There by the seashore, he sits, long after the congregation has departed, and inscribes all that is told to him. Collecting the sayings is as though he, and others, are putting Jesus' life back together, reconstructing his presence.

On that morning, Miriam, the daughter of Peter, recalls a saying Jairus had not heard. She recalled he had said, "The harvest is abundant, but the workers are few; beg, therefore, the master of the harvest to send out workers into his harvest." A farmer from Chorazim said he would never forget Jesus saying, "No one who puts his hand to the plow and then looks back is fit for the kingdom of God."

"Do you recall the situation?" Jairus asked the farmer. "There must be more to the saying, the reason behind it."

"Verily, I do," the farmer responded. "Someone had said to Jesus, 'I will follow you, but first let me say goodbye to my family.'"

"Many thanks, my brother," Jairus says. "That gives the saying a context. Blessings on you," and he continues writing what the man had told him.

In this manner, line by line, page by page, his sayings of Jesus grow.

# CHAPTER FIVE

*Jerusalem, Israel, May 26, 2012*

The entry into Jerusalem was sudden. One minute Chris and Kate were on the highway, the next they were quickly in a different world of low level buildings and narrow streets. They could see holes in buildings where bullets had struck from conflicts over the decades. Hasidim, ultra-orthodox Jews, strolled along the street with soldiers, automatic rifles slung over their shoulders. A mixture of ancient and modern, religious and secular.

"Here we are," she announced, as she pulled in front of the Olive Garden Hotel. A bellman came out to help with the luggage, but Kate asked him to park the car, that they could manage their carry-ons. Chris marveled at the orange and mauve flower beds surrounding the front entrance. Once inside, he understood why it was called The Olive Garden Hotel. It was built around a large ancient olive tree which sprouted from the center of the lobby floor. The place had an elegant but comfortable bar. Two attractive female clerks were attendant and efficient, checking them in quickly to separate rooms.

"At least we're on the same floor," he noted as they walked to their rooms on a maroon carpet runner crossed with gold stars of David.

"So they are," she said breezily, and smiled.

By American standards, the rooms were small but efficient, tidy and clean. He changed clothes into something more comfortable, khaki pants and a knit short sleeve shirt, loafers with no socks. Even late in the afternoon, the temperature outside was still hot.

It was almost six o'clock when they met back in the lobby bar. She was wearing dark pants, a white blouse and flats, nothing to attract attention. Both looked like tourists. She ordered her usual, Glenfiddich over ice. He settled for a glass of chardonnay. They clinked glasses, toasting their reunion.

"Who do you think was in that Suburban?" he asked, looking left and right, assessing the small number of patrons in the bar.

She took a soundless sip from her glass. "I don't know. Apparently, they knew who we were."

"Maybe Passport Control alerted them."

"Possibly," she replied. "I doubt the source is our American student. That would have defeated his whole purpose for requesting aid. To your point, airport security may have alerted someone." She raised her eyebrows skeptically. "But then, since November of last year, our faces have been in the news and on social media. Our incognito tourist days may be over."

"Okay. Let's review the options," he offered. "The most logical choice is the Israeli Antiquities Authority and their Robbery Prevention Unit. After all, the Syrians accused us of stealing the Markan scroll. It was all over the news."

"We didn't steal it," she retorted. "We purchased it from a beggar at a fair price."

He drummed his fingers against the bowl of his wine glass. "But, against Syrian law, we took it out of the country. Assad had his legal team file charges in a New York federal court—"

"—British court, too—," she reminded him.

"—which threw it out along with the extradition demands."

"A reminder, dear Chris, that we're out of our comfort zones."

He held his glass up, swirled the wine contemplatively. "I would not think that Syria would be an option as long as we stay in Israel."

"Think twice," Kate advised. "Reality check: Damascus is only a hundred fifty miles from the Golan, a three hour drive in light traffic. Syria has spies and operatives in Israel. They maneuver regularly and unchallenged from a position in the Golan which is even closer to Jerusalem." She raised a brow. "Rest assured, Chris, Assad has not forgotten that the most valuable biblical relic in recent times was taken from Syrian soil … and by us."

"Hmmm," he murmured stroking the stem of his wine glass. "What are our other options?"

"That's it," she said. "Unless, there's one we're missing."

"Freelancers. Bounty Hunters."

She tilted her head thoughtfully. "Possibly. But they're not sophisticated enough to have known we were at the airport."

There was a lull in the conversation as they enjoyed their drinks.

"I presume we'll eat dinner," he finally said, "then have an evening stroll around the old city. It's not far from the hotel, you know."

Following a long sip of her scotch, she gave a single nod of acknowledgement. "Dinner, yes; the stroll may have to wait."

"Why's that? We don't meet our young American until tomorrow."

"Plans have changed. He texted me while I was in the room. It seems he's antsy. He's meeting us here in the lobby, at six thirty." She glanced at her watch, then her drink. "Which is about the rest of this one drink away."

"How will we know him?"

"I asked him the same question and he laughed. He said he was from Texas, that I'd recognize him. He speaks with a pronounced drawl."

"How will he know you?" he asked.

"He said that was irrelevant, that I would know him. He has an ego."

"Does he know you're not alone?" he pressed.

"I told him you would be here," she responded, her eyes scanning the bar. "From what he'd gleaned from the media, he knew about you as well. He seemed pleased, not threatened."

"We need to make sure he's not just using us for another purpose."

"I made that clear," she stated. "We were involved only to assist in research and assessment and that he must report the find to the IAA, if it's their dig, or the Palestinian Department of Antiquities, if it's theirs."

"And his response?"

"An absolute 'no' on the Palestinians," she said. "A weak 'yes' on the IAA. We can prevail against him. It's two against one," she declared looking firmly over her drink. "If he will not report the find, *we will*."

He looked to his right and didn't believe what he saw swaggering around the olive tree. "I believe this is our man coming now."

"My God," she said under her breath.

"It may be one against two," Chris clarified.

The man striding in their direction was over six-feet tall, broad-shouldered with wide ears, wearing a white ten-gallon Stetson, brown leather tooled cowboy boots, a sheepskin vest, a long-sleeved denim shirt and blue jeans. As he got closer, a thin Amish-looking beard became visible. His boots clicked loudly, too loudly. In his left hand, he held a book.

"He said you'd recognize him," Chris whispered again.

"Obviously he recognizes us," she said, as he approached their table.

Both rose to greet him.

The young man stopped in front of Chris and, smiling through clenched teeth and shaking his hand, said, "I'm Jones," with an excess of familiarity and in a high thin voice that had less volume than his physical presence.

"Dr. Chris Jordan. And this is Dr. Kate Ferguson," he said, palming a hand toward her.

She extended a hand. "At last, face to face, Mr. Jones."

"Please be seated," Jones said. He had a small mouth in a broad chin and a mannerism of pursing his lips before he spoke.

They all sat.

"Would you like a drink?" Kate asked.

"A Coca-Cola," Jones answered.

Chris raised a hand. A server came quickly and took the order and asked, "Would you like another scotch and wine?"

Kate leveled a hand over her glass.

"We're fine," Chris confirmed.

Jones removed his Stetson and hung it on the back of his chair. A shaved head reflected the lobby's high hanging lights. He placed the book face down on the table. He sat straight-backed and commenced pulling at each finger one by one emitting little snapping noises.

Chris gestured at the book. "Mr. Jones, is the book related to why we're here?" he probed, ignoring the finger-popping.

"In a way," Jones said. He finished pulling his fingers and turned it over for them to see the title, *Through My Eyes*. "It's by Tim Tebow," he said, without mentioning the co-author, Nathan Whitaker.

"Who's Tim Tebow?" Kate inquired.

"Whaooo," Jones said, leaning back exaggerating a flinch. "He's a famous Christian football player," he said, popping a finger he'd forgotten as if for emphasis, then laid his palms flat on the table. He had a habit of jiggling his legs when he spoke.

"They don't keep up with American football in Scotland," Chris told him, nodding at Kate.

"I don't even keep up with Scottish football," she exclaimed. "How's the book related to two ancient jars?"

"Maybe it's not," Jones said. "I'm over here trying to trace the origins of Christianity, learn about the great Christians of that era. Tim Tebow's at the other end of that timeline. I always carry a book with me to read if people aren't on time."

Chris and Kate exchanged glances.

The server brought a bottle of Coca Cola with a glass of ice and set it on the table by the book. Two men in business suits sat down at the table to their right. Kate eyed them sharply and bumped Chris' shoe under the table.

Chris acknowledged the message. "Since we're eating here, Mr. Jones, why don't we move to the dining room?"

"Suits me," Jones said. He put his hat back on and grabbed his Coke and book.

Kate motioned to the server that they were moving to the dining area.

The restaurant was filled with the sound of clinking silver, clicking of tea cups against their saucers, tables being bussed.

The dining area was a long room with a buffet along one wall. Chris picked a corner table at the far end, frustrating the maitre d' who was trying to steer them to one closer to the entrance.

"Is there something going on I don't know about?" Jones said, as they seated themselves. "And please call me Emmanuel."

"Ever heard of the IAA, Emmanuel?" Chris asked.

"Sure," Emmanuel said. "The Israeli Antiquities Authority. They oversee the antiquities in Israel, discovered and undiscovered. Our site is under their authority."

"I take it you also know about Elad," Kate injected.

"If you mean the right-wing Jewish settlement organization, yes," said Emmanuel in a lecturing authoritative voice. "They have the backing of the IAA which monitors all archaeological work in the country and are funded by private donors."

Kate again: "They also use archaeology as a means of expanding settlements in Arab East Jerusalem. Case in point, Silwan is now listed in guidebooks as the City of David."

"What's your concern about IAA and Elad?" Emmanuel probed. "And why are you speaking in low voices?"

"When we went through passport control at Ben Gurion Airport," Chris said, "passport agents identified me and probably Dr. Ferguson. You know the rest of that story."

"In other words," Kate interrupted, "we are marked. Our discussions, particularly with you, must remain private."

"Gotcha," Jones said glibly and opened his menu. "A ham sandwich and glass of milk, that's all I want," and closed his menu with a decisive slap.

Chris and Kate decided to go through the elaborate buffet. She made a salad and collected some fruit. Chris settled for boiled shrimp, a slab of prime rib and vegetables. They returned to the table and sat down.

"Y'all go ahead and eat. Don't wait for me. But I'll say a blessing." He reached out for their hands which they obliged and said an extensive blessing. A server stood by until he finished and then placed his sandwich in front of him, flipped back the table cloth and put his milk on the bare table top.

"What's all that for?" Emmanuel exclaimed too loudly.

"Ham and dairy products cannot be served on the same spread," the server said. "It is Jewish law."

"I'll be darn," Jones said with a buckwheat grin. "Glad I'm a Christian."

Silence for several minutes while they ate, Emmanuel like a machine. As though they were something fragile, the jars had not been mentioned. That was something Chris and Kate had not discussed, how to broach the subject with their new associate.

"So, you are here on invitation from the Israeli government?" Chris attempted.

"Yep. Through my school I am. The Israelis like Liberty University."

"They like your school and others of like persuasion because you help finance their settlements," Chris said staring straight into his eyes.

"That's right," Emmanuel voiced. "Jesus won't return, the Rapture won't happen, until all Jews are back in Palestine," he paused, glanced at Chris then Kate, "including the West Bank."

"But you are withholding knowledge of artifacts from these Jewish friends of yours," Kate confronted him.

"I'm not withholding from them. We like the Jews more than they like us," Emmanuel said, finishing off a bite of his sandwich and dusting his lips with his napkin. "When it comes to archaeological finds, the Israelis look out for themselves. Look what they've done in Bethlehem, practically run all the Christians out."

"I can't argue with that," Chris agreed, "though the Arabs i.e., Hamas, had a hand in that exodus. Jewish holy sites in Jericho and Nablus have been burned to the ground while Palestinian police looked on."

"That may be," Emmanuel said. "But if there are documents in that scroll, Christian documents, they may never see the light of day. If they do, it'll be after years of red tape."

"You are certain the jars were part of the Israeli dig," Kate questioned.

"I was working on an Israeli dig," said Emmanuel.

"That's not her question," Chris jumped in. "This is a very sensitive issue."

"I can't see that on site, off site, makes any difference," Emmanuel contended flippantly.

Kate got in his face. "If you found them off the site, it could make a big difference for the Palestinian Authority, if and when they get wind of it. This coming September, Palestinians will petition the United Nations for membership as an independent state. Both sides are staking out territory for archaeological research and digs. Neither have oil, but they've got antiquities, tens of thousands of them worth fortunes."

"So?" Emmanuel exclaimed indignantly.

Chris arranged the salt and pepper shakers and napkin holder in a triangle. "Have you ever heard of the Oslo Accords?" he said, looking at Emmanuel.

"No."

"That figures," Kate said curtly then tried to soften her comment. "What I mean is, you are from the U.S. and probably not tuned into the nuances of Israeli-Palestinian relations."

"Under this agreement," Chris interrupted, "signed by both parties in 1993, the Palestinian Authority was to control most archaeological and heritage sites within the main cities of the West Bank, Gaza and East Jerusalem. That includes Nablus and your dig which, based upon your description, is east of Nablus." He lifted the salt shaker and set it down. "The Palestinians and Israelis were to have conjoint control over most inhabited villages." He lifted the pepper shaker for that symbolic representation and placed it near the saltshaker. "The third leg of the agreement gave the Israelis the remainder, or about seventy-five percent," he concluded, and pointed at the napkin holder.

"In that case," Emmanuel said, "if I found them off site, they'd belong to the Israelis. No problem."

Kate touched the napkin holder. "The Palestinians would argue that is a gray area, particularly if the site is near Nablus and ancient Shechem."

"It's not far from Shechem," Emmanuel conveyed.

"That heightens the tension," Kate said emphatically. "Many of the Palestinians reject the idea that the Israelis get the remainder of what is considered an autonomous Palestinian State. A significant finding in the area you have described could create a major conflict."

"In Texas parlance," Chris said, "the Palestinians will jump on this like a junebug on a mosquito, as they have other charges that the IAA is stealing Arab heritage. They can cite chapter and verse. All of this has been simmering a long time."

"Your find could ignite the tinder box," Kate warned. "This is why we feel you should notify the IAA, come clean and public with it. Let the IAA and the Palestinian Authority fight it out."

"And if I don't," Emmanuel said cockily.

Chris revisited his triangle. "This is Israel," he said pointing to the salt shaker. "This is Palestine," pointing to the pepper shaker. "And this," he picked up the napkin holder, "is the United States of America," then dropped the holder onto the table for effect, all of the napkins spilling onto the floor. "You drag your country into it, if you get my drift."

The server arrived quickly and commenced picking up the napkins and replacing them in the holder.

"I'm sorry," Chris apologized to him. "I got carried away."

In the distraction of the dialogue and enactment, no one had noticed that the two suited gentlemen had moved from the bar into the dining room and seated themselves at a nearby table. Chris nodded at Kate, but she had noticed. The intent of their move was not subtle. They could have chosen a table near the front of the restaurant rather than one toward the back of a large area of empty tables.

Emmanuel seemed oblivious to the men's presence. "My country is a Christian nation," he breathed patriotically. "Anything pertaining to the origins of Christianity should, I think, belong to a Christian nation, not a Jewish nation or Palestinian state."

Chris looked at Kate, a fork of salad on its way to her mouth frozen mid-air and behind it a wide-eyed dumbfounded look. Aware the men were probably hearing every word, he looked back at Emmanuel and formulated a challenge. "So, Emmanuel, is it your opinion that if a man from Tennessee visiting the Alamo finds, in a hidden compartment, a pistol belonging to Davy Crockett, he has the right to hijack it and take it back to Tennessee."

"Now that there's diff'rent. You're talking apples and oranges."

"It's the same principle," Kate confronted him.

"Where are you staying?" Chris said, changing the subject.

"In Jericho at the Sami Youth Hostel."

"Why not Nablus?" asked Kate. "It's closer to your dig."

"Nablus is not safe," Emmanuel said. "It's rough and has the highest level of resistance since the Israeli occupation. There's been a lot of damage and destruction. Two other American workers from other colleges on the dig were already at Sami and willing to share their room. It cut expenses for all of us."

"That certainly makes sense," Kate remarked, "but how do you get to and from your work site?"

"I've rented a vehicle," Emmanuel replied. "My roommates share the gas costs. It's really not a bad commute."

They needed to get to the reason the heart of the issue, the precise location of the jars and when they could see them. But with possible agents of AII or Elad two tables away, this was not the place or time. They were almost through eating. Chris waved a hand at the server signaling they were ready for the check.

"And furthermore…" Emmanuel began but Chris clamped a finger over his mouth and nodded at the company to their left.

"Let's wait," Chris admonished.

Emmanuel noted the men and nodded.

Chris signed the credit card slip. They quietly rose and walked toward the restaurant entrance and into the lobby.

"I'm sorry y'all," Emmanuel said. He was still holding his hat, rotating its brim in his hands. "I didn't really believe we were being followed."

"We don't know that we are," Kate said. "But as Chris told you, he had a minor problem getting through passport control. We are known entities. What we took out of Syria is common knowledge and you have knowledge of two artifacts here in Israel."

"And the Israelis have an effective security system," Chris said. "Elad has its agents all over the place."

Emmanuel glanced back into the restaurant. "Now that we've left them in the dust, we can move on to the next thing."

"Let's step into the parking lot out back," Chris urged.

They walked through double-glass doors into a spacious parking lot.

Chris looked around to insure they were alone. "The next level would be the jars," Chris said. "Where are they?"

"Where I left them, in the cave beside the rubble of rocks they were under that took a while to remove."

"You are sure no one saw you around the cave," Chris said.

"Positive. I looked around."

"You can't be too sure these days," Kate advised. "The Robbery Prevention unit has sly operatives with night-binoculars and surveillance equipment."

Chris looked at his watch. "It's almost eight. The site is east of Nablus which is fifty miles from here." He looked at Emmanuel. "Is it near the entrance to the Wadi?"

"Yes," Emmanuel confirmed. "Where the Wadi Faria enters the Jordan Valley."

Chris was amazed how supposedly informed people were still calling it the Wadi Faria and not Farah. But he was not going to challenge.

"It's about an hour to the site from Jericho," Emmanuel said. "I would guess it's about the same from Jerusalem."

"You're not taking into consideration the checkpoints," Kate cautioned.

"There's just two main checkpoints between Jerusalem and Nablus," Emmanuel advised, "the Kalandia at Ramallah and the Katara south of Nablus."

"What about the Huwwara checkpoint just outside of Nablus," she questioned. "That's the most notorious one."

"I don't know. I always go from Jericho."

"They dismantled it last year," Chris advised. "I saw a news item about it." For once, he was one-up on his partner.

"But that's not counting the 'flying' checkpoints," she said, "the ad hoc ones they set up at any moment."

"I understand," Emmanuel acquiesced. "So it might take longer than an hour. We still have plenty of time. You can follow me in your car. That avoids your having to bring me back here and I can go to Jericho from there."

Chris looked at Kate. Both were thinking, tried to speak at once and Chris deferred to Kate.

"That's okay with me," she said and looked at Chris who shrugged his shoulders and weakly nodded in agreement.

"That's a plan," Emmanuel said. "My vehicle's right over there," and he pointed at a late model Land Rover. "For the two months I'm here, Hertz gave me a deal on this when I flew into Tel Aviv. It can navigate the terrain like you wouldn't believe."

"I'll bet," Kate said. "I've driven one before. It can climb a mountain."

"It'll have to get us to the cave," Emmanuel said. "Otherwise, it's a hike," as he began pulling on driving gloves, black leather ones with airholes in the back.

"Our car is nearby," Chris said. "We'll follow you. Which route will you take?"

"North on Highway Four-forty-three to Ramallah. You know about the check point at the wall before Ramallah."

They nodded.

"Then Route Sixty to Nablus," Emmanuel continued. "There are several checkpoints around Nablus but Katara, the main one, is on Route Sixty. That road can be closed for security reasons at any time. We may have to alter the route if that happens."

"And if it doesn't happen and we get through," said Chris, "What next?"

Kate was taking notes.

"At a major intersection due east of Nablus," Emmanuel continued, "we take Route Fifty-Seven, follow it along the Wadi Faria ridge. Just before the Wadi ends in the Jordan Valley, about two miles before the road intersects Highway Ninety coming from Galilee, I'll stop. You'll will need to leave your car somewhere and go with me in the Land Rover."

Kate driving, they pulled out of the parking lot into St. George Street, the Land Rover in front of them. Chris kept glancing in the passenger side-view mirror and saw no lights following them. Perhaps they were wrong about the two men, but their behavior was suspicious.

"There is something about this that doesn't feel right," Kate exclaimed.

"There's a lot about it that doesn't feel right," he agreed. "Including the driving gloves he put on. I think we made a mistake."

"We may have made more than one," she countered. "Which one do you have in mind?"

"That we're not all in the same vehicle. I'd feel more comfortable having him with us."

"I'd feel more comfortable if we were driving a Land Rover or Jeep," she said.

"The way he describes the place," he added, "we might need a tank."

# CHAPTER SIX

*Capernaum, Galilee, November, A.D. 66*

Jairus rises early before daybreak. He sits waiting for that early light to shine through the window, the first soft rays of the new day to fall onto the pages open before him. He likes to write early in the morning, when the house and village are quiet and the light comes from a softer sun. When the smell of the earth and grass are fresh. When he can feel the cool breezes from the sea. Hear its waves lapping softly on the shore, the sounds of the birds. The soothing sounds and touches of the land's soul. When his concentration is sharper, his hand steadier.

Sixteen years have lapsed since he began collecting and recording the sayings of the prophet Jesus, much of the time spent traveling, interviewing others. He is growing older and feels an urgency to begin compiling his work. Travelers from the north tell of conflicts. At Caesarea Philippi, Greeks sacrificed birds to their god in front of a Jewish synagogue. A Jewish Temple clerk, Eliezar ben Hanania, ceased prayers and sacrifices for the Emperor. Greeks of Caesarea attacked Jewish neighbors. Jews responded in kind expelling Greeks from Judea, Galilee and the Golan Heights. Tensions are rising. He fears this is just the beginning.

He watches the shade of night recede across the sea and then the sun fling shafts of sunlight, like a long-legged spider, over The Golan brightening the pages of the codex and the open scroll. This is the final stage of his work, copying the sayings of the master from his parchment codex notebooks to the scrolled papyrus. He knows the work will be tedious. He is accustomed to writing in Aramaic. The sayings in the codex are in Aramaic. But he wants the world to see them, so he will be translating and writing in Greek. The letters will flow differently, from left to right, not right to left. When he made errors on the parchment, they were easily erased and corrected on the leather surface. Writing on the papyrus scroll will be different. Erasing an error leaves a smudge on the delicate surface, one not easily cleansed.

He purchased the scroll from a passing caravan. The vendor, who made the transaction seated atop his camel, said the papyrus was fresh from Egypt. He had purchased it from a chartaria in Cesaraea Maritima for twenty-six drachma and would sell it for twenty-eight. It was a full ream of twenty sheets glued together and wound onto oak rods. The amount was more than Jairus needed to pay but the vendor refused to break the scroll and sell him less. Later, he could break the composite and begin another scroll.

The sayings fill two codices. He keeps them in a large leather casing. He is glad he purchased two instead of one. He looks at the codex to his left, runs his finger up the page to the first line then moves his eyes to the open scroll on his right. He dips his reed pen into the small jar of ink he has made by mixing soot, gum and water. He leans forward, his eyes close to his work, and drops the first letter, *Epsilon*, followed by the second letter, *Nu*. The next letters and words come with difficulty, but he knows the rhythm will improve. He sits back and looks at his beginning: "In those days the word of God came to John the Baptist, the son of Zecharia, in the desert of Judea."

He has been writing several minutes and feels her hand on his shoulder.

He turns and greets his wife's soft morning smile. She is peering over his shoulder.

"Can you read it?" he says.

"It is in Greek, not Aramaic. But I recognize some of the words. I see John the Baptist, Zecharia and Judea."

"You are correct," he says then reads the line to her.

She bends her head closer. "You write well, dear one. Your letters are well-stroked and evenly spaced, like the work of a professional scribe."

"You are kind. The work is slow and tiring. I dare not err on the papyrus."

"You can erase them," she says. "I've seen you spit on the end of your finger and use the rag tied to your waist."

"That is much easier on the leather parchment. Papyrus is thinner and fragile. Erasing creates smears."

"Why do you not use parchment on the scroll?"

"The leather leaves of the codices," he gestures with his hand, "cannot be bound end to end like papyrus sheets. They must be sewn together. The long strip would have been too unwieldy to roll into a volume. The stitches would make disfiguring ridges. For a scroll, papyrus is better."

"You have chosen the more difficult procedure," she responds.

"Yes. My eyes will tire. My hand will cramp. I must take rests."

She stretches her hand, the blue net of her wrists, to the top of the open scroll. "What is this?" she questions, pointing to a small dot at the top.

He picks up a needle lying on the table beside the scroll. "I make small pricks with the needle at the top of each page to set my margins."

"And these?" She moves her finger down thin horizontal lines lightly drawn across the page. "They must guide your writing."

"Yes. I write two narrow columns on a page. This helps prevent the scroll from becoming bulky and difficult to unroll."

"Clever," she avers. "But I see your writing is not at the beginning of the scroll. Did you skip the first leaf?"

With a hand he rolls the left rod taut to the first leaf. "This is called the protocol," he says, and points to an inscription. "You can see it includes the date and place of manufacture. Romans date their years by the two consuls in power at the time. The names here, C. Luccius Telesinus and C. Suetonius Paullinus II, are the current reigning consuls. The papyrus is from Egypt but was manufactured in Caesarea Maritima. I purchased it in May from a caravan vendor who said he bought it in that city."

"I have read scrolls before and never noticed a protocol."

"Some scribes remove the protocol," he says. "I have chosen to leave it. Otherwise the new first sheet would have to be reinforced by pasting another sheet to it and reattached to the rod, the umbilicus, and that would be extra work."

She pats him on the back. "I will leave you to your writing and prepare breakfast. Then you can rest."

He looks back across the sea, the sun now well above the rim of The Golan. He thinks how fortunate he is to have a wife like Rebecca. There were times he had thought of abandoning his project. Though errors were not difficult to erase on the parchment codex leaves, he was making far too many. On some pages it seemed a child, not an adult, had been at work. He had spilled and wasted precious ink. He also questioned his right to record the master's sayings. He was not a disciple. But Rebecca had encouraged him.

He had been in the presence of Jesus, heard him teach. A man named Paul was writing about Jesus and had seen him only in a vision.

He copies a few more lines and Rebecca calls him to breakfast. Around the hearth she has set bowls of olives, dried figs, and carob, a plate of bread and a cup of watered-down wine. They are eating in silence and a commotion outside occurs. It seems to come from the south on the main thoroughfare that passes in front of their house. He gets up and goes to the door. A small crowed is gathered around a man who apparently has just entered Capernaum. By the hysterical tone of their animated voices, Jairus can tell something of significance has occurred. As he nears he hears the words *Romans, garrison, Jerusalem.*

He stops Mathias, a neighbor, leaving the group heading his way and inquires.

"Several months ago," Mathias says, "Florus, the Roman procurator stole vast amounts of silver from the Temple. Jewish rebels responded by overthrowing the Roman military garrison and lynching all of the Roman soldiers."

"Yes. I knew of this. It occurred in early autumn, in September. Surely, the Romans retaliated," says Jairus.

"Indeed," responds Mathias. "The emperor sent the Twelfth legion, under the Syrian Legate Cestius Gallus, to restore order and quell the revolt. He massacred thousands at Jaffe, captured Narbata and Sipphoris, but the Jews ambushed and defeated them at Beth Horon."

Jairus does not believe his ears, an undisciplined rabble of Jews defeating a disciplined Roman legion. The first emotions sweeping through him—pride and joy—evaporate quickly, replaced by a feeling of terror that makes him tremble. "I fear we have stung a giant," he says, "one that will step on the ant who bit him and grind him into the earth. But that is not all I fear. Four years ago, High Priest Ananias illegally seized power and ordered the death of James, the brother of Jesus called the Messiah. You remember?"

Mathias shakes his head. "It was a murderous act for which Ananias was deposed as High Priest."

"I fear that now the Romans have been defeated, Ananias will again be in power."

"It has happened, dear friend," says Mathias. "Ananias is the rebel commander of Jerusalem."

"What about the Roman ruler, Agrippa?" Jairus says. "Is he still in the city?"

"No. I was told he left with his sister, Bernice, and other Roman officials to come here, to Galilee, to Tiberius. Others, including many followers of Jesus, fear reprisals and have abandoned the city to the radicals to face the inevitable," predicts Mathias.

"It is inevitable," says Jairus. "Thank you, friend, though the news is not good," and he turns to head back to his house.

Rebecca is waiting in the doorway, an anxious look on her face. "I see by your look that what you learned is foreboding."

"It is, dear one," and he tells her the news he had heard. "Two years ago I watched the comet cross the sky and recalled the quote from the Book of Numbers in the Scriptures: 'A star shall come forth out of Jacob, a scepter shall rise out of Israel.' Some say it is a prediction of the Messiah."

"But our messiah will not bring destruction," she says. "He will bring a reign of peace."

"This is true. But he foretold destruction and desolation before his coming."

"The destruction you heard about is in Jerusalem. Surely, it will not involve Galilee. Our capital, Sepphoris, and Tiberius, are pro-Roman. Agrippa has come here for safety. Jesus healed the paralytic son of the Roman officer who lived here. He even said of the officer he had not seen greater faith in Israel."

"But Galilee," he reminds her, "has a reputation of being independent and harboring dissidents. Jesus was from Galilee. He was crucified for being an insurrectionist. He said Capernaum would go to hell."

"I do not recall him making that statement," she utters.

"I will show you." He opened the second codex, turned the first page then another. "Here," he pointed, drawing her face closer: "It will not go as hard with Tyre and Sidon at the judgment as with you. As for you, Capernaum, do you think will be exalted to the heavens? No, you shall go fall into Hades.'"

"Jairus, if you believe the last day, the eschaton, is near, why do you write what no one will read?" she questions.

"Because no one knows," he responds. "The son of man 'will come like lightning flashing from one end of the sky to the other.' Jesus said we must be vigilant and prepared. His word will prepare others."

The look on her face he cannot decipher, whether it is one of disbelief or doubt, indifference or confusion. It is not one of affirmation. She is supportive of his writing, but often differed on issues of faith. Her next comment is helpful.

"He told us not to be anxious," she reminds him. "That is a word I choose to believe. I am prepared, and you as well. If your work helps others, then they, too, shall be prepared. Will you finish your breakfast?" and she points toward the hearth.

"No. I have no appetite. Perhaps later. With the news we have heard, I must waste no time finishing the scroll before the Romans come. Believe me, they will come and show no mercy."

"Very well," she says and kisses him on the cheek. "I share not your opinion. We are not the Jews they seek. We are not radicals in Jerusalem but followers of Jesus the teacher."

He shakes his head in disgust. "My dear naïve one. We are Jews. The Romans do not know the difference. They still only remember they crucified a Jew from Galilee who claimed to be the Messiah."

He returns to his desk, runs his finger on the codex page to where he stopped, and copies the next words onto the scroll: *For the son of man is coming at an hour you do not expect.*

# CHAPTER SEVEN

*Jerusalem, May 26, 2012*

Before they had left the hotel, Chris had checked his laptop regarding Israeli checkpoints. There were 522 in the West Bank, up from 503 in 2010. Most were not on the West Bank boundary, but scattered throughout the territory. That did not include the temporary "flying" checkpoints Kate had mentioned that average about 500 a month. All were staffed by Israeli Military Police and Israel Border Police.

The evening was coming on, the sky changing from blue to dark blue. They expected the passage through the Kalandia Checkpoint at Ramallah to go smoothly, but Emmanuel was held up fifteen minutes, security guards shining bright halogen flashlights over and under his Land Rover. He finally passed through and Chris and Kate watched his tail lights pull over and stop.

As they drove up to the gate, they learned the reason Emmanuel was held up. He had carelessly told the guards the identities of the individuals in the car behind him and where he was taking them. Chris let Kate do all of the talking. On their last venture into Syria, he had learned that she was smooth at border crossings and checkpoints.

She did not disappoint. She told the guard she was with the British Museum and her companion was with the University of North Arizona and that they were in Israel to assist a research crew on the site where the young man in the Land Rover was taking them. Yes, they understood it was an IAA dig. Yes, it was unusual for them to be going at night, but they had just arrived in Israel and had little time before returning and they understood the site was well lit. No, they were not there to exploit artifacts. Yes, they understood Israeli law about archeological findings. The official stepped into the booth, made a phone call, spoke briefly with someone then returned, handed back their passports and waved them through.

They pulled up beside Emmanuel who was waiting and obviously perturbed. He rolled down his window. "Can you believe that?" he said with a nervous shallow laugh.

"Believe it," Chris said. "This is Israel. Now they know who we are, why we're here and where we're going."

"I didn't know what else to say," Emmanuel blurted. "The guy was giving me twenty questions."

"What's done is done," advised Kate. "If we lose you, call or text me. You've got my cell number."

Emmanuel gave a cocky thumbs up and pulled ahead of them.

The four-lane bypassed Ramallah. They passed lit up convenience stores, gas stations and motels, their eyes on Emmanuel's taillights. Behind them lay the city, a distant blaze of busy lights. Soon they entered Al-Bireh.

"You know much about this place?" Chris asked.

"Al-Bireh. Yes, it's where Palestinian government ministries, cultural organizations and women's groups have their offices. If I'm not mistaken, it's also the location of UNESCO, now called the World Heritage Center."

"That's right, you would know that in your job with the British Museum," he said mockingly.

"And my reserve status with the British Special Forces," she added smugly.

He laughed. "You might have to go back into active service before we're out of here."

She shot him a hard look. "That's not funny," she said in a testy voice. "If this find turns out to be nothing or a hoax, we leave peacefully, no one will even know we've been here." She tilted her head back and hiked her mouth to one side. "But if it turns out to be something significant and we don't handle it right, we may not leave at all."

"That's a touch dramatic," he said ironically.

"Perhaps a *touch* of history will help you understand, dearest one," she said with a bite of sarcasm. "In 1974, Israel's membership in UNESCO was stripped because of its archaeological damages on the Temple Mount in Jerusalem."

"I knew about that."

"But, did you know it was reinstated in 1977 when the U. S. threatened to withdraw forty million in funding?"

"No," he admitted.

"Did you also know that your U. S. of A. passed laws in 1990 and 1994 prohibiting financial contributions to any UN organization that accepts Palestine as a full member? Palestine was added to UNESCO in 2011. Israel immediately froze funding for the organization and placed sanctions on the Palestinian Authority."

He twirled a finger. "Go on, you're on a roll."

"I need to unroll a year," she said. "In October, 2010, UNESCO gave world heritage status to the sites of the Tomb of the Patriarchs and Rachel's Tomb stating they were significant to the people of Jewish, Muslim and Christian traditions and accused Israel of highlighting only the Jewish character of the sites."

"Now I *did* know that," he nodded, "along with the zinger that followed. They were declared an integral part of Palestinian territory and any unilateral action taken by Israel would violate international law."

"You are well informed," she said. "Then you're aware that UNESCO wants to add the Church of Nativity in Bethlehem to the World Heritage list. Decisions at its next meeting this June could set off more conflicts. UNESCO also recently reprimanded Israel over a cartoon calling for the bombing of its headquarters in Ramallah."

"You are much better informed than I," Chris admitted.

"Bottom line," she continued, "these two jars could be an archaeological powder keg. A wrong step would spark its explosion."

"I get it," he demurred. "In a lighter vein, Al-Bireh is supposedly the place where Mary and Joseph lost their preteen son before finding him in Jerusalem at the Temple challenging grownups with his questions. It's also the site of Arafat's tomb. He'd be fogging the lid of his coffin if he knew what was going on now in the West Bank," he said and pointed to a hilltop. "That must be Tel-al-Nasbeh over there."

"That one I don't know," she said.

"It's the biblical city of Mizbeh. Taybeh, a small Christian village, is not far from it."

"Taybeh is a beer," she said. "It's sold in the UK."

He nodded. "The place is more popular for its beer than its Christian heritage. Townfolk enjoy raising a glass to the place they believe Jesus spent his last hours with the disciples."

"Speaking of last hours," she said wistfully, "the last we had together seem long ago."

*Long ago.* Distance. Time. Two words that defined his work. Coming from her, they cut. *The last we had together seem long ago.* Was the comment an opening for discussion? Was she testing the waters? The last time they were together was in Arizona, when he proposed and she accepted. It did seem like long ago. She was sensing *his* distance, not hers. He knew the reason. It wasn't the physical distance. Or the time. It was the other person in the distance and the time.

His mind slid off center. He didn't know how to respond. He looked out the window, into the darkness, allowed his thoughts to expand. He did not love, or fall back in love, with Allyson. That romance was dead. But she had some mysterious claim on him. Was it the past that wouldn't let go? Was it his sons and grandchildren to be, the family politics, bringing someone new, a stranger, into that emerging mix? Was it fearing the leap of faith, the risk. He could get another teaching job in Scotland. If he couldn't, she could get one for him, but without tenure. He wouldn't be out of work. The famous discovery in Syria was bringing the mountain to Mohammed. He was turning down more digs than he could manage. Or did he need psychological help? Was he just passive and couldn't make up his mind? He needed to square with her, that anxious thought circulating and she let him off the hook.

"What's your read on this guy?" she questioned, breaking up his thoughts. "One minute he strikes me as Texas macho and the next as an overgrown wimp."

*Wimp* turned him around in the seat so he faced her. "The bravado is ingrained," he said. "Most central Texas males project that tough mental exterior. I'm unsure why he unraveled the way he did. He could have told them where he was going. He didn't have to tell them he was leading us. Too much information."

"He never answered whether he was off or on site when he discovered the cave."

"We're going to find out soon," Chris concluded.

For a while, they drove in silence. There was a question he wanted to ask her and now was as good a time as any. "Did you bring the gun with you?"

She looked sharply at him then back at the road. "Yes. It's in my purse. Why?"

"Israel is not Syria. Here they don't cotton to people carrying guns through checkpoints."

"Cotton?"

"I'm sorry. That's a term our man ahead of us would use. It's euphemistic in the South for tolerate. Don't ask me its origin. I'm from Arizona."

"And I'm from the UK and I carry British and Israeli permits. So let's just let it go at that," she bristled and laughed coldly. "If we have problems at this next checkpoint, we need to have a talk with our friend."

*Long ago* was turning into *here and now.*

The bright lights of the Katara Checkpoint came into view then the guard tower and the checkpoint booths. There was little traffic. Emmanuel pulled in behind a car at the shortest queue and they followed. One of the two guards made Emmanuel exit his vehicle and began interrogating him while another began thoroughly searching the Land Rover, beaming his flashlight beneath the carriage, under the hood, in the rear compartment.

"I've never had to get out of a car in Israel at a checkpoint," Chris said.

"Nor have I," she concurred. "The phone call from the last checkpoint is probably why."

"If he'd take off that ten-gallon, it might help," Chris complained.

"I don't think anything is going to help at this point," she said. "They've pulled him over and are motioning us forward."

The two guards repeated the routine. Chris and Kate exited the car, presented their passports. One guard interviewed while the other searched the car. Kate answered the same questions, gave the same responses. During the interrogation, the guard searching the car interrupted.

"Do you have firearms?" the guard questioned.

Kate's eyebrows flew up. "I do. A Glock Seventeen. It's in my purse. I have an Israeli permit." She immediately presented it from a breast pocket along with her Special British Forces identification.

The guard asked to see the gun.

She withdrew the gun from her purse and handed it to him. "It is unloaded, the clip is also in my purse." She pulled it out and showed it to him. "I have been in Israel many times and never had this problem."

"Yes, but we are under high alert," the guard interrogating her said, turning the gun over in his hand and examining it.

"A rocket attack alert?" Chris injected, knowing he'd probably get a none-of-your-business response.

Continuing to hold Kate's gun, the guard glanced up at him. "That's classified."

"I understand, but we've heard nothing about a high alert," Kate said diplomatically. "We are foreign nationals and if we are in danger, we should be notified."

"No need for alarm, madam," the guard said politely. "You are not Syrian, not Hezbollah."

Kate and Chris exchanged glances.

The guard continued. "But you are wanting to go to an archaeological site that is closed."

"Closed?" Chris shouted at Emmanuel who had been witnessing the unfolding drama from his Land Rover.

"It's not open at night but we should be able to go and look at it," Emmanuel shouted back.

"Now he tells us," Chris whispered from the side of his mouth.

"The site is not open," the guard said, continuing to assess the gun. "We cannot let you pass unless you have valid reasons."

"I guess that's that," Kate said. "I get my gun back, right?"

The guard looked again at the papers. "Yes. Your papers are in order. Just make sure the gun stays unloaded."

"Unless I'm attacked by Syrian terrorists," she quipped.

The guard nodded.

Kate got into the car. Chris walked over to the Land Rover, said something to Emmanuel, then returned, joined Kate in the car and twirled his finger. She turned the car around and headed back down the road, Emmanuel, this time, following.

"What did you say to him?" she asked Chris.

"I said we need to talk, follow us."

"I am ready to drop this," she said angrily. "So far, the only good purpose it has served has been bringing us together. And now we may be having to contend with Syrians."

"I heard that, too," he said. "But the Israelis are constantly on the lookout for Syrians."

"That's the norm," she remarked. "'High alert' makes me nervous."

The only time Chris had seen her nervous was when they were almost caught in Syria and barely escaped. If he admitted, he was nervous, too. But he was also becoming more aware that they may be on top of something big. "I'm inclined to see it through. Emmanuel may have just accidentally and innocently stumbled onto something."

"I don't see how you can say that?" she looked at him critically. "So far he's onto a site we can't get to, and he's never specifically stated where he found the jars."

"Did you see the small fish symbols around the lip of both jars?" he queried.

"No."

"I enlarged the photos," he continued, "and spaced about two inches apart, are small fish symbols, two arcs intersecting, similar to those we've seen in early Christian digs. They were known colloquially as the sign of the fish, or Jesus, and were used to mark meeting places and tombs. When a Christian met a stranger on the road, the Christian might draw an arc of the simple fish outline in the dust. If the stranger drew the other arc, this was the indication they were both Christians."

"I did know the fish is a symbol for Christ," she affirmed. "The letters of the Greek word for fish, ichthys, carry symbolic meaning: iota for iesous, chi for Christos, theta for theou, ypsilon for hyios or son, and sigma for soter or savior."

Chris picked up the thread. "Saint Augustine explained the meaning in his *Civitas Dei*. Before him, Clement of Alexandria recommended that his readers engrave their seals with the dove or fish. They are visible in the sacrament chapels of the catacombs of St. Callistus."

She nodded. "We saw it in the caves of Maaloula in Syria. Did you see any crosses on the jars?"

"No, just fish," he responded. "Crosses are uncommon. I've seen them in the catacombs of Rome, on tombs, but never on jars. These jars are similar to those used at Qumran, only they're a different color, different clay. And," he gestured with a raised finger, "they have Christian symbols on them, symbols that were not on the Qumran jars. I want to see these jars. If I'm in for a dime, I'm in for a dollar."

"And maybe Syrians breathing down your neck?" she added ironically.

He didn't respond and they rode for a while in silence.

"I even wonder if he sabotaged the plan intentionally," she surmised breaking the quiet.

"Why would he do that, go to all the trouble to call the museum, entice the museum send you here, then torpedo it?" Chris questioned.

"Perhaps he didn't like his feel for us," she said. "Or saw something he didn't like or there's a reason we don't know. One thing is for sure."

"What's that?"

"We're not going in separate vehicles again. I've got a different plan."

"Go a different way."

"Yes, through Jericho," she said. "There is only one checkpoint between East Jerusalem and Jericho and only one between Jericho and the dig, about half way. I'm more familiar with those checkpoints and they are more familiar with him. After all, he goes and comes through them daily. They know his face and vehicle. I think someone else tipped off the first checkpoint tonight and perhaps the second."

They came to a pull over and turned off. Emmanuel stopped behind them, got out and walked to their car. "What's the problem?" he complained, his bottom lip quivering slightly.

"The problem is a flawed plan," Chris said.

"We need to go from Jericho," she added emphatically.

"Fine with me," Emmanuel said nonchalantly with a shrug and a smile. "We can go now."

"What time do the workers arrive at the dig?" she asked.

"Eight a.m.," Emmanuel said. "Some come earlier when it's cooler."

"When do they shut down?" Chris asked.

Emmanuel looked at them quizzically as though he wondered where all of this was going. "Around five."

"What time is sunrise?" asked Kate.

"About five thirty," Emmanuel said.

"That's when it rises," Chris said, "It is light before then, when its first rays break the Jordanian plateau."

Emmanuel nodded in agreement.

"So, we go in the morning," she said. "We raise no suspicions. We go in your Land Rover. You can tell guards at the checkpoints that you are taking workers to the dig. They know you, see you pass through every day."

Emmanuel nodded again. "I'm sorry about this," he said, falsely apologetic. "But the jars aren't going anywhere."

"Unfortunately, we don't have that luxury of time," Chris said. "We must leave within a few days."

"We'll meet you in Jericho," Kate said. "You've given us the name of the hostel. We can find it. We'll be there at four o'clock. That will provide enough daylight for you to return us here and get back on the dig without raising suspicions."

Emmanuel signaled okay, walked back to his Land Rover and zoomed off around them.

# CHAPTER EIGHT

*Tiberius, Galilee, December, A.D. 66*

The weather is dry and balmy, the skies deep blue and cloudless as he follows the paved road along the seashore, his sandals making a dry, dragging sound on the highway stones. If he were in Jerusalem in December, the weather would be cold and blustery, perhaps even snowing. He marvels how Capernaum, only fifty miles away, can be so warm and comfortable, like eternal spring. A wise man once explained to him that Capernaum was below the level of the Great Sea and Jerusalem was much higher, that a mighty calamity within the earth caused the land to drop from Mount Hermon to the Salt Sea and beyond. He asked the wise man why that made palm trees grow in Jericho but not in Jerusalem and the sage said, "Only God knows."

A few miles out of Capernaum, Jairus can see Tiberius. In the distance, the walled city appears as a small crown on a hilltop. The hill is called Bernike for King Herod Agrippa's sister. Two decades into the new century, Herod Antipas, son of Herod the Great and Jewish ruler of Galilee at the time, founded the city and made it his new capital. He named it after the Emperor Tiberius Caesar. King Aprippa built a fort around the crown of the hill to protect his palaces and government buildings.

Jairus has been to the city a few times and each time sees more buildings and more streets. He enjoyed strolling along the paved colonnaded street that ran north and south through the city, observing the local people in their busy routine, eyeing the wares in the various shops, stalls of fresh produce brought in from the countryside, fresh fish from the sea. He would walk all the way to the southern gate with its two imposing towers and beyond to the warm springs and baths, a main attraction of the area. He would return to the city and explore the theater on the west side, the baths and other public structures located nearby, then descend to the piers and lake on the east side. Each time he was awed by the city's architectural extravagance, the fine clothes the people wore, and their expensive houses. And each time, he was glad to leave and return to his rural hometown with its rustic buildings and simple pastoral lifestyle and understood why Jesus chose Capernaum as his home.

Jesus would have been about twelve years old when Herod Antipas founded the city. Twenty years later, in the city Jairus was approaching, Jesus would stand before the same ruler and refuse to speak to the man who beheaded John the Baptist. A little more than twenty years after his death, many recall the sayings of Jesus but to Herod Antipas, he was mute.

Jairus covered the ten miles from Capernaum to Tiberius in little more than a half a day on the paved Roman road. He made better time than he would have made on a dirt thoroughfare and his feet were cleaner when he arrived, but they also hurt from the constant slapping of his sandals against the large hard stones.

The road into the city becomes a wide colonnaded street, shops and houses aligned on separate walkways behind the columns. Pedestrians fill the side passages while carts and horsemen move noisily in the main thoroughfare. He proceeds further into the city, noting the signs over the shops, looking for one that says CHARTARIA. He has been told it was on the right side of the street, near the main intersection where the Decumanus, the other central artery, crossed the city from east to west. He weaves among the vendors hawking wares and produce. One man has chickens hanging around his neck and he passes an elderly woman seated with her back against a column selling cloth sacks of beans. Except for the fishermen and their daily catch and the farmers on certain days, these are not scenes he sees in Capernaum. In Capernaum, one can hear the waters of the lake lapping on the shore from his porch. In Tiberius, one noise drowns another.

He sees the shop and enters, greeting the man he presumes is the owner. "Peace be to your house."

The shop owner, stooped and ancient in years, looks up as though surprised and returns the blessing. His voice, worn by time, is raspy and rattles as though from deep in his chest. He has a long white beard that emphasize the hollows of his face and only sprigs of hair on his head. The light through the doorway reveals a web of fine lines around his eyes. He wears a colorful cloak over a white robe and fashionable sandals on his feet. His attire reflects he is prosperous but the deep lines in his face and dark circles around his eyes suggest he has known much pain in his life.

"I have come a long distance to purchase writing supplies," Jairus says, his speech pressured with a sense of urgency for he hopes to return home before dark.

"Sadly, I have none," the shopkeeper replies. "My writing supplies— papyrus and ink—were requisitioned by King Agrippa when he and his staff arrived. They were fleeing the rebellion in Jerusalem and brought only their clothes and some food with them."

Jairus is downcast. "I could have purchased them at Caesarea Philippi, but that is a two days journey from Capernaum. Now I have a three day journey."

"I have sent a courier to Jerusalem to purchase more supplies," the shopkeeper says. "Due to the turmoil there I cannot predict his return, but he is a strong youth and fleet of foot. He could return tomorrow." He raises his hands into the air. "Only God knows."

"I was aware Aprippa came here," Jairus says. "We heard the news in Capernaum."

"Yes. They are staying in the procurator's palace. Roman soldiers are everywhere."

"I have seen many. They seem friendly."

"Until they get bored and demand your identification papers. Listen, my friend." He raises a firm finger for emphasis. "I am a Jew, a Sadducee, but I want no part of a rebellion. Life here is good. Tiberius is a peaceful place. Prosperous and well-to-do people live here. It is like a Greek polis with an elected ruler assisted by a committee and a town council. I am glad the King and his soldiers are here. They will ensure order. You are from Capernaum. If they knew you were from north of Tiberius where the pockets of rebels are, they might not seem so friendly." The man shakes his head dolefully. "Do not forget, Nero is Emperor."

"Nero," Jairus whispers the name as though he dare not speak it aloud. "He was behind the burning of the ghettos of Rome to make room for his palaces."

The shopkeeper adds, "And he blamed the Jews for the fire—Sadducees and aristocrats and their friends, even Jewish Christians—all thrown to the coliseum and butchered for arson. That was only two years ago." He shakes a finger in the air. "I tell you, my friend, he dislikes Jews and the followers of Jesus. The man is ruthless."

"I am concerned about Capernaum," Jairus comments sadly.

"Capernaum may not be safe," the shopkeeper declares. "The conflict has spread. The revolutionaries have divided Judea into seven districts and set a general over each. Joseph ben Matityahu, called Josephus, has taken command of the Galilean forces in the north. He is only twenty nine years old with no military experience. As we speak, he is fortifying Galilee. We have received word that soon he will be coming to Tiberius to reinforce its walls."

"How can that be with Agrippa here?" Jairus asks

"Agrippa took his army and departed."

"To where?"

"No one knows for certain," the shopkeeper says. "It is rumored he has gone to Caesarea, possibly to join Vespasian, one of Nero's successful generals sent by the emperor to quell the revolt."

"This is news, Agrippa joining Romans. I have heard he is not an admirer of Romans."

"You heard correctly," the shopkeeper affirms. "He tried to draw Tiberius and Galilee into war against them. Justus, the historian and his private secretary, is associated with the Zealots. Justus wants it both ways. He wants Agrippa to continue his rule with Roman support and yet support the revolutionaries. It will be an interesting state of affairs."

"Some of these things I know," says Jairus. "Josephus' family lineage extends to the Hasmoneons. The local politicians who have spent their lives building a power base resented the intrusion of the haughty Jerusalemite. Leading the opposition is John of Gischal."

"I know of him," says the shopkeeper. "Many Jews in Tiberius buy his kosher olive oil. He is a successful and wealthy merchant who wants more."

"He is hungry for power," Jairus says. "He has accused Josephus of being a traitor and attempted to assassinate him."

"He and one of his associates, Jesus of Shapat, have plotted against him here in Tiberius."

"They are battling among themselves," Jairus comments. "This is not good."

"They should make peace soon," the shopkeeper says hopefully. "The Romans may strike first in Galilee. Do you have family?"

"Yes, my wife, a daughter and her husband, their three grown children. Two sons and their families."

"Bring them here," the shopkeeper says cheerfully, palming a hand around the room. "Tiberius has pro-Roman sentiments. In a war, it will probably be spared. My wife is deceased, my children gone. I would welcome the company, along with food cooked by someone other than myself." He smiles and points to a nearby table. "You could write in peace."

"You are most kind," Jairus says gratefully. "I am unsure my family would leave their homes, perhaps my daughter and her family. Our capital Sepphoris also has pro-Roman factions. We are hopeful Galilee, as well as Tiberius, will be spared. Regardless, Capernaum has done nothing. If there is open conflict, we pray the village will be spared." *As for you, Capernaum ... you shall go to Hades,* the silent words of judgment springing from his memory. The Romans are a mixed blessing. Nero, the emperor, is unpredictable. Capernaum cannot be safe as long has he is in power, Jairus thinks.

"At least, you can stay the evening. It is a long walk to Capernaum. Robbers and thieves lurk in the hills and shadows."

Jairus thinks a moment, looks out the door at the sun's height. He jiggles his money pouch. The amount he brought for papyrus and ink would cover lodging and a meal with more to spare. "Your kindness overwhelms me. I will gladly pay for this hospitality."

"Nay," the shopkeeper gestures, raising a hand. "Treat people as you would like them to treat you. Give and there will be gifts for you."

The familiar words stun Jairus. "Are these your own words or did you hear them from another?"

"From another, someone you know."

"How do you know this?"

"Your greeting when you entered my shop, 'Peace be to your house.' Only one person said this. The rest of the saying is as important. 'If a person who loves peace lives there, they will accept your blessing. If not, the words will come back to you.' You, too, have heard Jesus."

"Yes. He healed my daughter. I heard him often in the synagogue in Capernaum. I have been collecting his sayings, copying them from codices onto a papyrus scroll. A man from Bethsaida said a group of Jesus followers in Caesarea Philippi heard of my work and wanted a copy. Shortly after, a man came from Jerusalem. He had heard Jesus' words were being committed to writing and wanted a copy for the ecclesia there. He knew of others who were writing a gospel, the life of Jesus, and he, too, wanted a scroll. I need more papyrus and ink. Friends in Capernaum told me of your shop, that you were a chartaria, a seller of papyrus."

"Are you a scribe?" the shopkeeper asks.

"No. But I was once president of the synagogue, caretaker of the Scriptures, the scrolls. I speak Hebrew, Aramaic and Greek and write in those languages."

"You need a scribe, perhaps more than one," the shopkeeper suggests.

"Do you know of any? There are those in Capernaum who could help me, but there are no scribes, no one who could produce quality scrolls quickly and I fear time is of essence."

The shopkeeper raises a shy hand and smiles. "Allow me to introduce myself. I am your scribe. My name is Ezra."

"I am Jairus."

Both raise open hands of salute and embrace.

"With the name Ezra, I would expect you to be a scribe," says Jairus.

"For over thirty years I have been copying last testaments, property deeds, pamphlets, books. It might surprise you the things people want put in writing and saved," he says, passing a hand over rows of jars of various sizes lining one side of the small room where a stairway ascends to the second level.

"Perhaps not," Jairus says. "We store our valuable documents in jars as well, but none like these. Are you a potter also?"

"Nay. The potter is another vendor down the street. But I sketched what I wanted and he made them from the sketches. They are specially made for scrolls. He gets his clay along the shore, at a place just north of here."

Jairus walks over to the jars, touches the lid of one, runs his hand around the smooth lip. "I have never seen any like them. You are creative, Ezra. An artist as well."

"I cannot take credit. Please sit." He points toward a small stool near the jars while he pulled one from behind a short counter but Jairus is not ready to sit. "These images around the top curvature of the jar, did you etch those?"

"Yes," he says proudly.

"I copy scrolls for different Jewish clients and occasionally for Greek Gentile clients. Jewish clients generally want ornamental or ritual scrolls.

The small inscriptions I make help identify the customer who has ordered the documents. Sometimes, Gentile clients want only initials."

"You are a Jewish follower of Jesus", Jairus confirms. "How do you identify their scrolls?"

"You are my first Jewish Christian customer. I will put whatever you want, whatever is meaningful for you."

Jairus seats himself on the stool so they both sit facing each other and Ezra continues. "I heard of a group who dedicated their lives to writing and preserving the Scriptures. They are call Essenes and live in a small community south of Jerusalem on the shore of the Salt Sea. I went there to observe them. They are truly fascinating."

"I have heard of these people, that they are very disciplined and practice baptism."

"Indeed," Ezra agrees. "They arise early in the morning and begin writing with the sun's first rays in a second story scriptorium, a room with benches and tables with inkwells. It is a large room, windows facing east and west and ceiling openings. They were very gracious, invited me to stay an evening and join their group."

"Apparently, you preferred only to visit," Jairus assumes.

"Yes. I could not practice their form of religion. I am too much involved in the world. But I learned much, which returns our discussion to the jars. They would not allow me to take one, but I made a sketch, paying particular attention to the lid," and he points to one, "how well-sculpted the fit. Once in place, it is sealed with wax. When the wax dries, the contents of the jar are protected forever. Unless, of course, the jar is damaged or broken or unless the owner wanted a jar that could be opened."

Jairus sits listening with rapt interest, nodding his head as though all he hears fills his head and is sealed. "With no paper and ink and pens, how can you help me, Ezra?"

"Ah! The pens! I have many types." He gestures. "They are there in trays at the end of the counter. I think soon I will have papyrus as well as parchment. The dried animal skin of parchment is more difficult to write on and sensitive to climate as it often warps, which makes it more difficult to transport and store."

"I've also been told that parchment is sturdier and more durable than papyrus," Jairus offers.

"This is true," confirms Ezra. "Though you are already using papyrus, the other option is available."

"I will continue with the papyrus."

"The ink we can make if Raphael, my courier, finds none in Jerusalem. Again, please accept my invitation to stay the night. We have much to discuss, my new friend."

"How can I resist such generosity? But I must depart in the morning. My wife will worry."

"Then you can return with your codices and scroll and we can record the words of Jesus for others."

Jairus reaches out and lays a hand on the man's shoulder. "You are an answer to prayers, Ezra."

# CHAPTER NINE

*Jerusalem, May 26, 2012*

Back in Jerusalem, Kate parked the car. Chris looked at his watch. It was almost nine o'clock. "How about that stroll through the Old City," he suggested.

"Excellent idea. I was thinking the same."

The evening was cool and dry. Hand in hand, they walked passing a number of upscale hotels and a few minutes later entered the Old City through the Damascus Gate. During the day the narrow streets were noisy and full of motorbike traffic. Tonight, except for the murmur coming from the shops, they were unusually quiet. They strolled along a wide street, then she pulled him to the right at the Hashimi Hotel, the only hotel in the heart of the old city, and onto a narrow twisting passage. Street lamps hung above them like caged white moons in their iron brackets, the shadows in the narrow streets like a black sheet, a geometry of light and darkness. They took in the unique fragrance, aroma of Jerusalem—sage, jasmine, coffee, leather, cypress and eucalyptus. They passed shops, some closed with corrugated gates and an occasional beggar's shrill voice calling out "Bakshish." Strings of colored lights looped overhead.

"You know this is the Via Dolorosa," she said, her tone light and pleasant, "where Jesus walked from Pilate's Praetorium to Golgotha."

"Yes," he said. "But the real Via Dolorosa is twenty feet below current street level. Some of the original stone slabs have been preserved. You can see them at a nun's convent down a flight of steps."

"I guess all of antiquity here is twenty feet below," she mused, as they continued strolling. "Each time Jerusalem was destroyed, they just leveled off the rubble and built on top of it."

"This is true," he agreed. "The landscape we will see tomorrow has been shaped by wind, rain and sun. The side of a wadi has been eroded so that the trickle of a man's urination seeped through a thin mantle of soil to a cave. Originally, it had probably been covered by rocks. I haven't even seen the place, but that's my read on it."

"So, when the cave was first entered, the jars were visible, not hidden behind anything," she said.

A store owner called to them in accented English to view his rugs draping in folds from hangers surrounding the entrance to his shop. Shaking their heads, they politely declined and kept walking.

"Tomorrow, we will see," he said. "The cliffs are pockmarked by small caves, some only a few feet deep. My guess is that whoever put the jars there was in a hurry, passed a small indenture, a shallow cave, placed the jars and covered them with large stones and rock, possibly with the idea of returning to retrieve them. Later in geologic time, an earthquake slide perhaps completed the concealment."

"But our original jar owner never made it back," she conjectured.

"We'll probably never know. I'm curious why these jars appear to be replicas of those at Qumran, yet are miles away from that site."

"Perhaps they are just that, replicas, and didn't come from Qumran," she said. "I'm not the archaeologist, but it would seem the Essenes didn't have a monopoly on jars designed to hold scrolls."

"They did on this design," he responded firmly. "At least, archaeologists have not seen it elsewhere. These two jars differ only because of the fish images, a Christian symbol, that would seem to set them apart from the Qumran sect which, in part, preceded Jesus. Or hadn't heard of him."

Ahead of them loomed a large dome visible through the aperture of buildings lining the narrow street. In front of them, a young couple was posing for a photo op. Kate held Chris back, then they continued when the couple moved on.

"That church, the dome," she said pointing at it, "the Church of the Holy Sepulcher. It marks the spot where Jesus was crucified and probably buried. At least that's the traditional speculation."

"It may not be speculation," he continued, a little ruminative. "Noted British archaeologist Kathleen Kenyon went below the city streets, into the sewer system, and discovered the existing walls at the time of Jesus. Where the Church of the Holy Sepulcher sits would have been just outside the walls at that time, where the Jerusalem-Joppa and Jerusalem-Samaria roads converged on the city. Golgotha was situated between their convergence."

"It gives me the chills," she said, "that it all happened right here." She squeezed his hand and they continued walking. "Why do you think we, you and I, are so attracted to, and enamored, with things that are old, that we have chosen the professions we have?"

"I think part of it is a reverence," he said softly. "We render them sacred because they endured."

"They have indeed," she said with a sigh. "The Church of the Holy Sepulcher is one of the oldest structures in the Western world. You know the story, how Constantine, the emperor converted to Christianity, sent his mother Helena to find the location of Christ's crucifixion."

"Yes," he responded. "An interesting story. Following the Roman destruction of Jerusalem in 70 C.E., the Emperor Hadrian, began rebuilding a new Roman city, *Aelia Capitolina,* and ordered that a cave containing a rock-cut tomb be filled in and the spot leveled to create a foundation for a temple dedicated to Jupiter. Three centuries later, enter Helena."

"You're headed somewhere with this?"

He nodded and continued. "Sensing that the temple stood on a sacred Christian spot, Helena had the temple to Jupiter destroyed. When the soil was removed, the rock-cut cave was discovered." He extended an upturned palm. "*Voila!* This had to be Christ's tomb, thus the location of his crucifixion and resurrection. The basilica, with some remodeling and modifications over the centuries, we see now. It was dedicated in 325 C.E."

"Amazing," she exclaimed wistfully. "Absolutely amazing."

Gazing at the domed structure with the same fascination, he said, "I find comfort being around old things—buildings, monuments, walls. Perhaps that's another reason I'm an archaeologist. I am fascinated by the grandeur of ancient rubble."

She wrapped her hands around his arm. "Interesting."

"That I became an archaeologist?"

"Interesting that we're both attracted to archives, to antiquity, to its magic," she said. "That we would travel a great distance because of two jars ... and what they might ... or might not, contain."

He thought about the two jars, the distance, the time. *Long ago.* How some vessels held up over time, their contents insulated and protected. How some were so fragile and lost everything, including the sacred words within them. He thought of the two of them and what they held, their pledge of love. His first marriage did not stand the test of time and distance. Would his new love for Kate stand the test of a lifetime? Or would their venture together be just one more wild scramble for antiquity, the thrill evaporating after the discovery? He felt her eyes on the side of his face and thought the moment as good as any.

"Kate, there is something I've needed to tell you."

Her hands slid down his arm and her face slowly turned where he could see the night reflected in her eyes.

"When you asked me on the phone if I was having second thoughts and I told you 'No.'" He paused.

"Yes?" she said, her dark eyes eager, nervous.

Facing her, he anchored a hand on her shoulder. "I was less than honest with you."

She blinked and her head flinched backward slightly, as though dodging a pest.

"When I returned home from our Syrian venture, and after our rendezvous at my place and the Grand Canyon—"

"Where you proposed to me," she reminded him matter-of-factly.

He shook his head. *You're not making this easy for me.* "Allyson, my ex-wife, called me. I told you that she and I have never been on bad terms."

She nodded.

"We've never really been on any terms," he added.

"Now, she wants terms," Kate surmised, her eyes pinning his.

"I don't know," he responded absently. "She may think fortune has followed fame. She is not desperate financially. She receives a nice alimony. But she's called a few times." He swallowed deeply. "We've been out."

Kate blinked as though stung.

"That was the hesitancy, the distance you heard over the phone." He paused again, waiting for the next words to come. "She's just"—he looked up, away from her, then back into her eyes—"She's the mother of my two sons. She's just—"

"A part of your life," Kate said empathically, finishing the sentence for him.

She placed a hand on his shoulder so they looked like two people about to wrestle, and drove her eyes into his. "My turn." She took a deep breath. "Geoffrey has been dead seven years and he is yet, to this day, with me every day. I still love him. I've often wondered if I could remarry, if I could have strong feelings for a new person not overshadowed by my previous love. At times, after his death, the pain was unbearable. Selfishly, I wanted to meet someone, but for the wrong reasons. I wanted a distraction, something to help me forget ... to fill the emptiness," her words a long sigh and she stopped.

In the moment, he didn't know if the struggle he felt was his or hers.

She squeezed his shoulder and again fixed him with a steady gaze. "Are you tracking with me?"

He tipped his head.

"Then I saw this movie, an old one that was playing one night on television. *A Man and a Woman*. Have you ever seen it?"

"No. I've heard of it."

"You must see it, Chris. We must see it together." She removed her hand from his shoulder, leaned into him and lay both palms upon his chest. "Following the sudden deaths of their spouses, a young widow and young widower meet through their children who attend the same private school in northern France. The couple become attracted to each other, one thing leads to another, and they make love with passionate tenderness." She patted one hand on his chest. "But something is not right. While making love, they have memories of their deceased spouses. The woman feels uncomfortable continuing the relationship." She paused again.

He could see her emotions in her eyes, felt them in her voice.

"I'm waiting ... to hear the rest," he said patiently.

"She takes a train back to Paris. Once separated, they realize something greater is missing and they reunite. It is a marvelous love story." He liked the way her face moved up and down when she talked, her features turning attractive then unremarkable, then attractive again. "Walking out of that movie, back into the real world, I decided to embrace my loss and the wonderful memories of Geoffrey. They are a part of me. This is life. I did not want to meet anyone, love anyone else. Then ... *you* came into my life."

"That bucket travels both ways from the well," he said.

She chuckled at his homegrown idiom.

"But there is a difference, Kate," he resumed, "between my situation and yours. My ex-spouse is still alive."

"That's not a fair comparison," she quickly countered.

"I don't understand," and looked at her uncertainly.

"In a way, Geoffrey is still alive," she sighed. "There is a phrase that when someone dies, it is said they 'pass away.'"

She paused.

"Yes?" he said, and rolled a finger for her to continue.

"I wish people would stop saying it," she said with irritation. "It is inaccurate. Loved ones do not 'pass away,'" she gestured with quotation marks. "Strangely, they are more with you than when they were alive. That was the point in the movie. Death is not a brain trauma. Unless we have an aneurysm or dementia, death does not diminish or eliminate memory, but magnifies it. You can walk away from Allyson and not miss her. One cannot walk away from a cherished memory."

"So, the saying," he responded, "'Absence makes the heart grow fonder' refers to a different distance."

"Perhaps," she said. "The poet Bayly was referring to a particular place, an isle, when he wrote those words."

Ah! Thomas Haynes Bayly. The name he had forgotten. The English poet.

"But death cancels distance," she continued, her face slightly lifted, the expression meditative, unruffled. "Spirit takes over. There's an immediacy about spirit. It does not know distance."

They were moving into deep waters, like the discussions on Jesus' resurrection when they were pursuing Mark's lost scroll. She had insisted Christ's rising was spiritual, not physical.

She bit her lip, then smiled at him brightly. "We agree on one thing," she said in a soft considerate voice.

"That is?"

"Old things."

They were still standing on the Via Dolorosa, before the looming Sepulcher dome, looking at each other, engulfed in the shawl of night in the murmur of the old and new city around them. They were postured in such a way that his thigh had moved between her legs. Had he done this, or had she? It didn't matter. The contact against his groin was causing his heart to race.

"Perhaps that is one of the reasons we are fond of old things," he said, attempting a distraction. "They never pass away."

"Not if we can help it," she added and looked at her watch. "We must get some sleep."

He wanted to continue the warming conversation, all that was left unsaid, but she had grabbed his hand and steered them back to the hotel. He put his arm around her waist and left it there for just a minute. Just a minute.

# CHAPTER TEN

***Tiberius, Galilee, December, A.D. 66***

After a meal of fish, olives, bread and wine, Jairus and Ezra sit in cushioned chairs around the hearth and talk.

"Have you lived here in Tiberius all of your life?" Jairus asks.

"Nay. Only the last twenty years. Before that time, I lived in Jerusalem." The old scribe went on to tell that he was born four years before the new century and grew up in a Sadducee family in the shadows of Herod's Temple. He told how his father was involved in Herod's rebuilding of the Second Temple and that Herod's effort extended to smoothing the Temple Mount and replacing the foundation stones. "Because my father was a priest, Herod had him and hundreds of other priests, more than a thousand, trained as masons and carpenters. Only priests could work on the sanctuary and the Court of Priests. When I became of age, I was allowed to accompany my father as a helper." He pauses and looks wistfully into the hearth where the flames of the fire he had built had died down to a nest of quaking embers. For a moment Jairus thinks he sees tears gather in the corners of the old man's eyes then smiles at himself for thinking "old." The man indeed looks ancient. But based upon the story he tells, they are the same age. Jairus waits for him to continue.

"I recall one day I was there with my father. We were walking through one of the outer Temple courts to resume our work where we had stopped the day before and there was a crowd of other priests gathered around someone. We stepped closer and saw it was a young boy. He was about my age. He was asking the priests and scribes gathered there about the law. I tell you he was asking profound questions. He had these older men scratching their heads. I wondered to myself, who is this brilliant youth." He looked back into the glowing coals. "I saw him again, two decades later. I was awakened in the middle of the night. Caiaphas, the chief priest, had called the meeting. Someone claiming to be the Messiah and the son of God was dragged before the quickly assembled body. He looked haggard, much older than his thirty years. He looked as though he had been beaten. But I knew the face. It was one I would never forget. It was that of the boy I had seen in the Temple court years before." He stops.

Tears were forming and running in streams down the man's face, falling from his chin onto his robe. Jairus cannot think what to say. He wants to console the man but does not know how. "So, you were there that night?"

"Yes," he struggled. "I fear I was. It is the reason I live now in Tiberius and not Jerusalem. I did not agree with the other members of the Sanhedrin. Some of them were present that day in the Temple, the same who were having trouble answering the young boy's questions. It was as though they were getting even. Everything was happening too quickly. I felt Caiaphas rushing too hastily to judgment. I felt they were looking for false evidence to frame the man. Another Pharisee defended Jesus, but, besides me, he was the only other. I wanted to know more, hear more from this young man almost my age."

"Did you learn more?"

"No. Those testifying against him contradicted each other. There was no evidence. Caiaphas asked him, 'Are you not going to answer to what these witnesses are saying against you?' The man did not answer. He would not defend himself. He remained silent. Only when Caiaphas asked him if he was the Messiah, the son of the Blessed One, did he respond. 'You say that I am. You will see the Son of Man sitting at the right hand of the Mighty One and coming on the clouds of heaven.'" Ezra stops again.

Jairus is anxious in the long silence. "What happened after he spoke?"

"Caiaphus became very angry and ripped the young man's clothes from his body. He said, 'We need no more witnesses. You have heard the blasphemy. What do you think?'"

"What did you think?" says Jairus, suddenly feeling very uncomfortable, that he is in the presence of one who convicted Jesus.

"I thought he only quoted scripture, referenced the son of man and used words similar to those in the Book of Daniel. That was not blasphemous. A vote was quickly taken. Every man in that room condemned him to die.

Everyone but this one," he says, raising a finger as though pointing toward heaven.

Jairus relaxes. "I do have one question."

Ezra nods.

"How were you on the Sanhedrin at an early age? You must have been about the age of the Master."

Vertical creases appear between his eyes, like someone trying to remember a vital past. "My father had died that year and I was allowed to take his place until I could prove my merit."

"But you never took his place."

"No. I could not belong to a body that condemned an innocent man. I never went back. Within a short period I sold my house in Jerusalem and moved here to Tiberius. It was a new city. Herod Antipas, its originator, was encouraging Jews to move here. A moment ..." He gets up, crosses the room to a table and opens a drawer. He removes a small pouch that jingles with movement and pulls out a coin. He re-crosses the room and hands the coin to Jairus. "Look at it, look at the name,"

Jairus holds the silver coin in his palm and sees the word TIBERIUS arched around the edge.

"Antipas had the coins minted here with the name of the town on them. This was part of his propaganda. I thought a ruler who would go to that extent must believe in his settlement. But there was another reason. There are healing springs just south of here. My wife had an ailment and the move seemed right for her. With the money from the sale of my house in Jerusalem I purchased this building, my shop downstairs and the living area above."

"But your wife is no longer with you."

Ezra looks into the coals again. His eyes turn misty again. "No. She died a few years ago. But we would go to the springs several times a week and I think their healing powers gave her more years than she would have had in Jerusalem."

"I know about healing powers," Jairus says.

"Tell me."

"My twelve-year-old daughter was seriously ill, at the point of death. All medical treatments had failed. Jesus was nearby in Galilee and I went to him. I must tell you I was not that impressed with the man until I saw him cast out a demon and heal a man with a withered hand in the synagogue. I doubted his claims of being holy, but I was desperate. He could heal."

Ezra listens quietly, his eyes have cleared and his head is bobbing up and down.

"The details are unimportant. I did go to him on bended knee, something difficult for the synagogue leader to do. My daughter was dying, I told Jesus and he went with me. We were rushing to my house. Then Jesus stopped to heal this woman with a bleeding disease, all because she touched his robe. I was frantic. My daughter was dying. We were approaching my house and men came running toward us crying, 'Your daughter is dead.' My heart was crushed. I was angry with Jesus. We arrived at the house and he put a calming hand on my shoulder and said, 'Don't' be afraid, just believe.'"

Ezra's head has stopped bobbing and the tears are back.

"We arrived at the house, everyone is wailing and weeping and he said, 'Why all of the commotion and crying. She is not dead, she is only sleeping.' He took my wife and me and the disciples into the room where she lay. He knelt and took her by the hand and said, "Little girl, I say to you, get up."

Ezra moves to the edge of his chair.

"Immediately, she stood up and walked. Jesus told us to give her something to eat and to tell no one. If he is listening, he is upset with me, as I have told this story hundreds of times. I cannot help but tell it. My daughter still lives and has a family."

With the sleeve of his robe, Ezra is wiping tears from his eyes.

Jairus feels moisture warming his as well. "This is why I became a follower of Jesus and why I am committed to preserving his word."

"You know I am a Sadducee," Ezra says. "We Sadducees do not believe in life after death. But your story is compelling."

"Your story is also most interesting. But there must be more, something equally compelling."

"There is, but first some more wine for your cup?"

Jairus nods and his host lifts the decanter from the table between them and fills the cup of his guest, then his own cup. "My mouth turns dry when I talk too much and I fear the rest of my story may be lengthy."

Jairus extends an open palm, directing his host to proceed.

"It begins that night at the house of Caiaphas where I and other members of the Sanhedrin were summoned. Unconvinced of the guilt of the man I saw then and recalled from the Temple years before, I began investigating. I spoke with those who knew him ... "

"Considering you were within the camp of the opposition," Jairus says, interrupting him, "how was this possible? Who would help you?"

"That is a good question, my friend. I knew two men who had known Jesus when he was alive. One was a prominent Pharisee named Nicodemus—the one earlier I mentioned who defended him—a member of the Sanhedrin but absent at that evening court. Had he been present, the results might have been different. The second was Joseph of Arimathea, a friend of Jesus who claimed his body and buried him. It was Nicodemus who referred me to this second man. Both served as intermediaries with others, including four of the disciples who lived in Galilee—Simon Peter, James and John and Matthew."

"I knew them all," says Jairus. "They are all dead now."

"Yes, but that was another reason I moved to Tiberius. I would be closer to Capernaum, where I eventually met with each of them."

"I am surprised I never met you then, that our paths did not cross."

"Perhaps God's will is all a matter of timing. We are meeting now at a critical point, a turning point, I think, in the life of our land. I did not wish to speak of this earlier, but I, too, have been collecting information on our Lord ... "

"I am sorry, Ezra, if I may call you that."

"Please do."

"You just said 'our Lord.' Were you converted as I was? Are you a follower?"

"Verily, without doubt," Ezra says. "I feel I touched the truth in my quest, or rather it touched me, and my life was changed. I, too, am one of the many followers of Jesus."

"You have not used the word Messiah or Christ," Jairus notes. "Perhaps there is a reason."

"I confess the omission is intentional. I am uncertain what Jesus meant by the title of Messiah and just as uncertain about the meaning of his death on a cross and his reported resurrection. You noticed I wept when you told of your daughter's apparent resurrection. These are important events to some people, perhaps to you, but for me, the words he spoke about living from day-to-day, how to treat your neighbor, how to avoid evil and follow good ... these are more helpful to me."

The coals of the fire have darkened and a cool breeze begins blowing from a window above them. Ezra leans over and throws some twigs on the coals then small sticks of wood. "There," he says. "We can speak by the warmth of a fire to match the one that burns within us."

"I would like for you to read what I have collected," says Jairus. "What I hear from you is consistent with the sayings of Jesus I have collected and committed to writing. They are about one's concerns about daily life. There is no mention of a crucifixion or a resurrection. I will look again, but I do not think the word 'Messiah' appears."

"This is not to say they are not circulating," Ezra comments. "A man named Paul, a Pharisee who persecuted followers of Jesus, has written letters to some churches in Asia Minor. I have read none of them, but those who have say he speaks highly and eloquently of the crucifixion and resurrection of Jesus."

"He also takes a very dim view of Jewish Law," injects Jairus. "Some of which I still find helpful. I speak not of the rituals but the early commandments which I believe Jesus affirmed."

"We are in agreement. Our obstacle is papyrus, or the lack thereof. If my courier does not return by noon of the morrow, I will send him to you with your needs, including ink and, of course, pens."

"I am grateful to you, Ezra. I sense we are both tired. I must rise early and journey home."

Ezra leads him up the stairs to his sleeping quarters, a bed in a bare room upstairs, and bids him goodnight. Ezra brings an oil lamp and a scroll which Jairus eagerly opens. As the script slides beneath the yellow light of the lamp, he is astonished at the words he reads.

# CHAPTER ELEVEN

*Jerusalem, Early Morning, May 27, 2012*

To avoid drawing attention, Chris and Kate had decided to meet in the hotel parking lot and not in the lobby. Kate was carrying a large cloth purse and he had a small bag of archaeological tools he might need—tweezers, brushes, trowels, root cutters, a sieve, utility saw, dust pan. He was wearing his standard archeological uniform—blue jeans, khaki shirt and multi-pocketed traveling vest.

"I guess we are announcing that we're archaeologists," she said, gesturing at his attire. Her hair was pulled back in a ponytail and she was carrying a wide-brim felt hat. Dark glasses hung over the V of a white blouse. Khaki pants and desert boots completed the ensemble.

"You are the best looking archaeologist I've ever seen," he said. "'Dashing' is the word."

She waved off the comment with a forget-it-look.

At 3:30 a.m. sharp, they departed the parking lot and almost immediately were onto Highway One. They followed the four-lane around the northern tip of the Old City, its spotlighted fifteenth century walls silver against the dull glow of the city, then around Mount Scopus, its dark mound sprinkled with lights. Shortly, they merged with the tunnel road.

"Get your passport out," she said as they approached the West Bank Barrier and a checkpoint. "They may not ask for it. They didn't ask for mine the last time I was here. This car also has Israeli plates."

No cars were queued at the booth, only a single uniformed female guard inside. Kate slowly rolled to a stop. The guard peered in and waved them on."

"That was easy," he said, looking back to ensure the experience was real.

"It's smoother without the cowboy," she said.

Further away he could see the barrier wall, its length and looming prominence, deviating significantly from the Green Line into occupied territories captured by Israel in the Six-Day War of 1967. The wall was an illegal attempt to annex Palestinian land under the guise of security, violated international law and undermined negotiations. "I've never understood how the Israelis could get away with building this wall of separation," he commented.

"I agree," she said. "But most Israelis support it. And the wall works. Before it was built, all a terrorist had to do was walk across an invisible line to terrorize the Israeli population. Now this barrier makes it harder for them to penetrate Israeli security."

"But it makes life difficult for the innocent Palestinians," he complained. "Two hundred thousand people are forced to use detours that are much longer than the direct route to their closest city. And four of the five roads leading into the Jordan Valley are not accessible to most Palestinian vehicles."

"It gets worse," she groaned. "Much within the Jordan Valley is off-limits to the Palestinians. It is taken up by Israeli settlements, 'firing' zones, and nature preserves."

"That's the reason our cowboy friend's discovery could set off a small war."

"Bingo!" she said glancing at him then back at the highway. "We agree on that."

They were beginning their descent from Jerusalem. Appearing on their right was the high-rise honeycombed complexes of the Jewish settlement Ma'ale Adumin. A sign past it said Speed Limit 90 km/h.

"Interesting, the psychology of speed," he commented.

"Meaning?"

"The needle is on ninety which makes you think you're going fast, but it's only fifty-five miles per hour."

"Wait until we intersect with Highway Ninety and head north," she said. "The speed limit from Jericho to the first checkpoint is sixty. To you Americans, that's less than forty miles per hour."

"Why wasn't that mentioned?" he asked, tension rising in his voice. "At that rate we may not make it to the site to retrieve the jars, get him back to

Jericho to drop us then return to his site on time without drawing suspicion."

"You're right," she agreed, an alarmed look on her face.

"We need to refigure," and began talking to himself. "Emmanuel said it was an hour to the site from Jericho. We arrive at his hostel at four, get to the jar discovery site around five, take half hour with the jars, back to his hostel at six thirty, putting him back at his dig by seven thirty."

Listening to him, she cautioned, "That's pushing it."

He pulled a map from the dash and opened it. "Using the map legend, and if he's shooting us straight, it's roughly twenty-five miles from Jericho to the jars' site. I keep forgetting this is a small country, about the size of Massachusetts. We should cover that in no time."

"Under normal conditions," she said. "Emmanuel is probably obeying the speed limit and allowing down time at checkpoints. Every minute counts."

"Which prompts my usual question," he voiced.

"It's in my purse."

He slapped his forehead. "Oh, God."

"Loosen up, Chris," she said with exaggerated annoyance. "This is Israel. People carry guns. They have permits. I have one. Do I look like a terrorist?"

He scanned her up and down. "Nope. With that felt hat on I thought you might pass for Ingrid Bergman in *Casablanca*."

She released a hand from the wheel and back-handed him playfully across the chest.

Between Ma'ale Adumim and Jericho, the highway widened to four lanes and curled down the valley rift wall. They were paralleling the old Roman road from Jerusalem to Jericho.

"Speaking of terrorists, do you know what this road was called in the time of Jesus?" He answered the question before she could respond. "The 'bloody pass'. It was the roughest, rockiest, most robber-infested road in the world."

"Today it is one of the safest highways in the world," she added. "They have more checkpoints in Mexico than here, and I wouldn't drive a golf cart into Mexico."

He continued. "About half way down this road the Good Samaritan tended to a victim and stayed in an inn. Some say it was in Jericho, but I think it was near where we are now.'"

"You do know your Bible," she remarked ironically.

"You keep forgetting I have a degree in New Testament from your beloved University of Edinburgh."

"I don't keep forgetting it. There are times," she cut her eyes at him, "I wish I could."

They passed a sign that said SEA LEVEL. When they reached Jericho, they would be over two thousand feet below sea level, having dropped over three thousand feet in seventeen miles. Chris thought about where they were going. Jericho, Tel es-Sultan, home to the oldest and longest continually inhabited city on earth. Remains from the walled old city dated back to 9,000 B. C. E. The weather there was dry and warm year-round. That was why so many ancient artifacts—pottery, tile, manuscripts—had been found there intact. That was also why Jericho was the only place in the world where balsam, known for its medicinal uses, grew and the area, in biblical times, contained large balsam tree groves. That was also why it was a considered a resort by many, why it was called the "jewel city of the plain," why Marc Antony gave it to Cleopatra as a wedding gift.

On both sides of the road, lights burned dimly in the distance. They were the campfires of Bedouins who lived in tents, makeshift shelters and metal boxes. Chris had heard somewhere that most had traded their tents for metal boxes which means they were no longer Bedouin wanderers. They were mired in poverty.

"Take it as a compliment to your navigation savvy," he said, "that I didn't even ask if you knew where you were going, how to find this place, the Sami Youth Hostel."

She pointed to the GPS window on the dash. "There's my savvy. I set the address before you got in. It's on the Jerusalem-Jericho Road, Aqabat Jaber Camp, across the road from the Hotel Intercontinental and its closed casino. I also Googled the name and got a phone number."

"My compliment was in order. You don't miss a trick."

"I'm assuming that's American slang for our Scottish 'doss' and not a compliment one would pass to a whore," came the haughty rejoinder.

"Doss?"

"It means brilliant, good," she responded.

"Okay, 'doss,'" he said deferentially. Then: "You're a touch edgy, aren't you?"

She shot him a stern glance. "Yes! Where we are and what we're about to do is on the edge of edge," and swung her eyes back onto the white dashes stapling the highway.

"What's the worst case scenario?" he asked, turning and facing her.

"Worst case, we get shot and killed by either Israelis or Palestinians or both for looting an archaeological site, at that point it wouldn't matter. Next worst case scenario, we get arrested and spend the rest of our lives in an Israeli prison for antiquity theft. Third worst case scenario ... There is none."

"Are all Scots this pessimistic?" he quipped.

"No, but they are realists and we are currently playing with fire."

"What happened to our original noble intentions of rescuing what potentially could be valuable artifacts, possibly manuscripts?"

"Nothing," Kate said. "We just need to be careful. I don't trust this guy. He may be using us for another purpose."

"I don't trust him either," he agreed. "I can't figure his angle. He's got this corrupt thin smile, like he knows something we don't know or we can't sense. You said he didn't open either jar."

"That's what he told me and the photos he sent are consistent with his story. At least the jars appear sealed."

"I was thinking he knows what's in them and needs a cover to get them out of the country."

"Or a diversion," she offered.

"How would that work?"

"Authorities become over-focused on us and under-focused on him. He's not even on their radar, and for all we know they've been tracking our every movement." She glanced at the rearview. No lights.

"Somebody seems focused on us," he said.

"The Israelis are the best spies in the world. An infra-red camera may be following our every move."

"Damn, Kate. That's a touch paranoid. Your years in the British Special Forces have taken their toll."

"What you call paranoid, I call caution. I'm still alive, thanks to what I learned in the BSF."

He wasn't going there. There was no counter for the truth. She probably was still alive because she was cautious. He tried to think of something else, change the topic. But none came to mind.

They continued in silence.

Overhead was a thin shell of moon and each star shined like a new cut diamond, the sky awash with their glitter, the Milky Way a gossamer river. The highway spiraled down the valley rift wall and it seemed the two of them were dropping, descending into some vast darkness that would clamp shut upon them.

A few more miles and she flipped on the blinker at the intersection of Highway 90 and turned left onto the direct road to Jericho. Just before the Jericho city limits was a checkpoint.

"I thought this checkpoint had been removed," she said surprised, as she steered the car between the walls of concrete slabs and came to a stop at the booth.

The only soldier manning the booth stepped forward, gathered and quickly scanned their passports, returned to the booth with them and picked up a phone.

"Here we go again," Chris exclaimed. "That's all we need is a stall."

The soldier returned and asked the same questions everyone had been asking—reason for being in Israel, their occupations, previous trips to the country, had they been in the country before, were they excavators.

They were not excavators, Kate told him emphatically.

The soldier then asked, "Why are you coming to Jericho this early in the morning?"

Chris was about to answer and Kate preempted him. "We are in Israel to see a friend who works on an archaeological site and wanted to see him before he goes to work," she glanced at her watch, "in two hours." To provide more credibility to her story, she told him the name of the hostel where Emmanuel was staying.

The soldier bent over and, glancing back and forth suspiciously between the open passports he was still holding and Chris and Kate, he said, "Do you have any firearms?"

Chris stopped his hand before it slapped his forehead.

Kate's mouth flattened into a grimace. "Yessir, I do." Anticipating the next question, she reached into her bag and withdrew the gun, then presented her credentials for possessing it.

Chris was beside himself, looking at his watch, out the window at the sky, tapping his foot on the floorboard. The soldier took his eternal time reviewing Kate's permits, turning them one way, then another as though they were some hieroglyphic he could not interpret and finally returned them to her.

Before the guard could speak, Kate said, "And I know to keep it unloaded with the clip out." She opened her mouth to comment further and Chris injected, "And she will, sir, I will see to that."

The soldier nodded and smiled and waved them on.

She threw Chris a hard look. "You didn't have to say that."

"A little levity for the situation," he responded and smirked

"You mean *leverage*," she said angrily.

"It's a good thing we are switching to Emmanuel's Land Rover," Chris said. "What are you going to do when security finds out we're actually going to a site to see a mystery relic? Because you know when the guard got on his phone he was spreading the word about us to other checkpoints."

She snapped her head back. "We *are* here to see a friend—"

"A stretch," he interrupted.

"He *does* work on an archaeological site."

"Now that is *fact*!" he agreed.

"And we *do* want to see him before he goes to work."

"Another stretch, but true."

"And I am perfectly capable of coming up with other stories to support those if needed," she snipped with a nodding jerk of her head.

# CHAPTER TWELVE

*Tiberius, Galilee, December, A.D. 66*

Jairus leaves Ezra's house at daybreak and is immediately detained by a soldier who demands his papers. He politely hands them over, but the soldier is condescending and rude. Noting Jairus is from Capernaum, the soldier does not ask, but demands, his business in Tiberius. Jairus tells him he came to buy writing supplies, that none were available and he will have to return in a week, a partial untruth. He did not want to draw attention to Ezra who had become his friend. The soldier inquires what he is writing. Again, he partially lies to him and tells him he is copying some documents for friends.

The soldier persists. "What documents?"

Jairus thinks. The soldier was not a Roman. He could tell him he is copying Jewish Scriptures. But with Nero in power, and Jews recently persecuted in Rome as well as Caesarea Philippi, he must be careful. "Some deeds and wills," he says. The guilt of his lie penetrates.

"Proceed then," the soldier says, practically throwing his papers back to him.

Halfway to Capernaum, Jairus sees a plume of smoke. Or is it dust rising into the sky? He cannot tell, for the land before him bows upward. Moments later, he crests the rise and sees the source, a large army moving toward him. It can not be a Roman army. He has heard nothing of Roman troops arriving at any ports of the Great Sea, or traveling south from Syria.

To evade their forward movement, he leaves the paved road and begins ascending the mount. Other travelers, he observes, are doing the same. The elevation will give him a better vantage point. And, if they be foe and not friend, it will afford an escape route. As the army nears, he can see the banners and infantry standards in the front ranks. They are Jewish. This must be Josephus' army coming to reinforce the walls of Tiberius. He climbs higher and cannot see the end of the column which seems to stretch to Capernaum.

Surely, Rebecca saw the troops, he thinks. The road through Capernaum passes before their house. He is concerned for her. Did the sight frighten her? Did she run up the mount as he has done? Did she go alone or meet with neighbors and go with them? The entire city was surely anxious when they saw a large army making its way around the northern shore, arcing towards them.

He quickens his pace.

Moving northward and paralleling their southward movement, Jairus sees the end of the procession. He begins descending the mount, down-stepping at an angle to intersect the end of the column's baggage train. These are the cooks and laborers, the prostitutes, vagabonds and wayward types that trail in an army's wake. The gossips who will give him information.

As he nears them, one from the ragtag group calls out. "Come, join us to fight the Romans."

Jairus raises a hand but says nothing. They are too far away for his weak voice to be heard.

Another cries out, "Fall in. We are going to Tiberius."

Now he knows their destination. He draws closer to the column and shouts, his voice reedy in the wind. "I am an old man. I cannot fight."

The first voice, distinguished by its gruffness, shouts again: "No one is too old to fight the Romans. Look at me," and he slaps a hand proudly against his chest.

Jairus comes closer to the man. He is gray-headed with a long gray beard but he looks stout and hardy. "I am an old farmer," Jairus says. "I can feed you but cannot fight beside you."

Someone within the baggage section shouts, "If you live in Capernaum, you have already fed us."

The comment alarms him and increases his concerns for his wife and others in the village. Has it been pillaged? Has anyone been harmed, any dwellings burned? He does not want the troops to tell him how they have been fed. That might cause agitation. Only a few more hours and he will learn the answers to his questions. He is in need of information that could determine the future of his family. And the master's teachings.

He is closer to the baggage train and a young man in shepherd's garments leaves the column and comes out to meet him. "Greetings, countryman," he says, raising his hand.

"And greetings to you," Jairus says in similar gesture.

The man approaches Jairus and with his foot draws an arc in the gravely soil. Jairus knows the signal, steps forward and compliments the arc with another counterposed. Both smile in acknowledgment of the fish symbol.

"My name is Andrew," the young man says. "All of us are Jews. We march with Josephus. Some of us are followers of Jesus."

"And I, also," says Jairus. "Where is Josephus taking you?"

"To Tiberius, to fortify the city's walls. The Romans are coming," announces the young man named Andrew.

"I have feared they would," laments Jairus, "But I did not know the time or the place?"

"Nero has sent Vespasian to quell the revolt," Andrew says excitedly. "The Roman general has arrived in Antioch with two Syrian legions. His son Titus marches north to meet him, we are told, at Ptolemais with a legion from the garrison in Egypt. They are being joined by Agrippa and his troops."

"But I have just departed Tiberius, and Agrippa's soldiers are present."

"Those were left for security, to guard his palace," informs Andrew.

"The main body of his troops are with him in Ptolemais."

"I have heard Agrippa does not like Romans," Jairus presses.

"Agrippa is an opportunist who is trying to save his skin," Andrew says.

"What is their objective?"

"Galilee."

"Why Galilee?" Jairus questions. "Sepphoris and Tiberius, the region's largest cities, support Rome against the rebels. Why not Jerusalem where the zealots hold the fortress and the Temple, where the rebellion began?"

"This is true, my friend. But leaders of the rebellion, John of Gischal and Simon bar Giora, are in Galilee preparing to fight. The Romans will strike in Galilee first," Andrew warns.

"I have heard this from others. This is not good news."

"Are you from Capernaum?" Andrew inquires.

"Yes. You passed my house. And you hail from where?"

"Chorazin. If you had orchards and crops, the trees have been stripped, your grain harvested by the soldiers. If you had livestock, they," he nodded at the long column of soldiers, "left only enough for you to survive."

"But why," Jairus asks surprised. "Surely the soldiers brought food with them."

"Josephus' orders. His army would not have enough food for the long campaign and little was left for the Romans."

Jairus glances down at the fish symbol in the dirt. "Thank you, good brother. I must hurry home to my wife. She is surely in much distress."

The man named Andrew claps a firm hand of friendship on Jairus' shoulder and moves on.

The sky is clear but the air is filled with the clouds of dust stirred by the continuous tramping of the multitude. When he was higher on the mount with a broader view of the long column of soldiers, he estimated their numbers to be several thousand, considerably less than the tens of thousands Rome would send, that thought sending a shudder through him.

# CHAPTER THIRTEEN

*Jericho, May 27, 2012*

Chris and Kate entered the Jericho city limits, the wheels of their car sounding like distant thunder running over the cobblestones. The GPS guided them to Samis Hostel, across the road from the Hotel Intercontinental. Emmanuel was standing outside in his dig grubs, the ten-gallon hat perched atop his head like a misplaced artifact. Kate parked the car and she and Chris got out. She grabbed her cloth purse that sagged with the gun and pushed the car's lock button. Emmanuel was clearing the back seat of the Land Rover, tossing walking shoes, and notebooks and what looked like a backpack over the backseat to clear space for his new passengers. The interior smelled of dust and heavy male deodorant. The front seat was clean and unfettered.

"Y'all are right on time," he beamed. "Four o'clock straight up."

"And we must not waste any either," Kate said firmly. "We didn't know we were going to get held up at a checkpoint and that the speed limit from Jericho north was sixty kilometers per hour."

"I figured that in," Emmanuel said cockily.

Chris rolled his eyes. "What about the checkpoints and road blocks?"

"There's only one checkpoint between here and the dig," Emmanuel said. "They've never held me up. Road blocks can occur at any time but I've not encountered any on this stretch."

"Let's go," Kate instructed. "We're wasting time talking."

She got in the back seat and motioned Chris toward the front, which he thought was a good move. He was not the one with the gun. Emmanuel wheeled out of the parking lot and onto the access road which would take them back to Highway 90.

At Highway 90, they approached the check point to the city's northern entrance. In the early morning, there was no queue. Two soldiers manned the booth. Emmanuel pulled up and stopped. A female guard stepped up to the car, pistoled a finger at Emmanuel and requested his passport. The male soldier in the booth behind said something inaudible to her.

The female guard thumbed over her shoulder at the guard in the booth. "He knows you," she said. "But your passengers." Her pointed finger swiveled to Chris and Kate. "We need to see their passports."

Chris and Kate handed their passports to Emmanuel who gave them to the guard. She looked at each, then through the window at their owners then again at their pictures on their passports.

"The other guard says this is early for you. You normally come through later."

"These two with me are just temporary with the dig," Emmanuel stated. "Their time is limited, they have to fly out tomorrow. We're getting an early start with daybreak."

The female guard listened intently. She handed back the passports. "They are returning with you?"

"Yessum," Emmanuel said, nodding his head.

"To Jericho?" she said

"No. They're staying in Jerusalem."

"Where?"

"At the Olive Garden Hotel," Emmanuel answered.

The guard studied them a moment, had that look of someone or something she might recognize. "Do you have a gun, any firearms?"

"Nope!" Emmanuel clipped. "Don't even own any."

*He's lying*, Chris thought. Fundamentalist evangelicals are the biggest gun toters in the country.

"Very well. You may pass. But drive carefully. You know the speed limit is sixty kilometers per hour."

"Yessum," Emmanuel said again with exaggerated politeness. "Thank you."

*That was close*, Chris thought and breathed a sigh of relief that Emmanuel knew nothing about Kate's gun and that the guard took his answer to be generic for all of them. Apparently, the word had not been passed along from the previous checkpoint or the guard was unaware Chris and Kate were the same people.

Emmanuel drove slowly through the corridor of concrete slabs and back onto the highway.

"That was good, Emmanuel," Chris said. "Only one problem."

"What's that?"

"We are coming back through here in a couple of hours or less, depositing us, then you are going back. Assuming those two guards will still be there, they're going to be scratching their heads."

"I'll just tell 'em you got a call and needed to get back to the hotel," Emmanuel said. "Besides, the guards go off duty at seven."

"Hopefully, we'll be back before then," Kate said. "What if they start in with twenty questions? We need to think this through."

Chris turned around in his seat again. "We're not sure how soon we're coming back. Depends on what we run into." He winked and pointed at her bag.

She rolled her eyes, said nothing further and he turned back around.

For the first few miles, except for an occasional eighteen wheeler, the drive north on the broad stretch of Highway 90 was quiet and deserted. The three shared pleasantries about sleep, or the lack of it. Emmanuel pointed to the dark mass scraping the sky on their left.

"That's the Mount of Temptation," he said with an authoritative air.

"It's Arabic name is Jabal al-Quarantal," Kate said. "It's from a mispronunciation of the Latin word *quarentena* for the forty days of Jesus fast in the wilderness."

Emmanuel shrugged his shoulders as if to say *So what!* And launched into a lengthy discourse about Jesus' experience and how the sacred spot was desecrated with a crusader castle on the top.

"Have you been to the top?" Chris asked.

"No," Emmanuel quickly responded. "It's a thirty-minute hike up a steep path and you have to go through a cliff hanging church."

Kate again: "That church, Emmanuel, is a Greek Orthodox monastery, Deir al-Quarantal that was originally constructed by the Byzantines in the sixth century above the cave where tradition says Jesus stayed during his forty-day fast. And you don't have to walk up, you can take the cable car that leaves from Tel es Sultan."

"I'll need to do that," Emmanuel said unconvincingly and opened his mouth to say more but Kate was not finished.

"And, that is not a Crusader castle on the summit. It is a modern wall built around the ruins of a church the Crusaders built. Before that, it was a Hasmonean castle built in the second century B.C.E."

Tiring of Kate's scholarly admonishment and the history lesson, Chris had been eagerly waiting for an opportunity, then lunged. "Were you off your dig site or on it when you discovered the cave with the jars?"

"I'll have to let y'all determine that. The site is not roped off or anything like that. The Israelis can pretty much determine the site area, if you get my drift."

"Not sure I do," Kate said directly.

"The Israelis do what they want," Emmanuel stated. "They call the shots. If they want something within a site, they just expand the site perimeter to include it."

"That's precisely what concerns us," Chris said. "The Palestinians can do the same. When they overlap, there are fireworks."

Emmanuel did not respond.

Kate picked up the loose end. "Emmanuel, are you aware that the Palestinians will bid for statehood at the United Nations in September this year, just a few months away?"

"No, I was not," he replied.

"They are racing to claim heritage sites on the West Bank," Kate informed. "They are channeling money into excavating, developing and branding sites as their own. They are underscoring connections bound to history and identity."

"Yes, ma'am," Emmanuel said. "That's all happening now."

"And that's all the more concerned we are about this find," Chris said. "If it turns out to be something related to Arab or Israeli heritage, there's going to be a squabble."

"I don't think that's going to be a problem," Emmanuel advised calmly. "Did you see the fish symbols around the top of those jars? Bet you ten to one, those jars are of Christian origin."

Chris spun around and looked at Kate.

Noticing Chris's reaction, "Y'all saw 'em, too, I see," Emmanuel drawled excitedly.

Chris turned back around. "Yep. We saw them. That doesn't necessarily mean they're of Christian origin. The fish symbol is represented in other religions."

"I don't think so," Emmanuel said adamantly. "I've never read that anywhere and I read a lot."

*Let's just see how much*, Chris thought. "For starters, there was Aphrodite and Artargatis. In their company are Dagon, Ephesus, Isis, Delphine and Pelagia."

"You read a lot, too," Emmanuel said bemused. "We must read different books."

Kate leaned forward from the backseat. "Try Barbara Walker's book *The Woman's Dictionary of Symbols and Sacred Objects*. She points out that Ichthys was the son of the sea goddess Artargatis and represented sexuality and fertility."

"Not to mention the fact that the fish sign has been used to symbolize Pisces in the Zodiac configuration," Chris added.

That shut the cowboy evangelist up for a few minutes, Chris thought, and hopefully dampened any spirits he had about claiming ownership of the jars. But his fundamentalist orientation didn't need to be fed.

"Emmanuel, do you talk about your faith with your coworkers?" Chris queried.

"Every chance I get. I've met some converted Jews who said they were converted by witnesses like mine."

Chris wanted to ask if they ever asked him to shut up, decided on a different approach but Kate pre-empted him.

"Emmanuel, does it bother you that many Christians have left, and are leaving, Israel because of the Israelis and their heavy-handed tactics? Has that behavior not caused any friction?"

"No, ma'am. Some may be leaving but Christians come here in droves to see the sites of the Holy Land."

Chris pressed. "How much longer do you think those sites will be managed and run by Christians, if there are none left in the country?"

"I don't think that will happen," Emmanuel snapped. "First of all, they like evangelicals. We support their existence and are helping get all of the Jews back into the promised land. Second, too many of *us* will be around."

"Last night, Emmanuel," Kate addressed him, her head over the backseat, her mouth almost in his ear, "you said they liked you, meaning evangelicals, less than you liked them. You also said that when it came to artifacts, the Israelis looked after themselves. You said the Israelis had run the Christians out of Bethlehem. I'm not sure I understand your position. It seems conflicted."

"It's like I said last night, or you helpfully demonstrated with the salt and pepper shaker and napkin holder act," Emmanuel said and nodded at Chris. "If those jars once belonged to Christians and if they hold Christian documents or artifacts, they belong in Christian hands. That's why I called you," he glanced back at Kate. "After all, you hijacked the Gospel of Mark from Syria."

Not once had he called either by their name, professional or otherwise, Chris noted. The reason for their presence was becoming clearer. They had not been called by their new Texas friend to prevent the mishandling of a potentially great discovery. He and Kate were there to legitimize a possible heist by a far right Christian Fundamentalist. Chris was sure Kate was getting the same drift.

She spoke again. "Emmanuel, when you called the British Museum, you said it was a delicate situation and you needed help. You were concerned about these jars falling into the wrong hands and getting caught in the type of conflict Dr. Jordan has described. Now, we may be doing something that will cause the very conflict you wanted to avoid."

Emmanuel seemed agitated. Chris could see the ripple churning along his jaws and up into his temple, his hands squeezing the steering wheel.

"I thought I was doing the right thing," Emmanuel said, grinding the words through his teeth.

"If it is an Israeli dig, you need to notify them as soon as possible," Kate said.

Emmanuel did not respond.

"Is it an Israeli dig or not?" Kate pursued, her voice rising.

Chris was concerned she was losing her patience with him. "Emmanuel, does this have anything to do with the onsite/offsite issue?"

Emmanuel did not answer.

"My God, what is going on?" Kate exclaimed in a voice no louder than a sigh.

Headlights appeared behind them, out of nowhere it seemed. Emmanuel glanced in the rearview and noticed them.

From his side view mirror, Chris monitored them. They were neither gaining nor falling behind but keeping the distance between them constant. Emmanuel was driving the speed limit. It seemed the Land Rover was creeping. *It could be anyone,* Chris thought. Then again, *maybe Elad agents.* He glanced at his watch. It wouldn't be just anyone at four-thirty in the morning. Did the female guard recognize them and make a phone call? Did they tell them about Kate's gun. Even if she did, the three of them had done nothing wrong, not yet at least. He couldn't vouch entirely for Emmanuel Jones, which was the reason for the concern. Emmanuel said he didn't take or move the jars. Chris had crossed an ocean and Kate had flown from Scotland at the request of the British Museum to assist in evaluating an archaeological find. If Emmanuel had other ideas, an archaeological heist from an Israeli or Palestinian dig would put them on everybody's radar. He and Kate would be considered accomplices. He looked again. The lights were still there. If they followed when Emmanuel turned off Highway 90 toward Nablus, he'd get concerned. In the meantime, he kept telling himself they were law abiding professionals assisting in an archaeological discovery which may or may not be authentic and, if authentic, may or may not be of significance.

Emmanuel drove on in a fragile silence, constantly, and nervously, glancing in his rearview. After a few miles, he turned on his left blinker.

"Why are we turning?" Chris asked urgently. "I thought we went all the way to Highway Fifty-seven and turned left there?" From the back seat, Kate suddenly pulled herself forward.

"The dig is on this side of the Wadi Faria," Emmanuel said, "on its southern ridge. This is the route I follow every day, Route Five-o-Five, a regional road that goes through Ma'ale Efraim, to Route Five-o-Eight, through a village called Gitit, if you can believe that." He smirked as though he'd said something funny.

Chris was more concerned about the lights behind them, to see if they turned.

They turned.

"Did you see that, Emmanuel?" Kate exclaimed.

"See what?" Emmanuel responded.

"The car behind us," she said.

"I'll lose them at the next intersection. The road does some funny things before it gets to Ma'ale Efraim."

"Like what?" Chris asked nervously.

"You'll see," Emmanuel said confidently. "Just up ahead I can take a long detour that loops to the right. If that vehicle's still behind us, they're following us. That road goes nowhere and hooks back into Five-o-Five a few miles ahead. It must have been built to accommodate settlers. It passes a few houses but that's it."

"You seem to know your way around here," Kate said, the comment nuanced with sarcasm.

"Been driving it every day for a month now. I've taken some turns here and there just for the heck of it, to see where the road went, if anywhere. And a few are dead-ends, like one just past Ma'ale Efraim. It goes a few hundred yards and stops. Why don't I just take it? That way, if the lights turn, we could have ourselves a little confrontation."

"Take the first one," Kate ordered. "We don't want a confrontation, not yet."

"I agree," Chris said.

Emmanuel veered right at the Y intersection, everyone conscious of the direction the car behind them might take.

The car continued straight.

"That's good," Emmanuel said. "Now when we come back into Five-o-Five they'll be ahead of us. The followers become the followed," and he chuckled at his joke.

"If that doesn't happen," Kate said, "they know the road configuration as well. They can simply slow to a crawl, wait, and pick us back up."

"Then we can do the confrontation number," Emmanuel said.

"No confrontation," Chris asserted. "That would blow our objective. You want us to take a look at these jars, make an analysis, and determine if they are worth pursuing."

Emmanuel snapped a hard look at him. "You're already pursuing that, good buddy. Why else would you two fly half way around the world to see them?"

Chris flinched at the 'good buddy' comment but let it pass as typical Texas jargon. He was about to clarify his statement and Kate did it for him.

"We came because you asked for help with what we, and the British Museum, think could be an important discovery. You said you needed help because you were in a delicate situation, one you never fully described. Our sole motive is to assist in analyzing and protecting ancient artifacts."

His eyes riveted on the road, Emmanuel said nothing.

"All you needed to do was report it to the IAA," said Chris.

"I don't trust the Israelis with religious artifacts," Emmanuel said hostilely, "especially when the artifacts are of Christian origin. Anything the Israelis find will go into an Israeli museum. Then there's the black market mob. I'm sure y'all have heard of the Elkingtons from England."

"Oh, yes," Kate acknowledged.

Emmanuel continued. "They found seventy ancient lead and copper sealed books bound in wire in a remote cave in eastern Jordan, a region where early Christians fled after the destruction of the Temple."

"Just a second," Chris said. "They didn't find them, a Bedouin farmer in Galilee found them and they are considered to be a hoax."

"That's beside the point," Emmanuel said. "It caused a ruckus. The Elkingtons were shot at and had to flee, not only back to England but from their home to a remote Gloucestershire hideaway. I could see something like that happening here."

"So, you called us to put our lives in jeopardy," Chris clipped.

"I didn't want anybody's life in jeopardy," Emmanuel said. "But you two pulled off the archaeological find of the century in the middle of a revolution in Syria. Dr. Ferguson was the only person I knew to call that could help in this situation. I didn't ask the British Museum for help. I felt I would feel safe with you."

"We can help you recover the jars," Chris said. "I can conduct an analysis, perhaps arrive at some conclusion of their origin. If they hold documents, Dr. Ferguson can possibly provide a preliminary assessment of their identity and authenticity. That all depends upon the circumstances and if the conditions are adequate for her to perform her assessment." He glanced at her and she gave a confirming nod. "We can help you get them to the appropriate authority. Otherwise, I'm still unsure how we can help."

The road converged with the main 505 route. No lights were ahead or behind them. The only lights they saw belonged to a town ahead.

"How much further?" Kate asked.

"About five miles," Emmanuel replied.

They approached a city limits sign that said Ma'ale Efraim and drove through its sleepy streets, only a few people on the lighted sidewalks, and then they were quickly back into the dark night. A few more miles, the lights of another town appeared but they saw no light beams on the highway.

"You'd think we'd at least see their taillights ahead of us," Emmanuel said nervously. "Daylight's not long away and then we won't be able to tell."

Chris looked to his right and saw the dim bulge of sunlight along the eastern plateau pushing back the dark.

"We're not far from Shechem or Tell Balata," Kate estimated. "It's near Nablus, on this side. The Palestinians have been upgrading the ministries of antiquities and tourism including sites around Jericho, Bethlehem and Nablus," she apprised. "Israel is competing with them."

"Perhaps that's why the Israelis have a dig nearby," Chris conjectured. "It's an in-road."

Emmanuel was mute.

"A find near the dig Emmanuel is working on could escalate hostilities," Kate stated.

They both looked at Emmanuel who seemed not to have heard them and continued his silence.

Emmanuel turned off Highway 505 onto 508. A few more miles they passed through the small village of Gitit. Less than a mile out of Gitit, Emmanuel stopped and pointed to a narrow dirt road on their left. "We turn here," he said. "The dig site is a couple of miles up this road."

He turned left and the Land Rover bumped over the crude corduroy road.

The dig site looked like most Chris had seen. A couple of support buildings, a backhoe. It was not roped off, as Emmanuel had said, but crude fencing surrounded the area.

"Don't we stop and get out?" Kate said.

"Nope," Emmanuel said. "Got a little further to go," and he took his foot off the brake and continued slowly over the rough terrain.

Chris and Kate looked back as the dig site faded then vanished from sight.

"I thought you said you had to take a leak and you walked away from the site," Chris said.

"I did but I didn't walk from the site."

"How much further?" Kate questioned, concern rising in her voice. "If I know my directions, we're headed toward Shechem."

"We are," Emmanuel agreed. "But we're not going *to* Shechem."

He drove on a couple of miles over the poorly kept and unpaved road, axles jouncing, tailpipe slapping. Chris understood now why Emmanuel insisted on going in the Land Rover. The sky was turning lighter behind them, but it was still dark ahead.

Emmanuel finally brought the vehicle to a halt. "This is the place," he said.

Chris and Kate looked at each other and immediately knew where they were.

# CHAPTER FOURTEEN

*Capernaum, December, A.D. 66*

Jairus enters Capernaum.

The village is quiet.

The streets are empty.

He can see his fields and orchards up the mount behind his house. If the young man named Andrew was accurate, the soldiers took some of his livestock and crops of barley and wheat, probably some herbs and legumes closer to the house. But Jews could not eat the first fruits of grain until they had been offered on the day after the Sabbath of the Festival of Unleavened Bread. They would have to wait at least another month. He wondered about the number of committed Jewish soldiers, if they would abide by their law. The Christians would not have to wait. The Romans would not care.

He quickens his pace.

Rebecca stands in the door. Her hands are on her cheeks, her eyes red. She has been crying. She sees him and runs toward him, her robe flying behind her. She slams into him, throws her arms around his neck. He feels the tremors along her body.

"Jairus, Jairus, thank God you have returned."

"I was just away over night. I told you I might not return until the morrow."

"Yes, yes," she cries into his shoulder. "But much has happened."

"Much has happened also with me. Walk with me." He turns her toward their house, an arm around her waist holding her close.

Once inside the house, he removes his sandals and outer garment. He sits in a chair beside the hearth, places one opposite him and gestures for her to sit. "Josephus' army marched through Capernaum. They took crops and some of our livestock."

"This is true," she says, wiping long tresses of hair that seemed damp with tears from her face. "You saw the army. How did you know about the crops and livestock?"

"Someone, a man named Andrew from Chorazin, a follower of Jesus, told me. When did they come?"

"You left early morning. They arrived shortly after you departed. They were camped between Capernaum and Bethsaida."

"How much did they take?"

"Half of the sheep and goats, one cow," she says speaking rapidly, excitedly. "They harvested much of the grain. Their leader, Josephus, could not control them. He fell from his horse and injured his ankle near Bethsaida. His men took him to Miriam's house. She and some of the elders treated him. He ordered his soldiers to take only what they could carry but many took more and ..."

"Calm, my love." He reaches for her hands and holds them in his. Their knees are touching. "Breathe deeply and slow down. All is well. We have our home, each other. We can plant more grain, the trees will again ripen with olives. Remember the words of Jesus, 'Give to the one who asks you; and from the one to whom you have lent, do not demand back what is yours.'"

She looks up at him, drawing his strength. "And this one: 'Who among you through worrying is able to able to add an arm's length to his height.'"

He completes the saying: "'Do not worry about your life, what you might eat, nor about your body, what you will wear. Is not life more than food, and the body more than clothing.'" He points a finger toward the north. "The Romans are coming, their army many times the size of the one we have just seen. But, if they come, they come."

She glances toward the door where he had left his sandals and outer garment. "Papyrus. You did not bring the papyrus. Was it stolen? Did you lose it?" She was always the perceptive one.

"Neither. The chartaria had no papyrus or ink. All had been purchased by Agrippa for his scribes and court documents."

"Agrippa?"

"Agrippa had to flee Jerusalem and could not bring his supplies with him."

"But others wish to read the sayings of Jesus," she complains. "They clamor for them. Soldiers stopped me as they passed and asked if I knew him for they knew he was from Capernaum. What will you do?" her voice almost frantic.

"My work will not stop," he replies calmly. "The paper vendor, his name is Ezra, said he would help me. He is a professional scribe. He showed me a scroll written by the man named Paul of Tarsus. We have heard of him."

"Yes, please continue."

"The scroll was a letter from Paul to the ecclesia at Galatia," Jairus proceeds. "I stayed up all night, as long as the oil lamp provided light, and read. I could not read the entire letter because I wanted to rise early and see you. I missed you, my love, even as I was leaving Capernaum."

"And I missed you." She leans over and kisses his cheekbone, beside his eye, a casual peck. "This letter from Paul that you were reading, it was important?"

"Indeed!" He says excitedly. "At the beginning of the letter, Paul speaks of others deserting Jesus and turning to a different gospel."

"Yes?" she says, her eyes boring into his to tell her more.

"There is no other gospel except the one I am compiling," he says. "The world of Jesus followers is waiting. Paul needs my help. I must make haste."

"Will you return to Tiberias when the chartaria has supplies?" she inquires anxiously.

"He is sending a courier to me with the supplies when they arrive."

"How long?" she presses.

"I think not long," he replies. "He was expecting supplies from Jerusalem at any moment. But the courier has gone to Jerusalem where there is much upheaval. We may not wait. Ezra, and the man named Andrew I met along the way here, said the Romans would strike first here, in Galilee. Ezra has encouraged me to bring you, our daughter and her family to Tiberius. He has spacious living quarters above his shop. We will be safe there. It is a pro-Roman city."

She reaches and holds his hand. "I do not disagree. But when will this happen?"

"The Roman general, Vespasian, is said to be moving from Antioch to Ptolemais, joining his son, Titus, with more troops from Egypt. If they are now in Ptolemais, they will move soon." He glances toward his writing area. "I have enough papyrus and ink to finish my first draft. I will write steadily.

Then we go to Tiberius where I can make copies. Ezra said he would help, possibly others could help also. We need to get the scrolls out to other communities before the war, if this is possible. Tell our daughter and sons to be prepared."

"Yes, certainly," she exclaims and departs immediately.

# CHAPTER FIFTEEN

*Near Shechem, Israel, May 27, 2012*

Kate got out of the Land Rover, slammed the door with her hip and walked briskly around the front of the vehicle to the driver's window. "Roll down the window, Emmanuel," she commanded, her face livid, eyes glacial.

Emmanuel lowered the window.

She leaned over and got in his face. "Emmanuel, this is nowhere close to the dig, " she said.

"I know," Emmanuel said apologetically. "Please forgive me." He remained folded into the driver's seat, his huge knees jammed against the wheel. He began pulling on his fingers again and cracking his knuckles.

Chris got out, walked around and stood beside Kate. He could feel her anger rising.

"Why did you lie to us?" she continued fiercely.

"By my estimation," Chris said, looking west where a vault of stars hung overhead, then toward the dawning east, "we are about midway between the Israeli dig and Shechem, which the Palestinians have been posturing to control."

"Let him answer my question," she demanded, her face still inches from Emmanuel's.

"I was afraid if I told you where the cave really was you wouldn't come," he offered weakly.

"Because we would be in the gray area of contention," she said. "Now I'm beginning to see why you needed us."

"To legitimize your find," chimed in Chris, "and why you seemed eager to come from the other direction. Coming from Nablus we wouldn't pass the dig and know where we were in relation to it."

Gazing at his lap, Emmanuel nodded.

"Is there even a cave here?" Kate questioned, her voice rising higher. "Are there even jars in it or was the photo rigged? If they're there, did you open them and already know their contents, if they have any?" She continued hammering away at the side of his face.

"I answered that already," Emmanuel said. "Look!" His palms flew up in defense. "The photo was not rigged. It's authentic. The cave is just a few steps from us. You are right. I skirted the truth on the location of the discovery. I was afraid the IAA and the Palestinians, once they heard of the find, would begin squabbling over it and I would have no way of protecting it. In your hands, the jars would have legitimate protection. At the time I called, I did not know the British Museum would be involved."

"Until they throw us in jail," Chris exclaimed. "You know we must report the find, and probably to the Israelis since technically, according to their laws, this is their country."

"You said you had to pee and walked away from the site rather than use one of the portables," Kate said.

"That was partially the truth," Emmanuel confessed. "I did need to relieve myself, but I was driving back from Nablus where I'd gone for some supplies. I don't like getting in those job potties they have on the site. I decided to stop before I got there."

"You said it was in daylight," Chris said.

"Yes," Emmanuel responded.

"Anyone could have seen you," Kate said alarmed.

"I didn't see anyone," Emmanuel replied. "I looked around."

"But ELAD and the Robbery Protection Unit have eyes everywhere," Chris exclaimed flabbergasted.

Emmanuel opened the door. Chris and Kate stepped back as he emerged. "The cave is just over there," he said pointing.

Exasperated, Kate slapped her arms against her sides. "Well, we're here. Might as well check it out."

Emmanuel reached back and retrieved a flashlight from the dash, aimed its beam on a huge boulder at the base of a cliff facing. Behind them the dawn was developing but it was still dark where they were standing.

"That is a mammoth boulder," Chris said. "It was probably once a part of the cliff and broke apart during an earthquake, covering the cave entrance for centuries."

Emmanuel swept his flashlight beam left and right along the long cliff revealing a continuous accumulation of rocks as far as the beam extended.

"There's no telling how many caves are sealed behind all that debris," Kate said. She had her flashlight out assessing the geologic malformations. "When the IAA and Palestinian Antiquities Authority learn of this, there will be one colossal hiatus."

"Several hiatuses," Chris added. "A fight over each cave as they are discovered." He looked at Emmanuel. "How did you manage to even get into it?"

"I had to get on my hands and knees and crawl through a small opening I made with my handpick," Emmanuel said. He walked to the rear of his Land Rover, popped the upper hatch, removed a pick and shovel and headed up the rocky slope. Chris grabbed his tool kit and he and Kate followed. Midway up the rocky incline, Emmanuel stopped.

"The cave is behind the rock. You can take the pick," he said handing it to Chris.

"It's bigger than the hand pick I brought," Chris replied, accepting the tool.

"Once I realized there was something behind the rock," Emmanuel continued, "it took me forever just to to breach the entrance enough so I could crawl through. Someone must have sealed it aeons ago. As you will see, the cave is shallow."

"Many of them are in this area," Chris said. "A few around Jericho are human-made."

"Once you get through the narrow opening, the jars are in full view," Emmanuel said, "almost as though whoever left them wanted them discovered. The big rock was probably not there then, but, like you said, fell from higher up."

Chris nodded in agreement, took the pick and began chipping around the edges of the jagged hole Emmanuel had scratched out earlier. The place had a scent of old stone and dust. Opposite him, Emmanuel shoveled debris to the side. Kate stood and looked on then returned to the Land Rover to get her digital camera. They were about thirty minutes from sunrise. The sky was getting brighter by the minute and they no longer needed the flashlights. She unhooked the Brookstone binoculars from her belt, lifted them to her eyes and panned the road and rock strewn panorama east as far as she could and then scoped west.

Observing her, Chris said, "Do you see anything?"

"Nothing," she replied. "Daylight is a mixed blessing. In the dark we could see car lights, any light that hinted of an intrusion. Now we'll have to watch and listen."

"Keep looking, not just at the road but the hills, atop the ridge-line," Chris advised. "Keep an eye out for someone who might be looking at you."

"I know," she said, casting an irritated glance at him. "Palestinians come into these hills with metal detectors and farming tools searching for artifacts that could bring them a few hundred dollars from antique dealers. The Israelis have cracked down on antiquities theft and the looting of ancient sites. We are not far from a dig they surely know about."

"The IAA patrols these hills," Emmanuel said. "We've seen them at the sight. They carry pistols, flashlights and walkie-talkies. Some of the dig workers said they carry night-vision scopes."

Chris stopped chipping. "That's comforting news, Emmanuel," he said snidely. "Were you thinking about that when, in broad daylight, you unveiled the cave? Is there anything else you haven't told us that could keep our butts out of jail?"

"Sorry," Emmanuel apologized again. "I didn't think about it until I saw her with those binoculars."

"Keep digging, Chris," Kate directed then shot Emmanuel a hard aggravated look. "You, too, Emmanuel."

Chris looked at her as though he didn't hear her, not at her, but at something behind her. Sunrises and sunsets in the desert had no spectacular play of changing light on clouds that one might see in Rome or San Francisco or Tahiti. Desert sunrises possessed a stunning brilliance, usually against a cloudless horizon, a singular piercing orange light, like the color of a horseshoe before its hammered, a display of light one never tired of seeing repeated. The hem of night was pulling away. He called Kate to him, hit a few more licks with his pick as she made her way.

"What?" she responded.

"Turn around," Chris said. A bright bulge of dawn was pushing upward over the trans-Jordan plateau, the features of the land to the east appearing and falling into place as though in a developing picture, the Jordan a stream barely discernible in the morning mist rising above it and the Dead Sea deep turquoise at its end like a tethered balloon.

"It's breathtaking," she exclaimed.

"And it's only beginning," he said in awe.

"It's big enough now," Emmanuel shouted, pointing at the cave opening.

Chris refocused on the task and with his hands began moving some of the large rocks aside.

Kate took a photo of the two beside the larger opening, then kneeled down to help, all three now lifting and tossing rocks until the sun's first rays threw a golden splash against the entrance now large enough for them to crawl through. In the rear of the shallow cave the two jars appeared. They looked as they had in Emmanuel's photo. Kate took another picture of the jars bathed in a swatch of early morning light that pierced the opening. The cave was about ten feet deep and six feet high, a pock mark on the cliff face compared to other caves that had been discovered in the area.

"Were they standing up like that when you first saw them?" Chris asked.

"They were lying flat on the ground," Emmanuel said. "I propped them against the wall to photograph them which is how you saw them and I left them like that."

Chris looked at his watch. "It's five thirty. We can't waste time. Whoever put them here was in a hurry."

"I forgot to tell you," Emmanuel said, "They were covered up with rocks and dirt. I could see part of one sticking out."

"You may have been right, Emmanuel," Chris said. "This was not a careful case of hiding something."

"Maybe whoever left them was on the run," Kate said. She had crawled in beside Chris.

"I don't know," Chris said. He looked back through the mouth of the cave. "It's not that elevated from the road. If someone was on the run, or being chased, they saw the cave, could get to it without difficulty, quickly covered the jars, then planned to return and get them. This may have been just a temporary hiding spot." He turned to Emmanuel who was standing behind them leaning on his shovel, looking on as if he were a disinterested spectator. "Are the jars in the same spot when you first discovered them?"

"Yes," Emmanuel said. "They were lying down. Like they might have been standing at first, then knocked over by something."

"You said they were partially buried under rubble, that you saw part of one exposed," Chris said wondering how much damage may have been done to the jars removing the debris around them.

Emmanuel nodded.

"That would support the theory they were buried hastily, loosely, not like some Qumran scrolls."

"There's another possibility," Kate suggested, glancing up. "An earthquake could have shaken the rubble from the ceiling. There has been multiple seismic activity in this region over the past two thousand years."

"There was one last August just off the Israeli coast, registered four point one on the Richter Scale," Emmanuel said.

"That's possible," Chris considered, scanning the roof of the cave. "Earthquakes almost sealed the cave in Syria where we found Mark's autograph intact."

"It left enough of an opening for a renegade ex-Syrian army officer to eke out a home," Kate added.

"Thank the Lord they did a better job here," Emmanuel said, looking at Chris. "It took me a lot longer than the two of us working to clear a way in."

"Emmanuel, do you have some type of cloth in your Land Rover, something we could lay down?" Chris asked.

"I've got a chamois."

"Perfect!" Chris said.

While Emmanuel left to retrieve the chamois, Chris pulled a small spiral notebook and pen from his shirt pocket and began making notes. He looked at Kate. "Would you estimate this cave depth to be about ten feet?"

"Yes," she agreed, "and width and height about five feet. A tall person would have had to crawl."

"My thoughts exactly," Chris said and they momentarily looked at each other. He glanced again at his watch. "We are in clear view of that road should anyone come along."

Emmanuel returned with the chamois and handed it to Chris. He spread it onto the pebble strewn ground and laid the jars upon it. From his pocket he removed a pair of surgical gloves and Kate, observing, did likewise. Carefully, he picked up the smaller jar, held it up in the bolts of dawn hammering the cave. He pointed at the small fish symbols around the lip. Then to the same etchings on the larger jar.

"Whatever the contents—and based upon the Qumran design probably scrolls, writings of some sort—they belong to the early Christian Era."

"The Christ symbol," she added.

"Yes," Chris confirmed.

Ears cocked, Emmanuel was observing intently.

Chris reached in his tool bag, removed a small brush and began lightly stroking the lid then whisking down the sides of the small jar and around the bottom. Dirt and dust particles fell onto the chamois. He repeated the procedure with the large jar.

Emmanuel continued looking on as though mesmerized. Kate watched attentively. Occasionally, Chris would glance at her, look straight into her eyes then back on his work. He knew she had performed similar procedures and rituals with old manuscripts and would apply them later to any texts the jars might contain. He was feeling closer to her now than he had since he'd arrived.

He put down the brush. "The jars don't look as dark in the sunlight as in the pictures." He turned to Emmanuel. "You said you stopped here during daylight. Did you photograph them in early morning or late afternoon?" He looked over his shoulder at Emmanuel.

"Late afternoon."

"That may explain the reason they look darker," Chris concluded.

"Can you tell anything about the clay?" Kate asked.

"To a degree," Chris responded. "The jars are darker than the Qumran jars, yet not as dark as I had expected. The color of the clay—yellowish-red to reddish-brown—is possibly from a sandy clay loam with elements of basalt. The sequin effect you see in places, like for example here," and he pointed toward the middle of the small jar, "are probably quartz from igneous basalt."

"Where would you find that kind of clay?" Kate inquired. "Jericho?"

"No," he voiced. "Galilee, which has a heavy basalt concentration."

"So, the pots were made in Galilee but look remarkably like those from Qumran," Emmanuel commented. "That's quite a ways away,"

"That's the initial assessment," Chris said. "I'll have to run a chemical analysis to be sure. It's doubtful someone would have hauled this clay to Qumran and had the pots made there. More probably they were made where this soil was available and, for whatever reason, we don't know, transported here and left."

He drew a measuring tape from his shirt pocket, laid it across the lid of the small jar then down the side measuring its height. "This jar is shorter, but wider, the opening almost twice that of the other. Eight inches across the lid or twenty point three centimeters. Record that for me in my notebook," he said to Kate who picked up the spiral pad and pen and made the notations. "And lengthwise, ten and one-half inches or about twenty-six point seven centimeters."

Next, he measured the large jar's lid and called out, "six inches," turned the ruler over, "or fifteen point two centimeters." The height was nineteen and one-half inches or forty-nine point eight centimeters. "That's about the size of the scroll jars at Qumran." He looked down briefly. "The contents may be different, if anything is inside them. And we assume there is since they are sealed."

He deposited the brush back into the tool bag and looked around. "If we had time, we would need to scour this place with brushes, see what lies beneath this thin layer of soil, what might be hidden by the elements and earthquakes."

"We don't have time," said Emmanuel. "It's six o'clock. We have to pass the site and the workers know my Land Rover. We'll have to stop. They'll ask questions."

Chris retrieved the mason trowel from his bag and two small vials. With the trowel he scooped up loose dirt and dust that had fallen from the small jar onto the chamois, sifted it into one of the vials and with his pen marked the label: content, time and location. He did the same with sediments from the other jar, then shook and folded the chamois and handed it back to Emmanuel. He then reached again into his bag and pulled out two large cloth bags and two plastic Ziploc packets. "We'll put the scrolls in here," he said, pointing to the cloth bags, "and what's left of the leather bags into the Ziplocs. UNESCO's antiquity authorities will be impressed with our thoroughness." He carefully, and gently, slid the two jars into the protective covers and did the same with the fragile leather wrappings into the large Ziplocs. He peeled back his gloves, picked up his tool bag and handed the small jar to Kate. He gathered the larger jar snuggly in his arms, cradling it as though it was an infant and they proceeded to the Land Rover. Emmanuel followed.

Emmanuel opened the rear hatch. "There's a bunch of dirty clothes I was going to take to the cleaners in Jericho," he said. "You can put the jars on top of them."

Chris nestled the jars among the loose laundry. He then unzipped his tool bag, placed the two small vials and the Ziplocs containing the samples inside, zipped it close and placed it between the jars.

"Which authorities will you deliver them to?" Emmanuel asked nervously.

Remembering what Emmanuel had said the evening before at dinner, Chris thought carefully about his response. "We are in Israel ..."

"We are in the West Bank," Emmanuel interrupted.

"We understand," Chris said, "but the West Bank has not yet been recognized by the United Nations as an independent country. So, by law, technically, we must report the find to the IAA."

For a few seconds, Emmanuel was mute, looking at them as though they had lost their minds, betrayed their profession, or both. "When do we have to do that?" he said.

"We do have another option," Kate suggested. "UNESCO. It's neutral."

Chris looked at Emmanuel to assess his reaction but Emmanuel's eyes were distracted with something he saw coming up the road.

# CHAPTER SIXTEEN

*Capernaum, Galilee, March, A.D. 67*

It has been almost three months and no courier, no papyrus or ink. Jairus diluted the ink remaining and made notes on extra blank pages he had on hand. There was room left on the scroll for additions. He had interviewed several more who had heard Jesus and acquired some new sayings he had committed to memory. Without papyrus and a fresh supply of ink, all he can do is review what he has written.

His wife comes and stands behind him. She leans over and observes the passage he is reading, where Jesus pronounces judgment on Capernaum. He feels her shudder, her hand tremble on his shoulder.

Her voice quavers as she speaks. "We were there, in the synagogue, the day he said those words. 'Capernaum will you be exalted in heaven? No, you will fall into Hades.' I remember trembling then as I do now. I remember others startled by the comment. Perhaps some among us feel exalted, I do not," she concludes.

"Nor I," he says gazing at the words before him.

"Why do you record Jesus' words if the world is going to crash?" she questions.

"Because they are words that teach us how to live until that time comes. I preserve them for the living, not for the dead."

She gives him a nod of understanding and kisses his forehead. "I sense the restlessness inside of you. It is the sound of your soul."

He acknowledges her comment. "Are our daughter and her family prepared, our two sons and their families?" and sees her face drop before he even finishes.

"Hava and Abner are ready," Rebecca says. "I alerted them yesterday of our plans and they were in agreement. However, Aaron and Benjamin and their families will not go."

"They are being stubborn," Jairus says. "They do not understand the gravity of the situation."

"They say it is you who does not understand," she replies. "They say the Romans are interested in Jerusalem, not Galilee."

"Very well. I will not argue with them," he says. "Tell them they are welcome if they change their minds. We are staying with a man named Ezra, the chartaria. His shop is on the main street."

She kisses him on his neck and departs.

He wonders what happened to the courier. Perhaps he could not acquire supplies or he secured them and could not bring them. He could have gone himself to Caesarea Philippi, two days journey away, but there were rumors of armies in that direction. If papyrus and ink have arrived from Jerusalem, he and Ezra can begin immediately copying. Perhaps his courier could carry the new copied scrolls to Jerusalem and Casarea Philippi, cities he had placed at the top of a compiled list that included, Antioch, Alexandria, Ephesus and ... eventually Rome.

His grandchildren now grown and unmarried, still living with their parents, have never been farther from home than local villages near Capernaum. When told they were going to Tiberius, Asher and Dan and Michal became excited. They recalled the times when they were younger and their father had been and returned bearing gifts—for the two boys, stone marbles and spinning tops; and for Michal, a wax doll. To all he brought sweets he had purchased along with tales of adventure.

As Jairus and his family draw near to Tiberius, they can hear the muted din and clamor of the city. Once through its city gate, the noise is louder than Jairus recalled in December. The main street is clogged with people, mostly men, Josephus' army. The noises he hears—hammers, stone on stone, metal on metal, men barking orders—at first he cannot place. He looks around. Men are on the walls, hauling up stones and putting them into place, constructing towers. He recalls what Ezra had said about Josephus coming to reinforce the walls.

Standing in the door of his shop, Ezra sees the family and runs to greet them. "Jairus, my friend," he says joyfully, embracing him, "I have worried about you. Thank God you are safe. And this must be your family."

"My wife, Rebecca," Jairus says, extending a deferential hand, "and my daughter Hava and her husband Abner, their children Asher, Dan, and Michal," pointing to each as he calls their name.

"Yes, yes, of course, come in, come in," says Ezra ushering them with open arms.

Rebecca and Hava and Michal scurry inside. Ezra rushes to help Jairus and Abner and his sons with the bundles and items in the cart.

"Do not leave the cart outside," Ezra says. "This is not the quiet city it was. There are problems," and he helps Abner and his sons tilt the cart sideways and carry it through the door into his shop. "I have a place for it behind the shop, but later." He turns to Rebecca and Hava. "My home is upstairs, please go and be comfortable. There are fruits and olives and cheese on the table. Please enjoy."

Rebecca and Hava nod and Hava motions to her three, who are inspecting the shop, and leads them up the stairs.

Jairus unslings the leather bag from his shoulder and sets it at the foot of the stairs. "The codices and scroll," he says, pointing to the bag. "I will leave them here for the moment."

Ezra nods approval, then says, "But only for the moment. Things of precious value must be guarded with care."

"You say there are problems," Jairus says. "What problems?"

"Josephus," Ezra pronounces.

"But he comes to protect," Abner says. "That is the reason we are here and not in Capernaum."

"One wonders," Ezra says. "Josephus has taken control of the city, destroyed Herod's palace and entrapped pro-Roman Tiberians. By the grace of God, he was able to halt the pillaging of the city by his Jewish army. To quell his opposition, he imprisoned many of the city notables, including the historian Justus and his father."

"We've only avoided one danger for another," Jairus says downcast.

Abner nods in agreement.

"Perhaps not, my brother," Ezra says, looking at both of them. "We have received word through Josephus' spies that Vespasian is moving his legions from Antioch to join Titus at Ptolemais. From there, it is likely they plan to cross our Galilean borders."

"When will this take place?" Abner asks.

"Who knows?" Ezra says. "If the information is accurate, Josephus and his troops must leave to defend our borders."

"Let us hope that is soon," says Jairus. "This city sounds like a bubbling caldron about to spill over. I may have a revolt of my own, my daughter and husband leaving to return to Capernaum." He glances at Abner but his son-in-law, arms folded across his chest, says nothing. He is a large quiet man, a good husband and father, one not easily upset. But when riled, he makes decisions quickly and does not look back. It took Jairus days to convince him he should bring his family to Tiberius out of harm's way. Should he change his mind, they would leave as quickly as they arrived.

"Hopefully, you will stay," Ezra says. "Papyrus and ink arrived from Jerusalem two days after you left for Capernaum. Josephus' men barred my courier from leaving the city. They believed him to be a Roman spy."

"Where is he now?" says Jairus.

"He is in Tiberius with his family. Only at my pleading, did Josephus' men not imprison him. But he is forbidden to leave the city. I tell you, Josephus is doing more harm than good. I hope he leaves the city soon and takes his men with him."

"The rebellion is a horrible thing for Jews and the followers of Jesus," Abner says.

"Allow me to show you your lodgings," Ezra says.

The three men ascend the stairs and find Rebecca, Hava and her two sons and daughter standing on a small balcony, observing men working on the walls and the steady flow of traffic below. They turn around as the three men enter the open air area of the upper floor.

"You are surely tired," Ezra says. "Please, allow me." He directs them to rooms and pulls out straw mattresses where they can sleep. "If the weather is clear, you may wish to sleep beneath the stars," he suggests.

"We are grateful to you, sir," Abner says, "but inside will be less noise and dust from the traffic below and the men working on the walls. Tomorrow my sons and I can join and help."

"Very gracious of you," says Ezra. "I am sure they can use the help."

"We will only need one room," Hava says. "We can sleep together on the mats as we do at our home."

"Splendid!" Exclaims Ezra. "When the sun sets," he glances at the sky, "and that is but hours away, the city grows quiet. Rest and later we eat."

"We brought food with us," Jairus says.

"This is good," says Ezra. "Josephus monitors the food supply, ensuring his soldiers will have enough. If they are leaving soon, they will hoard before they go."

Jairus and Ezra return to the ground level and adjourn to Ezra's private quarters, the one large room around the hearth and a raised platform along one side where he sleeps.

"On clear bright days, I write in the courtyard," Ezra says. "I did not show that to you when you were here. Allow me," and with an open hand guides Jairus to the small enclosed area at the back of the building. "Please sit." He points to a stone bench and seats himself on another. "This is my sanctuary."

Jairus is impressed with the cobbled patio, its protected walls draped with ivy and colorful flowers in pots spaced around the perimeter. A lone olive tree stands in the center, its branches shading the benches where they sit. "It truly is a sanctuary," he says. "In this place one can draw inspiration to write."

"And we shall," Ezra says, "beginning in the morning. The papyrus Raphael brought back from Jerusalem is of fine quality, Hieratica. Perhaps you've heard of it."

"Yes," Jairus affirms. "It is a large sheet distinguished by its whiteness. The priests like it because of its sacred color."

"This is true. It is more durable than some of the other papyrus types. There is room in the courtyard for both of us. Or, you can use the table inside."

"Indeed. I can work from the two codices, freeing the scroll for you to copy."

"This is a good plan," Ezra agrees, "for there is an urgency."

"Something other than the impending war?" Jairus says curiously.

"While Raphael, my courier, was in Jerusalem, he encountered a man in the same chartaria shop. The man was purchasing writing supplies and, Raphael said, several bundles of papyrus, of the same type he had purchased. The man told Raphael that a friend of his, a disciple of Jesus for whom he was purchasing the supplies, was writing a gospel about Jesus and in search of more material about Jesus' miracles and healings, but especially, his teachings."

"And this man, this friend of the master," Jairus says, a sudden joy jumping in his chest, "did he give a name?"

"The name of the disciple writing the gospel?"

"Yes."

"No. But the man inquiring was one called Theophilus."

"That is a Gentile, Greek name," says Jairus. "It means 'friend of God.'"

"That is of little importance," Ezra says.

"It could be of much importance," counters Jairus. "The sayings in the codices are in Aramaic. I translated them in Greek to the scroll. Whoever receives our scrolls must be able to read and write in Greek, not Aramaic or Hebrew."

"Forgive me that lapse of reason," apologizes Ezra. "But it is imperative we get a scroll of the master's sayings to Jerusalem. I know of no one who has collected his sayings and teachings of Jesus and committed them to writing. You are the only one. Have you knowledge of anyone in Galilee who has done so?"

"I do not," Jairus responds, "and I think I would. Many, especially in middle and lower Galilee, know of me and my efforts. Some have come to me with remembrances of Jesus' teachings and works."

"You said you brought the codices and scroll with you," Ezra affirms, "in the leather bag by the stairs."

"Yes. Allow me," and he pushes himself up from the bench and enters the house. All is quiet up the stairs. Everyone is resting. He will join them soon. He picks up the strap of the leather bag, takes it to the courtyard, places it at his feet as he sits.

"You are wise to carry your documents in a bag of strong leather," Ezra says.

"I bought it several years ago in Caesarea Philippi to carry scrolls I purchased in that same city for storage in the synagogue in Capernaum."

"You could have purchased more writing supplies there instead of waiting for a courier who was not coming," bemoans Ezra.

"I still had room to write on the scroll and ample writing to accomplish and I trusted you would deliver."

"I failed you, my friend," Ezra nods sadly.

"Nay, you did not. I am here. I would have come regardless to begin our mission. And you have the supplies. God's will prevailed. It is fortuitous. I may wish to copy my scroll onto your finer papyrus, if that is permissible."

Ezra smiles and claps his hands. "But of course. Which do you want me to see first, one of your codices or the scroll."

"The finished work, the scroll, from which we will copy others. You can review the codices later if you wish," and as he talks, he removes the scroll from the bag. Carefully, he unwraps the layers of linen cloth encasing it then unties leather thongs threaded through a leather tab that is clamped to the end sheet of the scroll. Untying the thongs loosens the scroll and readies it to be unrolled and read. In that state, he hands it to Ezra.

Ezra moves to the edge of his bench and, like a father receiving a new born, receives the scroll, at first fondling it as though it was his own. He looks up and Jairus sees the tears in his eyes. "I am holding the first recorded words of Jesus."

"And they will not be the last, my friend," Jairus confirms. "Together, we will spread them."

"Do you have a title for your scroll?"

"Yes. The Sayings of Jesus."

"Excellent. I cannot think of one better. I know you are tired, my friend. Please join your family and rest. Your wife is lovely. I now understand your concerns of her worrying about you. Your daughter is beautiful. If there was a name for 'healed by Jesus,' she would surpass it."

"Many thanks, kind one. We will join you later for the evening meal."

"Your family returns an air of joy and happiness to this house," rejoices Ezra. "I feel twice blessed."

"My family is your family," Jairus says, then joins his wife and family and rests.

# CHAPTER SEVENTEEN

*Near Shechem, Israel, May 27, 2012*

The sun was blinding over the trans-Jordan plateau, the sky a murderous blue and they could not make out the type of vehicle headed towards them. Kate pushed her sunglasses over her forehead and glassed the moving conveyance with the binoculars.

"Palestinian officials," she said. "They're in a jeep."

"How do you know they're Palestinian?" Emmanuel questioned.

"The Palestinian flag flying from the pole on the jeep," she said, taking another look. "Black, white and green with a red triangle indent. And they are in uniform."

"They could be fake," Emmanuel quipped. "We've seen that before. Palestinians dressed like officials looking for artifacts, not protecting them."

Listening to him, Kate was still standing by the Land Rover. She pinched the front of her blouse, billowed and shook it a few times then drew her hand across her brow, gestures she was getting hot. "He could be right," she murmured to Chris who was watching the jeep. Pulling her blouse from her waist, she opened the back door of the Land Rover and stepped behind it, shielding herself from Emmanuel's view. Chris knew what she was doing. His heart raced. He stepped between her and Emmanuel shielding her as she unsheathed the gun, inserted a clip and slipped it inside the back band of her pants.

The jeep was traveling fast when it left the small local road, bouncing its driver and three passengers up and down over the rocky slope. It seemed the two on the back seat might eject. The one behind the driver had an automatic assault rifle strapped around his shoulder anchoring it with his arm. Binoculars hung from the neck of the companion seated beside him. All wore dark sunglasses.

Trying to remain calm, Chris stood beside Kate who was still standing behind the open door of the Land Rover, Emmanuel a few paces to his left. Chris could see all the jeep's passengers were male, dressed in blue camouflage and wearing dark berets, uniforms worn by Palestinian security units. The jeep came to a jolting stop and the men bounded from it as though assaulting a strategic point. Kate stood akimbo, her right hand edged closer to the gun.

The small security force stopped and aligned thirty paces from them. The one holding the rifle had it pointed at them and the one wearing the binoculars, apparently the spokesperson, pushed it aside. Kate relaxed her posture, dropped her hands and stepped from behind the Land Rover door.

"You speak English?" the spokesman said and pointed at Emmanuel, first at his boots, then his hat. The Palestinian looked official, bars on his shoulder.

"Yes," Kate said though the question was not directed at her.

"Your passports, please," he commanded, rubbing his hands together as though washing them.

Kate faced him squarely "First, identify yourselves," she said, her voice authoritative, demanding.

"We are special unit. Palestinian Authority."

"How do we know you are not imposters?" Chris enquired.

The spokesman pointed to the official insignia of the National Security Forces on his left shoulder, the pan-Arab "Eagle of Saladin" with the shield of the Palestinian flag holding a scroll with the word *Filistin* in Arabic.

Chris observed an intimidating movement he'd seen before, Kate lowering her eyes so they leveled out like a laser, and he knew what was coming. In a firm tone, she said something to the young officer in Arabic.

Her aggressiveness startled the official and Chris was reminded she spoke seven languages fluently, including Arabic. He leaned over and whispered to her: "What did you say to him? We don't need to start something."

Her eyes still on the officer and in the same firm pitch, she said, "I demanded to see his papers and documentation."

Emmanuel was looking on dumbfounded, his mouth hanging open.

The spokesman glared at her. "You speak Arabic, but I speak English. All respects, Madam, I am requesting *your* documentation," he commanded, thrusting out his hand.

Kate swallowed and fished her passport from her rear pocket and Chris did likewise from his shirt pocket. Emmanuel had to go to the Land Rover and retrieve his. Chris and Emmanuel handed theirs to Kate, who in turn, handed the three passports to the spokesman of the group. He opened each passport, glancing at each of them as though he had difficulty matching photos with faces.

"Where you from?" He pointed again at Emmanuel as if, in his attire, he'd drawn the center of their attention.

"I'm from Texas, the U.S.A.," he drawled, "and these other two are—"

"I am from the United Kingdom," Kate interrupted, "and he," she thumbed to her left at Chris, "is from the United States."

"I am Doctor Christopher Jordan and this is Doctor Kate Ferguson," Chris added.

"And the other one with you, he is doctor, too?"

Emmanuel was about to answer but Chris preempted him. "He is a student."

The spokesman was listening with his eyes. "Why you are here?" he said.

"First," Kate said, taking a few steps toward him, "Why are *you* here and may we have our passports back?"

"We are here because you are here," the spokesperson replied.

"I don't understand," Chris said.

The spokesman pointed at his binoculars. "We have been watching. Many people come, including Palestinians, and steal our history. This against the law and the Oslo Accords. You know the Oslo Accords?"

Chris said, "We understand about the Oslo Accords. Heritage sites with a Jewish history remain under Israeli sovereignty. That was Prime Minister Netanyahu's position in 2010. And it's the same position today."

The spokesperson countered. "UNESCO ruled heritage sites in Bethlehem and Hebron are Palestinian."

Chris and Kate nodded in agreement.

The young official continued, his hands carving the air as he spoke. "Palestinians say location, not religious history, determines a site's sovereignty. Israel violates international treaties it has signed. Israel excavates the West Bank. He is with them." He pointed at Emmanuel.

"Let's see if I understand," Kate said. "You've been monitoring the dig nearby and you think we are involved."

"He is involved," and again the officer pointed at Emmanuel. "*Perhaps you are.*"

"No," Chris said emphatically. "*We*," he thumbed his chest,"are not involved," then pointed to Emmanuel. "This student is involved. He was invited by the Israelis."

"Then why are you *here*," he speared a finger at the ground, "in *this* place?" "We saw you," then turned the same finger to the binoculars dangling around his neck. "This is a new dig, new overnight. You removed archives."

Kate threw up a palm to halt any comments from her companions. "We have two jars and the leather bags they were in. To our knowledge, they are of little significance. They may not be authentic. We are considering taking them and turning them over to UNESCO."

"*Considering?* The security guard questioned tartly. "You give them to us. *We* take to UNESCO."

"By the rules of UNESCO, if they are genuine, they will have to return them to you. We would like to conduct our own preliminary evaluation," Kate explained, "to ensure we are not turning over something that is bogus."

"Bogus?" The young spokesman asked nonplussed.

"Fake," Chris injected. "False."

"Why do you evaluate jars first, before turning them over?" the soldier asked.

Kate spoke again. "Because we are experts. Dr. Jordan is an archaeologist and I am an ancient manuscript expert. I work with the British Museum. We trust ourselves before we trust anyone else. You surely know that in the past antiquities have fallen into inexpert hands, including UNESCO, and later they were declared forgeries, hoaxes. Our reputations are on the line."

"Oh yes, I know this." He slapped a hand on his chest. "My reputation, my job. We have our own experts." His voice was rising and they could tell he was getting impatient. "You turn them over to us, not the Israelis. Israelis steal our heritage. This is Palestinian area. Read the Accords. Read UNESCO's rulings. Tell the Israelis to read them."

Chris became intrigued with Kate's argument, and also sensed she was losing.

"We understand," Kate said, and took an intimidating step forward.

The gunman standing next to the spokesman swung his gun around. The spokesman again pushed it away, glowered at him, then looked back at Kate. "We do not want trouble. I repeat. We have our own antiquity department. We evaluate. So, if you please, hand the jars to us."

He began walking toward them. Kate's hand flew to her hip.

"Naw now," Emmanuel erupted. "We're not handing anything to you. We are Christians and these may be Christian relics."

Kate put up a hand to stop Emmanuel from saying more but the spokesman did it for her. "I am Christian. This one," he pointed to the driver, "and this one," then the one who was the front passenger side, "are Christian. We are all Christians. Palestinian Christians here before Muhammed was born."

Emmanuel stood stunned and mute, like a balloon had burst in front of him and he was looking at the empty space.

"We understand," Kate said, her tone moderating and soft. "This is not about religion; it is about your heritage."

The spokesman thumped his chest. "Yes. Our heritage. You understand. Now be so kind and hand us the jars."

"We're not handing you anything," Emmanuel blurted.

"Emmanuel, be quiet," Kate snapped and shot him a hard squinty-eyed look.

"But we are within rights," Emmanuel said.

"We are within somebody's rights," Chris joined in, "but it may not be ours. And you probably knew that when you skirted us from pillar to post before getting here." He glanced at his watch. "And you may have some explaining to do to your buddies down the hill when they see us go by."

"Hold off, gentlemen," Kate said to her two companions and turned back to the four men across from them. "Sir, we have no idea what is in these jars. For all we know it may be nothing. Ancient jars are a dime a dozen in this area of the world. You are surely aware—"

The spokesman's hand went up to stop her. "A dime a dozen?"

She looked at Chris, the moment near comical, then back at the spokesman. "A mil a dozen," she said to him smiling, referencing the lowest denomination of Palestinian money.

The man then understood. "Yes, yes, but still they, the jars, were on Palestinian property. They belong to us."

There was a pause. Kate's head down, thinking. Chris wondering about her next tact. Then she said: "Your antiquities department has an office in Jerusalem, yes?"

"Yes, East Jerusalem, the Jerusalem Governate. But East Jerusalem is Israeli territory. We are in the Nablus Governate."

Kate looked at Chris. "That's not going to work. I thought they could follow us into Jerusalem."

"That could start a war," Chris said.

Emmanuel was tapping his foot nervously, shifting from one to the other, heaving great dramatic sighs, making it obvious he was having a problem remaining silent.

They stood staring at each other, the four Palestinians and the three discoverers, no knowledge of what had been discovered except two jars. No knowledge of their contents. Yet they were faced off as though the hopes of the world hung in a balance. The spokesman was clutching the passports, looking down at them, then up at his new adversaries.

Kate backed up a few steps to the open door of the Land Rover. She reached in, retrieved her purse and from it a slender black wallet. She opened it and pulled out a lacquered card, put the purse back. Holding the card in one hand and the wallet in the other, she approached the spokesperson. Chris had seen the slight bulge of the gun made beneath her blouse and hoped she wouldn't turn around when she returned to the Land Rover.

She handed the colorful card highlighted with the sword of Excalibur to the spokesperson. He passed it around to his companions.

Kate proceeded. "I am a member of the British Special Forces, Army Reserve, counter-terrorism and reconnaissance unit. It is similar to your Palestinian Security Forces. I am bound by the protocol of the Geneva Convention, as are you, that was in place long before the Oslo Accords. I am obligated to abide by the laws of your territory but also the laws of Israel which, currently, supersede the laws of the West Bank. So far, do you understand?"

"I understand Geneva Convention and Oslo Accords. I do not agree Israeli laws are over Palestinian laws," the spokesman said.

"Believe me," she asserted, "I do not blame you. But this is the real world. If we give you these jars and the Israelis hear about it, and they would, this will cause major problems. It will cause major problems between the Palestinian Antiquities Authority and the IAA, not to mention the problems it will cause for us with the IAA. But there is another more peaceful way to solve this," she said then added something in Arabic.

"What did you say to him?" Emmanuel blurted angrily.

"I asked if he would be satisfied if we took them directly, now, to UNESCO in Ramallah? Don't interrupt me again, Emmanuel," and waved him off.

Frustrated, Emmanuel began kicking the dirt with his boot.

Chris, too, was flummoxed.

Noting Emmanuel's frustration, the security guard seemed to understand her reason for not speaking to him in English. He questioned, "How will we know?"

Kate spoke again in Arabic, and, as if to placate Emmanuel, she switched back to English. "There are two jars in the Land Rover. We will see that they go to the proper authorities. We are sympathetic to your cause. Please, write down the information about me from my UKSF card. My word is the word of the British Special Forces."

The spokesman was listening with bright, intent, quick eyes.

"Kate, do you realize what you're doing?" Chris popped.

"Yes!" she fired back. "Don't interrupt!"

The spokesman huddled with his men. They kept studying the card, looking at Kate, then Emmanuel, then back at the card. "How will we know?" the young spokesman pressed.

Continuing in English, Kate said, "I am asking you to trust me. We will take the jars to the UNESCO office in Ramallah. You can call UNESCO now, tell them we are coming with the jars. We will contact the Palestinian Antiquity Authority. What is your name?"

"Ahmed."

"How can we contact you, Ahmed?" she asked.

"Nablus!" While one of the other men was hastily copying information from her UKSF card, he pulled a card from his shirt pocket. "This is the Nablus Governate address and telephone number. You can ask for me or leave information," and handed the card to her.

Emmanuel stepped forward, "Look—"

Kate flung an arm back toward him and snapped her fingers. "Emmanuel, button up!" Her cheeks were hot, her eyes flashing. "Get in the Land Rover."

"Well, I've got something to say," Chris interrupted.

"You, too," she said, then turned her attention back to the Palestinians. "Mr. Ahmed, if you would return our passports and my UKSF identification card, we need to move along."

Ahmed looked at the passports, opened them again, closed them and fanned them across his palm.

"The sooner the better, Mr. Ahmed," she emphasized impatiently.

Behind her, Chris and Emmanuel were getting into the Land Rover. Emmanuel turned the ignition and started the motor.

Ahmed handed Kate the passports and her UKSF card. "I do not like this," he said.

"But it is better than starting a war," she quipped. "Tell your commanding officer you prevented a war. Again, we will follow through accordingly. I give you my word."

"I am trusting you," Ahmed said.

"Dr. Jordan and I are staying at the Olive Garden Hotel in Jerusalem. We will be there until we can get these jars documented. One way or the other, I will contact you. You may also contact UNESCO yourself to verify."

From inside the Land Rover, Chris was watching and listening, relieved she didn't give them any information about Emmanuel. He was turning out to be a loose cannon.

Kate clicked her heels, saluted Ahmed and returned to the vehicle. She opened the door and stopped, her eyes averted.

"What is it?" Chris asked.

"I don't know," she responded. Her binoculars still hung from her neck and she raised them and peered at something in the distance, her fingers rolling the focus knob, then they stopped.

"What do you see?" said Emmanuel.

She raised an open palm, a signal to wait, her face serious.

"What do you see?" Emmanuel repeated impatiently.

"I don't know." The back door was open and she was about to enter, then turned to the Palestinians and addressed their leader. "Ahmed, the Syrians are on the Golan, not far from the East Bank. Do they cause you problems, do you ever see them?"

"Occasionally we see them, but rarely here," Ahmed replied, looking around and palming his hand in an arc, "in this area."

"But they have spies in Israel, in the West Bank," she asserted.

He nodded. "But we usually catch them," he said and slightly grinned.

"Thank you, Ahmed." She got in the Land Rover and shut the door.

"What did you tell him about the jars?" Emmanuel immediately snapped.

"That we would ensure they got to the proper authorities," she fired back at him.

"Why did you say it to him in Arabic?" Emmanuel continued pressing.

"To make sure he understood. Now, no more questions. Let's go!" she ordered and Emmanuel accelerated the Land Rover forward down the slope, past the sullen faces of the Palestinian security force.

Chris turned around and looked at Kate. "And you're comfortable with what you said to them?" he asked

"Yes," she said quickly removing the gun from the back of her pants, ejecting the clip and slipping both back into to her bag. "The Palestinians have a point. The Israelis are heisting their heritage, using archaeology as an excuse to claim West Bank land."

"That's been my position all along," Chris agreed.

"Israel argues it is not occupying the West Bank," Emmanuel said, "that it has a legitimate legal claim. They did not take the land from the Palestinians but the Jordanians. They are occupying the occupiers." He paused, glanced in the rearview. "And the Palestinians in the jeep are following us."

"Let them follow us," Kate said.

"Emmanuel, face it," Chris said. "Most of the international community believes Israel is occupying the West Bank."

Emmanuel wasn't going to let it die. "The Palestinians are not capable of protecting the sites from damage or destruction. Israeli government archaeologists are just following local antiquity laws." He looked again in his rearview. "They quit following us. The jeep turned off north toward Nablus."

They were approaching the Israeli dig. Chris glanced at his watch: 6:45. A couple of vehicles were pulled off the road's shoulder. "There are some of your buddies. Are you going to stop?"

"I'm thinking about it," Emmanuel responded.

"Keep going," Kate directed. "Explain later."

Emmanuel pretended he didn't hear her, pulled off the road and stopped.

He got out and approached one of the workers at the site. Chris and Kate remained in the Land Rover and out of ear shot. Talking to the worker, Emmanuel pointed to the Land Rover then up the road from where they had come. He pointed south toward Jericho then west.

"Surely, he's not telling him what we have," Kate said.

"No telling," Chris exclaimed, turning around and facing her. "He's giving some kind of directions. For all we know, he may be telling them he spent the night in Nablus, our vehicle broke down and he picked us up."

"I don't trust him," she murmured under her breath.

"Nor do I," Chris responded. "But he's our only way back to Jericho, then we can leave him and proceed with the jars." He glanced back and observed her retrieving her phone from her purse. "Who are you calling?" He asked nervously.

"UNESCO. To make sure they know we have the relics and are on our way with them to their office."

She made the call and he listened to one side of a brief conversation in Arabic.

"I'm glad I did that," she said and breathed deeply. "Our friend Ahmed has not called their office yet and it portrays us as proactive and not defensive."

"Good for you," he said reaching a hand over the seat back and giving her a high five.

"I surely did not want to say that in front of Emmanuel," she said and placed a finger over her lips. "Here he comes."

Emmanuel returned to the Land Rover and got in.

"Okay, sorry about that," he said. "I couldn't just drive by and say nothing."

"So, what did you tell them?" Kate asked. She was leaning forward, her mouth almost in his ear.

"I told them I met you two in Jerusalem, told you about my work at the dig and you were interested in the area. I was just giving you a tour and taking you back to your car in Jericho."

She sat back and Chris said to Emmanuel. "That is the most helpful thing you've said and done."

"And I presume you are returning to the dig after you drop us off at your hospice," Kate said sternly.

Emmanuel chewed on his lip. "At some point."

"Emmanuel, if you go with us, that contaminates our objectivity," Kate warned. "You are working on an Israeli dig. We're outsiders not working for anyone on any dig. We need to keep this discovery neutral. That was one of the reasons you called me, or have you forgotten?"

"You told the Palestinians you were sympathetic to their cause," Emmanuel shot back. "You lost your neutrality."

"I *am* sympathetic to their cause," she retorted. "But I also want to obey the law. If an appropriate authority can tell me that the location of the find gives it Palestinian ownership, I will abide by that. I'll do the same if that authority gives it Israeli ownership. I believe Dr. Jordan will as well."

Chris nodded.

"Where does that leave me?" Emmanuel inquired anxiously.

"Back at your dig," Chris said.

Continuing south, Chris glanced in the passenger rearview, at the highway narrowing into Na'ama, the small Jewish settlement they'd just passed, and saw a speck rapidly enlarging. "We may have company," he said in a raised voice.

Emmanuel glanced up in the rearview. "It's just a white pickup. They're all over the place. It probably pulled out from Na'ama."

"Whoever it is, they're in a hurry," Chris said.

Kate turned around to see through the rear window. "Maybe not just any white pickup," she said, her voice slightly alarmed.

"Maybe not, why?" Chris pressed as he continued observing the vehicle gaining on them.

"Before we left the Palestinians, that's what I saw with the binoculars," Kate said. "There were two men standing beside it, one with binoculars that appeared trained on us. I didn't want to say anything at the time."

They were moving through an area of bare rock-strewn hills on the west side of the road, the Mount of Temptation looming above them. On the east side was desert sloping toward the Jordan River.

"Emmanuel, do you know another route into Jericho?" Kate asked, still peering through the back window.

"Yes, ma'am. It's a local road, avoids the check points," he said.

"I'm not thinking check points right now," she replied.

"Gotcha," Emmanuel said glancing again at the truck just car links behind them.

"There's an unmarked dirt road up here on the right, past this guard rail," Emmanuel said. "I've used it before as a short cut."

"Take it!" Kate directed, almost shouting.

The guard rail flowed past, the dirt road appeared, Emmanuel slowed. Suddenly, a muffled pop, like a firecracker going off behind them and a slight jolt to the Land Rover.

"What was that?" Chris cried out, turning around to check Kate's reaction.

"One of my rear tires hit something," Emmanuel reacted.

"Or something hit *it*," Kate exclaimed, still twisted in her seat peering through the rear window.

"Not to worry," Emmanuel shouted. "It's a General Grabbers, puncture free. It can go another fifty miles."

What Kate did next brought Chris almost out of his seat. In one calm singular movement she could have executed blindfolded, she slid her hand into the bag beside her, retrieved the gun then a magazine clip, slipped the magazine into the grip with a loud *click*—

"What was that?" Emmanuel snapped hysterically.

—pulled the slide and chambered the first round. "It's my gun, Emmanuel," she said matter-of-factly. "Does your rear window lower?"

"No! What are you going to do?" He asked alarmed. "That gun could get us into trouble."

Chris rolled his eyes.

"Getting ready to turn," Emmanuel said, almost yelling.

# CHAPTER EIGHTEEN

*Tiberius, Galilee, May, A.D. 67*

Jairus arises early but not on his own. He has been in Tiberius with Ezra for two months and a great stir in the city awakens him. For a moment he thinks to check on his family, but they are not there, not even his wife. She chose to return to Capernaum with their daughter and her family. After one week in Tiberius, with Josephus' troops disturbances, Abner had had enough. The workers had been rude to him and his sons, their effort to help unappreciated. Food was becoming scarce. "If the Romans come to Capernaum," Abner said, "we will go to the caves in the hills above the city. That would be better than in this hole."

Jairus could not disagree and made no attempt to press them to stay. He had used the time wisely, completed copying his master scroll on Ezra's fine papyrus, three days before Ezra had finished a copy. Today, they begin copying two more scrolls. Their plans are to distribute two scrolls to other churches then copy two more. Scribes in those churches would copy and send duplicate scrolls to other churches. In that fashion, the words of Jesus would quickly spread.

But now a war, with maneuvering troops and armies, challenges their agenda. By the noise he hears outside, the war might already be upon them.

He rushes down the stairs and finds Ezra standing in his doorway watching soldiers pass. Dust billows into the air and the sounds of their tromping and shouting echo through the main thoroughfare.

"Is the war beginning?" Jairus says.

"It is not far away," says Ezra. "Vespasian and Titus are moving from Ptolemais. They are headed toward the Galilean border. Josephus' spies estimate their strength at sixty thousand strong. He and his troops are going to meet them."

"These troops are marching toward the south gate," Jairus observes. "What is their destination?"

"Someone I know close to Josephus," Ezra responds, "says Vespasian's legions, which includes Agrippa's troops, are marching toward Gabara."

"How can they be sure. They could be going to Jotapata or Gischala."

"This is true," Ezra concurs, "but spies have seen engineers preparing the roads to Gabara."

"And if they take Gabara, where will they attack next?" Jairus poses.

"Jotapata," Ezra replies.

"At least their movements will be away from Capernaum."

"For your family, an answered prayer," says Ezra. Then solemnly, "But I fear Tiberius, due east of Jotapata, is in their path." He waves a hand in front of his face. "This dust and noise are too much for me. Let us retire to the courtyard."

Ezra closes the door and they walk back through the shop and the rear living quarters into the courtyard. They could still hear the din outside but it was muted beneath the louder chirping of the birds.

"You are trusting to leave your door unlocked, all of your merchandise vulnerable to theft."

He flaps a feeble hand in the air. "It is nothing. The people here know me."

"But the soldiers going by?"

"I will hear the door if it opens. We have more important things to discuss. As of last night, we have two scrolls completed. I have tied them with leather thongs and wrapped them in linen, placed them in strong leather bags of goat's hide."

"We decided the first copied scroll should go to Jerusalem, to the man named Theophilus," Jairus says.

"And the second to Caesarea Philippi," Ezra adds. "We are both too old to travel to Jerusalem, a hundred miles from Tiberius. There are dangers, too, along the way. With Josephus and his troops departed, Raphael can leave the city and take the first scroll to Jerusalem."

"I have an idea," Jairus says hopefully.

"If it shines like the brightness in your eyes, I must hear it."

"I am just past seventy but my legs are strong," Jairus boasts. "I had no problem walking from Capernaum to here, twelve miles according to the markers. I can take a scroll to Caesarea Philippi."

"My friend," Ezra says, an expression of dismay on his face, "you might be fit to walk from Capernaum, but Caesarea Philippi is twice that distance."

"I have walked it many times, when younger, in a day. I can make stops in Capernaum, spend time with my family and return here to continue our work."

"When will you leave?" Ezra says.

"This morning, before the last soldier exits the southern gates. Time is of the essence. The air will yet be cool. I can make Capernaum by dusk, spend a day with my wife and family then leave the next day for Caesarea Philippi. I can return here within the week."

"If the war does not interfere," Ezra cautions. "Despite their size, the Roman armies will not take Gabara and Jotapata within one week. Gabara might go quickly, but Jotapata is well defended, its walls reinforced. If Jotapata falls, I fear Tiberius will be next. All of us may have to leave."

"When will Raphael arrive to take the scroll to Jerusalem?" Jairus asks.

"Soon. I must prepare food for his journey."

Jairus climbs the stairs to pack. Abner has taken most of his belongings in the cart, so he is able to compact everything he will need in one shoulder bag. Papyrus and writing supplies he can leave for his return. He is almost finished and hears voices below. The din outside mutes their conversation, but he hears the name Ralphael. Quickly, he packs the last items and descends the stairs to meet the trusty courier he has heard so much about but never met.

Ezra is standing by the door speaking with a young man, his slender wiry figure backlit by sunlight streaming through the doorway. Ezra closes the door to block the dust and muffle the noise from the troops. The young man turns to face him and Jairus sees that he looks more Greek than Jewish, due possibly to intermarriage among Jews and Greeks encouraged by Herod Antipas, the city's founder.

Raising an open palm of salutation, Jairus speaks before Ezra can make introductions. "Greetings, new friend. Your reputation precedes you."

"And I with equal sentiments to you," Raphael says, lifting a hand. "Ezra says nothing of you but highest praise."

Ezra puts his arms around both as they embrace.

"Ezra tells me you are departing today," Raphael says, "for Caesarea Philippi by way of Capernaum to see your family."

"This is true. I have not seen my wife and family for two months. Though it has been time well spent on copying the words of Jesus, I have missed them. And you have family as well."

"Yes, a wife and two small children. My parents live in Jerusalem, so the courier trips there allow for time with them."

"Ezra tells me you were not allowed to leave the city."

Raphael chuckles. "Ezra compliments me highly. He thinks I am a Jewish spy, but I am more Greek than Jew."

Ezra nods in agreement.

"It matters not, Jesus would say," says Jairus. "One who believes in his teachings is neither Greek nor Jew."

"Raphael," Ezra says, "if possible, you are to leave today for Jerusalem while the Roman legions are occupied in western Galilee and before they move east then south, as most anticipate."

Raphael places a hand on Ezra's shoulder. "I have bid my wife and children farewell and prepared to leave immediately. I fully understand the importance of timing."

"Should the Romans move on Tiberius," Jairus says, "your wife and children are welcome in my home in Capernaum which may be out of harm's way."

"You are most generous," Raphael says.

"My house is on the main road through the village. Ask anyone. Ezra is welcome as well."

"Many thanks to you," Ezra says, "but I will stay here. Who would want to harm an eighty-year-old man. Besides, despite Josephus' presence, this city is pro-Roman. I doubt the ruling council will allow hostile gestures toward the Romans. The issue has already been discussed and they are willing to offer peace and safe passage through the area."

"Another reason I do not fear returning," Raphael says. "I equally thank Jairus for his offer, but I want to be with my family."

"What route will you take to Jerusalem?" inquires Jairus. "Surely, you will not go west to Nazareth, then take the highway south through Samaria. Troops, friends and foe, block the route west, not to mention the unruly Samaritans."

"No, protective friend," Raphael says, "I will take the road south from Tarichaea to Scythopolis. I know the safe places along that route. There are followers of Jesus in Salim and Alexandrium near Shiloh. They will welcome news of the scroll I bring. Other families I know live in Archaelus and Jericho. From Jericho, if I do not tarry, Jerusalem can be reached in a day."

"You are wise, Raphael," Jairus says. "Let us hope peace prevails here. I see the procession of soldiers has ceased. I must be away. God bless both of you."

"Give the members of the ecclesia in Caesarea Philippi my blessings," Ezra says.

"God's speed to you, Raphael," Jairus says, embracing the courier. "I will return in a week to copy another scroll, this one destined for Tyre."

"From Tyre to Rome," says Ezra, "the heart of the empire. While you are away, I will be working on the next scroll. We decided it should go to the church in Antioch."

"Amen," Jairus affirms.

"Be safe, my friends," Ezra says to Jairus and Raphael. "You carry the words of Jesus to churches that will give them new life."

"Those same words will carry us," Jairus says, bidding Ezra and Raphael farewell as he passes through the door into the street and settling dust. Just out of Tiberius, he notices the Arbel cliffs that rise above the city and mark its northern border. In the sun's early rays they cast a striking bronze glow. As he walks, he studies them, their faces darkly pocked by the many caves used by the Jews as shelters for the rebels against Herod; caves where his mother and father once hid; caves where Abner would take his family should the Romans come; caves where he could take Rebecca should that happen. Accessible only by ropes and rope ladders and not meant for routine living, they offered survival in times of distress. Some were man-made, others natural and enlarged to accommodate habitation. Should Nero's Romans come, hiding in a cave might be the best way to escape the Romans.

One more time, Jairus stands at the door to say goodbye to his wife. One more time, he bids farewell to Abner and Hava and his grandchildren. One more time, it is dawn, the sun not yet broken over the Golan plateau, and, one more time, he is leaving. *One more time*, he thinks to himself, *one more time*, then after, hopefully, never again. The master's words were the heart of his heart, but his wife and family were the source of its continuous beat, one that, at times, he heard in his ears when he missed them so. He was near the end, when he could rest. The master's word will have been completed and delivered. The rest of the world would hear.

As a youth, he had watched races in the arenas, how one runner would pass the baton to the next until the race ended. As though they were batons, he and Raphael were passing the scrolls. Raphael was on his way to Jerusalem. From there Jesus' words would go to Joppa and Alexandria. From Caesarea Philippi, his words would go east to Damascus, then north to Antioch. That was the plan he and Ezra had developed. They needed to copy two more scrolls, one to go west to Tyre and the other south to the coastal city of Caesarea Maritima. His master scroll and codices would be saved for perpetuity, put in a place yet to be determined. In case the chain of delivery was broken, the transmission faulted, the master would be preserved. Jairus thinks again of the caves in the cliffs of Arbel.

Those thoughts circulate through his mind as he stands in the door, his arm around his wife, her head on his shoulder. Over the crowded evening, he had told her about his stay with Ezra, about all they had accomplished, about meeting Raphael and his mission to Jerusalem. Though the courier had never met Jesus, he told her, the young man's energy and devotion was the future prologue to the master's words.

Holding his wife, Jairus tells Rebecca again how he will miss her and his family. Her eyes are filled with understanding and acceptance. But he can see the pain quivering beneath them.

"Which route will you take to Caesarea Philippi?" she asks. "It is reported the Romans are everywhere."

"The one I have always taken, the Via Maris."

"You do not think you should take less traveled paths," she says, a statement, not a question, her voice heavy with concern.

"Roman and Jewish armies are south of here."

"But the Romans will certainly prevail," she projects. "They will take Tiberius and then turn north."

"You are probably right about Tiberius," he agrees. "But after Tiberius, they will turn south toward Jerusalem, the stronghold of the rebels."

"I hope you are right," she sighs.

"If I am not, I will return from Caesarea Philippi to take my family to safety."

"Abner has already scouted the cliffs above us and located several caves," Rebecca informs him.

"I, too, am aware of these caves. But the caves in the Arbel cliffs are safer, more protected," he advises. "Before Abner's time, at the turn of the century, Judea was in political disarray. Roman rule was reestablished when the Herodians collapsed. I was but a child but remember my father taking us to the Arbel caves until calm returned to the area."

"Vaguely, I recall those times," she says. "But I was younger than you and recall no caves, only being awakened in the middle of the night and told to get dressed, we were leaving. I remember a place dark and damp, smelling of smoke, always that smell. The Arbel caves are difficult to access. Abner assures me the ones he has found will protect us. Families in Capernaum and Chorazim have used them in times past."

"Listen to those passing through Capernaum on the Via Maris," he says to her. "If the Romans are coming this way, we will go into the hills. I trust Abner's judgment. I will return within the week."

"It was comforting having you back on the Sabbath," she says. "Abner has been leading the services and reading the words you have gathered, but it is not the same, dear husband, as when you read them. Those listening can discern that of the two, you are the one who actually heard them from the master's lips."

"Let us hope they vibrate with equal freshness in the ears of others."

"They will vibrate," she says, "but always they will be second hand."

"Second hand is better than none," he says. "The spirit takes over. With that inspiration, dear wife, I must depart." He kisses her and steps into the road that runs before their house.

Outside of the town, he enters the Via Maris where it swings down from the hills and turns north toward Chorazin. Ahead of him, the snow-capped peak of Mount Hermon looms in the breaking dawn.

The first night he stays in the home of friends in Bethsaida. The second night he spends with friends in Gaulanitis near Lake Semechonities and the Huleh Swamp, rising early the next morning for the seven mile trek to Caesarea Philippi. He follows the higher terrain around the swamp and lake before descending into the Valley Dan.

At a point where the road takes a sharp turn, he sees what appears as a shadow on his right. The shadow jumps him and pulls him to the ground. In the struggle, Jairus finds himself atop the attacker. Surprised at his own strength, Jairus pins the assailant's arms with his knees, unsheaths his knife from his waist and presses the blade against the man's throat. He sees the mugger is a boy.

Jairus petitions him. "What do you want?"

"I am hungry ... food," he says in Greek.

His knees still on the boy's shoulders, Jairus slips his money pouch from his belt, opens it and tweezes out a drachma. "This should buy food for several days," sliding his knees backward. He stands. The boy remains lying in the road, his face showing disbelief, as though Jairus' outstretched hand holds a weapon and not a coin.

Jairus kicks one of the boy's feet. "Arise young one, in the name of Jesus, and do not steal again."

The boy jumps up, takes the coin from Jairus' hand and scampers into a fold of the hills.

Jairus looks around on the ground for the boy's weapon, sees only a small knife used to pare fruit and is touched by his young assailant's desperation.

He enters Caesarea Philippi at a place where the Jordan begins, a small stream issuing from a cave surrounded by temples of Syrian and Greek gods. Some have said it is the place where Peter affirmed Jesus was the Christ. The sun is beginning to set and he needs to find a person named James whose house is next to a market place on the city's main street. James is the leader of the young church in Caesarea Philippi. After stopping at several points and inquiring, he is welcomed by James and his family into the evening fellowship which is about to begin.

The timing is fortuitous he tells the group for he has brought the words of Jesus. The news arouses much celebration and joy. During the service, which is a fellowship meal, Jairus is asked to read from the scroll he has brought. As he reads, there is total silence. The eyes into which he looks are wide open, all ears attentive. It was as though he was Jesus himself speaking the words. When he finishes, there is continued silence, a hush. All are hearing these words for the first time, from one who heard them from the master. What Jairus had told his wife, is true. The spirit takes over and the words fall afresh with an energy of their own, as if uttered for the first time.

At the request and urging of the ecclesia, Jairus remains two more days, longer than he has expected. He struggles with the need to stay and bond with the group of Jesus followers that would help spread the master's gospel and concludes that two more days and nights would not conflict with his family duties. Rebecca, he reasons, will surely understand.

He spends his time in the city visiting households of those who belonged to the small group, sharing and witnessing his personal experiences of being in the company of Jesus and listening to his words and, each evening, reading again from the scroll he had brought. The last evening is special. As he is reading, his eyes, rising from the scroll, see a small face that looks familiar. Moving back and forth over the scrolling pages, he keeps noting the face, either of a small person or someone seated, he cannot determine.

When he finishes reading, the face moves quickly towards him and Jairus recognizes the young thief he had encountered on his journey. The boy extends a hand to him and in the hand is the drachma Jairus had given to him.

"I return this to you," the boy says. "I have been blessed by kindness," and he palms the other hand, gesturing to those around them.

Jairus embraces the child and, holding him close, thanks him for coming to the Jesus meeting and tells him, "You keep the coin, my young friend. It is from Jesus." The boy smiles and says he will return and bring his parents. Bidding the boy farewell, Jairus reflects on his decision to lengthen his stay in Caesarea Philippi and praises God for making His will known.

After sleeping soundly and contentedly that final evening, and following a hardy breakfast, Jairus bids farewell to his new friends and Jesus followers. More scrolls must be copied and sent to other communities. James promises the scroll he left will be copied by an able scribe and sent to Antioch with instructions that a copy be forwarded to Corinth to be reproduced then that duplication sent to Rome. A second copy will go to Damascus. This is thrilling news. Communities of Jesus followers in the major cities of Syria will have copies of the master's words. Within months, the major cities in Judea will have them, then southward to Alexandria. Before the year is out, the churches in Rome will have them and scribes there will make copies and send them throughout the western Empire. What began as a personal mission has turned into a major production. Words he has copied from the master's mouth are circulating far beyond Galilee where they originated.

Then comes a sobering thought. He knows only too well that once manuscripts are read over and over, the ends of the scroll become tattered and fall off. There are also enemy forces, the emperor Nero foremost, in the

Empire. Jairus has been told by some within the young church that Vespasian, following the Galilee campaign, plans to winter his troops in Caesarea Philippi. Romans are not friendly to the Jesus movement and less friendly to Jews who comprise the movement. Precious documents have been confiscated and burned, those who wrote them executed. Couriers have been ambushed and robbed. For the words of Jesus to endure they must find a permanent home for the ages.

# CHAPTER NINETEEN

*West Bank, Palestinian Territory, May 27, 2010*

Kate scooted to the right side of the vehicle so she was behind Chris and next to the passenger window and pushed the button lowering the window. "Listen to me, Emmanuel!" She said firmly but calmly. "If the truck turns off with you, as soon as you can, make a sharp right turn."

"My, God!" Emmanuel shouted. "Why?"

"Don't ask, just do it," she yelled back.

Chris was sweating and his heart was racing but he kept quiet. He'd seen Kate in action before.

"What are you going to do?" Emmanuel shouted, his voice tremulous. "You could get us put in jail."

"Don't worry, Emmanuel," Chris said, attempting calmness. "She was in the British Special Forces."

"Sharpshooter," she added, leaning against the door, the gun in her left hand, right hand propping her left elbow.

Emmanuel turned, the Land Rover descending onto the dirt road, dust billowing up behind, the white pickup turning and bumping downward with it. Between two small hills, the road curved sharply. In the turn Kate leaned out the window, leveled the gun and fired two shots then quickly slid back inside.

"Did you hit anybody?" Emmanuel blurted, his eyes wild with disbelief.

"Don't worry," Kate said confidently. "I don't miss."

"Your target?" Chris asked, strangely entertained by his partner's show of bravado.

"The radiator," she replied. "With the bumpy ride and dust, I knew I couldn't miss *it*."

"That'll put 'em out of commission," Chris said, managing a smile.

"That should delay them until we can reach safety," she said.

With the vehicle's uneven movement, Emmanuel was bouncing up and down clinging to the steering wheel. The road began to climb, snaking through scattered bare mounds. The pickup was still behind them but lagging, then disappearing between the hills.

"We may have lost them," Emmanuel said calmer but breathing heavily as though he'd run a long race. "We should call the police for help." He glanced at Chris when he said it and Chris looked back at Kate.

"Yes, Emmanuel," she said tartly. "We call the police. They come, make a report, check your vehicle, find the two antiquities we would have to explain, not to mention that we shot back and we'd be stuck here in the outskirts of Jericho for most of the day."

Emmanuel sighed deeply and said nothing more.

In the distance, about a half-mile ahead, buildings and utility poles appeared.

"That's a street up there," Emmanuel said pointing, still breathless.

"Presuming you'll take a left and continue south, where does it take us?" Kate asked, her eyes still peering through the rear window.

"Ein ad-Duyuk al Foqa," he replied between breaths. "It's a small village just north of Jericho. Lots of refugees live there. Israelis occupied it after the six day war. Now it's in Area A, fully controlled by the Palestine Authority, same as Nablus and Ramallah. Entry is forbidden to Israeli citizens."

"Can you get to Ramallah from there?" Kate said.

"Why do you ask that?" Emmanuel clamored.

Chris turned around and shot Kate a stern look.

"Just curious," she said.

Emmanuel thumbed over his shoulder. "Please, what was all that about back there."

Kate and Chris exchanged glances. "Not sure," Kate said. "Could be related to the jars we have."

"Maybe black market thieves," Chris added conspiratorially.

"You shot at them," Emmanuel said angrily.

"They shot at us," she retorted. "I just disabled them," her eyes still on the trail behind them that showed no signs of the pickup.

"What if they were Israelis?" Emmanuel suggested.

"Israelis or Palestinians, they'll have some answering to do when I file a report with the Israeli Police and the Palestinian Authority. Which I plan to do, in person, as soon as possible," Kate concluded emphatically.

"Which is when?" Emmanuel pressed as he drove the Land Rover onto the road before them and turned left.

Kate paused. "I'm not sure. When we're able to dispose of these jars."

Chris could see Emmanuel's teeth grinding through his jaws, his gloved hands twisting on the steering wheel.

They crossed a wadi, a narrow stream flowing through it, and began entering the outskirts of the village, small dwellings and stores appearing left and right, the Mount of Temptation hovering above them.

Emmanuel again: "There are several forks on this street but if we stay right, we could end up at the monastery on the side of the Mount of Temptation."

"That's a hike," Chris said.

"You can drive up to the path that takes you to it," Emmanuel countered.

"No thanks," Kate said, continuing her vigilance on their rear.

A fork on the street appeared and in its V, a small convenience store with gas pumps.

"Stop at the petro station," Kate directed. "I think we lost them." She was still holding the Glock. "They wouldn't try anything here."

Emmanuel flipped on his blinker and turned into the small store and parked in front of the pumps and left the motor running. They waited. Nothing appeared coming from the north on the street except an older man pulling a rickety cart filled with kindling sticks and a boy on a bicycle.

Eyeing a WC sign on the door beside the store entrance, Kate said, "This place has a toilet." She slipped the gun into her bag, grabbed it, opened the back door and got out.

Conscious that Emmanuel was remaining behind the wheel, Chris said, "I'll wait here," and stayed in the passenger seat.

In long quick strides that were almost a run, Kate approached the store and entered. Minutes later she returned to the Land Rover. Chris waited until she was at the rear door. "My turn," he said, opened the passenger door, got out and shut the door. Kate was reaching to open the back door and Emmanuel gunned the motor, swung the Land Rover sharply to the left and scratched off laying rubber to the left fork of the intersection.

# CHAPTER TWENTY

*Capernaum, Late May, A.D. 67*

The days are getting warmer, spring evolving into summer, as Jairus returns to Capernaum. His wife sees him coming and runs to greet him. The expression on her face is not one of joy. Her greeting is not warm.

"Dear husband, you are over ten days arriving home."

"I understand your anger with me, Rebecca," embracing her outside the entrance to their home. "I stayed longer in Caesarea Philippi than planned. But the young fellowship of Jesus followers was anxious to hear more about the man they, too, had once heard."

She pushes him at arm's length, her eyes wide with surprise. "They had heard Jesus?"

"Yes, the Master was once in their city. Many gathered to hear him. A few recalled the place where he was standing when Peter confessed he was the Christ."

"I did not know he had been to Caesarea Philippi," she says. "I knew he went to Samaria and Jerusalem but no further north than Bethsaida."

"He was there that one time with his disciples. The people were eager to hear more." He pulls her close to him, cups her head into his hand and speaks into her hair, a smell that always brings comfort to him. "Following evening meals, I read to them. The words fell on excited receptive ears."

"But, surely, you stayed longer for other reasons."

"Verily. One of their scribes had already been copying the scroll I had brought and asked me to review his daily progress. He was a Gentile and wrote his letters at a slant, but the words were the same, true to the original. The congregation decided that one would read and two would simultaneously copy. They could complete the copies faster and get them sooner to the churches in Damascus and Antioch, two of our major objectives."

"I question the accuracy of copying a text that is being read." she comments. "Is this a customary procedure?"

"Ezra informed me that the scribes at the Qumran sect south of Jerusalem and near the Salt Sea follow a similar procedure."

"But surely you know," she exclaims, "this does not ensure purity of word. I do not know the language these people are copying you mention near the Salt Sea. I suspect it is Hebrew, possibly Aramaic. Regardless, many Hebrew and Greek words sound alike. Errors will occur in the transmission from verbal to written word."

They pass some fishermen down the slope nearby tending their nets and wave to them.

"Rebecca, dear one, you astonish me with your insights. I have no control over the copying methodologies of others. But I have looked into the future and see a time when copies of the original will become so contaminated and compromised that scribes will need a corrective."

They are approaching the gate to their home and she stops again. "And this corrective?"

"The original codices and scroll must be protected. In later years, perhaps centuries, they will serve as corrections to the errors, redactions, and editing flaws which, as you have noted, will surely occur."

"How can this be accomplished?"

"I have not discussed this yet with Ezra, but he has sealed valuable documents of his clients in specially made jars that are hidden in secret places."

"That is nothing new," she says. "In the Book of Jeremiah, the prophet instructs Baruch and says, 'This is what the Lord Almighty, the God of Israel, says, take these documents, both the sealed and the unsealed copies of the deed of purchase, and put them in a clay jar so they will last a long time.'"

"You know the scriptures better than I," he says.

"Perhaps some of them. I knew this one because my father placed his deeds in a jar and buried them in the ground beside a tree behind our house."

They continue through the front gate and into the house. Hot from the warming weather and long walk, he removes his outer cloak, drapes it across the back of his chair, sits and sighs deeply. "We must speak of other events," he begins gravely. "Perhaps you have heard, Gabara has fallen to the Romans. Jotapata is next. People in Caesarea Philippi said Vespasian would then come to their city to rest his soldiers before moving toward Jerusalem."

"I knew Gabara had fallen," she confirms. "I knew not of the other movements." She crosses the room and returns, pours him a cup of wine, sets it before him. "How long are you home this time?" an edge in the tone of the question.

He perceives the sarcasm in her voice to be intentional. He had planned to go to Tiberius as soon as possible, while the opposing armies are locked in siege at Jotapata which had strong defenses, reinforced by Josephus. He needs to report to Ezra of his successful mission to Caesarea Philippi and the growth of the young church. He must also learn of Raphael's mission to Jerusalem. If the young courier succeeded in getting a copy of the scroll to Theophilus and the Jesus followers in Jerusalem, were they willing and able to make a copy and forward it on to Caesarea Maritima. Failure on either count, if the scroll was lost or stolen or if those in Jerusalem could not forward a copy, would mean another must be made and sent despite Vespasian's troops at large and Jerusalem in danger. He also needs to discuss plans with Ezra for the autograph's security for posterity.

But his wife had barely seen him in recent weeks. He must stay and spend time with his family, reassume leadership of the Jesus followers in Capernaum. There are times when care of family and loved ones supersedes other matters, even the master's words. "No one who puts a hand on the plough and continues to look at what was left behind is suited for the realm of God," Jesus told a man once who said he must first say good-bye to his family before following him. But Jesus did not have a wife and children, how could he fully understand such things. After all, he called God father. Must he, Jairus, not be a good father also, he reasons and, to the great joy of his wife, he tells her he will stay.

Her joy is short lived.

Her back is to him as she unpacks his travel bag and she suddenly wheels around as if spun by an unseen hand. "If Jotapata falls and Vespasian goes to Caesarea Philippi, his legions will march through Capernaum. We are in danger."

"I think not, dear one." He places a hand on her hand and calms her. "The lake route would be a diversion, out of his way. He will take the more direct route that passes near Gischala. If he does come this way, we can go to the caves."

"But what about your codices and scroll?" she says.

"If I had them, they go to the caves with us. But I do not have them. They are in Tiberius with Ezra."

"That explains."

"Yes?"

"When you returned from Tiberius last, you did not have the satchel that carries your scroll and codices."

"They were safer in Tiberius with Ezra, my devoted friend. If I met with thieves, they would vanish."

"Romans or no Romans," the timbre of her voice annoyed, "you will have to go to Tiberius again."

"Verily. But I am now with you and will stay as long as possible. But the gospel must have a lasting home. And I am its shepherd."

# CHAPTER TWENTY-ONE

*Jericho, May 27, 2012*

Hands on their hips, Chris and Kate stood gazing down the road where the Land Rover had vanished.

"He said he could go fifty miles on the tire," Chris said exasperated.

"That's enough to get him to Jerusalem," Kate said astonished.

"Surely, he knows he can't get away with this unless ... " He paused. " ... Unless he's planning on leaving the country with them."

"The jars would not survive customs," Kate said.

"The contents might," he countered, "especially if they're scrolls. We need to contact authorities."

"That's a last resort," she said. "Emmanuel is half-cocked. Maybe he'll calm down, rethink what he's done, that he needs us. At least, I had the presence of mind to take my bag," she said adjusting it on her shoulder, patting it, a reassurance the gun was still there.

"Well, I wasn't as fortunate," Chris said. "He's got my tools."

They stood beside the gas pumps, thinking, eyes on the ground.

Kate pulled out her cell phone.

"Who're you calling?" He asked.

"No one," she said. "Checking the GPS."

He watched her fingers working the buttons. A car pulled up to one of the pumps and they stepped away toward the intersection.

"According to this app, we're on Canaanite Dyook Road," she said talking to herself, "beneath the monastery on the mount," fingers scrolling, "not far from the intersection of Jerusalem Street and Ein Al Sultan Road," and she pointed toward the street Emmanuel had taken. "Jerusalem Street is a major thoroughfare. It takes us almost to Sami Hostel."

"How far to the hostel?"

She looked again at the screen. "About four miles."

"We can walk up to the monastery, take the cable car down," he suggested.

She looked up at the monastery and frowned. "That's an uphill hike." She looked back down at her phone screen. "We're about half-way between the monastery and the hostel. Let's start walking toward Jerusalem Street. It's a major thoroughfare. Maybe we'll spot a taxi."

They headed down the street Emmanuel had taken.

"Wonder what spooked Emmanuel," Chris mused aloud. "Maybe he's got an inside track on a black market deal." He paused. "Or maybe he's afraid being with us is going to get him killed or in trouble and needed to separate himself from you and the gun," the latter comments said snidely.

"Not funny," she responded. "It's about the jars," she said. "He doesn't want anyone to have them but him, a Christian."

"But he has no idea what's in them."

"We gave him a good idea. Fish symbols, first or second century origin, their Qumran shape," she said ticking off the reasons on her fingers.

"He could find a new home for them," Chris continued. "Plenty of caves in the area and he's in a vehicle that can get him to them."

"He can only go another fifty miles."

"He's from Texas, rolling the dice," Chris said. "A fanatic religious freak, thinks God is riding with him. Or he wants to whisk them to a safer place, back home to the U.S.A. But he'd have to change tires to get to the Tel Aviv airport. Regardless of what he does, he'll have to deal with the culprits behind us."

"I'm not so sure it was *he* they were after," she said. "Or the jars."

"What do you mean?"

"It could have been *us*," she said alarmed.

"*They* being Israelis or Palestinians?"

"Syrians."

"The men you saw in the white pickup."

She nodded. "Hezbollah bounty hunters. Regardless of what Ahmed said, the Syrians are a presence here. Assad tried unsuccessfully to get us extradited. He may have a bounty out for us."

"More like black market thieves after the jars," Chris conjectured. "Why else shoot a tire. No damage to the merchandise."

Walking side by side down the street, she looked at him and said, "Or the human merchandise. We'd be no good damaged—wounded or dead. Bad trade for Mark's autograph. We need to be vigilant," she cautioned, looking behind them at a car coming down the street.

The day was heating up, the air smelled of dust, fuel exhaust and eucalyptus. Chris was sweating, constantly removing his hat and wiping his brow. He noticed Kate doing the same.

They entered a long curve in the road and Kate pointed to the intersection ahead. "Jerusalem Street."

They neared the Y intersection and a yellow van with a small light on top approached from the opposite direction.

Kate stepped from the sidewalk into the street, waved her hand and shouted, "Taxi!"

The taxi made a U-turn and pulled alongside them. In Arabic, Kate told the driver their destination and he motioned for them to get in.

The driver was young and short, with a mop of hair that reminded Chris of Muhammed, their driver in Syria. "Muhammed the second," he said to Kate as they settled into the back seat and snapped their seat belts.

"Let's hope he's as efficient," she responded.

His ear cocked, the driver turned and looked at them.

"Do you speak English?" Chris asked.

"Yes," the young driver said and turned around and started his meter. The car lurched forward.

Chris and Kate began scanning for any sign of a Land Rover.

Within a few minutes they arrived at the Sami Hostel and the driver deposited them in the parking lot. Chris paid the fare in American dollars which the driver happily accepted and tipped him an extra ten dollar bill, far more than the fare.

The Land Rover was nowhere in sight. Kate pushed the unlock button on her key fob and they got into the LaCrosse.

"So, where to next," Chris asked. "I still think we should alert someone, Palestinian or Israeli. This occurred in a Palestinian controlled area."

Kate shrugged and started the car. "That's the problem, whom to call. No telling where Emmanuel is by now. Call the Israelis and he might be in a Palestinian area. And vice-versa. Emmanuel will pop up or we will find him."

Kate pulled up to the hostel office. She got out and went in. She remained longer than necessary, Chris thought. He checked his watch: almost 9:00 a.m. With all they'd been through it should be noon. She finally emerged from the office, a scowl on her face.

She opened the door and groaned, "That's a bummer. He's already checked out, paid his fee," she exclaimed as she slid behind the wheel and closed the door.

They sat in silence looking at each other, their eyes telegraphing their thoughts.

"That was fast," Chris remarked. "Did he clear out his belongings?"

"I asked and the young lady behind the desk said she did not know, that he seemed nervous and in a hurry."

"He didn't have much," Chris assessed. "His clothes. But you don't need much for an archaeological dig. Back at the cave in the rear compartment of the Land Rover, I noticed an empty duffel bag along with an empty backpack laying beside it. He probably stuffed everything in them."

"Including the two jars," Kate suggested tartly.

"Did she note which direction he took when he left?" Chris inquired.

"I asked that, too, and she did not. From where we sit now, it really wouldn't matter. He could have gone anywhere."

"Anywhere," Chris mumbled. "Maybe we should report it, let the police find him."

"We've been over that. If we report it, we have to explain why we didn't immediately report the find and we'd have to be available for questioning. We need to find him first. If he doesn't return and we can't find him, we'll report it. We've broken no laws, and I told the Palestinian security guard we'd take it to UNESCO. That was the deal. I feel certain Ahmed has filed a report and UNESCO is expecting us. We're sitting here talking and we need to be moving. We can talk on the way. Let's go."

"Where to?" he asked clueless.

"North!" and she headed the car into the street toward Highway 90.

"Surely, he wouldn't go back the way he came and got shot at."

"Correct," she nodded. "But, at some point, he'll have to contact his dig team, two of whom are his roommates."

"Were you ever a detective?" Chris asked ironically.

"Not *were*. *Am*. Present tense." She glanced at him. "And so are you. Occupational necessity."

He stroked a finger in the air.

They passed through the same checkpoint they had entered earlier that morning and Emmanuel was right. The guards had changed. The new duo requested their passports, asked the same questions.

"Your destination?" A young man, probably in his early thirties, asked.

"Just sightseeing," Kate said.

The guard returned their passports and waved them through.

"You are pretty glib with your distortion of the truth," he said grinning.

"That was not a lie," she exclaimed defensively, her back straightening. "We are seeing sites."

Mid-day traffic on Highway 90 had picked up. Caves mottling the cliffs north from the Mount of Temptation caught Chris's attention.

"Most of those caves have already been thoroughly excavated," he observed.

"Emmanuel got lucky with one," she replied.

"I'm still perplexed about where he found the jars," he said rubbing his chin.

"The contents, if any, will tell the story," she said. "There's something in them. Someone went to too much trouble. And there were only the two jars in the cave, nothing else."

"I agree."

"What do you think's in them?" she queried.

"I stick with the scroll theory, at least for the taller one," he said. "That would be the size and height of a first century scroll."

"So far, so good," she said.

"The shorter jar is puzzling. It is not shaped to hold a scroll." He paused, thought. "However, there were codices then, small notebooks."

"Paul carried them around with him, like tablets," she stated. "Codices, not scrolls, contained the letters he sent to the various churches."

He reached over and patted her shoulder. "That's impressive, Kate."

"What would you expect from an ancient manuscript expert," she retorted cockily. "Look to your left. We're approaching the place where

Emmanuel turned onto the dirt road. Keep an eye out for the pickup." She glanced into the rear view.

"I'd imagine the pickup is stranded somewhere over those hills," he said, pointing to their left."

"It's stranded somewhere," she remarked. "A vehicle can't go far without water in its radiator. When active in the British Forces, on a surveillance mission in Egypt, I was riding in a jeep that was following a suspected terrorist. A bullet fired from the vehicle in front of us hit our radiator. Within minutes, we had to stop."

"So that's where you got the idea?"

She nodded. "Whoever was following us was not official," she said, "Otherwise, we'd have seen flashing lights and heard a siren."

"And they couldn't report it for the same reasons we didn't," he said.

"Precisely. But we must be vigilant. Whoever it was may know our every move."

They were approaching Na'ama and she had to slow down behind an eighteen wheeler which she had to follow through the small village until she could pass it. Shortly after, they arrived at the dig where Emmanuel had been working and they had stopped earlier. Kate made a U-turn and pulled onto the road's shoulder. The dig site was about fifty yards from the road. Chris and Kate emerged from the LaCrosse and began walking toward the site. One of the workers saw them and walked to meet them.

"We don't need to tell them why we're here," Kate said, "just that Emmanuel has been showing us around and we got separated from him."

Chris gave a thumbs up.

The worker, a tall thin bushy mustached middle-aged male raised a hand to speak, but Kate preempted him. "Good day, sir. My name is Dr. Katherine Ferguson, British Museum and this is," extending a hand toward Chris, "Dr. Christopher Jordan, American archaeologist. Your co-worker, Emmanuel Jones, has been showing us around the area."

"Yes," the young man affirmed. "By the way, I am Leland Archer, archaeologist on staff at the University of Virginia. Emmanuel was by here earlier. Were you the two with him?"

"We were," Chris confirmed. "But we somehow got separated from him in Jericho and thought he might have returned here."

Kate cast Chris a quizzical look.

*Somehow,* Chris thought. *Why did I say somehow?*

"We've not seen him since you were here with him," said Leland.

"If I give you my contact information," Kate said, "could you notify me if and when he returns. It's quite urgent, you see," she said accenting her mid-Lothian Scottish brogue with a dash of British colloquialism.

"Surely, most certainly," the young man said then looked at Chris. "You're an archaeologist. Would you like to visit our dig?"

"We would like to," Chris said, "but we're a bit rushed," drawing another look from Kate.

They thanked the young site worker and returned to their car. Kate pulled onto the highway, waited for a car to pass, and made another U-turn heading them back north.

"Where to now?" Chris asked. "Galilee?"

"No! Back to the cave where we found the jars."

"We're not in a tank, you know," he advised.

"This Buick is an all-wheel drive vehicle, but I don't want to risk it on this terrain. We can park and walk to it," she said. "Emmanuel could have decided he was done with this venture, changed his mind and returned the jars."

Kate pulled onto the shoulder of the narrow road. They got out and walked the hundred yards to the cave, both of their heads turning left and right and up toward the top of the valley ridge, scanning for anyone who might be watching them.

The cave was empty and nothing to suggest it had been revisited. Standing near the boulder at the mouth of the cave, Kate unclipped the binoculars from her belt and scanned the ridge above them, the ground back to the road where she had parked the LaCrosse, then back at the rocky valley wall to the lip of the ridge.

"See anything?" he asked.

"Nothing except barren ground and rocks."

They were standing on the slopes of the wadi, the early afternoon sun beating down. Both were mulling over what to do next.

Moments passed, then Kate spoke: "When I was active in the British Special Forces, and when we knew we were being followed, the most prudent thing to do was not run, but stop and be still, let the stalkers come to you. The survivor of an assassination plot told me that. He said, 'There are times when the difference between life and death depends upon knowing when to act, and when not to act.' This is a time not to act."

"So, we go back to the hotel and wait," he said. "If no one shows up, then they were antiquity hunters."

"Possibly," she responded. "You Americans have these storms—hurricanes—which have an eye. Sometimes it is better to be in the eye of a storm, let everything swirl around you. Remain still, let a problem solve itself."

"What about Emmanuel?" Chris exclaimed.

"Eventually, one way or another, he will surface," she said reattaching the binoculars to her belt. "He'll screw up, get caught and we'll read about it in the news."

"And the jars?" he said.

She had been scanning the surrounding area as she spoke then turned and looked at him. "At this point, I'm not risking our lives for two jars that may or may not be of value."

"We risked our lives in Syria," he countered.

"That was different. We *knew* the stakes. Here, we don't. If any one is looking for us, let them find us."

"And make it easy for them," Chris added, "But you told the young Palestinian security guard we would take the jars to UNESCO."

"I did not tell him *when*," she replied. "Emmanuel cannot go very far with them. When he realizes he needs us, we may hear from him. If we haven't heard from him by tomorrow morning, I'll call our friend Ahmed and UNESCO. In the meantime, we wait."

# CHAPTER TWENTY-TWO

***Capernaum, Galilee, August, A.D. 67***

It is early morning. Jairus had worked in the garden plots the previous day and is sleeping later than usual. A noise outside in the courtyard, a gate opening and closing, awakens him. Then someone calls his name.

Rebecca hears them, too, turns over and lays a hand on his shoulder. "Someone is calling for you."

"I hear him," he says.

"Who could it be?"

He jumps from his pallet to the window and looks out.

"It is Raphael, Ezra's courier."

"Is something wrong?" she says alarmed. "Two months have passed since you have heard from Ezra."

"I do not know." He throws on a robe and rushes into the courtyard. By the sun's height over The Golan it is an hour past daybreak. "Raphael, what brings you to my home so early? You have surely run most of the night."

"I did run, sir," the courier replies. "The news is bad. Ezra has learned the Romans are headed to Capernaum."

"How does he know this?" Jairus anxiously questions. "We have heard nothing about the Romans except that they are in Caesarea Philippi resting after the long siege of Jotapata."

"The news from Jotapata is sad," Raphael says. "Romans surrounded the city with three lines of soldiers. There were attacks, defenses, counter-defenses. The Romans breached the walls but were forced back." He glanced down at a stone bench near the gate. "May I sit?"

"Of course, but continue."

"The Romans built earthworks to the height of the walls. Vespasian's son, Titus, and his men mounted the walls before dawn, broke through, and killed the sentries. Most residents were captured in their sleep. It was a general massacre. The dead are calculated to be about forty thousand."

The news takes the breath from Jairus. "Forty thousand? And women and children?"

The young courier nods.

"This is catastrophic," Jairus says with disbelief. "And the Jewish leaders," Jairus inquires, "their fate?"

Raphael continues. "Josephus and forty others escaped. They hid in a cave in the hills. Some say they had a suicide pact. Only Josephus survived. He was captured and taken before Vespasian and Titus in Caesarea Philippi. He told an incredible story of his survival by divine intervention."

"Josephus!" Jairus utters in disdain under his breath. "I do not trust the man. He is crafty."

"He is more than crafty," Raphael confides. "He told Vespasian about an ambiguous oracle that said *a star shall come out of Jacob, and a scepter shall rise out of Israel; it shall crush the forehead of Moab, and break down all the sons of Sheth.*"

Immediately, Jairus recognizes the passage. "That is from the Scriptures, the Book of Numbers. It is a prophecy of the Messiah."

"You know your Scriptures better than a Greek Gentile," Raphael acknowledges. "Regardless, Josephus converted it to a prophecy of Vespasian, that he would become emperor."

"This borders on the ridiculous," Jairus exclaims incredulously.

"Perhaps," Raphael sighs. "But Vespasian was impressed. An insurrection against Nero has begun in Gaul and Hispania. The Empire is on the brink of civil war. In preceding months, everyone saw the comet in the sky resembling a sword."

"I, too, saw the comet," Jairus says. "But I must correct you, it was two years ago, not preceding months. Josephus exploited the phenomenon to his benefit. He even manipulates the heavens. And the emperor's response?"

"Vespasian had mercy on his life," Raphael informs, "and put him into detention. He became friends with Titus, the emperor's son. They are about the same age. Josephus defected to the Romans. His name is now Flavius Josephus and he is the translator of Titus."

"Josephus is a traitor," Jairus exclaims angrily.

"Ezra is hopeful his treachery will benefit Galilee," Raphael says. "He has the ear of the son of the emperor and is with the legions marching toward Capernaum."

"And the other rebel leaders," Jairus says. "What of them?"

"Jesus ben Shapat, the leader of the revolutionaries, is in Tiberius. His spies brought the news I bring to you." Raphael has been pumping his legs up and down and rises from the bench. "But we must not talk further, we must go."

"Is there trouble?" Rebecca inquires, joining them. Her robe is pulled tight at her waist and her long hair uncombed so it curls fall wildly about her shoulders. "I heard 'Romans' and 'Capernaum.'"

"Dear wife, may I introduce you to Raphael, Ezra's courier."

She smiles and bows. "I hear many good things about you, Raphael."

"And I the same of you. Your beauty surpasses your husband's description."

Her face turns red and she passes a hand over her eyes. "My husband tends to exaggerate."

"Your husband," Jairus says, looking at her, "is not exaggerating the imminent danger."

"The Romans are marching toward Capernaum," voices Raphael. "I came to warn you and your husband and family."

Her eyes narrow sharply on Jairus. "You said they would not come this way, that they would take a more direct route."

"At the time," Raphael injects, "your husband was right. But, as I have told him, Jesus Ben Shapat, one of the leaders of the revolt, is in Tiberius. A rebellion is brewing there as well as in Tarichaea just south of here, only three miles north of Tiberius. Regardless of where the Romans go first, Capernaum is in their path."

"We must alert Abner and the others," Jairus says, "so we can evacuate to the caves."

"With all respects, Jairus," Raphael contends, "Ezra is hopeful you and your family will come with me to Tiberius."

"You said Tiberius is fermenting with rebellion," Rebecca interrupts. "Would we not be safer here, in the caves that have sheltered our families for hundreds of years throughout other upheavals?"

"If I may," Raphael says, glancing nervously at Rebecca then Jairus, "the valued autographs, your scroll and codices, they are safe for now with Ezra, but he fears they will fall into Roman hands or be destroyed if Tiberius suffers the same fate as Jotapata."

"Then we would be in harm's way," Rebecca implies fretfully. "Better for us to hide in the caves here, than to flee to Tiberias."

Raphael lifts a finger. "But Ezra is planning to evacuate Tiberius and go south to Scythopolis. Six hundred of Tiberius' nobles, Jew and Greek alike, have been taken to Tarichaea and imprisoned as traitors. Ezra managed to elude their net. But they, the Zealots led by Jesus ben Shapat, are still there and very active. My family and I go with Ezra as well." He is speaking rapidly with urgency, his eyes moving back and forth between the two of them. "Scythopolis, as you know, is a Roman city where we will be safe until the war is over. Current wisdom says the rebels cannot win against the Romans."

Her head cocked back, Rebecca crosses her arms stubbornly. "Abner and the others can go to the caves. But you will not leave again without me," she demands. And adds, "Regardless of your destination, I will be at your side."

"Dear one, with the scenario and plans just presented, I would not leave without you," he responds calmly. "It will be a long trek but we have a cart. I can hitch the donkey to it. When you tire from walking, you can let the donkey shoulder your burden."

Raphael gives an affirming nod, then says, "Scythopolis is not far from Tiberius, two days, slightly more perhaps if one stops for rests."

Rebecca loosens her arms. Her head comes down with a smile. "Now, I will be a part of your mission," she announced and laid an affectionate slap across Jairus' shoulder.

"You, dear one, have always been a part of this mission," Jairus professes.

"Aside from cooking for you and washing your clothes, buying papyrus from a caravan when you were away, I've contributed very little to the spread of Jesus' word."

He reaches and pulls her to him, embraces her. "My dear, dear Rebecca, you are the glue of my life. Without you, it would fall apart."

"This is good, this is good," Raphael says touched by the display of affection and commitment, "but we must hurry," and he rolls his hands. "The bird of time is aflight."

Jairus asks Raphael if he will notify their families who live nearby while he and Rebecca pack their belongings. "Tell them about the Romans, and that they are free to join us."

# CHAPTER TWENTY-THREE

*Jordan Valley, Highway 90*
*May 27, 2012*

Chris and Kate drove back to Highway 90 and headed south. They again passed Emmanuel's archaeological dig. No sign of his Land Rover. They drove past Na'ama, then the dirt road where the excitement had erupted. The traffic was sparse, no vehicles behind them, few headed north.

Silence in the car, a strange calmness settling within Chris. The fact Kate had a plan was part of it. But there was something else. Observing her driving, her fierce concentration on the road, Chris's mind was cycling elsewhere, back to the first time he had met her ...

At the request of his former New Testament professor, he had flown into Edinburgh unaware the reason was a quest, amid Arab spring, for Mark's original gospel. Unaware, too, that the woman Professor Stewart had sent to meet him at the Edinburgh airport would be his partner in the daring mission. During the drive to the professor's office, she had told him something about herself. She had a brother she rarely saw. Her parents were deceased. Her father had been an earl and she had moved to Dunbar in East Lothian to manage the manor and estate he had left.

*"How did your father become an earl?"*

*"Because his great-grandfather started stealing before everyone else did."*

At the time, observing her speeding and not wearing a seatbelt, Chris had imagined wealthy pedigree with a juvenile delinquent history.

*"Were you rebellious growing up?"*

*"Independent. There is a difference. But you don't want to hear about all that."*

But he did hear about it. He later learned her husband of twelve years had been shot and killed manning an observation post in Syria on the Golan Heights. He had been a military observer for UNTSO, United Nations Troop Supervision Organization. The incident occurred in 2005, the same year Chris was divorced. Her husband was older, Kate had said, and they had no children. She had flown to Syria, was escorted to claim his body and return home with it. At the time, she had been a linguistic specialist with the British Special Forces translating raw intelligence in different languages, which was how she and her husband had met. She had said she spoke multiple languages, including Arabic in different dialects, had been in and out of Israel several times and was in Cairo during the overthrow. She had said she had never gotten over his death, that her life had become a black hole. She had withdrawn from the Special Forces, immersed herself in analyzing ancient documents, in a different, safer world, and for a long time had no social life. On top of all that, she drank Glenfiddich scotch on the rocks and ate haggis. He had become convinced: If he was going into Syria during a revolution and hoped to get out alive, it would be with Kate Ferguson.

But there was something else seeping into the calmness and security he was feeling.

*"Were you rebellious growing up?"*

*"Independent. There is a difference."*

Christopher Jordan had been married to, and divorced, a woman who needed him too much. Now he was in love with one who seemed to need no one. At times, Kate could seem possessive. After all, she was the one who called him, pulled him into this mission for two ancient jars. Because she missed him, she had said, and wanted time with him. She could be tenderly affectionate to him yet so tough minded and macho, so fiercely focused on the task at hand, he wondered where he fit in. Perhaps that side of her was her real self.

Strong women ran in his family. His mother, and grandmother, were strong women. His mother once asked him why he married Allyson. He thought the question came from her awareness of his fascination with Scottish women, their enchanting highland lilts and brogues. Upon later reflection, the question carried a deeper wisdom. He couldn't remember his response to her question which, in retrospect, spoke volumes. If his mother was alive now, what question might she ask him about Kate Ferguson?

Though engaged, aside from the time together on their mission into Syria six months ago, and her brief visit to see him in Arizona in February, they had not spent much time together. What would his life be like if they were not on these missions in search of antiquities? She would not move to Arizona. She had made it clear, that was not an option. Would he be happy moving to Scotland and living in a small village like Dunbar, on a manse, presumably with servants and all the accouterments of nobility? Perhaps teaching archaeology at the University of Edinburgh or some other nearby college? Would he be able to continue with his archaeological excavations? Would there be more joint missions for them? Would he be needed enough in her life or would the current romantic flare give way to habitual conjugal life and he'd be stuck in the Scottish lowlands? *If*—that eternal subjunctive—they married, what would the long years turn into? Were similar thoughts of their future threading her mind? While they were alone in the quiet of the car, he considered raising these questions, and decided that was a discussion for another time.

He thought about where they were, on a barren stretch of highway at the lowest point on earth, following the same route Jesus took before making his triumphant entry into Jerusalem. His thoughts returned to the jars and why they were found in a wadi near Jericho and not in Galilee, their probable place of origin.

"I can't get the jars off my mind," he said to his silent partner. "Their shape, at least the larger, is similar to the Qumran jars and suggests a scroll. The fish symbols and their composition suggest Galilee, and not an off the beaten path wadi further south."

"That's not unusual for ancient jars to be found far from their origin of composition or even manufacture," she said, her eyes steady on the road, occasional glances in the rearview. "The Qumran jars were composed of clay from the Jerusalem area, possibly even made there."

"That is true," he replied, "but the ownership of those jars has never been questioned. The Essenes at Qumran hid them in nearby caves before they fled the Romans. These two jars are stray orphans, no identity of parentage."

"They may have been hidden for the same reason," Kate surmised. "The same Roman legions had earlier been in northern Galilee, headed south. If the jars had been fashioned in Galilee, with Galilean owners, they would have been fleeing south."

He recounted the first century history of the area: "You have the Jewish rebellion, Vespasian and Titus joining forces at Caesarea Philippi in 67 C.E., marching against the rebels, south toward Galilee, the turncoat Josephus with them. And something happened while in route."

"The Romans caught up with them," she said, picking up the thread.

"Or were hot on their heels." He paused. "Or they—whoever *they* were— were attacked by thieves and hid in the cave."

"It's also possible," she added glancing at him, "that they spent the night there and decided to unload some baggage so they could travel lighter."

At the Jericho exit, Kate flipped on her right turn blinker.

"I thought we were going on to Jerusalem," he questioned. "That turnoff is further down."

"His hostel," she responded. "He may have forgotten something, doubled back or called and left a message for his dig buddies."

They approached the check point at the Jericho city limits and she slowed. There were no cars ahead of them and one of the two guards manning the gate recognized them from their earlier passage and waved them through.

The same hospice clerk was behind the desk and told Kate she had not seen "the man from Texas," as she called him, "or his big jeep."

They exited the south Jericho checkpoint onto the Jericho/Jerusalem highway. The last of the sun was a fading taper of red to the west, the sky in the east plum-colored. Chris renewed the earlier discussion. "Knowing their probable Christian origin, Emmanuel will surely not destroy the jars."

"Not intentionally," she remarked. "If the occupants of the white pickup were antiquity thieves, they may still be on his tail."

"And if not antiquity thieves," he questioned glancing at his side view mirror, "then who?"

"We'll find out," she replied without emotion..

The re-entry into Jerusalem went smoothly, check points negotiated without delays. No one appeared to be following them. There were no conspicuous cars or occupants in the parking lot.

After refreshing in their rooms, Chris and Kate met in the hotel restaurant. It was early evening with only a few diners. Kate pointed to a table at the end of the large long room, against a back wall in an area that was mostly empty.

"We want a clear view," she said *sotto voce*.

He was nervous about the strategy, uneasy at waiting for someone to corral him. But there seemed little else he and Kate could do, except depart Israel and go home. And that, at this point, was not an option.

He noticed Kate had brought her bag, which meant the gun. They ordered drinks and sat in silence. He observed her eyes, like a broom dusting everything, scanning the room for any suspicious looking suspects.

A server came and took their drink orders.

An Hassidic young couple with a small child in a stroller entered the restaurant and took a table two removed from them. The woman wore a dark sleeveless hooded asymmetrical dress and the man dark pants, a white buttoned shirt, tie and sideburns. Chris thought about the ultra-orthodox sect, with its roots from Holocaust survivors and its fundamental principle: change nothing. Many of the men do not work but study the Torah full time. That would be like an unemployed Christian Fundamentalist studying the Bible all day. Observing Kate's keen attention to the young family, Chris thought about the Hasidic Christian counterparts, the Emmanuels of the world with inflexible mindsets that draw rigid lines, inflexible boundaries. That's what their lives boiled down to: the power of ancient written words. That's why he and Kate were in Israel. That's why they had risked their lives in Syria. Why they were sitting like gunslingers in a wild west saloon, their backs to the wall.

The server brought their drinks, took their orders and departed. Kate reached over and, holding his colorful beer bottle between her forefinger and thumb, turned it so she could see the label. "'Maccabee,'" she said. "Interesting name for a fermented drink."

"Symbolic!" he uttered.

"For you," she smirked, removing her hand from the bottle, "or the Jewish revolt and the independent Hasmonean Kingdom?"

He brought the bottle to his lips, took a healthy swig, tilted the neck towards her and grinned. "All of the above."

Her lips twisted into a wry smile. She tasted her scotch but gave no response. He thought the light banter might lead into that *long ago* discussion. Instead, she pulled out her cell phone and veered off citing texts from the caretaker of her manor in Scotland and minor problems there; from the director at the British Museum and updates on projects temporarily put on hold for her to pursue this venture; from a friend in Edinburgh whose daughter had just had a baby.

He was tempted to counter with scant news he had received from home, waiting for a chance to return the discussion to its point of departure. But she seemed distracted, almost too distracted, over-focused on trying not to appear distracted, as though there lurked within her designing mind another reason for seeking the storm's center, all the time her eyes alert and vigilant as a hawk's.

He, too, was casting his eyes about. After the Hasidic couple and infant, an elderly couple had entered. But he saw no conspicuous onlookers, no one who looked suspicious. No men in dark suits like those who had encroached their dinner rendezvous with Emmanuel. No one working too hard at being non-observant. No one with a pretense of mission, of urgency.

He decided to break the silence. "If Emmanuel is on the run, been chased and shot at, what's the first thing he will do?"

"Get rid of the Land Rover," she said.

"Precisely!" he said, a delicious mimic of her frequent use of the word. "He told us he rented it from Hertz at the Tel Aviv airport."

"But he wouldn't have to leave the city to unload it," she offered. "He could turn it in at a Hertz office in Jerusalem, change his attire, put the jars in the duffel bag or satchel that was in the Land Rover, hire a taxi to the Tel Aviv airport and he's out of here."

"I question if he'd be that proactive," Chris said, "have a plan formulated when he dumped us and move that quickly. My guess is he took off on a whim, probably holed up somewhere until he could decide on his next move, maybe even slept in the Land Rover."

"Regardless, at this point we don't have the luxury of speculation."

"Check the Hertz offices in the area," he suggested, "call and see if any Land Rovers have been returned."

She quickly responded, "I doubt they'd release that information."

He countered as swiftly. "They might if they knew you were Doctor Katherine Ferguson and your colleague left his archaeological tools in the rear compartment."

She smiled, her eyes narrowing alertly. She reached over and patted his arm. "You don't miss a trick either, my dear."

"And don't forget," he said lifting a finger to make a point, "in the kit are the vials and Ziplocs containing collected samples."

She picked up her cell phone. He observed the intensity of her beautiful face as her long delicate fingers danced over the small keyboard.

He waited.

"There are several Hertz offices in Israel, three logical sites: The one at Tel Aviv airport and two in Jerusalem." She pulled a note pad from her purse and jotted down the numbers. "I'll make the calls in private," and she rose and left the table.

He watched her disappear around a corner and used the vacant time to reassess the situation and diners around them, the entrance for any newcomers.

She returned, sat again and smiled broadly. "That was fortuitous," she beamed. "The clerks would not provide any information. But when I told them a famous archaeologist had left his tools in the rear compartment, that the tools were necessary for an excavation in Jerusalem and would they be so kind to just look, each confessed no Land Rovers had been returned. I left my number in case the tools surfaced."

"Clever," he remarked. "Very clever."

"And helpful information. He still has the Land Rover."

"He could still turn it in," he said.

"I doubt it. I caught them before their six p.m. closing time." She glanced at her watch. "And it is now six p.m."

"He could leave it in their designated parking area, drop the keys in the return box," he cautioned. "If he turned it in at the airport, he could sleep overnight there and leave on the first flight.

"That's a long shot," she said. "Tire change. Forty mile drive to the airport, in heavy traffic. Purchase a ticket. Negotiate customs and security. Your calculus—lay low tonight, depart the country tomorrow—is more promising."

"Check the flight schedule, time of the last international flight to the U.S.," he directed. "He's a student at Liberty University. That's in Lynchburg, Virginia, nearest international airport, Dulles."

She was still holding her phone, punched more buttons. "Last international flight to the U.S., Dulles International, a British Airways at seven p.m," she said.

"You're right," he said. "He would never have made it."

"We'll check Hertz again, first thing in the morning."

Their food arrived and they ate quietly. She made occasional remarks about the day's events but mostly ate with focused intensity. He thought again about sharing his earlier thoughts. But he had too much competition and decided to join her at the eye of the same storm. After all, storms moved.

He signed the dinner check and escorted her to her room.

"Must have been antiquity thieves chasing us," he said casually before kissing her good night.

"We'll see," she said. "The night is not over. And there's morning," she said with an ominous tone.

"Do you mind if I sleep on the floor in your room?" He said with no emotion. They were still standing outside the door to her room.

She looked at him quizzically. "Of course not. But why?"

"You have the gun."

# CHAPTER TWENTY-FOUR

**Capernaum, Galilee, August, A.D. 67**

Jairus pulls the cart from behind the house to the front of the courtyard gate. It is a small cart. The back slat is removable so someone could sit and extend their legs over the side. Hurriedly, they begin putting in belongings they will need for the trip and the extended stay in Scythopolis—undergarments, extra robes and sandals. Jairus removes money from a box hidden under a stone slab near the hearth and Rebecca gathers up the little jewelry she has, puts it in a leather bag and pulls the draw strap tight. In a larger pouch, she places some fruit and edibles, nuts, dried meat wrapped in linen. Jairus unties the donkey from his permanent stake behind the house near their garden and hitches him to the cart, the animal braying as though he knows he is going to have to work again. They are ready but Rafael has not returned. Rebecca remembers one other item. She runs back into the house and returns with a large scroll wrapped in white linen cloth.

"We cannot leave without The Scriptures," she says.

"Good," he agrees. "For without them, the sayings of Jesus would not exist."

Rafael comes running, followed by Asher, Dan, and Michael, and then their parents.

"I could not locate your other two families," says Raphael exasperated.

"Aaron and Benjamin are not at home," says Abner. "Their wives and children would not come without them."

"But they do know of the danger?" inquires Jairus.

"Yes," says Abner. "They will go with us to the caves."

"And you will leave soon," Rebecca says.

"Yes, Mama," says Abner. "This afternoon."

"That is wise," says Rebecca. "We do not know what lies between us and Scythopolis, hopefully nothing but the open road."

"Mother, stay with us," says Hava. "You are too old to make that trip."

Again, Rebecca's head tilts back and her eyes flash. "No, I will not be without your father again. I am older but I am strong. I can do this. I must."

Observing Raphael's anxiety, Jairus motions for embraces. Hava is tearful as she embraces her mother then moves to her father, places her arms around his neck and whispers in his ear, "I know the reason you go. To shepherd the master's words," and she squeezes him tightly, places a kiss on his cheek.

Raphael is motioning, rotating his arm forward. Jairus smacks the donkey on his rear and the small cart lurches forward. Abner's family waves farewell. At the edge of the town, Jairus turns to look and they are still waving.

"You must be tired," Rebecca says to Raphael once the city is behind them. "You arrived and are now returning without rest."

"I do not feel tired," he says. "For me, twelve miles is a short jaunt."

"You made the journey in less than the six hours it takes me," says Jairus. "You must have departed after the midnight hour."

"This is true," Raphael responds. "I did not want to awaken you in the middle of the night. Besides, I make better time at night and it is safer. The thieves are sleeping."

"Did you encounter trouble traveling to Jerusalem with the scroll?" Jairus inquires.

"Not on the trip *to* Jerusalem. But on the return trip to Tiberius, just out of Scythopolis, thieves tried to ambush me."

"Did it happen during the night or day?" Rebecca says.

"Bright daylight," Raphael says.

"Were you injured?" asks Jairus.

"No. They could not catch me. They chased me for a long distance but I ran into the Valley Farah and up its slopes and hid in a cave in the rocks."

"How long did you hide in the cave?" pleads Rebecca.

"Several hours," Raphael replies. "I waited until dark then took a different route out of the valley."

"And you had no further problems?" Jairus questions.

"None. Perhaps they thought I disappeared. I did not know there were caves in that area. I know we have them here," and he points at the cliffs they are passing. "Each time I travel between Tiberius and Capernaum, I see these caves and wonder of their history."

Rebecca says, "Our people, the Jews, have used them in the past to hide in times of trouble."

"I apologize to you, Raphael," confesses Jairus. "Our donkey is walking no faster than we. I fear we are moving much too slowly for your accustomed pace. You have matters awaiting you at home, please go ahead."

"Thank you for your consideration," Raphael says, "But, for me, moving more slowly is like resting. From time to time, a courier does need rest."

"You said you arrived in Jerusalem with the scroll," Jairus anxiously confirms. "Did you succeed in delivering it?"

"Yes, to the man named Theophilus," confirms Raphael. "I insisted on handing it to him personally because he is the patron of Luke, the physician who travels with the man named Paul."

"Did you get a commitment from this Theophilus that the scroll you delivered will be copied and copies taken to Caesarea Maritima and Alexandria?" Jairus entreats.

"Most assuredly," Raphael affirms and adds, "I also met one of the scribes. The Jesus group in Jerusalem is strong, led by members of Jesus' family."

"Surely, they were overjoyed to receive a scroll of the master's sayings," injects Rebecca.

"And it will aid Paul in his struggles with opposing forces," adds Jairus.

"Verily," says Raphael, "and they are as anxious as we to pass them on."

"This is good," Jairus says. "Scribes in Caesarea Philippi promised to copy and send scrolls to the young churches in Damascus and Antioch. But time takes its toll on documents, particularly scrolls of papyrus, which, as you know is fragile."

Raphael nods. His eyes are wide and attentive.

"Despite reinforcement with glue and bindings," Jairus continues, "the first and last pages of scrolls can become detached and lost. Entire scrolls had been known to disappear, lost or stolen. In times of cold weather, some had been used for fire fuel."

"Forgive me, Raphael," Rebecca interrupts, "If I seem bored with my husband's knowledge."

"She has heard it all before," Jairus says. "She could lecture in the academies."

"I could," she says with pseudo-cockiness. "I know about the originals, how they are copied and re-copied, how unscrupulous scribes make changes to suit their thinking. It troubles me much that the words of the master could become distorted."

"There is thus reason for Ezra's concern," Jairus says, "that the master copies of my codices and scroll must be saved for future generations of Jesus followers."

"You are wise, Jairus," Raphael says. "These are matters I have not considered."

A town appears down the road in the distance.

"Magdala," Rebecca says, pointing. "I had forgotten we would travel through Magdala. It has almost one hundred linen shops and the dyers make their headquarters there. Do we have time to visit some of the shops?"

"The Greek name is Tarichaea," Raphael says. "It means 'pickled fish' for which it is famous. The Jews in Jerusalem order them in barrels for Passover. And you are correct, madam, about the linen shops and dyers. But I fear we cannot go there today."

Her face drops.

"It is also a shipbuilding center and for that reason targeted by the Romans," Raphael adds. "The city is preparing for war. We are visible to posts on the city wall. Rebellion is more in ferment in Tarichaea than in Tiberius. My concern is ambushes, not from those who live there but from ruffians who have come to fight the Romans and pillage. The situation is volatile. I did not go there on my way to Capernaum, and we must not. Just ahead is a path, a small road big enough for your cart, that will take us up the mountain."

"Jesus came to Magdala after feeding the four thousand," comments Jairus, as if speaking to himself. "The incident is not in our writings, but many still remember and speak of it."

"Why is it not in your scroll?" asks Raphael.

"Because," says Jairus, "the scroll and the codices hold only the sayings of Jesus recalled by witnesses."

"Why not the events of his life?" questions Raphael.

"The sayings are his life," responds Jairus.

Raphael gives an approving nod as they turn west onto the small road. "Tiberius is four miles ahead," he advises.

Rebecca glances back wistfully as they climb the mountain.

"Jairus, how do you propose to save your writings," Raphael says picking up the thread of their earlier discussion. They are halfway up the mountain and approaching the cliffs of Arbel.

"I am sure you know, Ezra has told you," Jairus responds, "how those desiring the survival of precious possessions preserve them in sealed jars and store them in secret places."

"Of course." Raphael says, "That is one of the reasons I am a courier."

Rebecca trudges between them, looking at one then the other as they speak.

"Ezra also told me," Raphael continues, "that the scribes he visited in Qumran were already fashioning jars to protect their writings should the Romans or other enemies attack them. But where would you put them to be sure they were sealed and protected?"

"I am unsure, Raphael," Jairus responds.

They continue walking.

On the small road, they encounter traffic going the opposite direction, no people they know. Most were riding horses, a few camels and donkeys.

"They are zealots," says Raphael, "going to help the city prepare for the Romans."

Rebecca heaves a sigh of relief as they pass with cordial salutation. "They should turn around and follow us," she says, as they travel further up the mountain slope and away from Magdala, safe from any forays spawned by its brimming rebellion.

They are also safe from any Roman army, Jairus thinks, that would have to stop and take the city, which could take days, weeks. Its walls are heavily fortified.

But there is no city the Romans cannot conquer, his thoughts conclude.

# CHAPTER TWENTY-FIVE

*Jerusalem, May 28, 2012*

Chris' ex-wife was never on time for functions and Kate was never late. She expected punctuality. It was part of her military experience. So Chris was up early, sitting and waiting in the hotel lobby. After considering all the trouble and inconveniences involved, not to mention the awkwardness in their relationship, he had decided to sleep in his own room.

Exiting the elevator, crossing the lobby and making his way toward a table along the wall in the breakfast area, Chris had noticed receiving strange looks. He gave thought little to the extra attention and dismissed it. Until, at seven o'clock sharp, Kate emerged from the elevator, collecting more glances than usual.

She was wearing nothing striking, a white short-sleeve blouse and khaki pants and flats. Everything about her exuded anger—the way her hair whipped the air, her long sharp strides and the way her heels struck the slate floor, the tight-lipped look, a newspaper clenched under one arm.

He rose to greet her and pulled out her chair but she gave no indication she was sitting.

"You look like you could chew bullets for breakfast," he said. "What happened?"

She slapped the newspaper onto the table. "This was on the floor in front of my door. Did you get one, too?"

"Yes, but I didn't open it."

"Open it," she snapped.

"Okay, okay," he whispered, "but I'm standing here with your chair pulled out. Please sit down. We don't need to make a spectacle."

She sat. "We're already a spectacle." She pointed again at the paper. "Open it," she demanded again. When she got excited, a thick swirling Scottish brogue kicked in.

He picked up the newspaper, *The Jerusalem Post*, Israel's best-selling English daily. He unfolded it and shook it open, popped it once and flinched, his eyes recoiling. He leaned his head in for a closer look. Across the top in large bold type, the headline said **ARTIFACTS DISCOVERED THEN DISAPPEAR.** The subtitle was more alarming: Famed Explorers Involved. He read the story that followed.

> An anonymous source reported the archaeological find to The Jerusalem Post. Two jars were unearthed by ancient language expert Dr. Kathryn Ferguson of the British Museum and Dr. Christopher Jordan, American archaeologist, both are noted for their recent discovery of the original autograph of the Christian Gospel of Mark in Syria last year.

He peered at her over the top of the paper. "It says, 'an anonymous source.' Wonder who?" he mused. "The only people who knew about it were Ahmed and his Palestinian security guards ... and Emmanuel."

"The Palestinians would not have alerted the news media," she said, recovering her composure. "Especially *The Jerusalem Post*. They have their own newspaper and media outlets. Even if they had contacted the media, they would have mentioned the third party with us."

"That leaves Emmanuel," he said, then added, "and don't forget the white pickup. Its occupants might have known we had something. We may have been followed and scoped by the IAA's Robbery Prevention Unit. We just do not know."

"If they are the source, *they* would have mentioned a third party," she said. "That narrows it down. Emmanuel!" she exclaimed in a restrained but audible voice.

"And his motive?" he probed.

"Distraction! Takes the heat off of him."

"Possible," Chris replied, raised the paper and continued reading.

Sometime yesterday, Doctors Ferguson and Jordan discovered the jars in a cave east of Nablas, near the ancient site of Shechem. According to the anonymous source, the jars are the same type as those found at Qumran associated with the famous Dead Sea Scrolls and reportedly contain ancient documents. Due to the anonymity of the source, Israeli officials are filing no charges at this time.

Chris lowered the paper again and cast a concerned look at her.

"Where are you?" she pressed.

"Israeli officials filing no charges."

"It gets better," she said bitingly.

Before he could read further, a server came holding a stainless steel pot in each hand and asked if they wanted coffee, decaf or regular. Both indicated regular. The server poured their cups and Chris continued reading.

The discovery, not validated at the time *The Post* went to press, has created an overnight international crisis.The Palestine Antiquities Authority is claiming ownership of the jars and their contents, if and when they are found. The PAA claims if the artifacts were found near Shechem, an ancient archaeological site under its control within the West Bank, then they belong to it. The Israeli Antiquities Authority (IAA) claims ownership citing the artifacts were discovered clearly within its area of control of antiquities as set forth in the 1993 Oslo Accords.

He looked up at her again and she twirled a finger.

Israel and Palestine have long fought over heritage sites. In anticipation of a Palestinian bid for statehood recognition at the UN in September this year, they are racing to claim cultural heritage sites in the West Bank. If true, this discovery now magnifies and exacerbates the growing tension between Israel and Palestine.

He put the paper down, raised his cup, took a sip and returned it to the saucer. "You need to call the authorities."

"I have," she asserted, her face still clenched. "All of them: The IAA, Palestinian Authority headquarters, UNESCO and Ahmed. Because of our commitment to UNESCO, I called them first."

"What did you tell them?"

"I told all of them the truth," she said solemnly. "That we were here under the auspices of the British Museum and had indeed retrieved two jars of questionable value. That we were on our way to deliver them to UNESCO and that an American student who was with us absconded with them in his rented Land Rover." She lifted her coffee cup, drew it to her mouth, held it—"We didn't notify them sooner because we had every reason to believe the student would return with the jars and a crisis would be averted"—took a sip and he noticed a slight tremor in her hand as she returned the cup to its saucer.

"Did they seem interested in the student?" he pressed.

"Yes. I gave them a description of Emmanuel and the Land Rover and stated that we did not know his whereabouts. They also don't have a photo of him."

"And we do?"

She held up her iPhone. "I took one of the two of you at the cave when you were pulling back the stones." She showed it to him. "It's not that good, a side view," returned the phone to her purse.

"I would think they'd want us for questioning," he said in a low voice, glancing around nervously.

"Not at the time," she said, her eyes casting sideways with equal concern. "They know how to contact us. But, Chris," she inclined her head toward him, a serious look on her face. "We need to find him first."

"You'd said we weren't risking our lives over two jars."

"That was before this," she said exasperated, pointing at the newspaper. "Our lives, our reputations, are at stake. We could be charged with antiquities theft, serve time in an Israeli prison. Aside from the probability those jars may contain valuable documents of historical and cultural value."

He nodded. "What we know about them certainly points in that direction."

"We need to recover the jars and take them to UNESCO where they will be safe and properly evaluated. If the Israelis or Palestinians get possession of them," she said, her eyes widening, a fisted hand on the table, "those jars will be like two balls in a rugby scrum."

"Let's be realistic," he said skeptically. "You gave a description of Emmanuel and his vehicle. The Israelis will put that together in short order."

"I'm not so sure," she bristled. She blew across her coffee and took a sip.

"Other players are in the mix, including whoever chased us and put a bullet in his tire. We have no idea who might have been spying on us." Her eyes flashed. "But someone was."

He sat for a moment eyeing the headlines, her fierce visage above them, his thoughts circulating around the images of the two jars, the location of the find, the probable history, circumstances. He savored another sample of what tasted like Turkish coffee, then said. "I agree with you. We need to find him. But I think it must be a slow news day for *The Jerusalem Daily* to spread this on their front page. This is localized, a squabble between the Israelis and the Palestinians. Happens every day."

She reared up in her chair. "Localized, hell. Have you watched your television?"

"Haven't turned it on."

"It's all over the news—CNN, Fox, BBC."

"Are they expanding on the story or is it consistent with this article?" he asked, feeling more concerned.

"Nothing beyond this article," she declared. "The networks apparently know only what the newspaper knows."

"The article," he said pointing at the paper, "says we're involved but not implicated. Our action was appropriate and according to protocol. All of this explains why people were looking at me this morning when I came off the elevator, and you, too."

"Absolutely, the whole world knows," she said, her eyes flaring.

The server returned to take their order. Chris had lost his appetite but opted for a poached egg and bacon with orange juice. She ordered a bagel with creamed cheese and a spinach, tomato and bacon omelette, no juice.

"It seems your appetite hasn't been affected," he observed.

"No. I need energy," she said. "We've got work to do. We need to find Emmanuel and hopefully the jars before the Israeli police find him. We need to clear our names. I could lose my job, may have already lost it."

He wished she hadn't told him about the international media. The revelation made him feel hypersensitive. It also triggered another revelation. "Emmanuel is probably aware of the same news we've read and seen."

"Probably. He said he watched Fox News regularly," she said.

"So, he's vigilant. He knows he's on the run. What time does Hertz open?"

She pulled out her cell, pushed buttons: "Eight o'clock."

"Which office is closest to the airport?" He asked.

"The first one. It's on Highway One and a straight shot to Ben Gurion."

The server brought their meal and refilled their cups. They ate quietly. He was aware others were looking at them.

"Let's finish up and head out," he said, motioning to the server for a check.

With continued scrutiny of those around them, they hurriedly ate.

It took a while for the server to bring the check and take his credit card. Kate was antsy and ready to leave.

"I'm going to the room," she said. "Thanks for breakfast. Oh, and we need to check out."

"Check out?"

"I have a hunch we won't be returning."

"Your hunches are having a cumulative effect," he grinned. and glanced nervously around the dining area at others watching her walk toward the elevator. The server finally returned for him to sign the credit card slip.

He followed her through the door to the parking lot. She was pulling her carry-on with one hand and had her silver metallic hard-sided gun case in the other.

"You look like you're checking out of more than the hotel."

"You never know," she smiled. "Working for the British Special Forces, we had to be ready to leave at a moment's notice. Our bags stayed packed."

"But not the gun," he said pointing at the metallic case.

"Right. It's in my purse, unloaded. You drive," she directed as they walked to the car.

"Why? You know the city better."

"I'll explain later."

They got into the car. She entered an address into the GPS and he steered out of the parking lot.

She began punching buttons on her phone again, glanced at her watch. "It is now eight fifteen. We will arrive at Hertz about eight thirty. If our calculations are right, and he was on time when the office opened, he would be on his way to the airport in a taxi. The drive time from Jerusalem to Ben

Gurion is about an hour, longer with Monday morning traffic. And that, I know, is an expensive fare."

"Based upon those hand-crafted tooled cowboy boots and Del Norte Stetson he's wearing, he can afford it," Chris commented. "If he was not at the Hertz location when it opened, we might run into him."

She patted him on the shoulder. "That, my dear, would be divine intervention."

She didn't tell Chris what she was going to do, only said, "Don't say anything," before she opened the door and he followed her military stride inside of the Hertz rental office. He'd seen the look before, watched it throw macho types off guard and put them on the defensive. When she whipped her British Special Forces leather folder from her purse, flipped it open and held it beside that look and said, "Special Forces, we need information," the man behind the counter dipped slightly, as though his knees had buckled, and said, "Yes, absolutely."

No one else was in the small waiting area, which heightened the effect of her intimidation.

Before the clerk had time to get a closer look, she closed the slim wallet with a snap and slipped it back into her purse. "We have every reason to believe that an American male, Caucasian, who has stolen Israeli artifacts, returned a Land Rover he leased a few weeks ago at the Hertz Ben Gurion International office."

The clerk, who was short and thin with thick gray hair, became visibly shaken. "Oh, m-my God. A m-man, an American, just turned one in."

"Was he over six feet tall, muscular physical build, maybe wearing a cowboy hat and boots?"

The man nodded.

She pulled out her iPhone and showed him the photo. "Was this the man?"

His head pumped up and down. "That's the m-man. He was not wearing a hat but I did notice the boots."

"How did he leave?" Chris asked.

"I called a taxi for him," the clerk replied.

"Did he mention where he was going?" she probed further.

"He said the airport in Tel Aviv."

"Was he carrying anything?" Chris asked.

"A backpack and a duffel bag," the clerk said.

"Thank you," Kate said. "You've been helpful. Cheerio."

"Hold on," Chris said. "My archaeologist kit and tools were in that Land Rover. May I check and see if he left them."

"We're not supposed to let anyone unauthorized onto the lot," said the clerk adding, "and the vehicle hasn't been cleaned." He looked down and around as if searching for an answer then said, "I guess it's all right. The key is still in it. I'll have to go with you."

"Please do," Chris said.

Leaving Kate in the small office the two exited a side door and made their way to the Land Rover. The clerk opened the back hatch and, to Chris' delight, there was his tool bag. He unzipped it and checked. The two vials and Ziplocs were still there.

As they were leaving the office, heading to their car, the clerk shouted after them: "What did he do?"

They did not respond.

Chris opened the trunk and deposited his tool kit. As they got in, he said, "I checked the tires on the Rover."

"And?"

"The left rear."

"Yes?" she said, irritated at his delaying the point.

"It was the emergency spare."

# CHAPTER TWENTY-SIX

### Tiberius, Galilee, August, A.D. 67

The late afternoon sky is cloudless, an endless sheet of blue, and Tiberius appears quiet as the three approach the city, show their papers to the guards and pass through the gates. They would have arrived sooner but the donkey pulling the cart slowed them.

It is the Sabbath. As expected, Ezra's shop, along with most, is closed. Jairus and Rebecca stand behind Raphael as he knocks loudly. From inside, they hear the slow movement of shuffling feet.

Ezra opens the door and, with embraces, greets Jairus and Raphael, then acknowledges Rebecca. "Jairus, my friend, you return safely from Caesarea Philippi and again you bring your lovely wife. Wonderful. How long has it been, two months?"

"The city is quieter than last I was here in March," Rebecca observes.

"Be not deceived," Ezra heeds. "Beneath the quiet, Jesus ben Shapat's plots bring legions that follow on your heels. Just north of us, Tarichaea is in open rebellion, but I fear Titus will take Tiberius first, all the more reason we must hurry." He turns to his courier. "Raphael, alert your family. We gather at the south gate before daybreak tomorrow to leave for Scythopolis."

"Then I beg your leave," implores Raphael.

"Yes, yes," Ezra says, flipping his hand. "Hurry, time is of the essence. You and your family will join us in the morning?" the question begging confirmation.

"Aye, before dawn," and Raphael turns and steps into the street.

Ezra motions with a finger to Jairus and Rebecca, "Come, come," then sees the donkey and cart. "Rebecca, wait here in the shop for us. Guard my precious wares," he winks. "Even on the Sabbath, Tiberians steal."

Ezra grabs the donkey's muzzle, whips his head around, then guides animal and cart down an alley beside the shop. Jairus follows. Ezra leads the donkey through a gate into the courtyard then ties him to a small eucalyptus tree.

"This will secure him till morning," Ezra says. "Your belongings in the cart are safe here, but I will help you carry them inside if you wish."

"Leave them," Jairus says. "Except for this." He dips a hand into the cart and withdraws a large scroll wrapped in linen cloth. "Rebecca remembered we should bring The Scriptures with us."

"Your wife seems unhappy about the reason she is here."

"She does not say, but I believe she is more upset with me for leaving the scroll and codices here and not bringing them to Capernaum with me. No one has ever tried to rob her, so she is not sensitive to those issues of vigilance and safety."

"You have been robbed?" Ezra questions.

"An attempted robbery on my journey to Caesarea Philippi. The thief was a small hungry boy who was easily subdued. I gave him a drachma and told him in the name of Jesus to rise and steal no more. I did not know if he had ever heard of Jesus, but the last night in Caesarea Philippi he was present at one of the meetings. He sought me out to return the drachma. I insisted he keep it."

"So he had heard of Jesus."

"I learned others had as well, confirming that Jesus had gone to that city. Based upon what I heard, there is reason to believe that his presence in the city and his teachings influenced enough people that a small group began meeting and that group later became an ecclesia, the one I visited."

"This is good news," says Ezra smiling.

"Raphael reports success on his mission to Jerusalem," Jairus conveys. "I was concerned we would have to copy another scroll amid the turmoil of war."

"And I am concerned about the master copy and making additional copies, which is one reason, besides your and your family's safety, I summoned you. The weather is clear, the kind of weather armies desire and they are on the move."

"It is also extremely hot," Jairus says, "the kind of weather that exhausts armies."

Ezra raises a brow. "Not disciplined Roman armies. We must leave forthwith, at dawn."

They pass through the living quarters into the shop and find Rebecca examining the jars aligned below a front counter.

"Do my jars interest you?" Ezra queries.

"Not the jars themselves," she says. "I saw them when I was here last, but not the icons around the openings. Only now did I notice them. Are you a potter as well?" she probes, running her hand over the neck of one of the taller jars.

"Your husband asked me the same," Ezra confirms. "No. The potter is a friend. His shop is down the street. I tell him the size and shape I want and within a few days the jars appear."

"And these icons, there is a purpose?" she presses.

Standing behind Ezra, Jairus, impressed with his wife's keen observations, listens intently to hear the same response Ezra had previously given to him.

"They are symbols which identify the jars, their contents or owners or both," Ezra says. "For example, the one your hand is on has alternating symbols around the top."

"The Greek letters β and Σ," she says.

"Yes, they are the first and last letters of someone's name, which I cannot reveal. The jar beside it has the alternating symbols of Star of David and a crescent moon. The owner chose them to identify contents known only by the owner." Ezra moves toward the last two jars in the row, placing a hand on each. "These jars are of particular interest."

Rebecca steps closer, stoops to examine them. "They are intersecting arcs, the fish, the symbol for Jesus," she observes.

"Precisely," Jairus says. "They are, I trust, due to their different shapes, the jars we discussed for the master scroll and codices."

"Indeed," says Ezra. "The potter had them ready two months ago awaiting your arrival. The tall one will hold the scroll and the shorter, wider jar, the two codices. Nathaniel, my friend the potter, came here and measured them. With linen packing, they fit perfectly."

Rebecca continues scrutinizing the jars.

"Tonight we pack them for traveling," continues Ezra.

"What if we do not take them with us, but leave them here," says Jairus.

The comment surprises Ezra. "Where?"

"Perhaps conceal them in the caves."

Mention of the caves arouses Rebecca from her fascination with the jars.

"The caves?" says Ezra.

"The ones above Tiberius," Rebecca says, "in the cliffs of Arbel."

Jairus smiles approvingly at his wife's knowledge and involvement in the mission.

"I agree the jars could be stored in caves," says Ezra, "but not those caves."

Rebecca again: "But they are deep and run underground for hundreds of meters."

"Depth and distance are not concerns," says Ezra, "something I learned from the Essenes at Qumran. Moisture in the air, or the lack of it, is the major factor. Scrolls, even in sealed jars in Galilee, would not last."

"What, then, do you propose?" questions Jairus.

"I propose this situation has been created from above. Divine reason has determined we should leave this city and go south into the Jordan valley. The Jordan Valley is arid. There are caves along the cliffs south of Jericho. One of them, I believe, is destined as the depository, the keeper, of our gospel."

"You mean the gospel of Jesus," Rebecca gently corrects him.

"But, of course," says Ezra, embarrassed. "It is *his* gospel. And because of his authorship, divine reason, at another unknown time, will intervene again in history and the autographs of Jesus' words will be revealed to the world."

"I had never thought of caves south of Jericho until you told me of your journey to Qumran," Jairus injects. "The elevation decline from Galilee is great."

"So great," responds Ezra, "that even the cliffs of the Jordan Valley are below the level of the Great Sea."

Rebecca is listening and Jairus notices her concerned look. "But that would be further south than Scythopolis," Rebecca rejoins.

"About a four day journey," estimates Ezra. "I have walked it, though in younger days, of course," and he smiles shyly.

"So, we go to Scythopolis, get established—" Jairus attempts.

"I have friends there who will provide lodging," Ezra interrupts. "I have sent word to them with others traveling there that we are coming."

"Then after Scythopolis we embark on a four day journey to Jericho to find a cave for the two jars," Jairus confirms.

Ezra nods.

"That is a long journey to find a cave," says Rebecca. "I do not understand. How do you seal the jars?"

"With tar and pitch," says Ezra.

"If the jars are sealed," she says, "why would the documents not be protected? Why do you need a cave?"

"Your point is understandable," says Ezra. "Jar seals are not perfect. Over time, they often weaken and crack. I have told your husband about my visit with the Essenes in their small community south of Jericho which has existed for over two centuries. I saw their scriptorium, a room full of cubicles of unprotected papyrus scrolls, some as old as the village itself. These people are not concerned about moisture." He lays a hand on the taller jar. "They are concerned about desert animals nibbling on the tasty parchment and guano deposits from visiting birds and bats. There are also earthquakes and falling rocks that break the jars. Even sealed, the jars and documents they hold are not completely protected from harm. Yet, even if falling rocks break the jars, the arid climate, aside from varmints, will keep them from perishing."

"The location of our cave should be a secret," Jairus says.

Ezra looks at Rebecca and smiles. "At our age, we are not good candidates. Secrets will die with us."

"Do you not want the secret to die?" says Rebecca. "Perhaps, you have some doubts about divine intervention."

They laughed.

"Perhaps, Rebecca should be the one to hide them," Jairus quips.

The laughter died and there was a moment of silence.

"I think Raphael is the one," says Ezra. "He is young, dedicated and loyal."

"I agree," says Jairus. "He is the perfect choice, also young and strong enough to transport the jars to a cave and ensure their internment."

"The scroll and codices must first be put into jars and the jars sealed," Jairus says, "before we leave in the morning."

"This is true," Ezra says. "You can assist me later. But you and your wife have made a long journey and are surely hungry. First, we dine," and he extended a hand toward his living quarters.

# CHAPTER TWENTY-SEVEN

*Jerusalem, May 28, 2012*

Using Chris' phone and her British Special Forces persona, Kate had called airport security, given them a description of Emmanuel, the stolen jars he may have in his possession and the airline he would probably board. The security officer did not seem impressed or concerned. The person answering the phone at UNESCO, the same lady Kate had spoken with earlier in her call from the hotel, was concerned. She thanked Kate for the update and said she would immediately contact appropriate personnel.

Once back inside the LaCrosse, Kate set the GPS for David Ben Gurion Airport and took over driving. That was fine with Chris. He didn't like driving in cities, especially foreign cities, and she apparently loved the challenge. Once on Highway 1, perhaps they could talk. There would be no chance once they arrived at the airport.

"We're set," she said and pulled out of the Hertz parking lot onto the street and, following the GPS verbal instructions, took a couple of right turns then a left onto a major thoroughfare. "It's almost a straight shot from here to the airport."

"That's good," he said and grinned mischievously. "I like straight shots."

She looked at him as if she had a comeback, but said nothing.

They rode in silence, Kate turning as instructed by the smooth GPS female voice. Chris noted the street signs—Rehov Argon, Ramban, Derek Rupin—wondering about the heroes they were named for, the continuing Jewish struggle, the paranoia.

Then suddenly—"They may have come to us after all."

"What?" he exclaimed puzzled.

"We may have company," Kate voiced gravely, her eyes shifting back and forth between rearview and side view mirrors.

"How's that?"

"Check your side view. A black Suburban."

"I imagine Jerusalem has its fair share of black Suburbans," he said wryly.

She was not humored. "It's been behind us since we left the Hertz office. I've turned three times and it's still there."

Was the stress getting to her? She'd been on edge since breakfast. He was wondering what had happened to his Scottish lass of steel, then recalled the hand tremor at breakfast.

"In one kilometer bear right onto Yitzhhak Ben Zvi," the GPS voice directed.

Kate bore right. From his side view, Chris observed the black Suburban still following them.

The GPS voice again: "In one kilometer, bear sharp left onto Shazar Boulevard then in point two kilometers bear left onto Weitzmann Boulevard."

The black Suburban stayed with them.

"Perhaps it's going to the airport, too," he offered, his attention diverted to his side view, anticipating their next turn. "If it is following us, so what? They can't do anything."

"Unless they're Syrians," she quipped. "We're going to find out." She flipped her right blinker and, at the next intersection, turned sharp right.

The Suburban stayed with them.

"You have left the route," instructed the automated voice. "Please return to the route."

Kate turned off the GPS. At the next intersection she took a left turn, the Suburban on her bumper.

"You're watching," she noted. "What do *you* think?"

"I think you're right. Perhaps you should alert the police."

"Israeli police are the last thing we need right now. I have a plan."

"You going to lose them?"

"After they just arrived?" She said incredulously. "I want a closer look."

He didn't like the sound of her voice. He'd heard that tone before. Now he had a hand tremor. He checked to ensure his seat belt was tight and that hers was around her. He'd ridden once with her when she didn't wear it.

"They won't do anything here," she said. "Too many witnesses."

"What could they do?"

"They won't kill us. We're no good to them dead. Get pen and paper ready," she directed him.

He knew not to ask why and drew a pad and pen from his shirt pocket.

They were in the left lane of a steady stream of four-lane traffic. He observed her, the intense focus, eyes shifting from the road to the rear and side views, hands gripping the wheel, right foot brake-ready, everything timed, poised that said *eagle strike.* They were approaching a traffic signal. The light was green, then turned red. She glanced sideways and suddenly veered the car sharply into a right lane slot. The Suburban sailed by on their left and came to a stop at the light.

"Get the license number!" she commanded.

The maneuver was beautifully timed and executed, the Suburban one car length ahead, the plate in clear view. He scribbled down the license: 17-777-65.

"Well done!" he commended her. "What are you going to do with it. You had ruled out the Israelis."

"I need to make a call."

"You could call one of our embassies, alert them," he suggested.

"I thought of that," she said automatically. "But they'd have to make another call. I'm going to the top."

"What about the Suburban?"

"It's stuck in traffic. By the time the driver figures out what happened, we'll be back on route." The light was still red and she pulled her phone from her pocket.

Chris watched her fingers dance over the phone buttons, her face calm. She put the speaker mode on and set the phone in the hands free cradle on the console. The phone rang, short rings. She waited … and waited.

Finally, a male voice answered. "GCHQ."

"This is Kathryn Ferguson," she responded immediately, her military voice kicking in, "auxiliary British Special Forces, ID number 82846. Ian McCain please." It was not a question.

"Yes," the voice replied. "Please hold, I'll transfer you."

Another male voice: "This is Ian, may I help you?"

"Ian, this is Kate Ferguson."

"Kate, how are you?" Ian McCain said. "It's been a while. What's up?"

"I am in Israel with an American colleague, archaeologist Dr. Christopher Jordan. We're here on a mission for the British Museum. To the point, we are in a rented car on the outskirts of Jerusalem headed for the Tel Aviv airport and being shadowed by occupants in a black Suburban. I have the license number. Are you ready."

"Proceed."

Chris handed her the notepad. She read the numbers slowly, then a second time and asked that they be repeated. "Could you run a check on it. Also, can you tell us if any intelligence or counter-intelligence reports are circulating that involve two missing ancient jars we recently discovered that have been abducted by an American student, a story currently in the news."

"Sorry to hear this, Kate," McCain said. "Will get right on it. The news story's on the wire here in the UK. Understand your concerns. Stay safe."

The light turned green. The Suburban was boxed in with no choice but to cross the intersection. Kate turned right onto a two-lane street that, for a short distance, paralleled the four lane.

"Who or what, for heaven's sake, is GCH whatever?" Chris asked flatly.

"BCHQ. British Government Communications Headquarters," she replied. "It's a signal intelligence and security organization. At one point, I worked for them. I could have called the British Secret Intelligence Service known as M16 or even Defense Intelligence. I have their contact information. But I know Ian, have worked with him and trust him. BCHQ also possesses phone and online data. You may have heard about it regarding the Edward Snowden incident, his copying and leaking classified information."

"Did I ever."

"Within the BCHQ is the Joint Technical Language Service, a small department mainly for technical language support and translation and interpreting services across government departments. That is my connection with BCHQ and with Ian McCain."

Chris was becoming more impressed with his savvy sidekick's connections. But the connection stirred more questions. "And he can do what you asked him to do?"

"Yes!" she reacted decisively.

"How?"

"Because they *are* James Bond. They possess data mining software, pattern analysis, link analysis, watch lists. It's almost scary what intelligence systems can do."

This was all new territory to Chris, along with the circuitous route she was carving out in the Jerusalem suburbs until he saw ahead a sign directing them back to Highway 1 and ramping them back onto the route to the airport, the black Suburban nowhere in sight. "I think we lost them," he said.

"They're still out there," she said peskily. "Ian will scope it out."

For several miles, neither of them spoke. In the silence, Chris recalled the events of the past forty-eight hours, his anxiety mounting with the unknown ahead of them. From its cup holder on the console, the phone startled him with its loud ring.

Kate reached down and hit the speaker button.

"Kate, Ian."

"Go ahead, Ian," she said. "The speaker phone is on. Chris, my colleague is listening."

"Greetings, Ian. This is Chris Jordan. Thanks for your help."

"Much obliged," Ian said. "Do you also have a cell phone?"

"I do," Chris replied.

"Call me back from your phone on this same number," Ian continued. "I'll explain later."

"Will do," Kate responded and ended the call.

Chris unbuttoned his shirt pocket and pulled out his phone, put in Ian's number from Kate's phone, hit dial and pushed the speaker button.

Ian picked up. "Okay, this is better. Can both of you hear me?"

They responded affirmatively.

"I've got bad news," Ian continued. "You are being shadowed. Kate, your phone is not secure. Your calls are being intercepted. Also, you need to remove the batteries so your GPS route cannot be traced."

"That figures. Who's the culprit?" she asked, as Chris retrieved the phone from the holder, popped open the back of her phone, pried out the batteries and dropped them into a side pocket in the door.

"Hezbollah," Ian replied.

"That makes sense," said Kate. "Hezbollah is Lebanon-based. But in return for helping Assad with his civil war, Syria provides a foothold for it in the Golan Heights, providing a terrorist infrastructure against the state of Israel."

"Kate, you're on your game," Ian said. "Hezbollah has operations in the towns of Hadar, Quinetra and Erneh. It collects intelligence on Israel and Israeli military movements in the Golan and infiltrates Israeli communities in the adjoining area."

"I don't think of Hezbollah as being that sophisticated," chimed in Chris.

"Dr. Jordan, think again," responded Ian flatly. "Hezbollah has its own secret service, one of the best in the world, with allegedly specialized intelligence training in Iran and North Korea. Russia has augmented its electronic counter intelligence capabilities and Hezbollah also has complete dominance over Lebanon's official counter-intelligence apparatus. It is Syria's eyes and ears in Israel and has even infiltrated the Israeli army."

"I had no idea," Chris said astonished.

"Their operation gets even more sophisticated," Ian continued. "Hezbollah's counterintelligence apparatus also uses electronic and intercept technologies, software to analyze cell phone data and detect espionage. In the nineteen nineties, Hezbollah was able to download unencrypted video feeds from Israeli drones."

"We get the point, Ian," said Kate.

Ian kept on: "This is the rest of the bad news. Assad put a bounty on both of you, alive. Apparently—and this is all we've been able to determine—abducting the scroll from the British Museum was going to be too risky and costly for the Syrians in terms of their international status. Assad's political situation is complicated enough. He doesn't need any more heat. So kidnapping one or both of you and orchestrating an exchange was simpler. And if Hezbollah did it, Assad was in the clear."

"That was fast," Kate said.

"Yeah, how do you know all this?" questioned Chris alarmed.

"Through our surveillance and intercept capabilities, we are able to access Hezbollah's private telephone system," Ian replied. "Hezbollah, thanks to its Iran association, has a system which allows them to see our people and where they're going which, Kate, includes you with your Special Forces credentials and background. They've been shadowing you for the past two months in the UK. Apparently, and again this is partial supposition, kidnapping you from the UK was a logistical nightmare, then this bloke from the U. S. called the British Museum about the jars. The Syrians picked up the intercept and, *voila* Hezbollah came into the picture."

"Hezbollah is taking their bloody time," Kate said.

"Well, you're in Israel," Ian said, "which presents Hezbollah with a delicate situation. Hezbollah knows the Israelis know that Syria has operatives inside its borders, probably has them identified. Hezbollah wants to be the abductors, not the abductees. Apparently, based upon what we've been able to piece together, they tried once, when you were closer to their home base which is on the Golan Heights."

"A white pickup north of Jericho," Chris affirmed.

"Perhaps so," Ian said. "Don't know the particulars. But it's probably a good thing to keep the Israelis out of this. Otherwise, they exacerbate the dynamics."

"Ian, we are almost to the airport," said Kate, "and have not seen the Suburban since I left the route and circled back onto it. If they think we're leaving the country, they may get more brazen."

"Keep in mind," Ian advised, "that they're tracking your GPS, Kate, know where you are and can intercept your calls."

"I've removed the batteries," she said.

"Good," Ian affirmed. "It'll take them a while to reconfigure and intercept Dr. Jordan's phone." There was a pause as he seemed to take a deep breath. "One more thing," Ian continued. "You are considered to be in imminent danger. Take all precautions. Hezbollah has been successful with kidnappings. The M16 agency is on board. One of their Israeli agents has been dispatched to Ben Gurion Airport and is in route there now. He knows your ID's and is back up in case you need it. He is caucasian, athletic build and will be wearing Nike red wind runner pants, blue wind jacket and shouldering a Nike black tennis bag. His name is Nigel Blanchard. He will not make contact unless mandated. Got that?"

"Got it," Kate said.

Chris thanked him and terminated the call.

They passed a sign that said BEN GURION AIRPORT EXIT, 10 MILES. Traffic was light and Chris noted the absence of a black Suburban behind them. "I feel better knowing we've got support," he said. Kate's focus was intense, eye's darting back and forth between the road and rearview but he could tell by the muscles rippling along her jaw her mind was somewhere else. She didn't hold him in suspense long.

"I think we've been duped," she blurted angrily.

"By whom?"

"Emmanuel. Is it possible he is involved, and has been from the beginning, part of a bigger picture that lured us here?"

"But, Kate," he responded, "The jars are genuine. He could not have made them up."

She waited before responding. "I get it. But in his passion to protect all things Christian, has he allowed himself to be used? I mean, think about it. If they, meaning Hezbollah, has been shadowing us from the get go, intercepting phone calls, they are surely aware he is involved. We do not know what happened in the interval of time he dumped us and deposited the Land Rover this morning at Hertz."

"That's true," Chris agreed. "He could have abandoned us because he thought we were a liability."

"At some point, he had to stop and change his tire," she surmised. "The white pickup could have caught up with him."

"I've even wondered if he broke open the jars, has seen the contents and decided he has a mother lode ... ancient manuscripts which he can easily take out of the country ... or nothing ... or he has stashed the jars and with the breaking news decided he needs to get the hell out."

"That's why they didn't come to us when we were at the hotel," Kate said.

"They've known where we were all along," he said.

"Precisely. And have been waiting for another opportunity." She breathed deeply. "We need to quit thinking about it, quit speculating and act on what we know."

"What we know at this point," he said, "is that Assad, through Hezbollah, wants us as collateral for an ancient manuscript he claims we stole. We want Emmanuel and two ancient jars that Israel and the Palestinians now want."

"In the British Special Forces we were told a two-part rule in dealing with trouble. Have a plan and move first. In this case, stay focused on Emmanuel."

"Agreed," he said as she headed up the ramp to the airport entrance.

# CHAPTER TWENTY-EIGHT

*Tiberius, Galilee, August, A.D. 67*

Pre-dawn Tiberius. The city is asleep. To Jairus' ears, the clip-clopping of hooves and rumbling of cartwheels over the paved street sound too loud. Ezra decides to bring his donkey and cart carrying his effects which includes some of the finished work for his customers. In the distance, Jairus and Rebecca hear similar sounds, others making their way to the south gate, the agreed point of assemblage before departing for Scythopolis.

Rebecca walks beside Jairus and tugs at his arm. "Dear one, hopefully many have not heard of this plan."

"My concern is the numbers might be large and attract attention. We do not need to announce our departure from the city."

Walking ahead of them, Ezra overhears the comment. "This is true. Jesus ben Shapat might sabotage any plan that draws men from the city's defense."

Sounds given up by the sleeping city suggest a small army is moving through its dark streets. Arriving at the south gate, Jairus and Rebecca gladly find their fears unfounded. The sentries atop the walls must not be Jesus ben Shapat's men. Only a few families—Jairus counts five including Raphael, his wife Deborah and two young sons—are gathered, all with donkeys and carts. All are curious but ask no questions. They understand the situation.

The group waits a while longer. No one else emerges from the gate. Ezra, the former Sadducee official and designated leader, waits no longer. The first blush of dawn blooms along the eastern horizon and he gives the signal to move. In the lead with him are Jairus and Rebecca, followed by Raphael and his family. Behind them are other families who have joined the exodus. A full moon, small stream of clouds behind it, dusts the road with a phosphorescent glow, but not for long. Soon dawn breaks over The Golan. The men cup hands to their foreheads and the women shift their scarves to shield their eyes from the bright lateral rays striking over The Golan in a cloudless Galilean sky.

The route to Scythopolis follows the southern shoreline to Philoteria, a small village, then turns due south paralleling the Jordan River and will continue into the Jezreel Valley where the Yarmuk River empties into the Jordan.

Jairus knows if they continue due south in the hills, they will come to the village called Sennabris. By noon, they should reach Agrappina, then, barring any lengthy rests or interruptions, Scythopolis by dusk.

In the distance ahead of them looms the rounded shape of Mount Tabor and beyond it, Mount Gilboa, both rising from the land like rose-tinted twin breasts in the early light. They stop briefly at Sennabris to replenish their water at one of its outskirt wells, then continue on. Well south beyond Sennabris, the path angles east toward the valley and the Jordan.

Jairus' mind is working, assessing. After Scythopolis, then what? Do they stay in the city and wait for the rebellion to end? Or continue south toward Jerusalem, the home of the rebels and the core of the revolt? Surely they will stop and remain at Scythopolis. They are not rebels. The Roman garrison there will not be interested in them. These thoughts circulate through his mind, his eyes are on the ground and, suddenly, those in front of him stop. Ezra has thrown up his hand again. Jairus raises his head and peers around those in front of him. This time they have stopped because someone is approaching them. It is a man alone, running, breathless when he arrives. Jairus leaves the cart with Rebecca and quickly moves toward the front of their group to hear what news the man brings.

"The Romans are coming," he cries out to Ezra and others clotted around him, but loud enough for all to hear.

"The Romans are coming?" Ezra echoes. He turns and looks behind them, consternation on his face. "The Roman army is behind us, dear brother," Ezra corrects the man.

"Titus' army is ahead of you," the man says still breathless, "at Scythopolis, marching to Tiberius."

Ezra exclaims, "Just two days ago, Titus was in Caesarea Philippi."

"That was two days ago, dear sir," the man says, his face expansive, his eyes excited, dancing. "Titus marched his legions overnight through The Golan to Scythopolis, their new base. He departed there this morning and sent Josephus with a diversion toward Bethsaida and Capernaum." He begins pointing behind him, with both hands, his body half turned. "Titus is there. He is behind me, maybe five miles, coming this way."

Ezra inquires "Why should we believe you? Why are you running to tell us this? Who are you?"

By this time the entire group has left their belongings and carts and encircled the man and Ezra.

The man is trying to calm himself and catch his breath. "My name is Marcus. Your friends in Scythopolis sent me to warn you."

"Your name is Greek," Jairus says with suspicion. He is standing behind Ezra.

"True. I am a Gentile but a follower of Jesus. I belong to the small ecclesia in Scythopolis."

"What are the names of those who sent you?" Ezra asks sternly, suspiciously, his brows lowered.

"Zacharia and his brother Joshua. Just days ago, you sent word to them and their families you were coming."

Ezra looks around him, makes eye contact with Jairus. "This man tells the truth."

"What must we do?" Jairus asks, others mumbling in concert.

Ezra turns to the man. "Have they passed Agrippina?"

"Yes. The head of the column, but the rest of the army remains south of Agrippina. It is moving fast."

"I think we veer west," says Ezra. "Move to higher elevation and wait. Then once the army has passed, resume our course."

The man placed an arm on Ezra's shoulder. "But, my friend, the entire Army did not leave Scythopolis. One legion remained. It will join the others when they turn and march south toward Jerusalem."

Ezra looks south, turns and looks west then north behind him. "We continue south, moving higher. Keep to the mountains."

An opposing murmur rises from Ezra's followers. Jairus is not among them. He knows his friend has made the right decision.

"Then, after we go into the mountains, where do we go?" shouts a man in the group. He is standing beside Raphael who gives him a hard look.

"Jericho," says Ezra.

"Jericho?" the man shouts back angrily. "That is days away. We can be in Scythopolis tomorrow."

Ezra raises a calming hand. "This man says there is a Roman legion in Scythopolis. They may think we are coming to reinforce rebels. Jericho is not yet part of the conflict. We can bypass Jerusalem. We may go further. We can return when the war is over. What is a few days for our lives?"

The man does not respond.

To offer support for the decision, Jairus raises a confirming hand. "To Jericho!"

Others respond in supportive manner.

The man named Marcus bids farewell and turns. Ezra gives a pat of thanks on his back. Others move forward, responding in equal fashion. They watch the man as he heads back toward Scythopolis, then Ezra raises his hand and points toward the mountains.

It is near noon, the sun high overhead. Jairus stays with Ezra as they begin moving westward further into the mountains. "You said we may go further," he says to his friend, but in a low voice, almost a whisper.

"Qumran," Ezra responds. "I have been there. It is safe. The Essenes will shelter us. They have food and water. We can find a place for our documents."

"You should be a general," Jairus says smiling.

"Generals move men to fight. I move my loved ones to avoid fighting. I am a pacifist."

"And I, too," affirms Jairus, thumping himself in the chest. "So I should have said you are like Moses."

"You are too kind. I just want to save us and our writings. The scroll and codices are the master documents. Masters must always be saved. Perhaps in Qumran," Ezra concludes.

A man comes running beside them, falling into step. "Ezra, where will we stop. My wife is tired and we have not eaten since we left Tiberius."

Ezra continues walking, peering ahead. "We will rest soon, just up the way," and he points with his staff.

The man thanks him and returns to his family. Jairus stays beside Ezra.

Another mile when they are in a fold of the hills and in shade, concealed from anyone who might be observing from below, Ezra stops the group.

Briefly, they rest. Ezra signals for the men and they huddle to plan their route. All heard the messenger from Scythopolis and agreed that, without problems, they could not go to that city. They were several days ahead of a rebellion that was spreading south and Scythopolis was in its path. One man suggests they turn west toward the city of Nain, enter the Plain of Esdraelon and go to Mount Carmel and the sea. His plan receives a few nods, but Jairus points out that this is the route Romans soldiers will take from Ptolemais and the group will, again, be in harm's way.

Jairus is impressed how Ezra gives each man his say before presenting his own plan. With a small stick, he draws a crude map on the ground. Oval circles are Mount Tabor and Mount Gilboa and, further south, Mount Ebal. Due east of the mounts, a scriggley line is the Jordan River. With X's, Ezra drops in cities and calls out their names—Nain, Scythopolis, Ginae, Neapolis, Jericho.

"This is the plan," Ezra says, the small stick now a pointer. "We are here, on the south slope of Mount Tabor. We will continue over Gilboa, the western slope, the Plain of Esdraelon to our right and arrive at Ginae, if my calculations are correct, by dusk. At daybreak we will go due south to Mount Ebal, then to

Neapolis—"

"—But that is what the Romans named it," one man angrily interrupts. "It is Shechem, a Jewish city."

Ezra glances up at him. "This is true. The Romans are renaming many of our sacred places. But we carry something more valuable than all of those places, something they cannot rename."

"What is that?" the man asks.

"I cannot tell you," Ezra says and looks at Jairus. "Perhaps later. Do not be alarmed. We are all Jesus people."

They look at one another inquisitively but say nothing.

"As I was saying," says Ezra, referring back to his makeshift map in the dirt, on the other side of Mount Ebal "we will go to Shechem and overnight there."

"When we reach Mount Ebal," Raphael speaks up, "why not descend its southern slope, the Wadi Farah," he continues, pointing with his finger, "to the Jordan Valley and Coreae. From there the route is safe to Jericho."

Ezra gives the idea some thought. Before he can give his opinion, Raphael speaks again. "I have been there. It is where I hid in a cave not long ago to escape bandits. There are many caves along the walls of the wadi."

Ezra smiles. "Now I know why you are my courtier. Of course, the caves would offer us protection and a place to hide should we have to flee any situation. That is the plan. At Mount Ebal, we descend the Wadi Farah to Coreae. The next day we will be in Jericho."

"Do we stay at Jericho or move on?" a man asks, a new voice.

"We can stay at Jericho for a short while," Ezra says. "But the rebellion is moving in that direction. The Romans are moving with it. At Jericho, they will turn west toward Jerusalem where the rebels will most likely lose and the city be destroyed."

"So what do you propose?" another asks.

"That we go south to Qumran," Ezra says.

"Qumran?" several exclaim in surprised unison. One asks, "What is Qumran?"

Ezra had previously mentioned Qumran to Jairus, but Jairus discerns he should remain silent, that Ezra knew what he was doing.

"It is an Essenes settlement," Ezra says. "I have been there. They will remember me. They are peaceful and will give us shelter and food. They also have an ample supply of water."

Nothing more is said. Ezra signals with his arm and the small band moves from the shadows of the gulch where they have rested and toward Mount Gilboa looming ahead.

Jairus thought the caves could serve another purpose but did not speak. Where they hid the gospel documents must be a protected secret.

# CHAPTER TWENTY-NINE

*Tel Aviv, Ben Gurion International Airport, May 28, 2012*

By the time Kate and Chris negotiated airport traffic and parked the car in front of the main terminal, it was nine-thirty. Emmanuel was thirty minutes ahead of them. If he got his tickets on line, he was probably at security. Otherwise, he was standing in line at the British Airways ticket counter or on his way to security, none of those scenarios promising.

Using Chris' phone and her British Special Forces persona, Kate called airport security, gave them a description of Emmanuel, the stolen jars he may have in his possession and the airline he would probably use. The security officer did not seem impressed or concerned, but the young lady answering the phone at UNESCO did and said she was aware of the situation and would immediately contact airport security. She also mentioned a call she had received from Palestinian Security regarding its encounter with the three Americans on Highway 90 near Na'ama that the intent was to bring the artifacts to UNESCO and that UNESCO personnel had been anticipating their arrival.

"Can you believe that?" Kate said, hanging up and turning to Chris. "Neither the Israeli police nor Palestinians have alerted airport security about anyone who might try leaving the country with stolen artifacts. UNESCO is contacting airport security."

"The Palestinians have no authority at the airport," he replied. "But I would have thought the Israelis would have thrown a wider net."

"I agree with Ian. We don't need to call them. They would only confiscate the artifacts."

"We don't know that he's trying to leave with the jars," Chris said. "That would prove difficult. Israeli customs control is tight. They'd be quickly detected when his luggage was scanned. I raise my concerns again about his stashing them somewhere with a plan to retrieve them later. Or destroying them and repackaging to get the contents."

"Stashing them is a valid concern," she said. "Given his passion for antiquities, I doubt he would destroy the jars. We need the jars … for more than one reason." She looked at him grimly. "Or we might not be able to leave the country."

He nodded he understood.

They went first to British Airways checkin. In two long lines, no sign of Emmanuel or anyone resembling him.

"He's probably trashed his cowboy hat," Chris said.

"He couldn't get rid of the boots though," Kate pointed out. "Taking them off in security will hold him up at least five minutes."

"We can do a lot of damage in five minutes," he claimed, as they headed toward security at Concourse B.

Shoving her toughness before her, Kate flashed her British Special Forces badge at the first security check, a stern-faced female officer.

"We cannot give out information on passengers," the officer stated. She was broad-shouldered and stocky with bowling pin legs and stood unmoved with her chin protruding and arms crossed tightly over her chest.

"But you can receive information," Kate said addressing the guard politely.

"Yes, I can listen," the guard responded.

"An American male, about six feet two," Kate began, "is attempting to leave the country illegally with archaeological artifacts. His name is Emmanuel Jones. We have every reason to believe he is ticketed for British Airways flight two-four-three-two departing at twelve twenty-five for London, final destination Washington, D.C." She looked at her watch. "It is now almost ten. He has probably already passed through security and may be in a VIP lounge. Someone needs to stop him before he leaves, possibly with valuable antiquities that belong to your country."

Staring straight ahead, as though past them, the security guard said nothing.

"Can you tell us if you've received an alert from UNESCO about him?" Chris joined in.

"We have been notified," the guard said, over-articulating her accented English.

"So, you have a description of him," Kate said.

"Yes, we have been given a description," the guard said flatly.

"And you cannot tell us if he has passed through security," Chris said, testily.

"This is correct, now move along please. There are passengers in line behind you."

They stepped away from her and the line.

"Why didn't you tell her you had a photo of the guy?" Chris implored.

"Then she would unclip that walkie-talkie on her belt and radio to authorities that she had identified co-conspirators. No thank you."

"I guess then we buy a ticket," Chris exhaled.

"Unfortunately, I guess we do," she agreed.

"This is getting to be an expensive chase," he said, as they headed back to the British Airways ticket counter.

"We just reroute our tickets," she stated.

The attendant at the British Airways counter rerouted their old tickets to London, flight 2432, with London as their final destination. Kate had to go through the procedure of checking her briefcase with the gun and ammo checked. It was tagged and handed to an airline security agent. They headed straight for the security line, showed their boarding passes and passports to the same security agent who earlier had refused to give them information.

"In case we see this suspect," Kate said to her, "do you have a number besides airport security we can call."

"Yes." The agent removed a small notebook from her pocket and wrote down a number, handed the slip of paper to Kate who generously thanked her.

After passing muster through security, they headed for the gate.

"What if he's there at the gate waiting for the flight?" Chris asked.

"Trust me, he won't be there. That's why we're heading in here," she said, nodding at the British Airways Lounge sign.

A young attractive attendant at a long desk requested a special British Airways Pass which neither had. Kate pulled out her Special Forces badge again, and again it was to no avail.

"I am sorry, Special Agent Ferguson," but we cannot allow you in without a special British Airways Pass."

Again, Kate spoke for them. "We are looking for an American whom we believe to be on a twelve-twenty-five flight to London and believe he has special artifacts."

"I understand," the attendant said. "We have received an alert on this man."

"It would help us to know if you have seen him," Chris petitioned.

The lady looked left and right, behind her, and said, "I'm probably not supposed to tell you, but no person of that description has entered the lounge."

"No one about six-feet-two speaking with a Texas accent," Kate pressed.

The woman looked around her again. "No," she reconfirmed.

They headed toward the gate.

"Perhaps he took a later flight," Chris guessed.

"He would take the first flight out," she said adamantly.

"With the news coverage, he'd be high profile. He could have waited."

She said nothing. They kept walking toward the gate which was coming up.

"And, if he's here, what do we do?" Chris petitioned. "We can't arrest him."

"I thought about that," she said. "If we see him, let's hope he doesn't see us. We can call the separate security number the agent at security check-in gave us, then wait, make sure he stays put."

They approached Gate 25, the one indicated on their boarding pass.

"Slow down," she directed. "We don't want him to see us."

They moved left against a wall. Some passengers making cell phone calls were pacing back and forth at the gate entrance, Emmanuel not among them. Chris and Kate moved closer. Other passengers came into view, still no Emmanuel.

She was in front of Chris and he tapped her on the shoulder. "This is ridiculous," he whispered. "We should just walk in and, if he's there, immediately call the security number and sit on him."

"It's not that simple." She moved closer. "I can see most of the seating area and he's not there. Let's go," and she moved away from the wall. Chris followed her into the gate area, both looking left and right, scanning.

They looked at each other and murmured in unison, "He's not here,"

Chris looked down at his boarding pass. "Like I said, this chase is getting expensive. Every time we transfer these tickets it's a hundred bucks."

"Let's don't jump too fast," she cautioned. "The British Airways and gate lounges aren't the only place he could be lurking."

"Let's face it," he said exasperated. "The front security lady didn't tell us she had seen him. If she had, there would have been news flashes on all the television screens we passed."

"Right," she said plainly. "He's lying low until the news dies down."

They began walking back down the concourse toward the security checkpoint.

"Perhaps we erred about the country he'd leave," he offered.

"What do you mean?"

"If he flew out of Israel, where all the hype is occurring, he'd be easily detected and nabbed. But not if he flew from another country."

She stopped and looked at him. Her face expanded with a smile.

"I know," he said. "My brilliance overwhelms you."

"Let's look at the possibilities," she suggested, as they continued walking, their carry-ons clicking over the tiles. "Scenario number one, he arrived at the airport in a taxi but went to a car rental to drive out of the country."

"That's good, but which one?"

"Not Syria, there's a revolution going on there," she reminded him. "Not Jordan, he'd have to backtrack which would mean Israeli checkpoints. Not Gaza, more checkpoints. That leaves ... "

"Lebanon," he ventured. "He'd have no trouble getting a Lebanese tourist visa at the border, then head straight to Beirut and fly from there, which brings up scenario two: He didn't even come to Ben Gurion airport, or any airport, but had the taxi who picked him up at the Hertz rental take him directly to the Lebanon border."

"Or he hired a taxi at the airport, option three, to take him to the Lebanon border," she added to their speculations.

"Are you thinking what I'm thinking?" he asked.

"We call our old friend Dr. Krekorian in Beirut and enlist the services of our favorite taxi driver, Muhammed."

"Splendid!" he exclaimed. "You still have the phone number. Call him, tell him the situation then put Muhammed on. He can drive to the Lebanon-Israeli border and monitor any movements of our man. In the meantime—"

"In the meantime," she interrupted, "We retrieve my gun, then head for the border."

They made their way back down Concourse B and past security. The security guard who had checked them through observed them and gave them a strange look. The attendant at the British Airways counter was frustrated at Kate's request and asked for her bag check.

Kate quickly presented it. "As quickly as you can get it. This is an emergency."

"We will try," the attendant said. "But if it is already on the plane, there is nothing I can do. You'll have to claim it in London."

"But I'm not going to London. I've had to abort the flight."

"I understand." The attendant glanced at her watch, then at a screen. She called to a male attendant, handed him the check stub and told him it was urgent.

"This may take a while," the attendant said.

"Do you have to have the gun?" Chris asked exasperated.

"Yes! The gun is not mine but belongs to the British government. Except in circumstances like this, when I fly, it must always remain in my custody."

"Very well. We might as well sit and wait." He pointed to a row of seats along the sheets of glass in front of the main terminal that offered a view of arriving and departing traffic. "Use this time to call Muhammed in Beirut," he suggested.

"Might as well," she said with a deep sigh and sat down. She removed her phone from her purse then a number on a card. She began dialing then snapped the phone shut and shot up in her seat.

"What is it?" he said. "You look like you've seen a ghost."

"There," she pointed through the plate glass window. "Second row of cars from the left, headed this way."

Chris leaned forward, strained his eyes, blinked. "My God!"

"It's not just Emmanuel," Kate exclaimed. "Look behind him, about fifty meters."

Through the sun's glare on the sheet of glass, Chris strained his eyes. "Do you, by chance, have your binoculars?"

"Always." From her purse she retrieved a small pair of Brookstone's she usually wore clipped to her belt in the field and handed them to him.

He raised the binoculars to his eyes, spun the right lens for clarity. "Amazing," he whispered. "It's the two men from the restaurant. But what's Emmanuel doing in the parking lot? He's supposed to have taken a taxi here. And he has no luggage." He returned the binoculars to her.

She raised them to her eyes. "It all makes sense," she said under her breath.

"What?" he exclaimed, as they continued watching Emmanuel make his way across the expansive parking lot toward the entrance doors on the level below them at Terminal 3.

She looked at her watch. "It's ten after eleven. We must remember the time."

"I presume you're going to flesh this all out for me," he said exasperated.

"A few years ago, I had a lengthy layover in Tel Aviv, time for a quick trip into Jerusalem to conduct a personal business matter. I had to claim my luggage for the next leg of the flight to Cairo. I had one large bag and didn't want to haul it around with me. Ben Gurion has a luggage storage facility. They will store luggage, but for only twenty-three hours."

"Where's the luggage storage center?"

"You're looking at it," she said. "The baggage check room is in one of the parking garages directly across from us. He probably stored his backpack and duffel bag, hopefully containing the two jars. That's why he's coming from the center of the parking lot."

"Then why don't the agents just go in and take it?"

"We don't know that they're agents." She still had the binoculars to her eyes. "But wait," she said. "We have company. There are three men, further back. All in shirtsleeves."

"Antiquity thieves," he murmured.

"Perhaps," she said. "One of them has binoculars and appears to be tracking Emmanuel and the two men following him."

They watched as Emmanuel neared the terminal, the two suited men at a measured distance behind, the other three trailing between parked cars. Emmanuel came to the traffic lanes on the arrival level. He stopped. The men behind him stopped. He waited. No one moved. He hailed a taxi and got in.

"That was smooth," Kate said, as they watched the two men stand dumbfounded then scramble for one of the taxis parked along the arrival portals. The men behind them melted into an array of parked vehicles. "We don't know the identity of the men following him. The two men are possibly IAA. The other three, may be antiquity thieves. We do know, though, that they're after Emmanuel, not us."

"And there's a third party in the black Suburban still out there that's been shadowing us"

"Precisely! And somewhere in the mix, hopefully, is our tennis player."

"Dr. Ferguson," a female voice called from behind them. "We have your metal case."

The luggage facility at David Ben Gurion International Airport was located on first level parking across from Terminal 3. Unless you were looking for it, you would not know it was there. Thankfully, the small facility was not far from where Chris and Kate had parked. Located off a stairwell, Kate had used the services before and had no trouble finding it. A sign on a metal door said LUGGAGE STORAGE. Inside, a female attendant stood behind a counter with a chute at one end for luggage to be checked.

Kate immediately flashed her UK Special Forces badge. "I am Dr. Kate Ferguson with British Special Forces and the British Museum and this is Dr. Christopher Jordan."

"Do you have additional identification?" the young lady asked. She was dark-skinned, in her forties, wearing a white blouse with an official name tag on the pocket it. She spoke with a British accent.

Kate presented her passport.

*So far, so good,* Chris thought.

"How can I help you?" the attendant said. "You have luggage to check?"

In her customary air of authority, Kate cut to the issue. "We need to confiscate some that was just checked. A backpack and possibly a duffel bag that contains valuable antiquities looted from this country."

"I am sorry, but I can only return luggage to someone with a check. Do you have a check stub?"

Kate shook her head.

"I am sorry," the attendant said. "I would recommend contacting the Israeli Antiquities Authority. This would fall under their jurisdiction."

"Not unless it was discovered in Palestinian territory," Chris injected.

"That would be for someone else to determine, sir. I only check luggage."

Kate persisted: "Can you tell me if you have luggage matching the description of a backpack and a duffel bag?"

"Madam, we have many backpacks."

"This is most important and could stop a crime against your country," she pushed. "Do you have a backpack and a duffel bag together, ticketed together?"

The clerk paused, placed a finger on her cheek, thought. "I don't know if—"

"Ma'am, it's very urgent," Chris added.

"Well," she paused again, longer, "I do not guess it would matter if I told you. Just one moment," and she disappeared behind a door, was gone briefly, and returned. "Yes, I do have those two items, but I cannot tell you the name or tag number."

"We understand," said Kate. "But can you tell us when they were deposited."

"Yes," she said. "About half-an-hour ago."

"Thank you so much," Chris said.

They turned to leave and the attendant remarked, "But the person who left the luggage must reclaim it within twenty-three hours or it is confiscated."

Kate thanked her, calling her name, and they left.

"So now what do we do?" Chris asked, as they stood in the small landing area outside the door.

"We wait," she replied. "He'll be back. The same protocol was given to him. He's gone to this much trouble and will not allow the jars to be confiscated by the Israelis. Apparently, he's hatched another plan."

Chris looked at his watch. "It's past twelve noon, another twenty-two hours if Emmanuel pressed the time to its limit."

"We'll wait," she replied.

While Kate remained hidden from sight near the luggage storage room, Chris hurried to the main terminal and, at a Starbucks kiosk, bought sandwiches and sodas and snacks. When he returned, they found a spot about fifty feet from the luggage room, between a low wall and a line of parked cars, an EXIT door to parking levels four parking slots to their right. Sitting with their backs to the wall, they had a ground-level view beneath the cars of the storage room door.

"At least, we're surrounded by style," Chris murmured ironically, unwrapping a cheese sandwich.

They were sitting on the concrete floor of the parking level, slouched against a concrete retaining wall and facing a sporty Israeli-made Sabra and a late model Audi whose grills looked like large hungry mouths.

"It's what we can see beneath the styles that's important," she commented, pointing at the view they had of the bottom of the storage room door. She unpacked a Ziploc bag and groaned at the cheese sandwich.

"You liked cheese on our last trip," he remarked. He popped the top on a Coke can and took a swig.

She didn't respond.

"What did you mean by 'beneath the styles'?"

"You'll see," she said.

They heard footsteps in the distance, two distinct sounds echoing loudly, a sharp measured report and the second a slapping sound out of step with the first. The sounds grew louder. From beneath the cars, a pair of red slingback stilettos and men's leather sandals appeared approaching the luggage room.

"I see what you mean," he said. "If that's not a mis-match, I don't know what is. Love to know the story behind the feet in those shoes."

"A pair of cowboy boots will be conspicuous," she noted taking a bite of her sandwich.

The footfalls stopped. The two pairs of footwear disappeared. A vehicle roared to life several cars away.

"Wonder what those boots are up to now?" Chris asked.

"Trying to stay ahead of the IAA and antiquity thieves."

"Obviously, the authorities have not factored in the luggage unit," he said.

"Obviously, or they'd be camped out with us," she responded. "We may see them when he returns. Before we sat down, I neither heard nor saw anyone on this parking level. I think we're also safe from our Hezbollah pursuers." She paused and looked around. "The echo effect here, though, is eerily thunderous."

"It'll get more thunderous if our Syrian friends show up."

She said, "Their cover's been blown. They may have decided that what we took from their country is not worth the risk, at least for the time being. They could be in more danger than we."

"If we get the jars though," he said waging a cautious finger, "we have to take them to UNESCO. That means a trip back to Ramallah. We'll be out in the open. They'll get another shot at us."

"Understood," she replied. "We'll be vigilant," and she patted the metal brief case beside her. "On second thought." She opened the case and retrieved the gun and a magazine. "We'll be prepared."

He grumbled. "There you go again."

"They go or we go," she said clicking the magazine into the gun's heel, ensuring the safety was on. "It's them or us."

They ate, the sounds of their teeth at work reverberating around them. For a while they said nothing to each other.

Chris finished his sandwich and spoke. "Why do you think Emmanuel stored his luggage? What will he do with the jars when he returns. He can't take them with him if he's planning on flying out."

"One of several reasons," she responded. "He's confused and doesn't know what to do—"

"He's not confused enough to be one step ahead of everyone," he interrupted.

"I'm getting there," she said. "He knows he can't fly out with them, so he's trying to figure another escape route. Or, he's intentionally dragging this out hoping the salt shakers and napkin will collide and he'll slip away before the dust settles. After all, he was probably the one who broke the story. If he can park his luggage for twenty-three hours, he can hide it in another place for longer, perhaps rent another vehicle, park it in the airport, leave the country then return later and get it."

"Or park it forever, like the first writer did," Chris opined, "ironic for where we are now."

"I think you and I are on the same page," she concurred.

"But the pages keep flipping back and forth. We may be on the same page, but which one?"

"The one we are on is where we are now," she said. "Whatever his plans are, he's got to return here. He is not going to let the Israelis, Palestinians or anyone else have the jars." She re-zipped half of her sandwich in the Ziploc and opened a pack of peanut butter crackers.

"One additional scenario," Chris suggested. "He gives the check stub to someone else. They retrieve the documents and bring them to him."

"That's interesting," she remarked and gave him that look as though he'd said something brilliant. "I don't know who it would be but he could pay someone. We'll have to see what comes out of that luggage room."

"And ... "

"Get it back and rush it to UNESCO headquarters."

"Where I come from, that's called stealing," he said.

"In this case," she asserted, "it's called assisting the law. After all, we're not the only ones after the jars. The IAA and Palestinian Authority are both on the prowl for them. We're caught in the middle." She looked at her watch. "We've managed to kill two hours. Twenty-one to go."

# CHAPTER THIRTY

*Samaria, Wadi Farah, August, A.D. 67*

Jairus, Rebecca and their group of refugees are into the third day of their long trek. They are moving through a dry corrugated wilderness of trackless hills, above them desolate mountains and jagged ridges. They spent the night in Samaria, at Sebaste, a city north of Neapolis. At dawn, they head due east of Sebaste. They make good time in the cool early morning, the sun has barely risen over the Jordanian plateau. Colorful clouds stretch across the eastern horizon, promise of an early fall rain later. Visible to the north is Mount Ebal and to the south, Mount Gerizim.

Ezra is leading them toward a crease between the two mountains, a wadi well known to travelers as a shorter straight path to the Jordan Valley. Also, one well known to thieves. Raphael reminds Ezra this is the route where he was ambushed and outran bandits.

Ezra has told them they would reach Coreae in the Jordan Valley by dusk, but at the rate they are moving they might arrive sooner, Jairus thinks as he trudges beside his wife, a few steps behind their leader. He is proud of Rebecca. She has held up well and not complained, even when he knew she was in pain. Others in the group had whined, forcing Ezra to make more frequent stops.

Jairus mused upon the delays and the many obstacles Moses had to face with a group much larger. He reflects on where they are and the history of his people. Shechem, now called Neapolis, is south of them. The dry valley they are entering is the most direct route from Shechem to the rich Jordan Valley. Shechem and the plain of Moreh where Abraham's first stopped in Canaan. Later, Jacob bought a plot of land in Shechem and lived there a while. Centuries later, the children of Israel carried Joseph's bones from Egypt and buried them in the plot Jacob had purchased. A treasure more valuable than the bones of Joseph is on Jairus' mind as they begin the descent down the north wall of the wadi wall.

The angle of the slope is steep and some distance from the wadi base, a narrow wash carved over centuries by infrequent rainfall that, when it comes, gushes in torrents to the Jordan. They are treading single file. There is no path. They are creating their own. Each step they take dislodges rocks and debris that tumble down the slope ahead of them. Behind Jairus and Rebecca, a woman slips and falls.

"Hold to the cart," Jairus tells Rebecca. "Of the lot of us, the donkey is the most sure-footed."

At the commotion, Ezra looks back and calls to the others to do the same. "Hold to your animals or carts," he shouts. "Move slowly. Take your time."

They take their time. They must. They are at the point Ezra chose to descend into the wadi. The carts are wobbling and insecure on the pathless slope. The donkeys, with the weights of the carts behind them, have problems on the steep descent. Wheels and hooves skid and slide. People slip and fall. Taking the lead, Ezra signals everyone to veer at a more tapering incline. This helps, but the change in direction slows them considerably.

By noon, they are still not to the bottom where they want to be, not even near to the ancient path created by rain wash and by travelers over the centuries. Ezra confides to Jairus that he erred trying to move the group too quickly down the wadi wall. He also points to the gathering clouds ahead of them. Rain would slow them even more.

"But you did not know, dear friend," Jairus says. "You are a scribe, not a scout."

"Yes, but Raphael suggested a different tack," Ezra replies, "that I should have led our group further south to the western source of the wadi and followed the stream bed there. But I was trying to save time and reach our destination before dark. I should have listened to my courier's wisdom. On his travels to and from Jerusalem, he has trekked through this wadi. It was here he was once attacked by thieves. We must be vigilant."

Up in the mountains, the sky is bruising for a rain and Jairus can see the pale curtains distinctly farther down the valley which, through the rain, took on a wide softened beauty.

By late afternoon, they reach the descent of the wadi slope and merge onto its stream bed, the trackway that will take them into the Jordan valley and to Coreae, where there are other followers of Jesus and food and lodging. Veins of lightning flickering in the darkened clouds presage rain. The path is dry and wide and filled with large rocks and boulders heavy rains have carried down the slopes. If a heavy rain comes while they are in the wadi, they could be swept away. They need to move faster, but in the deep shadows of dusk, their movement is slower than the descent. The donkeys hooves move agilely but some of the carts mire in the thick gravel, their wheels unable to move over the rocks that must be constantly moved. Again, Ezra apologizes to everyone and, again, encourages them to be persistent and points at the clouds and says, "We are not far from our destination."

The words are no sooner spoken than a clatter comes from overhead. Thinking it to be thunder, everyone looks at the clouds. But the noise persists and they see rocks and gravel and dust erupting and boiling down the ridge above them. Brandishing weapons, a small group of men near the rim of the wadi wall are hurtling down the slope toward them.

"Thieves!" Ezra shouts. "Scatter!"

Immediately, someone steps around Jairus, grabs Ezra's arm and says, "Follow me!" In the deep shadows of the wide ravine, Jairus cannot see his face but the voice is Raphael's.

Quickly, Ezra follows Raphael and his family up the southern slope. Jairus and Rebecca scramble close behind, the donkey scurrying and the cart bouncing over the rocky terrain. The jars are wrapped in rugs but Jairus, concerned they might bounce, steadies them with a hand.

Raphael points ahead toward towering cliffs, odd rock formations beneath them. "There, at the foot of the cliffs, is a cave," he says excitedly, pointing to a crease in the sheer wall of cliffs rising five hundred meters from the rim of the wadi, then looks back. "We have time, the thieves are still descending the other slope."

Jairus looks ahead but sees no cave. There are pocks and holes along the the cliff wall that extends as far south as he can see, but he sees only large boulders, nothing resembling a cave in the cliff where Raphael is headed.

Raphael moves further ahead, his head scouting left and right. He stops, turns slightly to the right, then starts again, moving with confidence. Propelled by fear, the group continues scrambling up the steep incline. A sudden louder noise behind them obscures distant sounds of human movement in the valley below. Turning to determine the commotion, Jairus and the others see a carpet of gravel and tumbling rocks sliding down the slope. Their movement has triggered a small avalanche. They also see, moving in the wadi valley, a cloud of dust followed by another.

Jairus remarks to Ezra, "I fear the thieves have abandoned us and are chasing the others."

"They know to drop their baggage and run," Ezra says. "They are near the wadi entrance and safety."

Jairus then recalls the escape plan, if attacked by Romans or bandits. The baggage is all the thieves want. Their lives are all the Romans want. Ezra knows they cannot abandon the jars. Perhaps this is the reason he says nothing about leaving them.

Raphael continues his rapid upward climb.

"Where are you taking us?" Ezra shouts to him.

"You will see," Raphael calls back to him.

"I see only a cliff and a huge boulder," Ezra shouts in frustration.

"You will see," Raphael repeats.

They reach the huge rock. It leans against the escarpment leaving a small gap at the bottom, large enough for a person to enter. Raphael slips through the narrow breach and beckons the others to follow. Once inside, the cave is immediately visible. Jairus, the tallest in the group, can barely stand in the opening. The cavern is shallow, about fifty meters deep, and wide enough for a small group

"This is where I hid from bandits," Raphael says. "It was dark but the moon was full. I saw the large rock. I was going to hide behind it but it lay against the cliff. Then I saw the opening. I could hide between the rock and the cave. Once I was through the crevice, I discovered this cave."

"Blessed Lord!" exclaims Ezra.

All express their amazement.

"But what if the thieves decide to come looking for us?" Deborah says cautiously. "We can run no further."

"If they were looking," Raphael says looking at his wife, then at the others, "they saw us vanish in the air. Even if, by chance, they found the cave behind the rock, we are protected. As you can see," he moves a hand left then right, "there is only one entrance, the narrow crevice. The bandits can attack us, but only one at a time. Our position is impregnable."

"The Lord does provide," Ezra exclaims.

The others murmur agreement.

Jairus cannot believe his eyes, his mind locked on the word "impregnable." The large rock perfectly masks the cave. Its aperture cannot be seen by anyone from below much less if one were standing in front of it. The chamber is well off the traveled path and situated on the southern flank of the wadi where no one, unless they were running from someone, would stumble upon it. What were the chances of that happening in a hundred years? Emotion fills Jairus. Rebecca is standing beside him. He puts his arm around her. He was comfortable with the idea of taking the manuscripts to the Essenes but now different thoughts stir his mind. He must wait for a private moment to share his thoughts with Ezra. But Ezra is looking at him, his eyes conveying the same revelation.

Through the narrow opening, Jairus can see his donkey and the cart where the scrolls are packed, then he sees the problem, not just for him and his codices and scroll but the entire group. The donkeys can move through the narrow opening, but not the carts.

"Inside we are safe," Jairus says, "We can bring in the donkeys, but what about the carts?"

Ezra ponders. Raphael joins him. Between the two surely there is an answer, Jairus thinks.

"We are in no imminent danger," Raphael says. "The thieves, if they were thieves, are pursuing the others through the wadi. Pray God they are safe. We can empty the carts, remove the wheels and slide them sideways through the passage."

"But that will take much time," Rebecca, the analytical one observes.

"Rebecca is right," Ezra concurs. "We unload the carts, temporarily store their contents in the cave. In the deep corner on the other side of the rock, I do not think the carts will be visible."

All agree. Everyone, including Raphael's two young sons, begin working. Dusk is falling as Rebecca and Deborah keep watch while the men and boys unload the carts and stack the luggage inside. The donkeys are unhooked from their carts and led inside, then the carts rolled into a corner between the rock and the cliff. Jairus takes great care with the jars. Still wrapped in the rugs, he cradles them, one at a time, and lays them in a corner in the back of the cave where the rock roof tapers downward toward the ground. *Is this the place*, he questions himself.

Ezra, in the meantime, is pacing back and forth across the cave's entrance, looking up and down and rubbing his chin. He is a man in deep thought as though pondering a great plan.

Inside the cave, all wait for dusk to end and dark to take over when they can leave. The two women sit side by side and share stories from their homes, about their children. The two boys entertain themselves collecting and stacking rocks in the back of the cave until night descends and they can no longer see and they come and sit beside their mother.

Jairus and Raphael join Ezra. The three huddle in the cave's entrance, mumbling back and forth. Jairus notices Rebecca's intense focus on them. She knows the topic of their murmurings. The question in her eyes mirrors that of their discussion: What to do with the jars.

Whispering, Ezra shares his thoughts. "The cave is a perfect depository for the jars, if we could only seal it."

Raphael looks at him and returns the whisper. "Impossible. We do not have enough stones and nothing to hold them. Taking the jars south of Jericho, possibly to Qumran, is the best plan. They would be too quickly discovered here and probably destroyed."

Jairus has been peering at the crevice. "We cannot seal the cave, but we can seal this," and he points to the narrow opening that allowed them passage.

"We can close it with stones," Raphael says, "but without something to seal them, the closure will not last."

"We can cover the crevice, then bury the jars with rocks," says Jairus, a determination in his voice to make a plan work.

As they are speaking, a new sound fills the air. At first, they think footsteps and are startled. They listen. Above the soft murmur of the women, the mischievous whispers of the two boys and donkey's restless movement echoing through the cave, the faint noise is imperceptible. Ezra motions to them, claps a finger over his lips. The donkeys, as though they understand the gesture, grow still. Everyone is silent. The light patter on the ground outside the cave, on the boulder, grows louder.

Could it be? Jairus questions. This soon and not yet autumn?

# CHAPTER THIRTY-ONE

*Ben Gurion International Airport, May 28, 2012*

While they waited, this was as good a time as any to pick up the threads of their last conversation on the Via Dolorosa where it seemed their lives were raveling together. "A penny for your thoughts," he said, immediately wishing he'd been more decisive.

"Right now, they're not worth a pence," she said wistfully, her head against the wall, face upturned as if she might be looking for one. She turned and looked at him. "Well, they might be if I could pick one out. My head is too full. You go ahead," and she turned her gaze upward again.

He ventured: "How do we know this is real?"

She blinked and her brows jumped. "This?" she questioned.

"Us."

"Explain!"

"I'm just wondering where we, you and I, go from here," he said. "Two nights ago, when we were on the Via Dolorosa, we were talking about our marriages. They had different endings. Yours to Geoffery was for real, mine to Allyson was not, it did not last. Yours would have lasted. Like the old things we discussed, I want ours to last. I want it to feel right. I want it to be a done deal, that's all." He wanted to continue but felt he'd already said too much and stopped.

"The proof is in the pudding," she said with a slight smirk.

He felt her sensing his insecurity and wished he'd kept his mouth shut. But he had started the discussion so he might as well follow through. "Your turn to explain."

She shifted so their bodies were almost interfaced.

She looked at him seriously. "No marriage is a done deal. Marriages are adventures. Love is an adventure, always a veil of mystery. Take away the veil, the mystery, and it becomes cold. My marriage with Geoffrey was never a done deal. We had our ups and downs. We never knew each other completely." She paused, punched his shoulder with her finger. "There is much about you I will never know," then pointed the finger at her heart. "Much about me you will never know. There will always be much we will not know." She closed her eyes as if in search for her next thought. "The elusiveness of antiquity, the contents of those jars, the mystery, is what draws us on. In our work, it is the order of nature which, too, is a story we will never fully know."

This was not the direction he wanted the conversation to take and was feeling uncomfortable. But he had to admit, she had given their situation more thought than he had and had thrown that ball back into his corner. One thing he had decided was certain. He was not turning the page back. Allyson was not an option. Any fantasies about her were flirtations with what could have been. *What could have been* and *what could be* were two completely different possibilities and *what could be* was sitting next to him. He loved his work, his position at the University of North Arizona. But would he love his work as much, would it be the same without Kate? Could he return to excavations and caves without her beside him digging and picking, brushing and dusting? And his sons. They were grown with their own families. Was he going to grow old with them ... or with *what could be*?

He had started this dialogue and was ready take it to the next level and they heard footfalls. Fashionable black wingtips with tassels appeared then disappeared through the baggage door.

Short moments later the shoes reappeared.

He and Kate watched briefly then listened as the sound of the footfalls and plastic rollers on the concrete faded into the depths of the parking garage.

Chris started to speak, to pick up the thread of his thoughts and—

Footfalls again. Different. Clomping.

The steps came into view.

Boots.

Cowboy boots.

Kate raised slightly to see across the hood of the car in front of them, then lowered herself and said, forming the words with her lips, *It's him.* She placed a hand on Chris' arm and mouthed again, *Wait!* Then whispered, "Let him claim the baggage."

He nodded and watched as she retrieved the gun from her purse, checked to ensure the safety was still on. She sighted down the barrel.

He couldn't resist and murmured, "Surely not."

"Trust me," she replied, a firm hushed tone.

The storage room door opened. The boots disappeared. The door closed behind them.

They waited.

Several minutes elapsed. The storage room door opened. The boots reappeared.

Kate raised again to look and let out a slight gasp.

"What is it?" Chris whispered.

"He's coming this way."

Chris rose slightly to confirm. "He's headed toward the exit to our right," he whispered.

Still slouching behind the two cars, their backs against the low wall, they waited, Kate holding the gun in her right hand, her left hand on her right wrist steadying it.

Chris's heart was racing.

Emmanuel, backpack slung over his left shoulder and duffel bag gripped in his right hand, had not seen them and continued lumbering toward the exit. Paces before the exit door, parallel to Chris and Kate, he saw them and his mouth fell open.

Immediately, Kate rose and positioned into shooting stance, the gun in both hands leveled arm-length and shouted, "Stop!"

Emmanuel stopped, eyed the exit door.

"Don't even think it," she said loudly. "One move toward that door, and I'll shoot."

Emmanuel glared at her, a look between astonishment and terror.

"Gently, put the backpack and duffel bag on the floor," she commanded.

He let the backpack slide from his shoulder and fall and dropped the duffel bag.

Chris heard a muffled crack. *The jars.*

Her eyes and the gun steady on Emmanuel, Kate said, "Chris, get the baggage."

Cautiously, Chris stepped toward Emmanuel, picked up the two pieces of baggage and stepped back.

Emmanuel said nervously. "Someone is going to see you doing this."

Chris scanned the area and saw no one.

"Let's hope so," she quipped. "We'll all be arrested together. Dr. Jordan and I will be released for stopping an antiquity theft. You will be charged and sit in an Israeli prison for years. Where are the jars?"

Emmanuel pointed toward the duffel bag.

Chris bent over, unzipped the canvas bag to check. All he saw were clothes—blue jeans, T-shirts, underwear, socks—that appeared randomly tossed in. He rummaged, his hands moving slowly ... probing ... touching finally, at one end of the bag, grainy and sandy, wrapped in articles of clothing, he felt the contours of the large jar. Then the smaller one at the other end. He withdrew his hand and looked up at Kate. "They're there," he said. "At least he had the presence of mind to cushion them," and he re-zipped the bag.

Kate swung the gun toward the exit door. "Emmanuel, open that door."

Emmanuel wavered, cast a hesitant look at the door, then at her.

"Now!" Kate ordered, unsnapping the gun safety.

"What are you going to do to me?" Emmanuel questioned, his eyes ballooning in their sockets.

"That's up to you," Kate replied.

Emmanuel took a cautious step toward the exit, shot a side glance at them, opened the door, darted through and slammed it behind him.

# CHAPTER THIRTY-TWO

*Wadi Farah Cave, August, A.D. 67*

"Rain!" Ezra cries out and beams.

"You confuse me," Jairus says to him. "Rain means harder, slower travel."

"Rain means water," Ezra says with a broad smile, looking straight up into the sky as if looking for the end of the rain, the moment when it would stop.

"Now we can seal the crevice," joins in Raphael.

"Rains are brief, but heavy, in this area," Ezra continues. "We can mix the mud with small rocks and gravel. It will hold the stones together. Indeed, the Lord does provide."

Jairus is embarrassed. He knows this. He has built dwellings using the same materials and method.

Raphael picks up Ezra's thread. "When the mixture dries, it will be as hard as the rocks."

Overhearing the conversation, one of Raphael's sons begins scooping clay and gravel with his hands and making a small pile. The other mimics his brother's action.

"Well done, my sons," Raphael compliments proudly.

The women do not wait to be told.

Ezra gathers a cistern from his collected belongings and instructs the other two men to do likewise. The wives, as though concerned their husbands will not get the right vessels, leave their dirt work and move quickly to remove cisterns from their personal bundles.

Rain begins to fall with greater force, bouncing off the rocks, splashing around the entrance, currents rolling down the sides of the wadi and pouring in streams down the side of the huge rock. A curtain of water washes over the crevice. The cave entrance becomes soggy. The men place the cisterns under the heaviest streams. In short time, the jars are full. With a large flat rock, Raphael scoops up mounds of soil and pebbles the boys and women have scraped and collected with their hands and adds them to a larger mound he has begun. Everything is in place: water, clay, gravel. Then they sit and wait for the rain to stop so they can exit the cave and the men can seal the crevice.

A decision must be made about the jars that contain the two codices and the scroll. The entombment of the jars must be kept secret. Jairus knows Rebecca knows of their plan but she will tell no one. He is unsure about Raphael's wife and certainly the children. Who knows what they might remember of this night when they mature? The three men huddle away from the women and children, turn their backs to them and begin whispering.

"We can bury them in a hole at the rear of the cave," says Raphael.

Ezra stamps his foot on the ground then kicks it with his toe. "Beneath the loose surface, this ground is hard rock like the cliff." He points at the massive boulder before them. "The origin of that huge rock."

"Then we bury the jars beneath stones inside the cave," Raphael offers, the new idea shining in his eyes. "And seal the opening between the rock and cliff."

"If the seal breaks and the cave is found," Jairus counters, "the discoverers will see first the mound of rocks. The jars will be unearthed."

Ezra has been listening. Jairus watches him rub his chin again, a gesture that has come to mean deep thought. The old scribe finally speaks: "We do not want the manuscripts lost to the world forever. At some point in time, they will surely be found for the world to know."

"But at what point in time?" Raphael questions.

"It is now the year sixty-seven," asserts Jairus. "Even if the seal fails, who would come this way? Putting rocks over the jars risks breaking them, exposing the papyrus to the elements. I say we leave them as they are now, standing upright, for whomever comes this way to see. Leave their discovery to the will of God."

Silence among the three.

The rain stops.

The wadi is quiet.

The time is well into the night. A bright moon provides enough light. But also enough light to be seen traveling.

"It is still not safe to travel," Ezra says. "We will sleep here then leave before dawn,"

With the rugs they have brought, Jairus and Rebecca make pallets at the rear of the cave near the jars. The others find a place and bed down. One of Raphael's sons was already asleep and the other went quickly. The good leader and guardian he has become, Ezra sleeps across the entrance. Jairus is the last to fall asleep. He is worried about the manuscripts, if he is doing the right thing, if taking them on to Jericho and Qumran is the best plan. Will they be safe where they are? Who will discover them and when? When he is shaken by Ezra, one arm is around Rebecca and the other against the large jar.

Outside in the blue morning, the moon and a few stars are visible. The donkeys are led through the opening, their carts retrieved and hooked to the harnesses. One by one, possessions are brought out and reloaded.

"We will take a different route," Ezra says and points up the wadi wall.

"We are climbing?" Rebecca asks plaintively.

"Just to the top then we will descend," Ezra replies. "The robbers have done us a favor. This is the closer route to Coreae."

The morning air is cool and the breeze brisk at the top of the ridge where the sun strikes first in its rise into the new day. Immediately below, they can see the river Jabbok, a blue thread joining the Jordan and further to the south, the deeper blue of the Great Salt Sea. Over the fold of a ridge, they descend into another, smaller, wadi that takes them to a small tributary of the Jordan and a road beside it they follow into Coreae.

Each step of the way, Jairus is more concerned with what he left behind than what lies ahead. After the three men, with the help of the women and children, had worked so hard sealing the breach between the rock and the cliff, at the last minute he almost aborted the plan and retrieved the two jars. In his hands, they had a future in Jericho or Qumran. At least, they would be out of harm's way, if only temporarily. *If only temporarily*, that thought lingering, circulating through his thoughts.

Recalling portions of the writings which he knows by heart, Jairus also feels guilty. *No one lights a lamp and puts it under a bushel basket. They put it on a stand so that anyone can see the light.* Yet, what has he, Jairus, with the help of others, just done? And the story of the nobleman and his ten most trusted servants, giving each of them ten silver coins with the instruction, *See what you can earn with the money while I am gone.* Upon his return, each servant, except one, had multiplied the coins. One servant, fearing the loss of the coins, kept them wrapped in a handkerchief, reaping the anger of his ruler.

Jairus ponders upon these sayings of the master and another which comes to him as he sees the naked rumpled hills across the Jordan. *Jesus left the Jordan and was guided into the wilderness.* Now Jairus has taken Jesus' voice, his message, back to the wilderness, possibly forever. Only God knows these things. Perhaps children playing someday will find them. *Jesus said, "I thank you, Father for hiding these things from the wise and the clever and revealing them to the childlike."*

Perhaps the manuscripts are not permanently placed. He can return, retrieve them and inter them in Galilee. Or return with Ezra and take them further south where the weather is warmer, the air much drier. He wonders about Capernaum and Tiberius, if they have been spared or are in rubbles. And his family, of their safety. Rebecca trudges beside him. For comfort, he places his arm around her and says, "They are safe."

She leans against him, looks up and smiles. "Yes, dear one. Perhaps, too safe."

He stops. She stops with him. The donkey and cart continue rumbling down the wadi slope. "I think you jest. Our children can never be too safe, not in the caves above Capernaum."

"Nay. Not our children, the master's words."

"Ah!" she exclaimed.

They commenced walking. "Let us hope not too safe," he says. "Some day they will be discovered. Some day."

"How long?" she asks.

"Only God knows."

"And by whom? Only God knows that, as well," she says, answering her own question before he can respond.

Arm in arm, in the dusky new light of the beginning day, the hot white arc of the sun cresting the Jordan plateau, they continue down the wadi crest, toward Coreae where, hopefully, they will learn the fate of the others in their group.

"Let us pray the scrolls will be found by someone who knows their value," he laments.

"Someone who will protect them and spread them far and wide for the world to see," she adds.

# CHAPTER THIRTY-THREE

*Ben Gurion International Airport, May 28, 2012*

Chris lunged toward the door and Kate grabbed his arm.

"Perfect," she uttered, sliding the gun's safety back into place. "He's gone. We've got the jars. Our car is two rows back. Let's go."

Chris picked up the two pieces of luggage.

"Leave the backpack," she instructed and handed him the keys. "You're driving."

"You've driven more in Arab countries," he said surprised at her command.

"You'll be jolly good on the four-lane," she countered.

"Until we enter Ramallah," he snapped. "I've been there before."

She pointed at the dash. "We have the GPS. "

"If it were adjusted for a maze, that might work."

On their way to the car Chris said, "That was slick what you did back there with Emmanuel."

"He was terrified," she replied. "We didn't need him. That was the easiest way to get rid of him. He'll get picked up."

"You were bluffing, right?"

"Of course. I needed his attention. He's a big puppy."

"What about the backpack?" he questioned.

"It'll draw security's attention," she said.

The duffle bag securely on the floor behind the front seats, Chris navigated the parking level through the exit toll booth and onto the access road to Highway 1, then onto Highway 6 and Ramallah.

Kate removed the gun from her bag and put it on the seat beside her.

He said, "That's why you wanted me to drive. No more bluffing."

Her eyes on the side view mirror, she nodded "My cell phone is disabled and yours may have been compromised, too. Hand it to me," she said flatly.

He handed her his phone. She pulled out her notepad, flipped some pages, punched some numbers on his phone and activated the speaker phone.

"Yes," she said to someone answering. "Is this UNESCO?"

A female voice, a hint of Arabic accent, gave an affirmative response.

"This is Dr. Kate Ferguson with the British Museum. We have the two jars and are leaving Ben Gurion Airport now, bringing them to you."

The voice acknowledged then added, "The Ramallah UNESCO office is in a compound. If you use your GPS, please access the College Street entrance."

Kate concluded the call, powered off the phone, removed the back cover and with her fingernail, gently lifted the small battery, slid it into her pocket and returned the phone to him.

"So, if we get separated, we can't communicate," he said solemnly.

"We just won't get separated," she affirmed with a wink. "It's either that option or being a moving target. I've got the UNESCO College Street address." Flipping another page of her notebook, she leaned forward and entered the information into the car's GPS.

"This should be interesting," he said. "The shortest route to Ramallah from the airport would be Highway Four-forty-three. But it's tricky, especially for Palestinians who are restricted from using it. Vehicles rented in Israel are also usually not allowed in Palestinian Territory."

She replied, "We're okay. We're registered as tourists. Hertz has an affiliate with a West Bank rental. Emmanuel must have had the presence of mind to get the same deal."

"He's smarter than we give him credit," Chris voiced. "Wonder where he is now."

"We just need to know where we are," she said and pointed ahead. "Shortly, we'll right ramp onto Highway One. We'll be on it for about eight kilometers then up a right ramp toward Modiin which takes us to Four-forty-three."

He was familiar with Highway 443, known as the Bethron Ascent. It followed the ancient east-west trade route connecting the Via Maris, the old coast road, with the Way of the Patriarchs. The route was used during many battles in antiquity and is mentioned in a number of ancient writings, including the Bible." It was also the main route connecting Tel Aviv and Gush Dan with Jerusalem via Modiin.

"There will be a checkpoint at Modiin when we enter the West Bank," she continued and looked again at her side view.

"I haven't seen evidence of an M16 agent backup," he said.

"He's out there," she said unconcerned. "Trust me."

"Four-forty-three is not considered a safe stretch of road," he warned.

"Correct. It was closed in September 2000 due to the outbreak of the second Intifada. There were fatal shootings and bomb attacks on Israeli traffic. On road segments adjacent to Palestinian areas, anti-sniper barricades were erected, one of the reasons Palestinians are barred from using the highway."

"The poor Palestinians," he commented.

"They cannot even use the highway on foot," she lamented. "For many Palestinians, this road is the only way to their farmland. It's also the primary access road to Ramallah the villagers rely on for commerce and for their health and education needs. The Israelis provide alternate routes but they are circuitous and take much longer to meet Palestinian needs, including medical and hospital."

"I meant we are safe with the amount of traffic," he expressed. "I'm not concerned about snipers or bombs. We're no good to the Syrians dead."

"So far so good," she said.

Highway 443 ran along a ridge line and maintained a stable grade. They passed the Modiin junction and were approaching the Maccabim-Re'ut Junction where they crossed the Green Line into the West Bank and Palestinian Territory. Kate picked up the gun, removed the clip and placed both in her bag.

"That was smart," he said.

"No need to invite trouble," she replied.

"We may not be safe once we cross the Green Line," he opined.

She nodded. "Let's just hope they wave us through. With the two jars and the news that's out, thanks to Emmanuel, we'd have some explaining to do."

Chris pulled the car into the checkpoint line. They were two cars behind the first car. The guard waved it through. He halted the second car, examined the driver's documents and waved him through. He held up a hand for Chris and Kate, leaned over and peered into the car.

"Why do you enter the West Bank?" he inquired.

"We are tourists," Chris answered. He was about to tell him they were staying in Jerusalem, then decided against it.

"Your passports please," he said.

Chris handed their passports through the window to him.

"And where do you go?" the guard asked perfunctorily as he thumbed through their passport pages.

"Ramallah," Chris responded.

"And the reason you go to Ramallah," the guard pressed, closing their passports.

Kate was leaning over poised to answer, but Chris preempted her. "To see the exhibition at UNESCO then to Jericho."

The guard returned the passports to Chris and moved his face closer to the window, his scrutinizing eyes moving over their faces, then he backed away and said, "Enjoy your stay," and waved them through.

Once they were past the concrete barriers, Kate said sarcastically, "We lucked out. Is there even an exhibition at the UNESCO office in Ramallah?"

"If there isn't, he believed it," he countered, feeling a surging emotion to push back on her. "The guard wouldn't know. If they searched the car and found the jars, we have an excuse. We're taking them to UNESCO. They could check it out. UNESCO is expecting them."

She cocked her head back, stroked the air with her finger and said, "Touché!"

Past the Maccabim security checkpoint they rode in silence, Chris' thoughts turning to the last time he'd been to Ramallah. The year was 1990. He had been invited to make a presentation in Jerusalem to the Israel Expedition Society regarding a paper he had written about the archaeological history of Nablus. He was only in the country for two days and part of that time included a side trip to Nablus which involved driving through Ramallah. His Israeli host drove but Chris recalled the wild configuration of streets, as if they had been laid down on sheep trails.

Since that time, under the Oslo Accords, Ramallah and its immediate environs were classified as Area A and has become the seat of Palestinian authority and served as the headquarters for most international non-government organizations and foreign embassies. It also became a leading center of economic and political activity in the territories under the control of the Palestinian National Authority. The city had been the site of the

Second Intifada when two Israeli officers had taken a wrong turn and had been lynched by a frenzied crowd that was enraged by the Muhammad al-Durrah incident in Gaza. The mob mutilated the bodies of the two officers and dragged their bodies through the city's streets. Later that afternoon, the Israeli Army struck back with an air strike that demolished the police station. Twelve years ago, in 2002, the Israeli Defense Forces (IDF), in breach of the Oslo Accords, intervened again.

Now, eight years later, Chris wondered what he and Kate would encounter and doubted the infrastructure had changed much. Not much changes in a city five centuries old. And he was at the mercy of the GPS which would probably take them the shortest, but most congested route. They had been safer on the four-lane. They had been safer on Highway 90. They had been safer in their hotel in Jerusalem. If they got in congested bumper-to-bumper traffic on old narrow streets, in the midst of jostling crowds and honking horns, they could be dragged from their car and no one would notice. He glanced over at Kate clenching and unclenching her teeth, one hand inching closer to her bag.

At the Giv'at Ze'ev Junction and Ofer Prison Security Checkpoint, they were passed through, their passports not even checked. After several short turns they debouched onto Jaffa Street.

Jaffa Street was a long well-groomed boulevard, lined with palm and eucalyptus trees, fashionable modern homes and apartment buildings that sat behind low blond stone walls. The median was landscaped with trees, shrubs and occasional artwork, statues. Everything looked clean and landscaped.

One eye on his rearview, the other on the boulevard, *so far so good*, Chris thought, noting Kate's eyes glued to her side view. "See anything that looks like trouble?" he asked.

"A few cars behind us," she said. "They're a ways back. Leading them is a white van that was behind us when we ramped onto Jaffa Street. I'm keeping an eye on it." She pointed at the GPS screen on the dash. "The map shows us intersecting with Al Manara Square."

"That's the city center," he added. "A large roundabout. It will be busy."

From the passenger side-pocket, she pulled a map they'd been given at Hertz, opened it, flattened it on her lap, flipped it over and located the Ramallah city quadrant, her finger moving over the insert map, then stopping. "The UNESCO compound is a few blocks northwest of Al Manara Square. The lady there said use the College Street entrance."

"See anything on the map indicating a short cut bypassing the main square?"

She studied the map. "About a fourth of a kilometer ahead we could turn left onto Bulous Shi'hadeh Street. It looks like a short block, and then onto Almuntazan Street which would take us through a roundabout and onto Elias Odeh Street, a straight shot to College Street."

As she was speaking, Chris noticed a black Suburban suddenly emerge from a side street on their right and pull in behind them. "We may have company," he said with a backward gesture of his head.

She glanced in her side view. "Hopefully, just another black Suburban. Scratch the short cut. Stay on Jaffa," she said, adding, "There's safety in numbers."

"Unless the numbers turn into bumper-to-bumper traffic," he cautioned and pressed the door lock button. "Then, we're sitting ducks. Windows busted. Doors forced. Yanked from our seats at gunpoint."

She picked up her bag, removed the gun and clip, inserted the clip and quipped, "Think again."

He groaned. "Is the safety on?"

"It is *now*."

They passed Bulous Shi'hadeh Street. Chris maneuvered the car into the left lane. In the rearview he observed the black Suburban following.

"The Suburban switched, too," she noted.

He nodded. "So did the white van. It's been keeping a measured distance behind us since we entered Jaffa Street. That bothers me."

She didn't respond.

They were nearing the center of the city and the major roundabout intersection, traffic tightening. Chris's arms stiffened, his hands on the steering wheel constricted. The black Suburban was immediately behind them and behind it, three car lengths, the white van. Kate picked up the gun and moved it into her lap, kept her right hand on it.

"We are heading into the middle of protest history," Chris said somberly. "Especially during the First and Second Intifada. Blood spilled. People shot and killed. The square continues to be used to protest the actions of Israeli and Palestinian leaders."

"Let's hope we don't start another," she replied.

The GPS voice: "Approaching Al Manara Square. At Al Manara Square turn right onto the roundabout, then take the George Al Saa Street exit."

"I don't mean to be a back-seat driver," she said looking at the map, "but you'll need to be in the outer lane to veer right onto George Al Saa Street. It's the third exit once you're on the roundabout."

"Get into the backseat," he urged, glancing into the rearview. "Divides us up," and he pointed at the gun. "Just in case." If there was a shoot out, he didn't want to be in the line of fire.

"Got it," she said. Bag and gun in hand, she climbed onto the console, awkwardly squeezed between the seat-backs and positioned herself in the middle of the back seat where she had a better view through the side and rear windows.

He flipped on his right blinker.

"This is going to get interesting," she said peering through the rear window at the traffic behind them, the black Suburban close behind and further back, the white van. "The white van is hard to figure."

"We're about to find out," he said, guiding the Buick back into the right lane, noting the Suburban and van following suit.

"You're right," she said. "The van is in the hunt."

"Makes you wonder who's hunting whom," he remarked.

"The white van was there first," she said.

Al Manara Square was a smaller version of Times Square. It was a large circle with a stele monument in a center quartered with four lion statues, five streets radiating outward, and a teeming congestion of traffic, cacophony of honking and beeping horns and the nasal cry of a muezzin's call to prayer from a nearby minaret. Streaming by on their right was a blur of shops and cafes, umbrellaed vending carts, fruit and vegetable stalls and the incessant flapping of Palestinian flags.

The sunlight was brighter than normal, a fluorescent quality beating down. In the glaring kaleidoscope scrolling around him, Chris had been counting and saw what he thought to be the third exit on the roundabout, and he turned.

Immediately he realized his error. Kate did, too, and was on top of him but preempted by the GPS voice: "You have left your route. Turn around and return to the roundabout."

Chris was familiar with Al Isral. Its English name was Radio Street, the main transportation artery between Ramallah and Nablus. Several years ago he traveled it, and he recalled the destroyed flower beds, ripped up sidewalks, bent lampposts, abandoned buildings. Past the compound of Yassar Arafat, Israeli tanks. He recalled a Kentucky Fried Chicken restaurant where he'd wanted to stop and eat but there was no way to get to it because of the continuous median down the four-lane boulevard punctuated at regular intervals with utility poles, no U-turn breaks. Now, he was confronted by that same median, a GPS persistent voice barking that he needed to turn around, and his side-kick in his ear telling him two unknown vehicles were still behind him and in probable pursuit. Flashing across his mind was a time in San Luis Potosi, Mexico, when he was being followed by antiquity cartel thieves, how that scene ended, so he did the only thing he knew to do, what his instinct told him to do, and he gunned the Buick.

"Chris, what in God's name?" Kate yelled, reaching over and turning off the GPS.

"Hold on," he shouted. "I know what I'm doing." Then: "I think I know what I'm doing," he murmured to himself. Unless they lived in Ramallah, which he doubted, whoever was following him didn't know the street maze any better. Even if they did, they weren't in his mind. He was a GPS on the fly and only he knew his next move. That was the way it was in San Luis Potosi when he made a sudden right turn in front of a fire hydrant and the driver behind him tried to duplicate the maneuver and hit the hydrant totaling the car and flooding the street. Unless their pursuers started shooting, he had an edge. They were not far from the UNESCO office. He knew the general location and could work his way back to it. Once there, if it was a compound with guards, he'd be home free.

"You're going to get us killed," Kate blurted.

He didn't reply, his mind honed on strategy. He didn't believe in fate or luck, but there were times a person had to roll the dice and jump the rails even if it meant having a wreck. This was one of those times.

The traffic was lighter on the north side of the square, the median no higher than a speed bump, utility poles every fifty feet, he estimated.

"What are you going to do?" Kate demanded, this time leaning forward, her voice hard and high pitched in his ear.

"Get back and buckle up," he ordered, trying to keep his voice level. "I'm making a U-turn."

"God bless us," she moved back. He heard the buckle snap. He calculated and slowed.

If he timed the oncoming traffic in the other four lane and hit the median at an angle near a power pole, the move, like the one in Potosi, might take out the Suburban. And the van.

He waited.

*Now!*

Between a small tree and a pole, he angled the car toward the median.

"Whoa!" Kate howled. "You're mad."

The car bumped onto the median and he sharply spun the wheel, spinning the car right-angled into the oncoming lane, barely missing the pole, horns blaring and tires screeching then the sound of a crash.

Both turned and looked. The Suburban had glanced off the pole but was still behind them. The van, too. Suddenly, as if from nowhere, a desert-camouflaged Humvee appeared.

"See that?" Kate cried.

"Yes," he reacted.

"What do you make of it?"

"Don't know," he replied, eyeing a side street coming up on the right. He maneuvered into the right lane, waited until the last moment, then swung the car hard right bumping over a curb corner and onto a narrow bottleneck street lined with shops and sheltered markets and nice homes, weaving between cars parked along the side and on the sidewalks, the Suburban and Humvee close behind, the van further back. They were close to UNESCO, a few blocks away. He picked up the map she'd left in the front passenger seat and flipped it back to her. "What street are we on?"

Flustered, she caught the map and flattened it. "It's not on here, but the next is John the Baptist."

He shook his head in disbelief, then recalled that Palestinian Christians were a presence in the West Bank. *Somebody is going to get baptized*, he thought and he hoped it wasn't them as he observed the Humvee closing in.

"Take a left there, then a right onto George Saa," she advised, "and we're back on track."

Suddenly, behind them, they heard gunshots. Both looked and saw the Suburban weaving drunkenly, smashing into one of the parked cars along the shaded street, the Humvee closing in behind it. More gunshots.

"Keep going!" Kate shouted, almost screaming. "That's not us."

He came to the intersection, turned left onto John the Baptist, then immediately made a right onto George Saa.

"Turn left onto College Street," Kate said convincingly, the map in her hand, "Our destination's on your left," her eyes back on the rear window, at what was not coming. "They're gone," she shrieked.

Constantly glancing into the rearview, Chris, too, was puzzled that the three vehicles were not behind them, only a normal flow of traffic as the entrance to the UNESCO office came into view.

The building was a squat two story blond bubble-brick structure that looked more like a military bunker than a United Nations facility, and was part of a low-walled and chain-linked compound with a gated entrance and guardhouse. The gates were open and a lone uniformed guard stood at attention by the security booth.

"Mums on the incident," Kate whispered into Chris' ear as he rolled the car to a stop and the guard stepped forward.

"Later, when the jars are safe," he affirmed.

"Yes!"

Chris lowered the window.

The guard bowed and scrutinized them. "Identification!" he requested, at first in Arabic, again in English.

Chris heard Kate rummaging in the back, hopefully putting away her gun. Her passport appeared over the seat back. He took it and handed it along with his to the guard.

The guard quickly glanced at their passports. "Welcome. We have been expecting you," he said and with a smile palmed his hand for them to pass through the gate, adding, "The parking area is just ahead. Someone will greet you."

Before Chris could continue through the gate, they heard a sound behind them, another vehicle pulling up to the gate.

It was the white van.

# CHAPTER THIRTY-FOUR

*Trans-Jordan, The Golan, A.D. 67*

Ezra, Jairus, Raphael and their families have been traveling for four days, trekking mainly in the hills, steering clear of the paths of Roman armies, rebel-held territory and cities in the Decapolis with pro-Roman sentiments. To the west they can see the blue Sea of Galilee; due north, Mount Hermon's snow-capped peak; and to the east, wrinkling away to the horizon, the colorless Trans-Jordan wilderness.

At Coreae, a discussion had commenced among the group about where to go next. Several had wanted to stay with the original plan and continue south to Qumran. At Qumran were caves where they could hide and a community sympathetic to followers of Jesus. At Qumran, they could endure until the war's end and return to their homes.

But Ezra had voiced caution. Recent reports told of rebels leaving Jerusalem, headed for Masada, Herod's former mountain retreat, fortifying it as a last defense should Jerusalem fall. If this news is true, Ezra had warned that Jerusalem is sure to fall to the Roman war machine and Qumran lay directly in the path of a Roman march toward Herodium and Masada.

Some good news had created an air of optimism. Word had also arrived in Coreae that the traitor Josephus, leading one of Roman legions, had spared Capernaum, a town that had provided aid to him when he fell from his horse and injured his ankle at Bethsaida. Also, and to the great joy of Ezra and Raphael and his family, Tiberius had been spared. The seditious rebels had been expelled and the city's inhabitants had decided not to fight against

Rome. Unfortunately, most of the cities in Galilee, including Tarichaea, Jotapata, Gamla and Gischala, had been razed.

At the time, Jairus also had similar concerns but had remained silent. Ezra was older and wiser. Jairus was confident the group's needs would be met and he thought of one of the master's sayings: "So do not worry, saying 'What shall we eat?' or 'What shall we drink?' Or 'How will we be clothed?' Search for his kingdom, and all these things will be delivered to you."

Ezra had made the right decision to circle back through the Golan and enter Galilee from the north. The prospects of safety were more promising with the dangers behind, not ahead of them. Painful farewells were said to the group determined to go on to Qumran. They would achieve peace of mind for a while. But the Romans, in their drive to extinguish all resistance, would surely come.

The small group is descending the Golan plateau into the Jordan valley. In the distance, they can see Bethsaida and Chorazin and beyond them, a few more miles around the shoreline, Capernaum. Jairus and Rebecca are walking together, holding hands, Ezra and Raphael paces in front of them, others trailing behind.

Ezra turns and points ahead and with a broad smile says, "See, Jairus, our villages still stand."

Jairus returns the smile. "We are almost home."

Rebecca looks up at Jairus. "Thanks be to God," she sighs, then adds, "and for the hospitality of Capernaum, the home of him, who said, 'Give to the one who asks you.'"

"'And from the one to whom you have lent, do not demand back what is yours,'" he completes the saying. "But your meaning escapes me."

"Josephus, when he was still one of us," she says, "was cared for in Capernaum."

He stops, tilts back his head. "Ah, yes, dear one. And he spared the city." He puts his arm around her shoulder and draws her close. "And it was at Miriam's house, Simon Peter's daughter. How could I forget."

They continue down The Golan slope, nearing Bethsaida where they will cross the Jordan River before it empties into the Sea of Galilee.

Rebecca renews their dialogue. "If the Romans have moved further south, then you could retrieve the jars."

Ezra, only paces ahead, overhears the comment and turns around. "I, too, dear Rebecca, have had these thoughts. But, alas, I am an old man." He glances over at Raphael. "Perhaps, my trusted courier could achieve that mission."

Raphael nods.

Then Ezra eyes Jairus. "What say you, dear friend?"

In the seriousness of the moment, the group stops. Jairus does not have to think about his response. He has already pondered the idea, the possibility, weighed the pros and cons. It has threaded its way through his thoughts countless times. So when he responds, there is strength and confidence, an air of finality in his voice: "Let them remain entombed for future generations. From the stones and dust of antiquity, the words of Jesus will rise fresh as sunlight, as though just off the tongue of the young prophet from Galilee."

Except for the wind blowing off the sea through the trees, all is quiet when he finishes, as though nothing more is needed.

Except a final comment from Ezra: "Amen!"

They continue on to Capernaum, passing familiar sites, coming full circle to where it all began—the man, his words, his message.

Jairus puts his arm around Rebecca as they bid farewell to their Tiberius friends and cross the threshold of their home.

# CHAPTER THIRTY-FIVE

*Ramallah, Palestinian Territory, May 28, 2012*

Twisted in the backseat like a pretzel, Kate quickly withdrew her gun from the bag.

A Caucasian male wearing Nike red runner pants and blue wind jacket stepped from the vehicle, briskly approached the guard and, holding up his hands, flashed a badge. "Nigel Blanchard," his clipped, accent distinctly British. "M Sixteen agent."

The guard nodded acknowledgment.

Kate returned the gun to her bag. She and Chris exited the car, approached the agent and introduced themselves.

"Ian McCain told us about you," Kate said. "But we weren't sure of your M.O."

"What happened back there?" Chris pressed.

Agent Blanchard closed his badge wallet and returned it to his jacket pocket. "With your permission," he said to the guard, "I must speak with them privately."

"Of course," agreed the guard, then added, "you may enter the compound. The parking area is inside, about 200 meters."

Chris and Kate returned to their car. Blanchard followed them through the gate. Beneath a eucalyptus tree, they parallel parked and gathered beneath the tree.

Blanchard spoke first. "I received a call from BCHQ that you were being shadowed by Hezbollah. I alerted Israeli Security. They intervened. Two Hezbollah agents were arrested. You know the rest."

"There is a God," Kate exclaimed and thanked him.

"There is another person involved," Chris said.

"The student," Blanchard acknowledged.

"Yes," Kate affirmed.

"He is in custody," Blanchard confirmed.

"Others were following him," Chris said. "Three men we suspect were archive thieves and two more in suits we have seen at the hotel where we are staying."

"The three evaporated," Blanchard said. "The other two were IAA. They arrested the student. You have the jars now?"

"We do and are grateful for your intervention," Kate added.

"When do you leave Israel?" Blanchard enquired anxiously.

"When we finish here," Chris responded, "we're headed back to Ben Gurion International."

Blanchard lifted a finger. "Word of caution. You are not out of danger. Our office and the Israelis continue to intercept messages from Hezbollah. This failed effort may bring another. I will stay here and follow you to the airport. The Israelis are also monitoring the situation."

As they were speaking, two individuals, a woman and a man, were hastily descending the steps from the UNESCO building and advancing toward them.

"Hello!" greeted the woman who was older than the male accompanying her. She was thickset and wore a hijab and a dark western style business suit, white-ruffled blouse and low cut heels. The young man walking briskly beside her wore a white shirt, sleeves rolled to the elbows. A black mat of hair covered his forehead. Both were eagerly smiling. "My name is Nyla Abadi, I am the head of the office. And this is Nasir Abdallah, one of my associates. So glad you made it safely," the woman said, slightly breathless as she completed the welcome.

Kate introduced herself and Chris and stated, "This is Mr. Blanchard, British M Sixteen agent. There were problems. He will be accompanying us, if that is permissible."

"But, of course," said Ms. Abadie. "You *do* have the artifacts."

"On the floor," Chris affirmed, pointing to the back door. "In a duffel bag." He opened the door, gingerly removed the bag and set in on the pavement, his eyes shifting to the guard's keen observation of the process unfolding and the moving traffic beyond the open gate. *You are not out of danger.*

The young assistant named Nasir leaned over to unzip the bag and his supervisor said something nervously to him in Arabic.

Kate looked at Chris and whispered the translation. "She told him, 'not here, inside.'"

The comment reminded Chris. He quickly stepped to the car, opened the trunk and grabbed his tool kit.

Bending down, Ms. Abadie and her associate carefully hoisted the bag, gently cradled it into their arms and together began walking—Chris, Kate and Blanchard following—toward the building's entrance.

Once inside the building, the two UNESCO officials set the bag on a table in a small foyer. Ms. Abadie turned to Chris and Kate. "We will provide you with a receipt."

"A receipt would be helpful, in case we are questioned later. And one other thing, Ms. Abadie."

"Nyla, please."

"Nyla. Doctor Jordan is an archeologist from the United States, and I am an ancient manuscript expert with the British Museum in London and we—"

"—Yes, yes," Nyla exclaimed brightly, her hands coming together in a soft sultanic clap. "We know who you are. Your presence here at UNESCO honors us."

Hands steepled, Kate bowed in deference to the graceful comment. "Doctor Jordan and I traveled here under the auspices of the British Museum in a cooperative venture to assist with the recovery and safe placement of these jars."

Chris wasn't sure where she was going with this and jiggled his tool bag. They needed to move along swiftly. They had a plane to catch, and an M16 agent escort appeared antsy, but they hadn't come this far without knowing what was in the jars.

Kate continued: "We would like the honor and privilege of opening the jars here," she glanced at Chris, "and knowing their contents, before we must soon depart your country." She concluded, motioning toward agent Blanchard.

"This is an administrative office, not a research facility," Nyla said apologetically. "However, we do have a room that serves as a laboratory where we clean and prepare artifacts for cataloguing, labeling and transport, if that would be suitable."

Chris was anxious to respond, but Kate spoke first. "Splendid!"

A marble-topped island centered the rectilinear windowless room. Along one wall was a counter with drawers, cabinets above and below, a double stainless steel sink and small refrigerator, a microwave beside it. From the opposite wall, stools beneath it, extended a long worktable shelf and on it a laptop, a couple of adjustable LED desk lamps, a small scale, trays, sets of small plastic storage baskets, rulers, scissors, tweezers, assortment of brushes—the accoutrements of archaeology. In one corner was a survey instrument on a tripod and on the floor beside it, a large red fire extinguisher. Assembled on a table at the end of the room, and on shelving above the table, lay an assortment of artifacts—shards of pottery, stones, bowls, goblets, jars. Some of the items, particularly those on the table, appeared temporarily placed before being catalogued and labeled and moved to museums and other showcases of antiquity. The room had the smell of old things. Chris could only imagine their origins and how the international world heritage organization came by them.

The otherwise essentially bare room was far from the insulated, sanitized and well-equipped archeological laboratories he and his sidekick were accustomed to. But the room was clean, items neatly arranged and, with hanging ceiling globes and several strategically placed LED lamps, well-lighted. If Kate could meticulously unroll the millennium-aged scroll of Mark's autograph on a table in a professor's university office in Edinburgh, she could repeat the performance and he could remove the lids from two jars, probably as old, in this room.

Nyla and Nasir gently placed the duffel bag on the marble-topped island.

"You might need these," Nyla said, opening a drawer and removing two pairs of white surgical gloves. "And these," clear Ziploc bags of varying sizes with sheets of labels she took from another drawer. "You may also use the computer," she added, pointing at the laptop on the work shelf, "for entering your findings in our UNESCO data base."

"Thank you, Nyla," Kate said. "We will leave the labeling and cataloguing to you and your associates. We," she glanced at Chris, "only wish to open the jars and view the contents before we leave."

Besides Chris and Kate, the only people in the room were the two UNESCO officials and Blanchard, who had seated himself on a stool at the end of the work shelf near the entrance.

"As you wish," Nyla responded, the oriental bow again, hands folded. From another drawer behind her, she retrieved a folded white plastic sheet, unfolded it and spread it on the counter top beside the duffel bag, picked up a pair of the gloves, handed a pair to Nasir, Chris observing the methodical procedure with keen interest: *They've done this before.* Like two gloved surgeons about to operate, Nyla looked at Nasir. "Now."

Nasir leaned over, delicately touched the zipper and slowly, deftly, slid it the length of the bag. He removed first the small jar, set it carefully up right on the plastic sheet beside the bag. The second followed with a hush from Nyla, a sigh from Kate. The jars lay on the white plastic like high explosives. All could see the long thin fissure in the tall jar extending from the neck to the base.

Chris leaned over and whispered to Kate: "When Emmanuel dropped it." She shook her head.

Nasir, too, noticed the crack and, with Nyla's help, placed the larger jar on its side. Looking at Nyla, he pointed at the images around the lip. She nodded approvingly.

*Christian Arabs,* Chris thought.

"You may use our instruments," Nyla said, gesturing at the array of tools on the work shelf. "Also glue and labels. And this," she opened a cabinet door, retrieved a gallon of liquid labeled "Distilled Water."

Chris held up the small bag he was still holding. "Many thanks, Nyla, but I have my tool kit. The scale will be helpful. The jars will need to be weighed and the weights recorded. We measured them on site, but will need to do it again. As Kate said, we will leave the labeling and cataloguing to you and your staff."

Chris and Kate pulled on the gloves that had been provided. Chris moved down the island closer to the large jar and pointed at the fracture. "Hairline. I must be careful," he said gesturing at the lid. He motioned for Kate to move closer and said, "You agree," he said to her, "we should start with the small jar?"

"Yes."

He lifted the two vials and Ziplocs from his took kit and looked at Nyla. "Your research team will need these. The vials contain dust and fragments gathered at the cave site and are labeled accordingly. The Ziplocs contain the leather casings from around each jar."

Nyla thanked him.

Chris removed a small note pad and pen from his kit and handed them to Kate. "Take notes as I call out data."

She gave a restrained nod. She was not accustomed to taking orders, but she took the pen and placed the pad before her on a counter where she had full view of his work.

Nyla gestured to Nasir who found a writing pad on the counter behind him, clicked his ballpoint, and was poised to do likewise.

Chris scrutinized the small jar, moved his hands gently over it, particles of dust and clay smattering onto the plastic sheet provided by Nyla. He pointed at the sheet, smiled, and flashed an "OK" gesture.

"Kate, hand me a ruler from the shelf behind you, the one with the square."

She complied; he nodded thanks.

Others from the building began entering and gathering to observe, maintaining a distance from the procedure.

Once again, Chris measured the width and length of the jar and its top, called out the dimensions and Kate studiously recorded them. The measurements of the smaller jar were the same as the prior measurements, 8 inches, or 20.3 centimeters across the mouth and 10 1/2 inches/26.7 centimeters long. While he had the square ruler, he repeated the measurements of the larger jar. They, also, were the same: 6 inches/15.2 centimeters across the mouth, height at 19 1/2 inches/49.8 centimeters.

For the benefit of those looking on, Chris said, "The larger jar is about the size of the scroll jars at Qumran." He stood back and studied the small jar beneath the lights. His concentration had the immediacy and sharpness of sunlight. He carefully and slowly turned the jar to see the other side and saw again something he'd seen at the cave when shafts of early morning sun struck it.

"What are you thinking?" she asked.

"The jars have the same shape as those discovered at Qumran but the texture of the clay is decidedly different. A soil analysis will determine its origin. But one thing is for sure. These jars didn't come from Qumran, the Jericho area or where they were discovered. The composition of both jars has a volcanic origin." He pointed to several places around the middle of the small jar. "You see these granules covering the jar that flash in the light?"

"Yes!" Kate responded. "It's covered with them."

"It's mica," he said. "I've come across clay deposits like these before, on other jars discovered in Israel. The mineralogy of that type of clay has been thoroughly analyzed by others. Using several different analysis techniques, supplemented by electron-micrographs and chemical determination, we have all concluded the clay comes from basaltic soils." He picked up a small brush from his kit, swiped it gently over the mid-section of the jar and small particles sprinkled onto the plastic sheet. "It is manufactured from calcareous clay, limestone and marls, alluvium containing both basalt and carbonate grains. You can see the alluvial colors in grayish brown sandy loam soil." He moved the brush again, lightly, over the surface of the jar. "The clay comes from a sandy loam that is often grayish brown and occasionally yellowish red to reddish brown. The greatest part of this region where this clay is found is covered by basalts formed since the Miocene epoch."

"I'm impressed," she said, glancing around at the others listening in. "But you still haven't told me the location."

He put down the brush and looked at her. "To name the exact location, I would have to trace the pottery through its chemical composition to its place of manufacture. Every clay source on the earth has its own chemical composition. Once the chemical composition is known, it can be compare with what archaeologists call "local kiln wasters," misfired pottery lumps that are site specific. A chemical match between a pottery vessel and a waster means that one has found the place where the pottery was made. It's the chemical fingerprint. Without that chemical analysis—the basalt makeup and presence of mica—my hunch of the location of manufacture is Galilee, probably lower Galilee, which has a heavy concentration of basalt."

"All right," she said nonplussed. "But how and why did they get from Galilee to a remote cave north of Jericho?"

"The contents may answer that question."

He wrapped his gloved hands around the lid and tried a gentle back and forth clockwise, and then counterclockwise movement. The lid did not budge. "It's fairly encrusted. I don't want to force it off." He tried rocking it up and down. Nothing gave. "Wet that cloth hanging over the sink, please" he said, looking up at Nyla. "Just damp, not dripping."

Nyla walked around the island, turned on the water, ran the rag a few times under the faucet, shut it off and then twisted the rag over the sink until it quit dripping and handed it to him. He wiped the rag a few times around the lip of the jar's top. Excess dirt and particles fell onto the white plastic. With a small intake of breath, he tried again, a back and forth leveraging movement.

"Let me try," Kate said.

"Wait," he cautioned. "I felt it give."

He tried the same movement again. The lid turned.

"I saw that," Kate declared.

"Yes, it's coming," he confirmed. "But I must go slow."

Everything moved languidly like a fan at slow speed.

On the third try, the top loosened, came off with a plume of dust, chips from the lip splattering onto the plastic sheet, the occasion drawing audible breaths from the small gathering.

Chris laid the top aside onto the plastic. Kate stood beside him staring at the opening. The others in the room leaned forward in anticipation.

Kate lifted one hand and delicately pinched the bridge of her nose between her foreigner and thumb. "I feel we're opening the jar in Syria," she breathed emotionally.

"Except there, we had an inkling of its contents. Here, we haven't a clue." He leaned over and peered inside. "You're next," and he motioned for her to move closer beside him.

She carefully, and delicately, tilted the jar toward them for a better view through the opening.

At first, all Chris could see appeared to be packing material.

Then:

"It's not a scroll," he observed.

"It's two objects, side by side," she said, "packing cloth around them. Whatever they are, this will not be like the Markan scroll," Kate said. "They're not going to just slide out."

The only noise in the room was their voices.

She reached her hand through the opening, gently palpated the material with her fingers. "Cloth, folded pads, a common packing material for scrolls placed in jars."

"We'll need to remove the packing first, but carefully," he said. "It's also valuable." He moved a hand across his forehead. "This is a first for me. I've opened ancient jars before but never encountered packing material like this."

Nasir pointed to a pair of tweezers on the work shelf.

Chris acknowledged the gesture, but reached into his small bag and withdrew a large pair.

Agent Blanchard had left his stool and joined the onlookers.

Instinctively, Kate pulled a paper towel from a roll on the sink and laid it beside the jar onto the white plastic sheet.

"Excellent," Chris commended her. "We need to keep the particles from the contents separate from those from the jar. This shouldn't be a problem," he murmured. "The cloth is brittle and breaking apart." With the tweezers, he clasped an edge of dark padding, removed it and carefully released it onto the paper towel. The wad was shredded around the edges where he had pulled it from a larger piece. With the removal, two objects were in clearer view.

"Maybe we can pull one out," Kate suggested.

"Or tilt the jar. With luck, maybe it'll slide out," he said. Holding the jar by its neck and bottom, he lifted it from the counter and angled it downward. One object slid to the mouth of the jar, and stopped. Kate reached over, pinched the edge with her fingers and pulled a small notebook onto the paper towel.

"A codex," she exclaimed, her hands clasping her cheeks. "Oh, my God."

A murmur throughout the room.

Nasir spontaneously clapped and apologetically looked around.

Chris couldn't believe it either and stood gaping at the ancient booklet in wonder.

Kate reached down, placed a finger gently on the cover as if to confirm it was real, then removed her hand. "It's sheep skin," she said. "The pages are bound by leather thongs. These, too, can be analyzed."

"It's my understanding that codices did not come into prominent use until the third or fourth centuries. The codices Siniaticus, Vaticanus and Alexandrinus come to mind. But this is your area of expertise."

"That is partly true. The codex form came long before," Kate said, scanning the room addressing the onlookers. "Unlike a scroll, a codex could be opened flat at any page allowing for easier reading and could be written on both front and back, plus it was more compact and easier to transport."

"If I may," Nasir interrupted politely, raising a cautious hand.

"But, of course," Kate responded.

"The earliest surviving fragments from codices come from Egypt, tentatively dated toward the end of the first century or first half of the second. The Rylands papyrus containing part of St. John's Gospel is an example, dating from one twenty-five to one sixty C.E."

"You are well informed, Nasir," Kate affirmed.

He nodded shyly and continued. "I recall they were used early on as personal notebooks and for recording copies of letters. Paul mentioned them in his writings and may have used them to write his letters. Some New Testament authorities believe he created the first canon by binding his letters together in codices, and not writing them on a scroll."

Chris and Kate looked knowingly at each other, acknowledging her earlier comments about Paul's letters.

"They were also used to make rough copies, first drafts and notes," Nyla added, confirming again her probable Christian orientation.

"We are blessed by your knowledge," Kate said, glancing first at Nyla, then Nasir.

"And we, likewise blessed by your presence today," said Nyla with a slight nod.

Chris moved his right index finger carefully around the edge of the cover, then made a slight upward movement to see if it would lift, and it did. "The leather cover of this one is frayed around the edges and warped like the pages, but it appears to be in good condition," he said, casting his eyes about as though lecturing to those gathered around. "A stain in the lower right corner could be wine which can also be analyzed."

Gingerly, Kate lifted then immediately closed, the cover. "The pages are parchment, not papyrus. Parchment was used later by early Christian writers." She rotated the paper towel the codex was on so the others could see the spine. "From the looks of this, the author folded pages and bound them with thin leather thongs," she said pointing to the small cords. "My guess is there are three or four folios which would mean from twenty-four to thirty-two pages. Based on the thickness, the count is probably the latter. An analysis of the sheepskin and leather cords will reveal their origin."

"The other one inside must be the same," and Chris tipped the jar again. Nothing came out. He looked inside. "It can't slide over the neck of the jar's curvature. The first one could slide on the back of the one that's lodged."

"Can you shake it?" Kate asked.

"Slightly," he said. He lifted the jar, held it at an angle and lightly shook it. The item moved into the opening.

Kate reached inside and meticulously withdrew an identical codex. "This one is either a duplicate or the writer needed two to complete his task." She took a deep breath. "It's time for the moment of revelation."

The room was quiet, only the ticking sounds of a clock and whirring of the small refrigerator behind them. Chris and Kate leaned in close over the first codex, their heads nearly touching. She reached a trembling hand and reopened the cover, this time holding it open a moment and then pulling it gently along the outer edge until it lay flat. Chris remembered the opening of Mark's manuscript, the quiet hush in the professor's office in Edinburgh, the first page and impact of what they had discovered, his heart hammering.

Then.

"It's in Aramaic," Kate exclaimed

They looked blankly at each other.

"You don't speak Aramaic," Chris said. "Everything but."

"I picked up some in Maaloula," she said. "But just a few words."

The room was silent.

Movement stirred behind them.

Nasir stepped forward. "I know Aramaic," he said timidly with a half smile.

"Nasir!" Kate exclaimed. "How did you—"

"I am Arabic Christian, from Syria. I grew up with my grandparents who lived in Jabadeen."

"One of only three cities in the world where they still speak Aramaic," Kate said.

Nyla spoke up: "You, Dr. Ferguson, are also well informed. When the Syrian revolt erupted, Nasir and his grandparents escaped from Jabadeen to Palestine, to Ramallah. He had a degree in languages and applied for work with UNESCO. He is one of our best workers."

"In November, we were in Maaloula," Chris added. "Not far from Jabadeen."

"Yes," Nasir responded. "We know of your discovery in Maaloula."

"Please, Nasir," Kate said, rolling a finger, "come closer and translate."

He moved and stood beside Kate and Chris, breathed deeply and read the first words, the heading; "Sayings of Jesus."

Chris saw the tears brimming in Nasir's eyes. Others in the room sighed. Nyla's hand was on her neck, her mouth agape. Gasps and murmurs from the others.

Nasir leaned in closer, his eyes inches from the page and tracking right to left, continued translating the ancient Aramaic: "These are the sayings of Jesus ... In those days ... the word of God came to John the Baptist ... the son of Zecharia, in the desert of Judea ... He went throughout the Jordan area ... calling for baptism ... and a change of heart ... leading to the forgiveness of sins ... As it is said in the book of the prophet Isaiah ... a voice cries out in the desert ... Prepare a way for the Lord ... clear a straight path for him ...." He reached the bottom of the page and stopped.

A chill passed through Chris as he realized what they were seeing and he nudged Kate. "Can you turn the page?"

The pages were thin and warped from centuries of storage. He knew she was concerned about tearing them from their mooring, the leather strands that bound them together. She made a slow and careful attempt. The page was stuck. She worked the edge of the pages gently, deftly, with her fingernail. After several minutes, at once, several pages broke crisply apart.

"Please continue, Nasir." Chris urged.

"Nasir, wait," Kate said, "allow me." She reached over and, without touching the codex, trailed a finger down to the end of the page, then the opposite page and stopped midway. "Skip to here," she said.

Nasir leaned closer to the page, his head slightly bobbing as he scrutinized the passage, then he looked back up at them and said, his eyes glistening with moisture, "It's the beginning of the Beatitudes," and he began again, slowly, translating as he read: "Happy are you who are hungry now ... you shall be satisfied ... Fortunate are you who weep now, for you shall laugh." He stopped, turned and looked at Kate and Chris.

Kate rolled a finger for him to continue.

"Fortunate are the gentle ... for they shall inherit the earth ... Happy are the merciful ... for they shall be shown mercy ... Happy are the pure in heart ... for they shall see ... the face of God ... Fortunate are the peacemakers ... for they shall be called ... the sons of God—"

Kate raised a hand for him to pause and looked at Chris, "Do you realize what this may be?"

"Yes. So far everything you've read is from Q, the lost gospel of the sayings of Jesus."

"Do you want me to continue?" Nasir asked.

Kate and Chris nodded.

"No one lights a lamp ... and places it in a hidden place ... but instead places it on a lamp stand ... and it provides light ... to all those in the house."

"There can be little doubt," Chris interrupted. "These are the first recorded sayings of Jesus."

"Praise God," a female voice behind them exclaimed. It was Nyla, tears streaming down her cheeks. Nasir was wiping his eyes. Others in the room were looking on speechless. Even the stony face of the M16 agent appeared softened in awestruck wonder.

"If this codex is authentic," Kate said, "and we don't even know the contents of the other jar, "This is a greater discovery than Mark's gospel."

"In his own tongue," Chris murmured, "the *first* gospel."

# EPILOGUE

*Tel Aviv, Ben Gurion International Airport, May 28, 2012*

Chris and Kate returned to the Ben Gurion airport in Tel Aviv after opening the second jar and the scroll. As promised, and without further incidents, assuring their safety agent Blanchard had followed them and remained at their side until they entered the security check-in queue. They had no trouble negotiating passport control and passed easily through security.

At the gate in the business-class boarding line, they were approached by the two men wearing suits they had seen at the hotel's restaurant. Presenting their identifications, one of them, coldly and with a Yiddish accent, said, "We are ELAD agents and have a few questions for you before we can permit you to leave Israel."

Before Chris could respond, Kate lunged. "We have questions for you," she exclaimed angry eyes flashing. "You have been following us since we entered your country. In my country, the behavior is called harassment."

The other gentleman raised a calming hand. "Madam, Dr. Ferguson," he said with a similar accent, "we know who you are and do not mean to harass—"

She flung a military arm at the gate. "Can't you see we have a plane to catch," she bristled, her mouth set hard, her look defiant.

"We just have a few questions," the one who had addressed her said evenly, then added apologetically, "We have not been following you. We have been following the gentleman with you, Mr. Jones, whom our Robbery

Prevention Unit has had under routine surveillance predating your entry into Israel."

Chris and Kate briskly followed the two men down the corridor to an empty gate where there was privacy. Consistent with their earlier comments, the agents were concerned about Emmanuel's contact with The British Museum, when and how Chris and Kate got involved, and the sequence of events following their meeting with the student. In her intimidating style and confident voice, and with her British Special Forces credentials and the receipt from UNESCO, Kate answered their questions and provided a convincing story: How they saved the relics from being taken, "to God knows where"—describing the abduction of the jars at the Jericho gas station; their detective work at the Jerusalem Hertz office; the confrontation at the airport luggage room—spitting it all out in a lividly excoriating twirl of Scottish trills that when she was finished, left the two agents scrambling for expressions of apology and regret.

They were the last to board the Air France flight to London. The flight attendant was standing at the door anxiously waving them forward. No one was ahead of them, as they quickly made their way to the plane door, stowed their carry-ons overhead and settled into their business class seats. A flight attendant closed and locked the door and announced the plane was cleared for takeoff.

Buckling her seatbelt, Kate heaved a huge sigh. "I wasn't sure that was going to happen."

"To quote Yogi Berra, 'It ain't over till it's over,'" Chris said, prepared for the sharp look she gave him.

"That's not funny," she quipped. "What do you mean?"

"Don't look at me like that," he retorted. "You've flown before. Control tower can stop takeoff and we can be yanked back."

"At least Emmanuel's not on this plane," she said, "or any other."

"He's somewhere in an Israeli jail," Chris said. "But probably not for long."

"Connections!"

"Yep!" he clipped. "His relationship with Liberty University and its strong support of Israel will get him out. He'll probably be released to return to his work study program and face his friends. Or fly home and face disgrace or be a hero to some, his name and picture in the papers."

"Unfortunately, along with ours," she bemoaned.

A male flight attendant approached and asked for a drink order.

She opened her mouth and Chris preempted her. "Champagne. Your best."

Before she could object he distracted her. "They could be forgeries, it happens. But I think the codices and the scroll are authentic."

"They're authentic," she responded confidently, "especially the scroll. The papyrus is white, Kieratica, a very fine quality. Whoever penned the sayings, knew what they were doing. The Museum has some similar ancient papyrus documents. We won't know for sure until we get a report on the carbon dating. UNESCO agreed to keep me updated at the museum. That will tell us a bundle."

"The most convincing part for me," he added, "were the letters on the scroll. They hung down straight from the top line. Letters were not slanted until the second century C.E. I don't think a forger, unless highly sophisticated, would know that."

"I'm impressed you noticed," she said, a twinkle of amazement in her eyes. "When I opened the scroll, that was the first thing I saw, too, the vertical drop of the letters."

"The image of you opening and unrolling the scroll I will always remember," he continued. "Unlike that long dusk to dawn struggle with the Markan scroll in the professor's office, this one was different. No tension. No torture. No obstacles. Unbelievably, once the scroll slid from the jar, you were magnificent—your hands deftly rolling the scroll with your right hand, gathering it in your left, translating the Greek koine as you unspooled. The same words, passages, in the same order as they were in the codices. Oh, my! What a scene!"

"I had had some practice," she said modestly.

"What do you think happened to the ancient person, or persons, who hid the writings?" he questioned, shifting the focus. "Did they vanish? Were they persecuted and killed by the Romans?"

"We may never know," she said. "We do know the time frame. The two consuls listed on the protocol held the office in sixty-six C.E."

"Which was before Vespasian and Titus led their attack on the Jewish insurrectionists. Jerusalem fell in seventy C.E."

"Therein may lie the answer to your question," she suggested. "The author, or authors—as we had previously conjectured—were in the path of advancing legions, fleeing south to safety, and at some point had to deposit their literary treasure."

"Why the scroll *and* the codex? Your thoughts."

"That one's easy," she smiled. "For the same reason two of Marks autographs were discovered side-by-side: rough draft and final copy."

"I understand," he replied. "But this codex appeared to be a finished copy, not a working draft. There were no signs of smudges, erasures and rewriting."

"Perhaps, along with the scroll, it was a master copy," she injected.

"Or there was another codex he used, the original plus separate sheets he may have discarded."

"At least the're safe and in proper custody," she said, mildly irritated with his persistence. "That was the reason we came."

The plane taxied. It's engines roared. Soon, the blue Mediterranean was sliding beneath them. After several minutes of uplift, he turned to her and said, "Now we can relax. We're headed home."

"So?" A pause. "And where is home?" she asked.

He pulled a boarding pass from his coat pocket and handed it to her.

She looked at it. Her eyes widened. She pulled it down to her lap then raised it again to her eyes. "Chris Jordan!" She grasped his arm in a spontaneous gesture of affection. "How? When?" and she leaned over and kissed him.

"Back at the gate, when you went to the restroom, I went to the gate counter and had my ultimate destination rerouted from Phoenix to Edinburgh. I thought it'd be fun going *home* with you."

"What about your sons?"

"I sent them texts."

"And?"

"They're delighted and can't wait to meet you."

"*What* did you tell them?" she pressed excitedly, her face expansive, eyes bright.

"Later!"

The male attendant arrived with a bottle of champagne in a bucket of ice and set it on the console between them. He reached over to lift the bottle and pour the champagne and Chris held up a hand, "Not yet," and the attendant departed.

"My, my, aren't we being mysterious."

"That's what this adventure has been all about." He reached down, opened his computer bag between his legs, pulled out a thin book and handed it to her. "A small gift for you."

She took it, glanced at the cover and clutched it to her breast. "How in the world?"

"When you stopped at a kiosk to get some cappuccino, next door was a newsstand and book nook. The book was on display with different *Bible* translations. I didn't believe my eyes and snapped it up."

Looking for an inscription, she opened the front cover, turned a page and there it was. In a low voice, she read, "For Kate, my wife to be. And to the words that light the way. Chris, your husband to be." She was fighting back tears, her face dissolving, softening. She kept her eyes, tears welling in them, on the page, as the book shook in her hands.

"I thought it would make a nice wedding present. There are a number of books out on the Q sayings but this, *The New Q* is freshly translated with commentary. The upcoming revised version will be even better."

"Christopher Jordan, I love you," she said, unsnapped her seatbelt, leaned over and gave him a long embrace.

He whispered in her ear. "I think the little Methodist Church in Dunbar near your home would be a good place for the ceremony, the reception afterward at the Bayside Inn."

"Perfect!" she leaned back and beamed, but her attention was still on the book. She held it up, clutched it again to her chest and sighed. She opened it at random, and read. "'No one lights a lamp and places it in a hidden place but instead places it on a lamp stand—'"

"—And it provides light to all those in the house," he said, completing the saying of Jesus.

"And to the rest of the world," she added, and closed the book.

He reached for the bottle and filled the glasses they lifted.

"Here's to all that endures," he said.

"To us," she added with an affirming smile, and paused. "And to antiquities that endure, to mystery ... to love. May the adventure continue."

# THE END

# ACKNOWLEDGEMENTS

I am deeply indebted to my parents, William Edward and Joan Ferguson Morris who, on my eighth birthday, gave me an *Eigermeir Bible Story Book*. Thus began an epic journey exploring the scriptures, their origins and archaeology, all of which contributed to an imaginative portrayal of the how the sayings of Jesus could have been recorded and saved ... and found.

Jill Smith, Director of the Union County Historical Museum provided information on museums, their relationships with archaeologists and ancient finds. Dr. Jason Stacy, my step-son and neurovascular surgeon, gave technical details about late-model Land Rovers. Dr. David White is always a helpful reader of my early manuscripts. The staff at the UNESCO office in Ramallah, Israel, aided in contributing information about UNESCO and antiquities. Carol Killman Rosenberg, my personal professional editor, conducted a review of the early manuscript with constructive feedback that led to multiple changes and rewrites, and a much improved work.

Michael Hartnett, friend and fellow writer, read earlier, and final drafts of the manuscript offering invaluable suggestions, critique and, always, his warm affirmation.

I am always thankful to the publisher, Reagan Rothe, and his staff at Black Rose Writing for their assistance through the publishing process.

For first century historical information and details regarding the first century Jewish revolt against the Romans, the following sources were useful: *The New Q: A Fresh Translation with Commentary*, Richard Volantasis, T & T Clark, New York: 2005. *The Lost Gospel: The Original Sayings of Jesus*, Ulysses Press, Berkely, CA: 1996. *Excavating Q: The History and Settng of the Sayings Gospel*, John S. Kloppenborg Verbin, Augsburg Fortress Press, Minniapolis, MN: 2000. *The Early Church*, Henry Chadwick, Penguin Books, London: 1993 *The Jewish War: Revised Edition* (Penguin Classics), Flavius Josephus, trans. G. A. Williamson, Penguin Books, London: 1970. *The Jewish Wars: History of the Jewish War and Resistance Against the Romans; Including Author's Autobiography*, Flavius Josephus, Trans. William Whiston, Kindle Edition. *A History of the Jewish War: AD 66-74*, Steve Mason, Cambridge University Press, London: 2016. *Archaeology,* A publication of the

Archaeological Institute of America. *Josephus: The Jewish War*, Gaalya Cornfeld,

To my resident Editor-in-Chief, former English teacher, final reviewer of all manuscripts and wife, Sandi: Bravissimo!

# ABOUT THE AUTHOR

Joe Edd Morris is the author of *Land Where My Fathers Died*, *The Prison* (both awarded Best Fiction by the Mississippi Library Association), *Torched: Summer of '64* and non-fiction works including *Ten Things I Wish Jesus Hadn't Said*. Joe Edd is a psychologist and retired United Methodist minister. He and his wife, Sandi, live in Tupelo, MS where he has a private practice in psychology. He enjoys traveling, gardening, playing the piano and writing.

# NOTE FROM THE AUTHOR

Word-of-mouth is crucial for any author to succeed. If you enjoyed *The Lost Gospel*, please leave a review online—anywhere you are able. Even if it's just a sentence or two. It would make all the difference and would be very much appreciated.


Thanks!
Joe Edd Morris

Other Titles from
# Joe Edd Morris

## *The Prison*

In *The Prison*, Shell Ferguson visits his incarcerated grandson Cal with tragic news: his daughter, wife, and grandmother have perished in a fire. Cal must rely on his grandfather to uncover the suspicious circumstances of the blaze, as clues unfold to establish his innocence. Compelling revelations link the fire and Cal's innocence with domestic terrorism. From plots to blow up Mississippi River bridges to threats on their lives, grandfather and grandson take a series of risks, including Cal's daring prison escape, to save the remnants of their family and southern community so disturbingly infiltrated. A surprise addition to their efforts is Cal's six-year-old daughter (thought to have died in the fire), who was kidnapped by the terrorists and escaped from their camp. The trio, in a race against time, help the FBI and Coast Guard thwart the nefarious plot.

## *Torched: Summer of '64*

*Torched: Summer of '64* finds Sam Ransom at his first pastoral appointment in Holmes County, Mississippi, in the summer of '64. At a civil rights rally, he is reunited with two friends from his childhood. His decision to join their efforts to rebuild a black church torched by nightriders sets all three on a collision course with the Klan and two grisly murders. The story is about interracial friendship and romance, the ultimate sacrifice, atonement and redemption.

We hope you enjoyed reading this title from:

www.blackrosewriting.com

Subscribe to our mailing list – *The Rosevine* – and receive **FREE** books, daily deals, and stay current with news about upcoming releases and our hottest authors.
Scan the QR code below to sign up.

Already a subscriber? Please accept a sincere thank you for being a fan of Black Rose Writing authors.

View other Black Rose Writing titles at
www.blackrosewriting.com/books and use promo code
**PRINT** to receive a **20% discount** when purchasing.

Made in the USA
Coppell, TX
13 April 2023

15580824R10163